Praise for J. M. Hochstetler

"*Refiner's Fire* is not simply a story but an experience. Within its pages are all the upheaval, suspense, heartache, and romance that make the American Patriot Series unforgettable. The author's breadth and scope of our founding history is truly remarkable and each finely tuned character seems lifted from the actual historical record. Extraordinary!"

—LAURA FRANTZ, CHRISTY-AWARD WINNING AUTHOR OF *The Lacemaker*

"*Refiner's Fire* is an absolutely thrilling read! J. M. Hochstetler once again takes readers deep into the turbulent days of the American Revolution, bringing to life the battles, the spies, and the intrigue that belong solely to our forefathers and their struggle for our burgeoning country. Hochstetler's rich description, strong and unique characters, and impeccable attention to historical detail leaves readers wonderfully satisfied yet longing for more. Fans of historical fiction will adore this newest installment in the American Patriot Series.

—MICHELLE SHOCKLEE, AUTHOR OF *The Widow of Rose Hill*

"Painstaking attention to research and detail, vivid setting, peeks into some of the most obscure corners of an otherwise familiar history, all overlaid with a grand, sweeping love story that will break your heart before it takes your breath away . . . this book (and series!) has it all. If you're a fan of historical fiction and romance and haven't yet discovered this author, don't wait another minute to do so!"

—*Shannon McNear, 2014 RITA® finalist and author of* The Cumberland Bride, #5 OF DAUGHTERS OF THE MAYFLOWER

"J. M. Hochstetler's in-depth research and masterful writing combine for an exceptional novel, filled with history, intrigue, and romance. *Refiner's Fire* is an engaging and most satisfying read. As Book 6 in the American Patriot series, *Refiner's Fire* can be read as a standalone, yet the preceding novels fill in much detail, making *Refiner's Fire* even more enjoyable. It is rare to read a series with the intensity of historical understanding that you will find within the pages of the American Patriot Series. From every vantage point—the Native Americans, to the British, to the Colonial Americans—the complexity of the political and cultural ramifications brings a greater depth of understanding to the bigger picture than you will find in most historical novels. A series well worth mentally devouring."

—ELAINE MARIE COOPER, AUTHOR OF *Love's Kindling*

Refiner's Fire

THE AMERICAN PATRIOT SERIES
~BOOK 6~

J. M. HOCHSTETLER

ELKHART, IN
46514 USA

Library of Congress Control Number: 2019901579

ISBN: 978-1-936438-46-4 (softcover)

All scripture quotations are from the King James Version of the Bible. The
scripture verses quoted on p. 76 are Psalm 29:3, 10-11. The verses quoted on p.
92 are Isaiah 30:19-21. The verses quoted on p. 93 are John 5:24-25. The verses
quoted on p. 94 are Ezekiel 37:9*b*-12, 14*a*. The verse quoted on p. 224 is
Ephesians 2:19. The verses quoted on p. 308 are Psalm 91: 3*a*, 4*b*, 5. The verses
quoted on p. 420 are Ecclesiastes 2: 4; 3:1-2*a*, 4, 8*a*, *d*. Verses quoted on p. 421
are Song of Solomon 1:2:2:4. Verses quoted on p. 422 are 2:11-12*a*; 4: 9-10*a*, *b*.

Cover design by Marisa Jackson.

Cover image: *L'Attesa* by Arturo Ricci from Wikimedia Commons. This work
is in the public domain in the United States.

"Battle of Monmouth" map by Jim Brown of Jim Brown Illustration.

MANUFACTURED IN THE UNITED STATES OF AMERICA

This book is dedicated to the French heroes who came alongside in our country's time of need to help secure the independence of these United States.

"He shall sit as a refiner and purifier of silver: and he shall purify the sons of Levi, and purge them as gold and silver, that they may offer unto the Lord an offering in righteousness."

—MALACHI 3:3

"For You have tried us, O God; You have refined us as silver is refined."

—Psalm 66:10

An award-winning author and editor, J. M. Hochstetler is the daughter of Mennonite farmers, a graduate of Indiana University, a professional editor, and a lifelong student of history.

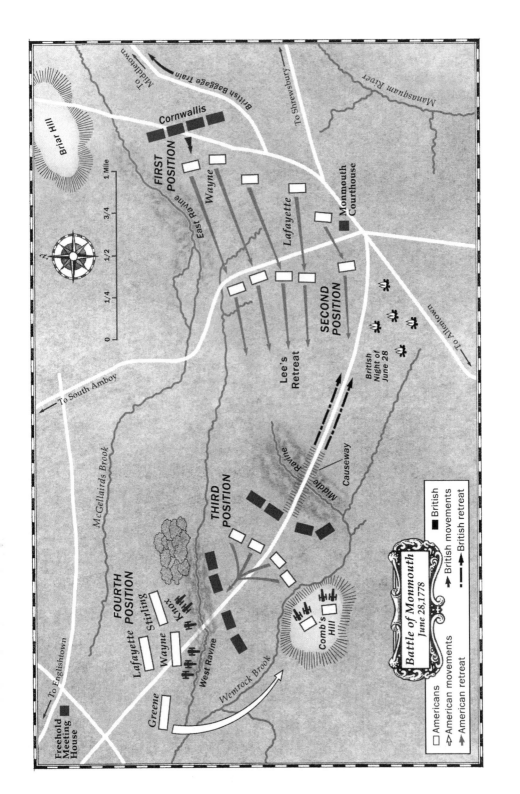

Battle of Monmouth
June 28, 1778

Americans
British

American movements
British movements

American retreat
British retreat

Freehold Meeting House

To Englishtown

Briar Hill

To South Amboy

McGellaird's Brook

FOURTH POSITION

Lafayette
Stirling
Wayne
Knox

Greene

West Ravine

Wemrock Brook

Comb's Hill

THIRD POSITION

Middle Ravine

Causeway

British Night of June 28

SECOND POSITION

Lee's Retreat

Monmouth Courthouse

Lafayette

Wayne

East Ravine

FIRST POSITION

Cornwallis

British Baggage Train

To Middletown

To Shrewsbury

Manasquan River

To Allentown

N

0   1/4   1/2   3/4   1 Mile

OTHER BOOKS IN
THE AMERICAN PATRIOT SERIES

DAUGHTER OF LIBERTY
NATIVE SON
WIND OF THE SPIRIT
CRUCIBLE OF WAR
VALLEY OF THE SHADOW

Forthcoming
FORGE OF FREEDOM

_____

OTHER BOOKS BY
J. M. HOCHSTETLER

ONE HOLY NIGHT

_____

NORTHKILL AMISH SERIES
WITH BOB HOSTETLER

NORTHKILL
THE RETURN

Chapter One

"IT WOULD BE SAFER for all of you if I'm away. Then General Clinton would have no further reason to send his agents here to . . . to murder me."

Elizabeth Howard looked from her father to her mother and younger sister, sight blurred, throat painfully tight. It was just past sundown on Thursday, February 19, 1778, following an attempt on her life early that morning by agents of General Henry Clinton, the British commander at New York.

"We're not going to let that happen, daughter," Dr. Samuel Howard snapped as he paced restlessly across the room, hands clasped behind his back. Rounding on French Admiral Alexandre Bettár, le comte de Caledonne, he growled, "I appreciate your concern, Alexandre, but I've no intention of allowing you to wrest my daughter from her home and family after all she's been through. Beth hasn't fully recovered from her ordeal aboard that wretched prison ship, and I'm afraid a long sea voyage would do her irreparable harm—if she even survived it."

"Aren't you being a bit dramatic, Papa?" Elizabeth objected. "Surely I'm fully recovered by now. It's been over three months since. . . " Her voice choked.

He stopped beside Elizabeth's chair to frown down at her. "There are still hollows in your cheeks, my dear, and you're too thin and pale. You eat hardly more than a bird—"

"I'm stronger than you think."

"You think you're stronger than you are!"

"That's why I enlisted Jean and Marie to accompany us to France—to ensure that her health isn't compromised," Caledonne pointed out, his calm demeanor a settling counterpoint to Dr. Howard's vehemence.

Forcing a teasing tone, Elizabeth said, "Faith, Dr. Lemaire, I'm astounded that you'd desert *Destiny* even for such agreeable service as that aboard *Néréide*."

Slender, handsome Dr. Jean Lemaire exchanged a wry smile with his companion, Marie Glasière. He and the beautiful, dark-haired young French nurse had kept Elizabeth alive after her rescue from the horrors of a British prison ship in New York Harbor.

"This hardly qualifies as desertion, mademoiselle, though I think General Carleton would not begrudge it in this instance," he protested.

He referred to Major General Jonathan Carleton, the man Elizabeth loved. Commander of Carleton's Rangers, a renowned brigade of the Continental Army under General George Washington, Carleton also owned a fleet of privateers including the 100-gun warship that had led the successful raid on the British stronghold.

"I know he'd not begrudge any means of keeping you safe and well," said Carleton's portly, balding French agent, Louis Teissèdre.

Elizabeth averted her eyes quickly from the Frenchman's searching gaze. He had arrived unexpectedly that morning as the attack against her unfolded. After ensuring that her aunt's property was secured, he had gone to fetch Caledonne and returned under cover of darkness with the admiral and his son, Lucien, accompanied by the physician and nurse. All of them had been heavily muffled in dark cloaks, with Caledonne also substituting plain civilian dress for his ornate French naval uniform.

"Should Beth go to France, it'll be a great comfort to know she's in your care," Elizabeth's Aunt Tess said to Marie and Lemaire. "God forbid that she fall ill again!"

She turned a warm look on Caledonne, which he returned with one that caused the color to bloom becomingly in her cheeks. Noting it, Elizabeth suppressed a smile.

"Jean and Marie will rejoin *Destiny* as soon as you're safely delivered to the home of my eldest daughter, Cécile, la marquise de Martieu-Broussard," Caledonne assured Elizabeth. "Once there, you'll be under the care of her personal physician."

"You see, Samuel, there's nothing to worry about." Anne Howard drew her younger daughter, thirteen-year-old Abby, onto the sofa between her and Elizabeth.

She was the source of both her daughters' delicately modeled features and slender, graceful forms. Abby had also inherited their mother's blue eyes and fair coloring, while, in addition to her father's passionate nature, Elizabeth had inherited his expressive brown eyes and curly hair, the latter a rich, dark auburn in contrast to his black locks.

"There's always something to worry about when it comes to sea travel, even for one who's in perfect health—which Beth is not! Surely you haven't forgotten the weather we endured on our voyage back from London last fall, my love. And the winter storms are even worse."

"There's equal, if not greater, danger if she stays here," Tess pointed out. Older than her brother, she shared his coloring and classically handsome features, though her hair was streaked with silver.

From his post behind his father's chair, leaning on the mantel of the drawing room's blazing fireplace, Lucien Bettár agreed quietly, "Mademoiselle Howard's very life is at stake, sir."

Elizabeth covertly studied Caledonne's son, whom she guessed to be slightly younger than Carleton. In appearance the two could not have been more different. Both were strikingly handsome, but Carleton was tall, lean, powerfully muscled, and deeply tanned, with blond hair and intense blue-grey eyes. In contrast, Lucien was slender, dark-haired, and pale complexioned, of middling height, his heavy-lidded brown eyes giving him a languid appearance. She detected little of his father's easy affability or martial discipline in him and more the manners of a French courtier.

As though sensing her scrutiny he met her gaze with a direct one that caused heat to rise to her cheeks. She dropped her eyes, unaccountably flustered, and hastily returned her attention to Caledonne.

"Beth will be much better able to regain her strength where she's safely out of Clinton's reach and needn't worry about further attacks."

"As much as I want to keep Elizabeth with us, I have to agree," Anne returned, her brow furrowing. "Samuel, after that . . . that horrible incident this morning you can't possibly believe we can keep her safe here any longer."

"You said it was not the first attempt, monsieur."

Teissèdre turned to Tess. "It was not, madame, and this time the effort came far too close to success. I shudder to think what might have happened had General Carleton's Marines not intervened in time. Nor was the man alone. Had I not arrived when I did—*mon Dieu!*" He pulled out his handkerchief and mopped the perspiration from his bald pate.

Involuntarily Elizabeth's hand flew to the plaster that covered the raw scratch on her cheek. She suppressed a shiver at the unsettling memory of the man she had briefly glimpsed prowling through the fog beneath her window early that morning. Convinced that he had to be Carleton, she had hurried outside after him only to have a bullet whine past her head, terrifyingly close. Had the crack of a rifle fired at the intruder not come first, startling her and causing her to slip and tumble into an ice-crusted snow bank, the musket ball aimed at her would have struck its target.

She was certain now that that brief glimpse of the stranger, whose height and form were uncannily similar to Carleton's, had not been mere coincidence, that he had meant to lure her outside to her death. Mercifully his malicious intent had been foiled by the Marines Carleton had secretly stationed around her aunt's estate not long after he had brought her home.

In addition to commanding a brigade of Rangers with Indian scouts, Carleton was also the feared Shawnee war chief White Eagle, the adopted son of the renowned sachem Black Hawk. It was the revelation of the latter that had caused the bitter confrontation with her parents in early December and his abrupt departure while Elizabeth slept upstairs, unaware. He had left behind only a poignant, hastily scrawled letter on her bedside table, a few items of clothing, and his treasured violin before vanishing into the night.

She had received no further communication from him. And at the turning of the New Year she had learned that he had taken all his warriors and returned to his people as Washington's envoy to negotiate the Shawnee's neutrality in the war with England.

Looking up, she met Caledonne's concerned gaze. Carleton's uncle was imposing in appearance, tall and lean with neatly coiffed white hair. His deep tan testified to years of service at sea, as did the fine lines that creased his forehead and crinkled at the corners of eyes an intense blue-grey disconcertingly like Carleton's. Indeed the close resemblance between the two men pierced her as forcibly as it had at their first meeting.

She felt suddenly as though she would suffocate despite the cold drafts that seeped along the floorboards. Springing to her feet, she went to the nearest window and pushed back the heavy winter draperies. With her handkerchief she violently scrubbed at the thick layer of frost that coated the panes until she cleared a circle on the glass large enough to peer through. Heavy clouds obscured the black heavens, and in the gloom she could make out only the dim shadows of the nearest trees buffeted by an icy wind, a prospect as bleak as her emotions.

Behind her she heard her father say, "Surely there's another alternative to sending Beth three thousand miles across the ocean."

"Where on this continent will she be safe from General Clinton's reach?" her mother demanded anxiously.

"You think she'll be safer aboard a French warship when England will declare war on France the instant they sign a treaty with us—if that hasn't happened already?" Dr. Howard's voice scaled upward.

Elizabeth glanced over her shoulder as her mother protested, "But from what we've heard it's only to be a treaty of alliance, nothing more."

"It's very much more, as the British well know," Caledonne broke in, his eyes glittering with anticipation. "It will have the same effect as waving the *muleta* in the bull's face. We've already passed through the *tercios* of lances and flags in this *corrida de toro,* and now will enter the third of death, our sword, our *estocada,* at the ready. Our countries will be fully engaged at sea by summer at the latest. That's why we must sail now to ensure Beth is safely in France before our navies collide."

Teissèdre lifted his shoulders in an expressive shrug. "There can be no safer place for your daughter than aboard such a ship as *Néréide* in the midst of le comte de Caledonne's fleet. I assure you that the British will think twice before they dare attack such a convoy."

Dr. Howard snorted. "I wouldn't be so sure of that, considering the number of naval engagements France lost to the British not so long ago during our French and Indian War."

"Touché," Caledonne conceded dryly. "But they will find that twenty years has done much to shift the balance of naval power."

When Dr. Howard began to speak, Anne turned to her sister-in-law in frustrated appeal.

"Samuel, for once please listen to what Alexandre and Louis have to say before you dismiss their arguments out of hand," Tess pleaded.

Elizabeth returned to her seat. Abby immediately clasped her arms around her waist and leaned her head on her shoulder.

"Please don't send my sister away!"

Anne reached over to gently brush straying tendrils of the child's hair back from her flushed face. "We may not have a choice, dearest."

"I disagree. I've no intention of doing so, Abby," Dr. Howard broke in. "We've been home from England for hardly four months, and I don't need to remind you how close we came to losing Beth then. But we kept her alive and safe, and—"

Marie had held her silence, but now enquired politely, "Will you keep her a prisoner in this house then? Otherwise she'll be in danger whenever she ventures outside."

"Obviously Jon's Marines have—though unknown to us—protected her quite effectively," Dr. Howard blustered.

"They cannot remain here forever," the young nurse pointed out.

He frowned. "It's to be hoped that General Clinton will finally abandon his efforts to get at her since they've all come to nothing. At any rate there are other methods of defense we can employ. I simply don't think it necessary to take such drastic action as sending Beth to live among strangers in a foreign land!"

He rounded on Caledonne. "Come to think of it, how is it that a French admiral of your reputation is free to bring his entire fleet to rescue my daughter?"

Caledonne raised one eyebrow. "As I'm sure you'll understand, Samuel, I'm not at liberty to divulge our mission. Suffice it to say that it involves something other than plucking Beth out of Clinton's clutches, important as that is to me personally. Officially, one of my squadrons escorted several merchantmen into the harbor loaded with supplies for your army, by now a not unusual occurrence. No one knows I accompanied the squadron; we came ashore at nightfall and will return the same way. We'd bring Beth aboard secretly as well."

Frowning, Dr. Howard rubbed his brow. "If I were to agree, can you assure me that there are no British agents in Louis the Sixteenth's court who might find out where she is and become a danger to her?"

"But of course there are such agents—as we maintain agents in George the Third's court." Caledonne leaned forward, the calculating light in his eyes reminding Elizabeth that despite his easy manner he was a man to be feared. "But all British officials will be recalled the moment we conclude our treaty with your government. As for agents who operate in the shadows, I guarantee to you that *my* agents are quite capable of . . . removing them should that become necessary."

Elizabeth shivered as he sat back in his chair. "You need have no fear for your daughter, Samuel. She's as dear to me as she is to Jonathan, and I will give up my own life before I allow harm to come to her—on sea or land. And once in France, she'll be under the protection of my son-in-law le marquis as well. He is also a man of high connections and power."

When Dr. Howard bristled, Tess snapped, "Oh, lay down your hackles, Samuel! Even you can't be in control of everything. And in case you hadn't noticed, Beth's a grown woman, in her right mind, and capable of making her own decisions. In fact, she's been doing it for years."

Bending in a slight bow Lucien cut off Dr. Howard's response. "You can trust my father to always keep his word, sir."

Elizabeth detected a subtle, barbed undercurrent in his tone and saw Caledonne direct an unreadable glance at his son, his mouth tightening almost imperceptibly. But her mother's voice distracted her from the questions the interchange aroused.

"What do you want to do, my dear?"

"Are you actually considering this proposal, my girl?" Dr. Howard protested.

Feeling her father's troubled gaze on her, Elizabeth hesitated, not certain what she did want. "France is so far from all of you and . . . Jonathan." Staring blindly at her hands clenched in her lap, she whispered, "But he made it clear he has no intention of ever coming back. So what does it matter?"

A strained silence hung over the room for some moments as Abby clung tearfully to her. Rising, Caledonne came to squat in front of her. He pulled from his pocket a folded paper and held it out—a letter, she saw.

"I received this from a messenger a short time after you left *Néréide* that evening."

The address, hastily scrawled on the outside in a hand she knew well, read: Admiral Alexandre Bettár, *Néréide*, Boston Harbour.

Caledonne pressed it into her hand. "Please read it."

She searched his eyes, then with Abby leaning anxiously on her shoulder, she unfolded the page, hands shaking, tears scalding her eyes even before she scanned the few short lines inside, written in French.

Uncle Alexandre,

It's become necessary for me to return to duty at once. I've given orders to my Marines to remain on alert for any intruders. Please instruct Louis to stay in constant contact with Captain Hartley and do everything possible to keep Beth from harm. If at any time he deems it too dangerous for her to remain at Boston, I desire that you take her to your estate at Marseille and keep her there until she may safely return home. Tell her it is my wish, should that make a difference—

Jonathan

Reading the last line, broken abruptly off, with only his name carelessly scribbled below, she bit her lip hard, fighting back a sob. Carefully she refolded the letter, conscious that the others watched as though hanging on her movements.

When she looked up, the kindness in Caledonne's eyes entirely undid her, and tears spilled. Taking her hand between both of his, he held it tightly.

"As it is his wish, I'll come with you—of course."

When she extended the letter to him, he motioned for her to keep it and, releasing her, stood. She pressed the page to her bosom and thanked him, voice choked.

As Caledonne returned to his chair, her father cleared his throat, then asked, "Beth . . . may your mother and I read it?"

The pain in his voice pierced her. Brushing away her tears, she held the letter out to him. He came to take it, read it slowly in silence, then handed it to her mother.

Elizabeth lifted her chin. "I won't be gone forever. I'll come home the moment it's safe."

"Well . . . it's doubtless for the best." Sighing, Anne folded the letter and handed it to Abby. She motioned her to carry it to Tess, who scanned it, frowning, and returned it to her.

As Abby brought the letter back to Elizabeth, Tess asked, "Didn't you say your daughter lives near Paris, Alexandre?" At his confirmation, she said, "But Jonathan asks you to take her to Marseille."

"Naturally he had no way of knowing that Cécile would offer to take Beth into her home. My younger daughter and her family reside at my ancestral estate near Marseille, and we'll visit at a convenient time. But Cécile and her husband have a large estate outside Paris that is much more secure and a more advantageous situation as they can introduce Beth to trustworthy people at the highest levels of society."

Lucien moved to stand beside his father's chair. "Let me assure you, madame, that you could not ask for a better situation for your daughter than in my sister's household. She is the best of women and a musician of great ability, whose guidance and contacts within the arts will be of great benefit to mademoiselle."

He spoke with reassuring sincerity. Seeing that her mother was clearly delighted at the prospects that residing with the marquise and her family would afford her, Elizabeth suppressed the nagging reflection that this was, nevertheless, not what Carleton had requested of his uncle.

Beaming, Anne said, "Then there's only the matter of a proper chaperon to decide."

"I'll have Marie and Jemma with me, Mama."

"That's hardly sufficient aboard a ship filled with sailors. You'll need someone older, with greater experience—"

"I believe I have a solution." Caledonne smiled at Tess. "I propose to take Thérèsa with us—if she's willing."

As both her parents gaped, Elizabeth clasped her hands in delight. "Of course! I can't think of a chaperon I'd want more. You will come with us, won't you, Aunt Tess?"

A becoming hue suffused Tess's cheeks as she met Caledonne's intent gaze. "Well, I . . . the last time I made an ocean voyage was when I came to Boston as a young woman. At my age—"

"You're not as old as I, Thérèsa," Caledonne scoffed, "and I've survived the sea. It's my very great desire that you come. You'll indulge me, will you not—for Beth's sake?"

And for yours too, I'll wager, Elizabeth thought, struggling to maintain an innocent expression.

"That would allay all our concerns, Tess," Anne said hopefully. "It's much to ask, but you'll do this for us?"

Struggling to hold back her own smile, Tess finally nodded. "Well . . . I suppose I must. After all, it's my duty to the family."

Seeing the light in Caledonne's eyes, Elizabeth reflected that her aunt had never married, and Caledonne had been a widower for a number of years. There was no disguising the attraction between them. As at his previous visit, he had immediately claimed a place at her side and made no attempt to conceal his warm regard.

"But if both you and Aunt Tess go away, I'll be left here all alone with only Mama and Papa for company! I was away from you ever so long, Beth, and—"

"Ah, but you see, little mouse, the second part of my proposal is to bring you with us."

Abby stared at Caledonne, openmouthed, before impulsively running across the room to fling herself into his arms. "Truly? Oh, *Onkel* Alexandre, you're not teasing—say you're not!"

Pleased by her affectionate appellation of uncle, he laughed. He tugged playfully on the blue ribbon that held back her golden hair and returned her embrace with a kiss.

"Not at all, *ma petit.* I must have you as well."

He turned to Elizabeth's parents. "I know it's a great deal to ask after having asked so much already, but I pray you'll consent to part with Abigail too—for a little while." Seeing Dr. Howard's face cloud, he continued quickly, "It was Cécile who suggested it as she can provide both your daughters the finest instruction in the arts—especially music, which is her forte, as Lucien mentioned. I assure you that she is a woman of the highest morals and discipline, and her youngest, Charlotte, is barely a year older than Abigail. They'll be delightful companions, and with Thérèsa to supervise them—"

Anne pressed her clasped hands to her bosom. "Oh, Samuel, think of what this means for our girls! I have such fond memories of my own education at the abbey in Paris—"

"Oh, very well," Dr. Howard conceded, throwing up his hands. "I can see I'm not going to win this debate—as usual! And . . . well, I can't deny my daughters the benefits they'll gain from a stay in France."

Abby ran to embrace him, and he bent to kiss her. Straightening, he turned back to Caledonne and shook his finger.

"But I'll not have my daughters turned into Papists, Alexandre."

"Even nuns didn't turn me into one, now did they?" Anne snapped in exasperation.

Teetering between dismay and laughter, Elizabeth began to speak, but Caledonne cut her off, from all appearances completely unruffled.

"I promise that no one will make any attempt to convert your daughters. I respect your Anglican faith as I hope you respect my Catholic faith. Are we not all Christians, after all?"

"Indeed we are," Elizabeth said firmly, fixing her father in a look that evoked a grimace.

"And I'll be there to supervise their religious instruction," Tess reminded him.

Dr. Howard raised his hands in surrender. "I meant no disrespect, but I'm sure you'd feel the same about your children were the situation reversed."

Regarding him with a wry smile, Caledonne said, "My greatest concern would be that they remain believers in our Lord Jesus Christ."

The heat rose to Dr. Howard face, and he inclined his head. "Point taken."

"How soon do you mean to sail, Alexandre?" Tess broke in.

He took her hand. "Can you be prepared to sail early Sunday morning? I cannot delay much longer."

Tess and Anne exchanged glances. "I'll consult with Sarah," Anne said, referring to her black housekeeper, Sarah Moghrab. "I believe we can manage it."

She bit her lip, and Elizabeth noted with a pang the shimmer of tears in her mother's eyes. Suddenly it felt all too real that she was truly to sail far away for an unknown time from the only place she had ever known as home.

Caledonne got to his feet, the others rising with him. "I hate to break up such charming company, but it's growing late and I must return to my ship."

Dr. Howard ushered their guests to the front door, where one of Carleton's Marines now stood guard, with others manning concealed posts all around the estate. Dark clouds scudded low overhead, driven before the icy wind. Promising to return to join them at dinner on the morrow, Caledonne's party wrapped their cloaks around them and hurried to the coach waiting on the graveled carriageway at the foot of the steps, while Teissèdre lingered.

He bent over Elizabeth's hand, then straightened and fixed her in an earnest gaze. "Unfortunately, mademoiselle, I'll not have the pleasure of joining you tomorrow as I leave at sunrise for Valley Forge, and from there for Ohio Territory." He paused before murmuring, "I'll find him and bring him back if it is a thing possible to do."

She looked up into his kindly face, tear blinded. "And if he refuses?"

His fingers tightened over hers. "Then you alone will be able to persuade him."

The knot in her breast tightened at thought of the letter she had sent to Carleton immediately after his disappearance, as yet unanswered. "Alas," she said tremulously, "in that I've had no success."

Chapter Two

A DIN OF GUNFIRE and savage, ululating cries pulsed on the bitter late February wind, underlaid by the deep throb of drums and silvery hiss of rattles. White Eagle tightened his grip on the reins to curb his restive stallion, his heart lifting on a wave of fierce joy.

The clamor rose from a palisade that crowned the brow of a broad rise of land a short distance before them to the southwest, overlooking the *Hathennithiipi,* called Mad River by the Whites for the churning waters of its rocky, winding course. From his vantage just within the forest's verge, he could make out the dun-colored, snow-capped humps of wigewas and the taller rooflines of bark-clad lodges and log cabins that extended beyond the partially completed walls. Grey Cloud's Town, named for its sachem, the headman of the Black Hawk clan of the Kispokotha division of the Shawnee. It was smaller now than when he had lived among them, White Eagle observed, evidently losing part of its population when the clan removed from the *Cakimiyamithiipi,* the Little Miami River, the previous fall to this more remote location forty miles north.

He held himself proudly erect, feathered lance in hand, indifferent to the buffeting gale that drove a fine, misty snow through the trees, shrouding forest and plain in a shifting white veil. With his deep tan, flowing, sun-bleached blond hair, and intense blue-grey eyes, his appearance was always striking. It was even more so now, clad in the regalia of a notable war chief.

For this long-desired homecoming he had put on his richly beribbon-ed match coat and painted his face in a broad band of crimson edged with thinner stripes of yellow and white. His hair was dressed in a roach at the crown of his head, from which protruded three snowy eagle feathers.

His cousins Red Fox and his younger brother Spotted Pony, along with White Eagle's close friend Golden Elk, drew their mounts along-side, their gazes questioning. They were all similarly arrayed but wrapped in luxuriant bear hides against the cold, their faces reddened by the wind.

"Our people have waited eagerly for your coming, my brother," Red Fox said, his resonant voice gruff.

The warrior and his brother were tall and imposing, with coppery skin, aquiline noses, and straight black hair shaved to scalp locks. Both men's countenances reflected the same emotion that filled White Eagle, and he could also feel the impatience of the other brilliantly garbed warriors who waited behind them in the pack train.

"I doubt they're more eager than we are," Golden Elk exclaimed, anticipation lighting his clear blue eyes as he clapped his gloved hands together to warm them.

Chuckling, Spotted Pony gave him a sly look. "Blue Sky does not conceal her joy at her husband's coming."

"And I feared she'd forget me," Golden Elk scoffed, laughing. "It seems as though many winters have passed since I've seen my wife and son. By now He Leads the Way must walk!"

"Even an infant as superior as your son will not walk at only four moons," Red Fox observed dryly.

White Eagle acknowledged their banter with a slight quirk of his mouth. Still he delayed signaling their advance, thoughtfully studying the vista before him.

To their right towering sycamores clustered along the stream's rush-ing waters, their pale trunks and crooked branches forking through the dark, bare limbs of the winter woods like silent, ghostly lightning. Directly ahead of them, nearer the bluff's foot, he could make out a graveled ford,

ice-crusted and scoured of snow by the relentless wind. The dark, hud-
dled forms of cattle and hobbled horses were visible against white-man-
tled fields that spread along the promontory's eastern side as far as he
could see. And to the west, across the river, lay broad meadowland deeply
swathed in snowdrift, swelling gently upward into forested hills.

No sign that anything was amiss though the road to the British stronghold at Detroit lay within a short ride. He could not help wondering
whether any of the towns in the region harbored their soldiers.

As though reading his thoughts, Red Fox said quietly, "When the
runner arrived from the *Sciotothiipi* two sleeps ago, I took a party of our
warriors and scouted a long distance out. The snows have kept away all
but a few traders."

White Eagle gave a curt nod. Regardless that he had asked the sachem
of the town on the Scioto River where his party had stopped not to send
runners ahead announcing their coming, the man had done so anyway.
Doubtless they had gone on to alert Black Fish, the Chillicothe division's
primary sachem who favored allying with the British. Frowning, he returned his gaze to the top of the town's walls, where between the upright logs'
sharpened points he could see guards gathered on either side of the gates.

It was Saturday, February 21, early in *Haatawi kiishthwa*, the Crow
Moon. He had been absent from his people for more than a year, ever
since love for Elizabeth Howard had drawn him unwillingly back to
General George Washington and the war against England.

During their long journey west, repeated blizzards, rainstorms, sleet,
and bitter cold had forced them to take shelter for days at a time at Lenape,
Mingo, Kickapoo, Wyandot, and finally a scattering of Shawnee towns
along their route. The provisions they carried for their clan had by necessity diminished in gifts to their hosts, as had the number of White Eagle's
warriors from the towns, who stayed to winter with their families.

The restless movements of his companions broke his reverie. He
squinted up at the sky, calculating that the sun neared its zenith behind
the grey clouds that shrouded the sky.

The town's gates were suddenly thrown open, and the townspeople began to pour out in a dancing flood, all heavily bundled in furs and blankets against the piercing cold. At their head strode a delegation of the town's headmen. White Eagle drew his horse off the path and raised his lance, signaling the warriors forward.

"It is for you to lead us," Spotted Pony protested.

"Go. I will follow." He glanced at Golden Elk. "Go to your wife, my brother."

Laughing, Golden Elk and the others spurred their mounts forward. The rest of the party quickly followed, adding mightily to the din as they answered the townspeople's calls with warbling halloos and fired their guns into the air, the scalps they had taken in battle held aloft on poles. White Eagle's brawny, middle-aged servant and adopted brother, James Stowe, called by the Shawnee Little Running Heron for his hunched back and energetic movements, grinned and touched his hand to his drooping hat brim in salute as he brought up the rear.

When the leading warriors ascended the bluff toward the jubilant crowd at the town gates, White Eagle dismounted to follow on foot, leading his sleek, black-stockinged bay stallion, Devil. At his approach Grey Cloud released Golden Elk from his affectionate hold and turned to greet him, while the townspeople quickly bore the younger man away in their midst. Red Fox lingered with the elders as the grey-haired sachem stepped forward to clasp the hand White Eagle extended before pulling him into an embrace.

"You've been gone from us too long, my brother," he said, stepping back to fix White Eagle in a searching look. "We began to fear we'd not see you again."

"Only death will keep me from returning to my people." White Eagle forced a smile, dismissing his somber words. "I was beginning to wonder whether we'd find you before spring—and if we'd survive the storms that set upon us on our journey. Our people remaining in the towns along the *Sciotothiipi* told us that you followed those favoring the British who moved here," he added, noting the wary glance the sachem exchanged with his companions.

As though to forestall what he did not say, Grey Cloud hastily replied, "Red Fox told us of the Long Knives' great victories over the British at the places called Trenton, Princeton, and Saratoga, where you and our warriors fought at our Father Washington's right hand. He also said Healer Woman had been captured by the British. When Spotted Pony came in this morning, he said you waged a great battle against their ships and freed her."

"Let it be clear to our people that the British can be overcome, by wile if not by numbers," White Eagle returned, eyes narrowed. "Those who wish to ally with them would do well to remember it."

Grey Cloud avoided his gaze. "Spotted Pony also told us of the message you bring from our Father Washington."

Before White Eagle could respond the shaman, Loud Thunder, spat on the ground, his face taut with anger. "This Washington is a Long Knife like those who murdered Cornstalk. How can you or any of our warriors fight for these dogs?"

"This is a matter we will speak of later," Grey Cloud cut him off abruptly before turning back to White Eagle. "We received messengers from *Shemeneto, Waweypiersenwaw, Catecahassa,* and *Cottawamago,*" he said, referring to Black Snake, the principal war chief of their own Kispokotha sept; Blue Jacket, a leading Piqua sachem; Black Hoof of the Maquachake; and Black Fish, war chief of the Chillicothe division. "They are eager to counsel with you."

Devil tossed his head and sidestepped, ears laid back at the press of the townspeople around them. Keeping his expression impassive, White Eagle tightened his hold on the reins and stroked the stallion's nose to calm him while weighing his response.

"Our journey has been a long and arduous one, brother," he said at last. "Let me first learn how the Kispokotha have fared since my leaving and enjoy the peace of my own clan and fire. After I've spoken our Father

Washington's words before our council, there will be time to call together the great council of our people."

Grey Cloud held his silence, but his keen glance made it clear that he noted his careful choice of words.

"Black Snake requested that we inform him immediately of your coming," Red Fox broke in. "When Spotted Pony arrived this morning, a runner was sent to tell him."

Only Grey Cloud would have sent the messenger, and White Eagle stiffened, meeting his cousin's warning gaze with a barely arched brow.

"His town is less than a day's journey south," Grey Cloud explained, his tone defensive. "It would be well for him to hear our Father Washington's words when you speak them to our clan."

White Eagle inclined his head. "Then let us delay our council until he arrives."

Grey Cloud relaxed perceptibly. Smiling, he clasped White Eagle's shoulder and motioned him and the others into the palisade.

The town still showed signs of the clan's move three moons earlier, with most of the domiciles consisting of temporary, hastily built bark-clad wigewas. These were interspersed by a number of larger arch-roofed lodges constructed of pole frameworks covered with bark slabs, and a few two-room log houses, with here and there others in various stages of construction, their completion evidently delayed by the cold and storms.

By now the arriving warriors had all dismounted, both men and laden pack horses engulfed by the celebrating throng. All were gaunt and many also showed evidence of illness, White Eagle observed with concern.

The moment he entered, the townspeople pressed around him, calling out affectionate greetings and reaching to clasp his hand or touch his arm or shoulder or back. He responded to each one by name, acknowledging those who belonged to the small congregation of believers in Jesus with especial warmth, exchanging jokes and laughter with all as he made his way toward the town's center.

Increasingly he heard angry shouts regarding Cornstalk's murder, along with demands that he abandon the Long Knives and lead his warriors in exacting vengeance for this betrayal. He raised his hands for quiet and responded with the same answer he had given Grey Cloud, which for the moment appeared to mollify the crowd.

Surrounded, he came to a halt in front of the great, gable-roofed *msikahmiqui* that served as both temple for the people's religious ceremonies and meeting house for the clan's council. The supplies he had brought were being unloaded in front of it for distribution, with the townspeople gathering eagerly around.

He was keenly aware, however, that a small party hung back: Raging Bear and the warriors formerly allied with Wolfslayer, the shaman who had been White Eagle's implacable enemy and who had died at his hand. Clustered near the council house door, they directed hostile stares at him.

As he turned, he caught a glimpse of Wolfslayer's widow, Walks Far, and his stomach clenched. Not looking in his direction, she ducked through the crowd and disappeared from his sight.

Because of the breach with Wolfslayer, his leaving had been fraught with pain for the entire clan. He had clung to the hope that during his absence the division would be mended, and indeed it appeared that much healing had occurred. Some who had held aloof from him then now freely welcomed him home.

Raging Bear and his faction, however, had determined to stay behind at their original home on the Scioto and continue the fight against the Long Knives instead of moving with the clan to the Little Miami the previous spring. That they had rejoined them on the move here to the Mad River did not bode well for the clan's unity. Or for their allegiance in the war between the Americans and the British.

Feeling someone jostle him, White Eagle looked down at Little Running Heron, who had pushed his way through the crowd to take his accustomed place at his elbow. With him was his wife, Sweetgrass, a short, plump older matron with a round face most often wreathed in a smile. Meeting her husband's fond gaze now, she beamed at him before greeting White Eagle.

He returned a smile and handed Devil's reins to Little Running Heron. Touching his forehead in a quick salute, the older man led the stallion off through the crowd with Sweetgrass bustling along close at his side.

Other joyful reunions were taking place all around him, he saw, gladness filling him. Spotted Pony moved through the throng with his arm around his tall, slender wife, Rain Woman. A short distance away Red Fox and his wife, Laughing Otter, were engaged in animated conversation with a cluster of the leading matrons.

Then his gaze fell on Golden Elk, who had stopped nearby to greet his adoptive mother, Autumn Wind. She held his infant son, and on her other side stood the young widow Mary Douglas, her baby snugly bundled in a cradleboard on her back, who had accompanied Red Fox's party on their return to the clan.

As White Eagle watched, Golden Elk took the hands of his wife, Blue Sky, who stood before him. Nearly as tall as he, slender and willowy, she had a serene beauty that stood out among the other women.

White Eagle felt as though he intruded on a deeply intimate moment, yet he could not turn away. For they gazed into each other's eyes as though nothing else in all the world existed but the two of them. And the radiance that lighted their faces cut through his heart with a force that came very near to staggering him.

IMPOSSIBLE TO FIND WORDS to tell her how much he loved her. Even while gladly returning the greetings of his father Grey Cloud and all the others, Golden Elk had sought her over the heads of the crowd. She had never appeared more beautiful to him than at this moment, and he ached to embrace her, to show her with his body how deeply his soul cleaved to hers.

To his distress, the color drained from her face at his look, and she dropped her eyes to the ground, head bent. "Forgive me, my husband. I disgraced you at our parting, and—"

Cutting off her words, he cupped her cheek in his hand and raised her chin until her eyes met his. "There's nothing to forgive, dearest wife. My heart was bleeding too. And now it swells with joy to see you and our son happy and well. It was a hard thing for us to do, *seela?* But it was right for you to return to our people."

Blue Sky's face bloomed into a smile so sweet that he gathered her into his arms, reveling in the feel of her slender form against his, not caring that the others watched. After a moment he released her and greeted Autumn Wind before nodding respectfully to Mary.

"You and your son are well?"

The young woman returned his smile with a glowing one. "*Seela,* General—Golden Elk," she amended hastily. "Everyone is kind to us here."

She spoke the Shawnee tongue with greater ease now, and he directed a grateful look at Autumn Wind, who clearly had taken the young woman into her care. She gave him a pleased nod, and he turned his attention to the squirming baby the matron held against her shoulder. Blue Sky took him from her mother-in-law and gave him into Golden Elk's eager arms.

At first the baby stiffened and looked anxiously to his mother and grandmother. Golden Elk stroked his small, ruddy cheek with one finger, smiling down at him as he hungrily took in his dark eyes, his complexion a shade paler than his mother's warmly dusky one, the thick fuzz of rich golden brown hair that covered his scalp.

The baby's fussing quieted, and he fastened his gaze on his father's face. Then crowing and kicking his legs against his snug wrappings, he grabbed hold of the fringe of Golden Elk's shirt, tugging on it before reaching to clasp a fistful of the hair that blew across his cheek.

He laughed at the unexpectedly strong pull of the tiny fingers. Gently disentangled them, he enclosed his son's small hand in his.

"He remembers me."

Blue Sky leaned on his arm. "Leads the Way does not forget his father any more than I do, my husband. We rejoice that you've come home to us."

"I bring gifts for you and our son—and for my mother and father," Golden Elk said, looking up at Autumn Wind.

With a broad smile she took the child. "Your gifts are welcome, my son, but we rejoice more at your return. We have gifts for you as well, but first go give pleasure to your wife, while I care for your son."

Golden Elk's face heated at his body's instant response to her plain-spoken words. He looked down at Blue Sky in eager anticipation . . . only to find her face furrowed, her attention fixed on White Eagle.

"My sister has not come? Is she safe and well?" she asked, referring to Elizabeth Howard, whom she had adopted as her sister Healer Woman to keep her safe from Wolfslayer.

Sobering, Golden Elk explained what had happened. While he was speaking, Mary came to put her free arm around Blue Sky's waist, and leaning on each other, the two young women listened with unconcealed distress. When he finished, Blue Sky caught his hand and drew him with her, the others following as she hurried to where White Eagle stood amid a cluster of men.

LAUGHING, WHITE EAGLE reached for Leads the Way. When Autumn Wind surrendered him, he cradled the infant, his heart melting at his beauty and innocence. The boy met his gaze with a solemn one, gnawing on his fist with toothless gums, and the realization that he might never hold a child of his own struck White Eagle with painful force.

After a moment he reluctantly handed him to Golden Elk and said gruffly, "You're greatly blessed." Transferring his gaze to Blue Sky, he added, "May the Great Father fill your quiver with many sons and daughters."

Delight lit up her face, but she quickly sobered. "I pray it will be so for you as well, my brother. How does my sister? My husband told me that you carried her safely away from the British but that she has been very ill."

White Eagle held his emotions in check with difficulty. Knowing that the question of Elizabeth's return would inevitably arise and have to be addressed in some way, he had given the matter considerable thought.

"Healer Woman came very near to death because of her ill treatment by the British." He looked around at the others as he added what he had mentally rehearsed many times, "She grows slowly stronger, but she will never be well enough to live among our people. I've left her with her white parents that they may care for her." He had no idea how he kept his voice from breaking and his expression unmoved.

Blue Sky's face crumpled. "It cannot be so! Am I never to see my dear sister again?"

White Eagle avoided Golden Elk's sorrowful gaze. Since the initial disclosure of his leaving Elizabeth, he had refused to speak of the matter even with this friend, closer to him than a brother, and his dismissive words clearly came as a shock.

Grey Cloud placed his hand gently on White Eagle's shoulder. "I am sorry for this, yet is not everything in Moneto's hands?" he said, referring to the Shawnee's supreme deity.

"All will be according to his will, indeed. It is good."

White Eagle found no comfort in his words though he believed the truth of them. It took all his resolve to fight back the black despair that so often threatened to submerge him beneath an impenetrable cloud. Indeed at that moment he felt as though his life blood flowed from a wound that would never heal.

Golden Elk clasped his arm. "The Great Father's will in this matter has not yet been revealed, my brother. He will do so in his own time."

White Eagle pressed his lips together in a hard line. Forcing a nod, he turned quickly away.

✳ ✳ ✳

HE LOOKED UP as the elderly woman grasped his wrist in a surprisingly strong grip. She clutched the brightly colored lengths of woolen stroud and linen with her free hand, her wrinkled face wreathed in a toothless smile.

"Thank you, my son! We are glad for your safe return and for the great victories Moneto gave you."

"May the Great Spirit bless you for your goodness!" echoed her middle-aged daughter as she eagerly accepted the smoked ham and bag of flour Golden Elk piled into her arms. "Game has grown scarce and the hunger time is upon us.

Nodding toward the rest his warriors, who were handing out the provisions they had brought—which he had announced came from Washington and Congress—the older woman said, "Your medicine grows ever stronger with the Long Knives. May our Father Washington and the Thirteen Council Fires give us justice for Cornstalk's murder that we may live in peace together."

Amen, White Eagle thought, the memory of his several altercations with his commander over the past months nagging at his mind. Particularly the one that had followed when Washington relayed the news of Cornstalk's death. White Eagle had come within a hair's breadth of shaking the dust from his feet and returning to the Shawnee at once to persuade his countrymen to wage all-out war on the both the Americans and the British.

Noting Golden Elk's warning glance and the slight shake of his head, he wrestled his anger back under control. He returned both women's smiles with one he hoped communicated his utter confidence in his ability to sway the American's entire military establishment and their foot-dragging Congress to do his bidding. Beaming, the two women moved off, to all appearances harboring no doubt as to his capabilities.

"Steady," Golden Elk muttered just loud enough for him to hear. He grinned at the bland smile White Eagle returned.

The distribution of gifts was almost finished: flour, cornmeal, and haunches of smoked meats; brass kettles, axes, and other household goods; brightly colored ribbons and beads, fine woolen stroud and linen cloth for the women, who received them with delight. And for the men, ample powder and lead, finely crafted rifles and muskets, and tools to repair them. Gathered in clusters around the council house yard, they admired and proudly compared their new weapons with equal satisfaction. His generosity would swell the ranks of his warriors, White Eagle reckoned, despite their understandable reservations about the Long Knives.

He had suppressed his misgivings and personally offered weapons and ammunition to Raging Bear and his adherents as well in spite of the vehement protests Red Fox had voiced in private. Though White Eagle saw that a number of them cast covert, longing glances toward the men handing them out, they had all turned their backs to him and walked away without the courtesy of a single word. White Eagle could not decide whether he was more relieved or angered at the rebuff.

He scanned the faces of the remaining townspeople pressing eagerly forward. With the exception of Raging Bear's party, everyone was obviously impressed and grateful to receive the bounty he had brought them. Yet they all first stopped to greet him and express their sincere pleasure at his return.

Ashamed of his cynical thoughts, he turned to the next woman in line, and his heart constricted. Falling Leaf, the young widow of one of his warriors killed in battle, stepped hesitantly forward with her two young children. She had not washed or combed her hair, and her clothing was in disarray. By custom she would observe the Shawnee's mourning traditions for a year, he knew.

He knelt to draw the boy and girl into his arms. They pressed into him while Spotted Pony and Golden Elk gathered the double portion of food and other supplies given to the widows at White Eagle's direction. When he released them and rose, Falling Leaf stood to one side, her posture slack, head bent as though she had no strength to raise it.

"I grieve for your husband, my sister, and for you and these little ones," he said raggedly. "Red Crow was *psaiwi nenothtu,* a great warrior. I ask your forgiveness that we could not bring his body back to bury him among our people. But we performed all the rites due to one of such great courage and strength, and he lies beneath the field of battle where he fell."

She nodded and looked up, eyes glimmering with unshed tears, to whisper her gratitude. After assuring her that he would supply all her and her children's needs, he sent them off with their gifts, feeling that .he had offered only cold comfort.

The townspeople were beginning to disperse to their homes, driven before the relentless wind. Watching them, he was reminded of how Jesus had looked upon the people who flocked to him with great compassion, seeing them as sheep without a shepherd. He also caught a glimpse of something akin to that although, in fact, many shepherds sought to lead them.

In the wrong direction. To their destruction. As blind guides, even though they meant well and believed they were right.

At least, it seemed so to him. His confidence was tempered by the piercing reflection that he also was but a man. As a mortal he could not see as Jesus did, in truth could not see much more clearly than Black Fish and the other leaders of his nation and those around them.

And yet everything he had seen, everything he knew warned him that the course they advocated was a course of destruction. The history of the preceding years strongly affirmed it.

It occurred to him how much Jesus must have ached at his people's rejection, their stubborn insistence on following their own futile ways when as their true Shepherd he longed to lead them to green pastures and living water. And he pleaded silently for godly wisdom and for the determination and courage to guide this people in it.

Somehow they had to find the path that would lead them away from danger to true life, if not in this world, than in the one to come.

Chapter Three

"WE WAITED AT WYANDOTTE Town just north of here until Red Fox came to bring us in." White Eagle scanned the sweat-beaded faces of the men gathered with him in the sweat lodge. "Dunquat was there," he continued, referring to the Wyandot half king. "Some of their warriors fight with us, but he spoke not ten words to Spotted Pony and turned his back to me and Golden Elk."

Grey Cloud shook his head, his seamed face grave. "You fight on the side of the Long Knives, and it is said he gathers his warriors to attack Fort Randolph, where Cornstalk and the men with him were murdered. I have heard that many warriors of our own people with those from the Mingo and Lenape have taken the tomahawk into their hands to join him. They wait only for the sun to melt the snow and warm the earth."

Golden Elk snorted. "Did he think such a plan could be concealed from us, my father?"

Grey Cloud poured water from a gourd dipper onto the hot rocks along the edge of the fire's seething embers, releasing a dense cloud of steam into the already stifling air. "Perhaps he does not wish to hear your arguments against it, my son. When one is determined to do a thing, the counsel of those opposed to it is unwelcome."

Seated cross-legged beside Golden Elk, with Little Running Heron crouched between him and Red Fox in the lodge's narrow confines, White

Eagle wiped the dripping sweat from his face with a cloth. This was exactly what he faced from his own nation's sachems, he reflected—and very likely from many members of his clan as well, including Grey Cloud.

"I read the letter Governor Patrick Henry of Virginia sent our Father Washington, professing his anger and sorrow over Cornstalk's murder. Governor Henry is my friend. He swore to investigate the matter personally, and I believe he will do everything he can to mete out justice for this outrage."

Loud Thunder waved his hand in dismissal. "He and the governor of Pennsylvania sent messages to the headmen of our people denouncing the murderers. Even the Americans' Great Council sent a fawning letter by the hand of George Morgan. But their words are hollow."

Not waiting for White Eagle's response, he crawled to the sweat lodge's low entrance on his hands and knees and pushed through the raw-hide door flap, letting in a cold draft. Steeling himself, White Eagle followed the others out of the stifling, humid heat, the breath expelling from his lungs in a gasp as he emerged into the thickly falling snow and the icy wind raked his naked body.

When they could endure the cold no longer, they returned to the glowing heat inside and poured more water on the red-hot rocks until the rising steam all but obscured their forms in the narrow low-ceilinged space. Grey Cloud chanted a prayer, echoed by Loud Thunder, and silence ensued for some moments.

At length, as though reading White Eagle's thoughts, Grey Cloud began to explain the reasons for moving the town. No sooner had they settled on the Little Miami and planted their crops the past spring, than great concern had arisen because of Black Fish's attacks on Long Knife forts in the Shawnee's ancient hunting grounds across the *Spelewathiipi,* the Ohio River, in Cantuckee. Raging Bear and a strong party of warriors from their own clan had participated in the raids.

"Those from the Maquachake division who followed Cornstalk in holding to peace have broken away from our nation because of this," Red

Fox said grimly. "They see no advantage in becoming entangled in the Long Knives' war with the British and hope to stay out of it."

Golden Elk nodded. "We came by Goshochking on the Tuscarawas and spoke to those from the Maquachake and Piqua divisions and also a few of our own Kispokotha who went to live under White Eyes' protection among our grandfathers, the Lenape."

Increasing numbers of the Shawnee, primarily the Chillicothe division, with a number of the Maquachake and Kispokotha, favored allying with the British to resist the Long Knives, Loud Thunder told them. These factions were steadily withdrawing from the *Sciotothiipi* to settle farther west and north along the valleys of the *Hathennithiipi,* the *Cakimiyamithiipi,* and the *Miyamithiipi,* called by the Whites the Great Miami, where they would be less vulnerable to American attack and from which they could carry out raids on white settlements and forts. Among them were also great numbers of Mingo, Lenape, and Twightwee as well as tribes from the north along *les Grands-Lacs*—the Great Lakes—the Wyandot, Ottawa, Ojibwa, and Potawatomi.

White Eagle listened without comment though he had been fully informed of the matter in discussions with those who remained along the Scioto. Now he concluded dryly, "So you chose to settle here on the road to Fort Detroit among those allied with the British, from whom they receive supplies as payment for their allegiance."

No one answered, but the glance Grey Cloud and Loud Thunder exchanged spoke volumes. "I did not choose it, my brother," Red Fox said, his dark eyes glittering.

"The council decided it was necessary in order to protect our elders and women and children from Long Knife reprisals," Grey Cloud said at last. "We heard this Governor Henry plans to send out soldiers under a man called Clark to wage war against us for Black Fish's attacks."

"We have not determined whether to ally with the British or seek peace with the Long Knives—if that is possible." Loud Thunder's tone made it clear that he had already decided it was not.

"Is it a coincidence that Raging Bear and those loyal to Wolfslayer have now returned to our clan?"

Color flooded into Grey Cloud's face. Avoiding White Eagle's stern gaze and ignoring his question, he said, "Many *Canadiens français* come among us, making fine speeches and giving us good gifts. They urge us to fight for the British. Is it surprising that our people trust them? They have long counseled and traded with us, even taken wives from among us. They do not take our lands, and they swear they will supply us with all that is needed to drive out these *shemanese*."

With supreme effort White Eagle bit back the bitter response that sprang to his tongue. Had they—unlike Cornstalk—learned nothing after pursuing this unfruitful path time and again only to suffer the same destructive consequences?

The memory flooded back of the turbulent council meeting at which the decision had been made for war and he had been left no choice but to give in to his clan's demand that he assume the mantle of war chief. Would they now again have to go through the same motions only to end up in the same place? He wanted violently to curse.

Little Running Heron laid his hand on his arm. He returned the older man's penetrating look, struck, as often, by how much he had come to depend on his adopted elder brother's steady presence since the Great Father had bound them together during a time of great need in England.

He became aware that Golden Elk, Red Fox, and Spotted Pony regarded him intently. These men, too, stood beside him, though they harbored the same doubts he did.

He drew in a slow breath, stiffening his resolve. He needed Grey Cloud and the other headmen of the clan on his side if he was to have any hope of preventing another futile repetition of history. His response now would be crucial in gaining it.

The trouble was that deep in his gut he understood his people's opposition to the Long Knives. More, he shared it—shared their rage at this latest betrayal. It burned in him, bringing back the bitterness of soul that had consumed him at Black Hawk's cruel, unjust murder by white settlers.

An equally great dilemma, however, was that he also cherished the ideals enshrined in the Americans' Declaration of Independence. There were many among them who lived out their convictions, good friends like Washington and Patrick Henry whom he deeply loved and admired despite the flaws that blinded them—as all men—to their personal hypocrisies.

Was it possible to find middle ground between the two sides any more than between Raging Bear's faction and his own? Cornstalk, his people's great sachem, had died for his efforts to bridge the two sides.

Great Father, give me wisdom, he pleaded silently.

"It was your council, my brother, for us to move farther west because of the danger of reprisals for your own raids," Grey Cloud pointed out.

"But our clan moved north with those who are for war," Golden Elk countered. "Is that not why Raging Bear and his party rejoined our clan after they had broken away—because of the 'good gifts' the British provide?"

White Eagle suppressed a laugh at Grey Cloud's and Loud Thunder's obvious discomfiture. Keeping posture and tone humble, he reminded them that along with Cornstalk he had opposed the war and had only agreed to serve as their war chief because both the men's and women's councils demanded it—and to refuse would have allowed Wolfslayer to take command.

He let his words sink in before deliberately softening his expression. "You did well in bringing our clan to a place where the people will be safer for now," he continued with an approving nod at Grey Cloud. "My concern is that the Long Knives will inevitably turn their eyes to the nest where their attackers bide. It is here they will come. And they will find our clan in the midst of their enemies just as they did during Lord Dunmore's War, when they began to wipe away the towns along the *Sciotothiipi* whether their warriors had joined in the attacks or not."

Gruffly Grey Cloud said, "Perhaps it had been better for us to go to White Eyes' people."

White Eagle considered this, at last shook his head. "When a great storm arises, it breaks first on those nearest at hand. I fear it will be so even for our grandfathers, the Lenape. Both the Americans and the British threaten those who do not fight on their side, and they are torn between the two even as we are."

"Then what are we to do?" Loud Thunder demanded. "There is no place of safety, for no one can live in peace with those who refuse to keep it!"

"When we went to war after Black Hawk's murder, Kishkalwa opposed it and separated from our people to lead the Thawekila division across the Great River to the Spanish. The time may come when it is necessary for us to do so as well."

White Eagle gave Spotted Pony an approving nod. "You speak wisely, my brother."

Before he could say more, Golden Elk abruptly cut him off. "You do not say it, but I know it weighs as heavily on your heart as it does on mine. The British offer a high price for both of us because we betrayed them—and that on yours is much greater since your victory against them at New York."

He turned a reproachful gaze on Grey Cloud. "My brother and I came all this way to find our clan, only to discover that we've placed ourselves—including my wife and son, your grandson—within reach of their hands."

The color drained completely out of Grey Cloud's face. And seeing it, White Eagle bit back the anger he had fought to contain since their arrival.

Chapter Four

WHITE EAGLE LED his warriors and their families into the *msikah-miqui*, where the townspeople had begun to gather for the evening banquet in their honor. Built of freshly hewn logs, the great structure was patterned on previous ones, standing roughly eighty feet long, thirty feet wide, and twenty feet high with a door at each end.

The air was laden with savory scents that caused his mouth to water as he took in his surroundings. All down the building's length large kettles bubbled over the shimmering embers in the fire circles. The fragrant steam that rose from them mingled with the coils of smoke twining upward to the holes in the roof. These were partially covered to keep out the snow, and a layer of smoke hung overhead.

Stout crossbeams spanned two rows of ancient wooden pillars that ran down the building's length, supporting its roof. They had been carried from the town's previous site, as with earlier migrations going back to the clan's first sachem named Black Hawk, the great-grandfather of White Eagle's adoptive father. Intricate relief carvings of all manner of creatures decorated each one. A fearsome, distorted face topped their front and back sides, hanging beneath a handful of twisted tobacco, while the outward and inward sides displayed carvings of the clan's totem: a great hawk in flight painted black, with iridescent clamshells inset for eyes, beak, and talons that glittered in the smoky firelight.

As always he felt his spirit deeply at home, held in thrall by the mystery of his people's ancient heritage that filled the space like a palpable presence. Almost he could perceive just beyond the range of hearing the distant, chanting voices of the ancestors who had gone before and feel a subtle vibration in the ground beneath his feet as if from their dancing.

A profound gratitude swept over him to be among this people again. Here he belonged as nowhere else.

The townspeople gathered around to greet him with a gladness that drew him back to the present. All were arrayed in their finest clothing, though he noted that much was worn and threadbare.

The women, most of them slender and straight in bearing, wore colorful trade cloth shirts and wrap-around, knee-length stroud petticoats belted at the waist, with the young maidens dressed in the finest fashion. Ribbons, quillwork, and beads edged leggings and moccasins, and a multitude of silver brooches adorned each article of clothing. Silver rings studded their ears and spots of red paint colored their cheeks. All wore their hair parted in the center, either tied behind the head to fall loose down their backs or clubbed and pierced through with dyed porcupine quills.

For the most part tall, lean, and muscular, with noble features, the younger men made an imposing appearance, while the elders were generally bent and wizened due to the rigors of their way of life. Like the women, however, every face was characterized by a lively good humor. Everyone wore collarless, thigh-length trade cloth shirts cinched at the waist with brilliantly colored woven sashes; a breechcloth; leggings adorned with ribbons, dyed porcupine quills, and beads; and thickly padded winter moccasins. Many had slit loose the rims of their ears and stretched them until they hung to their shoulders, with silver baubles dangling from them. Silver armlets decorated their arms, and silver nose rings and gorgets hanging from the neck were commonplace.

Most of the warriors shaved their heads, leaving only a long scalp lock trimmed with feathers or other trinkets at the crown, while others like White Eagle and Golden Elk pulled up the hair at the fore and sides of their head into a roach, which they trimmed as did the others. The rest of the townsmen wore their hair shoulder length, with a feathered headdress or a length of silk or linen wound around the head in the form of a turban.

That evening White Eagle had donned a shirt of finely woven grey-blue wool over richly beaded, quilled, and beribboned leggings and moccasins. Like the rest of the men, broad lines of red striped his cheekbones and a folded woolen blanket draped his shoulder, while a gleaming silver gorget and armlets completed his attire.

The customary trading of stories and jokes punctuated with laughter was subdued that evening. It was clear that Cornstalk's murder was on everyone's mind, along with the issue of whether their nation should ally with the British against the Long Knives.

Moving among the townspeople, he caught snatches of conversation—quickly silenced at his approach—about Healer Woman's absence. That they had obeyed the council in not marrying was spoken of with approval. Their restraint had brought them favor and helped to restore unity in the clan. He was glad for it.

But he also overheard whispers from more than one of the matrons that since Healer Woman was unable to return, he should take to wife a maiden born among the Shawnee. Healer Woman had been adopted into Blue Sky's Piqua sept, and if he were to marry another, she also could not be a member of Black Hawk's clan, according to the tribe's taboos.

It was a matter he wished heartily not to think about. But knowing it was one he would inevitably be forced to address, he allowed his gaze to drift casually across the assembly. He noted several families from other clans or divisions of the tribe living in the town who had daughters of marriageable age. More than one met his glance with a hopeful one before quickly averting her eyes, color rising to her cheeks. And the mothers nodded proudly to him with eager invitation in their smiles. He suppressed a sigh.

His warriors were finding places for their families along the near side at the building's front, and glad for the distraction, he took his place at their head. Little Running Heron and Sweetgrass settled close behind him as everyone found seats. Bending over his youngest daughter, Red Fox gently steered her to Laughing Otter and sat next to White Eagle with his younger son Little Deer pressing against his side.

White Eagle laid his hand on the boy's head. "You helped to protect our clan on the move here?"

The boy beamed up at him. "I did as you told me before you left us, grandfather."

Everyone fell silent as Grey Cloud joined Loud Thunder and the leading elders gathered before the fire at the building's head to sprinkle tobacco on the flames. Its fragrance rose to mingle with the succulent scents of cooking food. The shaman then led them in invoking the Shawnee's ancient gods, and together the people began to chant the prayers of thanksgiving.

White Eagle met the questioning gazes of the small fellowship of believers in Jesus seated nearby. He inclined his head to them, then closing his eyes, he raised his hands, palms upward, praying silently to the Great Father, as they followed his example.

When the prayers ended, he looked up to find Golden Elk studying Grey Cloud with a frown. "I fear my father straddles the fences between several fields."

White Eagle slanted a glance toward the sachem, who had taken his seat at the building's head as the women began to serve the food. "Trying to placate everyone is a sure road to pleasing no one."

Beginning with White Eagle and his warriors, the matrons carried the steaming kettles between the seated groups to spoon generous helpings of bean pudding, squash, and corn stew simmered with succulent bear meat into wooden bowls and on bark plates, while the maidens passed among them with baskets overflowing with corncakes.

A comely maiden of about twenty winters named Nettle Flower approached as she passed a basket around among his warriors. She was dressed in brilliant ceremonial garb, her hair sleekly parted and wrapped in a length of beaded red stroud at the back of her head. Coming to his side, she crouched, her arm brushing his as though accidentally. She held out the basket, taking him in with a slow, meaningful smile.

"Eat, my brother," she urged, her low voice seductive. "Strengthen your medicine among us and your hand against our enemies."

He took one of the few remaining cakes, keeping his expression non-committal. *"Neahw."* Thank you.

From the corner of his eye he caught sudden movement as Blue Sky snatched the basket out of Nettle Flower's hand. Passing it along to those on her other side, she fixed the maiden in a fierce, narrowed gaze.

"You may return to your mother now, little sister," she said, her tone causing color to flame on the maiden's face as though she had slapped her. "Your basket is empty."

Nettle Flower pushed to her feet. Dismissing Blue Sky with a poisonous look, she turned a beguiling smile on White Eagle before flouncing away.

White Eagle avoided Golden Elk's astonished glance, biting his lip hard to stifle a guffaw as Blue Sky settled back into her seat with a satisfied smile. He fought down a powerful urge to kiss her.

While they ate and traded jokes, he caught a glimpse of Walks Far, who was helping to serve at the building's rear. Her eldest daughter and son were with her, children of about twelve and ten winters. As before, she did not come near him and kept her face turned away.

The stark memory of her grief-stricken wails as she bent over Wolf-slayer, who lay at his feet, dead at the stroke of his knife, overwhelmed him suddenly, and his appetite fled. He had made her a widow and her children orphans, an act that had not ceased to torment him.

That he had prevailed over Wolfslayer had resolved nothing in the end. Indeed, it had only sharpened the conflict—as he suspected Raging Bear was determined to prove. And now Cornstalk's murder the previous fall complicated everything even more.

"Some sleeps ago, while on a raid into Cantuckee, Black Fish and Black Hoof captured several white men hunting there," Red Fox said in an undertone, interrupting White Eagle's painful reflections. "With them was a man called Boone."

Spotted Pony leaned around his brother. "Cornstalk's brother Nimwha has taken his place as the principal sachem of our nation. It is said that he also was with those who took Boone, as well as some *Canadiens.*" Deliberately he added, "Raging Bear and his men were with them too."

The bite of corn cake White Eagle swallowed stuck in his throat. "Why did Grey Cloud make no mention of this?"

Red Fox shrugged. "Loud Thunder and some of our elders favor allying with the British, and Grey Cloud's words are circumspect. I cannot tell on which side he stands."

Golden Elk handed his fussing son to Blue Sky. "We've heard of this Daniel Boone. He's led many white settlers over the mountains into Cantukee and built a fort they call Boonesborough."

Red Fox gave his empty bowl to Laughing Otter, who had risen to collect them. "Black Fish brought the captives to Chillicothe, and it's said he plans to take them with him to Governor Hamilton at Detroit."

"Some of our brothers say Boone promised to persuade his people to surrender to Black Fish when he returns in the spring." Spotted Pony gave Golden Elk a meaningful glance.

Using a fragment of corn cake, Golden Elk hastily sopped up the last of his bean pudding before relinquishing his bowl. As he chewed he mumbled, "From what I know of this man, Black Fish is mistaken if he believes Boone will cause his people to surrender to him."

Spotted Pony gave a derisive snort. "More likely he will attempt to escape and warn them."

White Eagle looked from one to the other. "I'm afraid you're right, my brothers. Boone is not our friend, though doubtless he'd have us think so now that he's been captured. Black Fish would be wise to watch him carefully."

As the women cleared away the bowls, bark plates, and leftover food, he glanced toward the members of the believer's fellowship. "Do the brothers and sisters remain faithful?" he asked Red Fox.

"Several now question the truth of the teachings, and a few have fallen away either because of Cornstalk's murder or because they wish to participate in the ancient ceremonials with the rest of our clan." Red Fox paused before adding reluctantly, "Autumn Wind stands firm, but Grey Cloud wavers in this as well."

Golden Elk studied Grey Cloud apprehensively. "I will speak with my father."

"It may be better to let this matter go for the time, my brother," White Eagle said gravely. "If you confront him, his heart might only harden further. Your life and that of Blue Sky and your mother are the strongest witness."

Golden Elk frowned, but nodded. "I'm anxious for his soul, but I'll wait on the Great Spirit's guidance."

He pondered the reasons why his adoptive father might have changed his position on the faith and the politics of their clan and nation. Certainly there must be pressures on him from within the clan that he had to navigate carefully if he was to maintain his leadership.

Despite the differences that appeared to be growing between the two of them, he felt a deep gratitude for this man who had become a true father to him. Even in the relatively short time they had spent together, Golden Elk had come to love and respect him, had given careful attention to his teachings on the customs, traditions, and protocols of their nation, division, and clan.

Golden Elk's white father had not been a father to him at all, nor had he been worthy of respect. He had never instructed, counseled, or advised Golden Elk in any way and had left him without steady moorings for his life. Indeed his family had been ruined because of the man.

But now—because of all that happened to White Eagle—he had found a true people and family, a wife and son dearer to him than life.

Day by day, even hour by hour, he felt his heart and soul being knit to them more tightly. To ever leave them had become unimaginable.

He looked up as Red Fox indicated a sturdily built man sitting with a woman and an attractive young maiden whom Golden Elk guessed to be his wife and daughter. In appearance and dress, they were not Shawnee.

"John Walk on Water and his wife and daughter settled among our clan last fall and moved with us here. He is Oneida of the Haudenosaunee, and Abigail Rising Moon is Tuscarora. They adhere to the teachings of a man called Samuel Kirkland. Walk on Water knows the words of the Bible and speaks strongly in our fellowship."

"Is not this man Kirkland a missionary among the Haudenosaunee?" Golden Elk asked.

Spotted Pony nodded. "He supports the Long Knives against the British. Our Oneida brothers who fight for Washington speak well of him."

Cradling her son against her shoulder, Blue Sky leaned around Golden Elk to speak to White Eagle. "Walk on Water told us he is eager to counsel with you, my brother."

At that moment Walk on Water looked up to meet their assessing gazes with a direct and open one. When White Eagle inclined his head respectfully, he smiled and nodded in response.

"I would speak with him as well," White Eagle said. "Let us call the fellowship together tomorrow after the council meets."

"I have a feeling we're going to need their prayers," Golden Elk muttered under his breath as Grey Cloud rose to face the assembly.

Chapter Five

WHITE EAGLE KEPT his expression neutral as Grey Cloud welcomed him and his warriors home, then concluded, "We are grateful for the many good gifts our brother brought us from our Father Washington and the Thirteen Council Fires."

He had no sooner finished speaking than one of his warriors, Brown Bear, sprang to his feet "Our brother is gracious to say this," he said, waving his arm in White Eagle's direction,. "but these things come from his hand, not from Washington or the Long Knife sachems! They are too poor to give any gifts, nor do they respect our people enough to do so even if they had the means. It is White Eagle alone we should thank!"

A loud murmur filled the council house. Hurriedly White Eagle pushed to his feet and held up his hands for silence.

He inclined his head toward Brown Bear. "My brother is a great warrior, one on whom I depend greatly in battle, and I thank him for his praise. These gifts indeed come at my hand as he says, but in the authority of our Father Washington and through him the Americans' Great Council. Indeed they do not possess the wealth the British do, but even so they won great victories against them at Trenton, Princeton, and Saratoga as Red Fox reported to you at his return two moons ago. Such victories are bought at a great price."

As the murmurs subsided, he continued firmly, "Our Father Washington appealed to me to bring these gifts to our people to demonstrate not only his and the Great Council's deep respect and gratitude for the part our warriors played in defeating the British, but also their grief and outrage at the murder of Cornstalk and those with him."

Turning, he strode to Brown Bear and clasped his hand. "Thank you, my brother, for your good words. You honor me, and I will not forget it."

Brown Bear's sullen expression cleared. He sat down with a proud smile and a puffed out chest, the warriors around him clapping him on the back in approval.

When White Eagle returned to his seat, Golden Elk murmured in English, "He is right, Jon."

"Though not exactly politic," White Eagle returned in an undertone in the same language, keeping his gaze fixed on Grey Clous.

They were interrupted by Raging Bear's contemptuous voice from the other side of the council house. "Do not White Eagle's warriors follow him because he supplies them many goods? Is this not why he now brings gifts to us as well—because he seeks to buy our agreement to lie down beneath the Long Knives' feet?"

Outraged, Red Fox objected loudly, "This may be true for a few who look only to themselves. It is not so for the rest of us, who follow our brother from our hearts because he is a man of a single tongue who does what he says, who speaks wisely and opens his hand to all who deal honorably. How many of our people speak proud words even as they lap up the gifts the British offer to buy their loyalty as dogs lick the hands of their masters who feed them when it suits them?"

White Eagle sucked in a breath and met Golden Elk's astonished gaze with raised eyebrows. His friend looked as though he worked hard to strangle a burst of laughter, while from across the council house, Raging Bear and his warriors appeared to be struck, for the moment, beyond speech.

"It is so," Spotted Pony was saying with equal anger. "I hear our men speak among themselves, and their allegiance is to White Eagle and our people alone, not to our Father Washington and the Long Knives. Our brother seeks the good of our people, not his own glory as some here do."

A roar of agreement rose from the warriors clustered around them. Across the expansive space the voices raised in approval of White Eagle drowned out those of Raging Bear and his faction.

As Grey Cloud attempted to quiet the tumult, Raging Bear shook his fist at White Eagle. "Had this Long Knife not stood in the way, Wolfslayer would have been our war chief, and we would have allied with the British and driven the Whites away forever," he spat. "Because White Eagle was jealous that Wolfslayer's medicine was stronger than his, he killed him so that he might persuade us to do the bidding of the *shemanese* like a tame dog. Even now he brings this message from Washington seeking to blind our eyes—"

By now all of White Eagle's warriors were on their feet, vehemently contesting Raging Bear's charges. Those clustered around Raging Bear instantly sprang up, shouting in return.

Reluctantly White Eagle stood up again, but before he could speak, Red Fox strode to the forefront. "Raging Bear speaks as a man who has no memory and no sense! Only one winter has passed, and have we forgotten already how Wolfslayer gave White Eagle no choice but to fight him to the death? If Wolfslayer's medicine had indeed been the stronger, why did he not prevail? Was his fall not the will of Moneto, the Great Father?"

Movement among the women at the back of the council house caught White Eagle's eye, and his chest tightened. Walks Far had also gotten to her feet.

She was a tall woman, still gaunt from the year of mourning for her husband that had ended several moons earlier, and she shook as though she would fall down. He had learned that she had left the town not long after his departure and had returned the previous fall, bringing with her only her two eldest children.

Voice trembling, she said humbly, "Since Raging Bear has spoken the name of my husband, may I be permitted also to speak of him?"

Grey Cloud silenced the tumult and commanded everyone to return to their seats. As White Eagle sat down, he met Golden Elk's dismayed glance with the slight shake of his head.

When a strained quiet fell over the council house, Grey Cloud said, "You may speak, my sister."

Walks Far drew herself to her full height with great dignity. "When Wolfslayer died I was filled with hate, even as Raging Bear and the men with him are. I desired vengeance more than any other thing." Indicating White Eagle, she added, "My heart froze like ice in winter when no one repaid him for killing my husband, the father of my children. Indeed I wanted to kill him with my own hand."

So great had her anger and hatred been, she continued, that she had not been able to stay among the clan even in White Eagle's absence She had taken her children and gone to live with her sister at Lichtenau, a town belonging to the people called Moravian, where she fulfilled the days of her mourning.

"My sister and her husband are believers in the Great God, the Father in Heaven White Eagle told us of. They took me to listen to one of the brothers called Zeisberger who spoke words of love and forgiveness I had never heard before. My sister's husband also spoke many such words to me and to our grandfathers the Lenape and some of our brothers and uncles who live among the Moravians. And slowly the ice in my heart began to melt. I saw the peace they had, the love and forgiveness they gave to all, and I wanted this for myself. For I knew if I did not choose this path I would either do terrible things or my heart would forever lie like a stone in my breast."

White Eagle listened, stunned, as with tears falling unchecked, she turned to face him and said, "I gave my heart to the Great Father, and he has taken away all my hatred as though it had never been."

"I did not want to fight your husband, my sister," White Eagle said hoarsely, fighting his own tears. "Can you forgive me for his death?"

"My brother, I have forgiven you already and ask that you also forgive me for my hardness of heart, for Jesus says that to think of killing another is the same as to do it. I see now that my husband was at fault for what happened. You tried to stop the fight, but he would not turn aside."

He rose and strode to her through the throng, many of whom now wiped their eyes as well. Standing before Walks Far, he took her hands in his and bent his head over them.

"I thank you, my sister. This matter has long troubled me."

"Let it worry you no longer," she said, smiling up at him, "and let there be peace between you and me."

GOLDEN ELK ROLLED OVER onto his side, his arm curved around Blue Sky's waist. After a quick glance at Leads the Way, who slept in his cradle-board, heavily swaddled against the cold, he took her face between his hands and kissed her. She responded with equal passion as she had during their lovemaking, and his heart swelled.

"How I love you," he whispered. "You're the most beautiful of women, not only in appearance, but also in heart and mind."

She snuggled into his arms, beaming. "What have I done to deserve a husband who is so kind and good, and a great warrior—" she broke off to look up at him "—and so handsome a man that all the other women envy my good fortune."

Raising up on one elbow, she reached to tuck the wrappings more tightly around their babe. "And our son is as beautiful as his father. Every day I pray to the Great Father that he will grow to be a man like you."

He chuckled and drew her back down beside him. "He'd do better to be as beautiful and as good as his mother."

It was incomprehensible to him that God had blessed him so greatly in this small family. His own, as a child, had been one of misery and want, with a father who squandered a rich inheritance in gambling and drink and a careworn mother who died because of his neglect. That this beautiful woman belonged to him now, and the child born of their bodies, that he had so unexpectedly and without his deserving been blessed with worthy adoptive parents and the connections of an entire clan with an honorable history astounded him.

Worry returned over the changes in Grey Cloud's manner. "Has my father turned away from our Father in Heaven?" he asked.

Blue Sky frowned. "He says little, but he no longer joins in our fellowship. Your mother is brokenhearted. Loud Thunder and some of the elders press him to return to our ancestors' ways and to ally with the British. From what I can tell, they do not oppose White Eagle, but they think he must turn his back to the Long Knives and join with Black Fish."

He released her and rolled onto his back. "They must know that is impossible—especially now after he took Healer Woman from the British."

She sighed. "It seems as though they've lost their reason. I pray they'll regain it when White Eagle presents our Father Washington's message before the council tomorrow."

"Black Snake has been informed of it and may come to hear this message with us."

Blue Sky hesitated, then said softly, "He agrees with Black Fish."

"So I assumed."

For some moments they remained silent. At length she laid her head on his shoulder, and he wrapped her in his arms.

"I wish my sister and White Eagle had the happiness we share. Has he truly given her up?"

He let out his breath. "He'll not speak of it even to me, but I fear so."

Briefly he told her of Healer Woman's letter detailing the bitter confrontation in which her white parents had insisted that unless White Eagle utterly renounced the Shawnee and left them forever they would never agree to his marrying their daughter. Blue Sky chewed her lip as she listened.

"He'll never do it!" he concluded. "He's one of us. Even his love for Healer Woman cannot tear him away from our people."

"But will she not come to him regardless of what her white parents say?"

"What the British did to her left her too weak to travel so far. And even if she could, White Eagle refuses to let her, for he won't be the cause of a rift between her and her white parents."

Blue Sky gave a reluctant nod. "Our people also value highly our relations with our families, our clan, and our tribe. To leave them or to lose them is unthinkable. But she is my sister and Shawnee too," she added disconsolately. "Has she forgotten me?"

He cupped her face in his hand and gazed fondly at her. "She does not forget you, dear wife, and she longs to be with you again. I know she'd come regardless of White Eagle's opposition if she was strong enough to bear the journey. But she may never be."

To his surprise she relaxed and smiled up at him. With a confidence in which was no shadow of doubt, she said, "Then we must pray to the Great Father. He will hear us, and he will overcome even this obstacle."

WHITE EAGLE SPRAWLED on the sleeping platform, hands clasped behind his head, staring into darkness softened only by the faint light reflecting from the banked coals on the hearth. From across the narrow room he could hear the soft snores of Sweetgrass and Little Running Heron, underlaid by the seethe of wind-driven snow around the cabin's exterior. From time to time a stronger gust shook the small building.

The gathering that evening had broken up early, Grey Cloud urging that they forgo the nightly dances and return to their homes before the blizzard blocked passage along the town's lanes. Hours had passed since the townspeople dispersed and he returned to Sweetgrass's cabin with the couple, yet his mind would not quiet.

He had hoped on his return to find the comfort and peace he had known as a youth and while he last abode with them, before the conflict with Wolfslayer came to its tragic conclusion. To take solace in the daily rhythms of the Shawnee's close-knit community, in their harmony with the mysteries of earth and sky and the great cycle of the seasons governed by the heavenly orbs, in the physical and spiritual sustenance the unfettered freedom of the vast wilderness afforded. But he was not to find it now, he realized with a sinking heart, and he doubted he ever would again.

He was deeply grateful for the reconciliation between him and Walks Far. But the sullen expressions of Raging Bear and his adherents made it clear that their anger would not be appeased. The foreboding that the days ahead were likely to be as tumultuous as the *Hathennithiipi* pierced him. He would have to cling to the Great Father with all his mind, heart, and strength if he was to safely navigate those churning waters.

As if that was not difficult enough, he also felt a mighty wind blowing before it all that had been. Irrevocable changes were sweeping away his people's world with the inexorable advance of white settlers. The invaders were changing the very nature and meanings of the land his people depended on for life, nor would they be turned back. The Shawnee along with all the native peoples were going to have to adapt in some way or another, but he could not discern a path forward that would not lead them onto dangerous, unknown shoals and to eventual destruction.

Was it possible to prevent that from happening or even so much as slow down its progress? he wondered bleakly. Indeed, he was only one man, and even if he gained reputation and influence among the Americans, the question remained whether their government could—or would—protect their native allies. Or whether, having won the war, they also would betray them when it became convenient and profitable to open native lands to settlement by their own people.

From the moment he had learned of the murders of Cornstalk and his companions and determined to return to the Shawnee, he had expected a confrontation with the tribal leaders. Every mile his party traveled westward, he had mulled the matter over between successive waves of rage, grief, and despair. He had discussed every possible course with Spotted

Pony and Golden Elk, yet the future seemed as trackless as the great, brooding swamps that interspersed the forests.

What he had not expected was the simmering resistance of the leaders of his own clan, much less the presence of Raging Bear, who again pressed the same stubborn opposition White Eagle had faced with Wolfslayer.

Repeatedly he had pleaded for the Great Father to reveal his will in all of this and provide wisdom as to what he must do. But the heavens remained as unyielding as iron. The more he sought understanding and guidance, the more he doubted the course he had chosen.

He was beginning to think that . . . he was asking the wrong questions.

Disheartened, he rolled onto his side and pulled blanket and bearskin more snugly around him against the seeping cold.

All during the journey west he had pushed himself past the edge of exhaustion, focusing intently on the needs of each day, driving his party to ride long and late, then sitting around the fire in conversation with his warriors as the night wore away, or counseling with the headmen of the native towns they stopped at and joining in their dances until mind and body were too numb to resist sleep any longer. All in the determination to avoid thought and feeling that would plunge him again into the anguish of that black void that ever hovered at the border of consciousness.

But in that dark hour stark reality broke through all the defenses he had erected to keep it at bay. That other time when Elizabeth had been wrenched away from him he had not given her up, not truly. Though he had told himself he had, still his heart had clung to her. Deep in his soul he had cherished the hope that somehow he might find her again—or that she might be drawn to him as to a lodestar and traverse the miles between them to find him there in the wilderness.

As she had!

He had concluded then that it had to be God's will and not just their own desire that brought her safely to him across hundreds of miles of wild and perilous terrain. And though it had riven his heart to leave his people, he had done it, believing he was called to do so.

Only for a time. That they would finally wed . . . and then return.

He could no longer believe any of it. Was he not, after all, to blame that her health had been so broken aboard that cursed prison ship that her life had been spared only by a thread? Was he not also at fault for the bitter confrontation with her parents? How could he ever have believed that they could accept, even tolerate, that he had become Shawnee, much less a war chief, and the actions that had brought her into such grave danger?

But this time he had truly given her up, refusing to be the one who caused a break between her and her family. His banishment as a three-year-old by his natural father for some unfathomable fault had left a gaping absence that lay forever unresolved in the deepest recesses of his being, and he would never be the cause of such shattering for her. He had harmed her enough by stubbornly clinging as long as he had to the illusion that they could ever have a life together. Thus loving her, longing for her, aching to hold her, he had released her freely into the care of the One who loved her more than even he did, the only One who could truly guard her body and soul.

And now he was discovering that to declare one's trust was an easy thing to do. To walk its path day by day was a never-ending trial that stretched him to the core.

In tha bleak night he despaired as Black Hawk's long-ago prophecy rang in his mind: that he would wander all the moons of his life yet never find a home. He saw the full meaning of it now with wrenching clarity: that he would always be spanned between two words, neither of which he could ever wholly be a part of; that he would always live on the outside, looking in as through a shaded glass, feeling the thin blade of separation twisting in his vitals.

"I am learning to trust you, Father," he whispered. "Truly."

It *was* so. Yet still that aching longing for home, for family refused to ease its grip.

Determined never to give in to unrighteous relations as he had once and so dishonor God again, he yet recognized that his need for a woman, both physical and emotional, made him dangerously vulnerable to temptation. Painfully he again faced the question of whether it would not be better to take a wife from among his people to tie himself more closely to them. Raise up children. Live a life. Make a home.

But it could never be what I might have had with her.

The thought struck him like a hard blow to the heart. Deep grief bore him into its depths, wholly shattering resolution and wresting from him a low groan.

"Beth—"

Blindly he shoved aside his bearskin, wrapped his blanket around his nakedness, and, careful to make no sound, groped his way outside. He stood barefoot in the swirling snow, oblivious to knifing cold and buffeting wind.

By degrees he became aware of a hand gently laid on his back. Glancing around, he saw Little Running Heron and behind him, Sweetgrass, both appearing ghostly in the pale reflection of the snow, their eyes dark with concern.

"It'll all come right, sir," Little Running Heron growled in English. "Give it time."

His grasp of the Shawnee tongue was not strong, while Sweetgrass spoke but little English and only a smattering of French. Yet somehow the two managed to communicate in a rough mixture of the three languages, interspersed with gestures, touches, and meaningful looks. Now she smiled and nodded encouragingly at White Eagle as though she completely understood what her husband had said and knew the truth of it.

The painful tightness of his chest eased a fraction. He was not alone after all. He had many faithful friends who stood with him, bore him up when he felt he could stand no longer.

The cherished lesson he had learned when a slave among the Seneca returned to him as well: The Father remained when all else was lost. And that mattered more than any other thing, even when it felt as though it did not.

He turned again to stare across the misty, snow-drifted roofs of the clustered habitations lying dark and silent in the storm's grip.

"Seela," he whispered. "Yes. All will come right in the end."

Chapter Six

WITH ABBY PRESSING against her on one side, Tess on the other, Elizabeth leaned against the *Aventure's* weather rail. Throat constricted, she scanned the familiar view of Boston's teeming waterfront, seeking to imprint it on her memory.

From behind her the sound of the chain rattling on the capstan signaled the raising of the 74-gun warship's anchor. Far too quickly she slipped her cables and slowly fell away from Long Wharf. Rigging and sails creaked as the wind and strengthening ebb tide brought the bow around to the east, and she angled outward, blocking Elizabeth's view.

Their maids had come aboard with all their baggage under cover of darkness. After taking tearful leave of her parents at Roxbury an hour before the bleak, clouded sunrise, Lucien had escorted the three of them to the docks in a closed carriage, disguised in rough men's dress and bundled against the raw wind in heavy cloaks with hoods drawn over their heads.

To explain their absence the Howards would give out that Tess had taken Elizabeth and Abby to Marblehead to visit cousins. Only after receiving confirmation of their safe arrival would they confide to family and close friends that they had gone to stay with acquaintances in France for the sake of Elizabeth's health.

Marie and Lemaire had greeted them when they came aboard. Soon the doctor excused himself and went below, but Marie continued to hover close to Elizabeth.

"Come with me up to the poop deck, where you'll be able to see the city for a while longer," Caledonne urged now, giving the three of them a kind look. "Captain Lafitt agreed that you may stay there until we leave the harbor. Unfortunately then you must go below to avoid getting in the crew's way or distracting them from their duties. I'm afraid you'll have to remain in your cabin until we rendezvous with the rest of my fleet and transfer to *Néréide,* which should happen before nightfall. After that you'll be allowed on deck briefly in the morning and evening until we land at Bordeaux."

"The last thing we want to do is interfere with your crew, Alexandre," Tess assured him as he and Lucien ushered them along the waist's gangway to the steps leading up to the quarterdeck.

Marie followed at Elizabeth's heels as though sensing her distress. The thought of the close quarters she would have to endure below deck for weeks on end summoned in full force unsettling images of her ordeal aboard the *Erebus* that resolved into the terrifying nightmares she had suffered since her rescue.

It was only by focusing her gaze intently on Caledonne's back that she could fight them back. He made a commanding—and reassuring—figure in the dark blue uniform coat of a French admiral with its red cuffs and facings and heavily ornamented with gold lace and braid; crimson breeches, waistcoat, and sash; and three-cornered hat crowning his neatly coiffed white hair. As they crossed the ship's waist, sailors respectfully ducked their heads and touched their fingers to their foreheads while quickly detouring around him.

It pleasantly impressed her to see that, although the ship's crew gave every sign of deference to their admiral, none cringed from him. In fact, he greeted a number by name and received genuine smiles and good-humored responses in return.

As though to punctuate Caledonne's point, however, it also became quickly clear that the masculine dress she and her companions had assumed could not conceal their sex at close proximity. They had become the focus of intense interest shortly after they stepped on deck.

Brisk commands rang out all around them, but as officers and sailors hurried back and forth across the deck or scrambled nimbly up the ratlines that webbed the towering masts, heads turned to follow their movements. Broad smiles, even occasional winks and the touch of chapped fingers to a hat brim or brow reddened by the freezing wind followed them until they mounted the steps to the quarterdeck, where Captain Lafitt paced.

After greeting the captain, they crossed the quarterdeck, eagerly climbed a few steps more onto the poop deck at the ship's stern, and clustered at the rear rail. The distance between them and the waterfront was already expanding far too rapidly.

Had it been almost two years ago when she had been the one standing on the dock, sadly bidding her parents farewell at their departure for England? Elizabeth reflected, emotions torn. Now she was the one going far away not knowing what the future held.

How often she had sailed these sea roads in sailor's disguise aboard the fishing sloop *Prudence* while serving as courier and spy for the Sons of Liberty, and afterward as an agent for General Washington. There had been little doubt of her soon return then, as the sloop made her unvarying circuit.

This time, however, there was certainty as to when she would return. How many months or even years might pass before she again saw the only home she had ever known? And her parents.

Were Mama and Papa even now standing at the morning room window sadly looking out over the bay, straining to identify the masts of the ship they were on? she wondered.

She heard Caledonne murmur something to Tess before he bowed himself off and hurried down to the quarterdeck to join Lafitt. Lucien took his place at the railing, his expression somber.

Gently Marie wrapped the blanket she carried around Elizabeth's shoulders to better shield her from the knifing wind. "You've endured this cold wind far too long, mademoiselle. You'd best go below before you catch a chill. Jean waits to see you in the surgery."

Forcing a smile, Elizabeth pulled up her hood and drew the blanket more closely over her cloak. "I'm fine, truly. Tell him I'll come down in a little while."

Marie clicked her tongue. Giving her a concerned look, she curtseyed and left them.

Elizabeth turned to see that the rest of the fleet had swung into line behind and to each side of *Aventure*. Spreading out, the squadron stood down the sea road that wove between the vast harbor's outlying islands and its mouth, five miles distant, while the city melted steadily into the haze.

She felt Abby abruptly turn and gathered her against her body, drawing cloak and blanket around them both. The young girl pressed her face against Elizabeth's bosom, shoulders heaving, and Tess enfolded both of them in her arms. The painful reality of this separation was sinking in for her little sister, too, Elizabeth thought sadly, and for the moment the exciting prospect of adventure had gone hollow.

Lucien squatted beside Abby and gently drew her around to face him, his hands on her shoulders. "Your parents will be well, and so will you," he told her with an encouraging smile. "I promise."

"I've never been away from Mama and Papa before," she answered in a small, quavering voice.

"I remember the first time I had to leave my parents, and it was very hard," he assured her. "But I grew so much and learned so many things I needed to know to be a man. I became stronger. You will, too, and in years to come you'll be glad of this experience."

When she nodded woefully, he continued, "You're going to have the most delightful time with my sister and brother-in-law and Charlotte. You'll do and see many new and wonderful things, and before you know it, you'll be coming home again to tell your *mère* and *père* of all your adventures. They'll be so proud of the young woman you've become. You do trust me and your *Onkel* Alexandre, don't you?"

Nodding, Abby brushed away her tears, her downcast expression giving way to a smile. "I can't wait to meet Charlotte!"

"You're going to love her, and she, you. I know you're going to be the very best of friends."

He rose and looked from Tess to Elizabeth. "And I assure you that you'll find Cécile and Eugène the most congenial of hosts."

Tess returned his smile. "We're very much looking forward to finally meeting them."

He turned a piercing look on Elizabeth. "I pray that the peace and safety you'll find with us will mend your health and spirits. Please know that I'll do everything in my power to make the voyage and your stay in France most agreeable."

Impulsively she touched his arm. "I know you will, Lucien. And I thank you very much."

He bent over her and laid his hand on hers. "My cousin is a very fortunate man to possess the affection of one so lovely and charming," he murmured. "I look forward to a closer connection between us."

Discomfited, she dropped her gaze from his intense one. He released her quickly and glanced toward Caledonne on the deck below them.

"*Mon père* beckons us to join him and Lafitt."

Tess and Abby followed him down the stairs, but Elizabeth lingered. As she turned to again look back, the eastern clouds broke behind her, and long rays of sunlight spilled across the winter sky and sea.

In the distance, just visible between Governors and Castle islands, she could make out the blue-misted buildings of Boston climbing its hills with the darker hue of the mainland's beetling brow at its back. Its white church spires stood out like graceful hands raised heavenward against the grey clouds massed above.

The strengthening light softened and gilded each detail, casting the scene in an unearthly serenity, so that city and harbor took on an almost celestial aspect. And for a fleeting moment it seemed to Elizabeth that she could see beyond the headlands that enclosed the harbor to the villages and fields and woodlands that stretched long miles to darkly forested mountains and still farther to the deep reaches of the continent's interior.

To where *he* was.

The memory returned to her of the day Carleton had first pledged his love and asked her to become his wife. Because she feared to trust him, she had rejected his suit then. And later, with the truth revealed and what seemed a joyful future before them, he had been torn from her against his will and carried far away as a captive.

This time, however, he had chosen to leave her, with no intention of ever returning. And the hurt of it took her breath away.

Before, the fear and anguish of not knowing what had happened, where he was, or even whether he still lived had tormented her ceaselessly. Now, knowing, she felt as though her very being was shattered.

"Dearest of my heart," she whispered, "wherever you are, remember me. Know that, though I never see you again, my love is yours forever."

Aunt Tess's words when she had poured out her anguish to her aunt a year after that first disappearance rose starkly to her mind. She had to live her life even if he never returned, her aunt had told her. Assuring Elizabeth that the pain would lessen in time, she had confided that she also had lost the man she loved, a ship's captain who died at sea before they could marry, and that in spite of her grief she had chosen to go on.

That day Elizabeth had looked toward the west, even as she did now. The same aching longing washed over her with the force of the restless waves that bore the ship on their breast, speeding them eastward and ever farther from him.

Trembling, she clutched the weather rail. Aunt Tess had been right, and live she must. Somehow she must find courage and strength to go on without him. Yet how she would find the will to do so escaped her utterly in that moment.

A glance toward the bow told her that *Aventure* approached the lighthouse at the harbor's mouth. With a sigh she left the rail, reluctantly descended the stairs to the quarterdeck.

Caledonne and Lucien had taken her aunt and sister to the forecastle at the ship's bow. Caledonne was bending over Abby, pointing out to sea ahead of the ship and saying something to her, while she looked up into his kindly face with a trusting smile as she had often looked up into Carleton's. Her gaze followed the direction he pointed, and clasping her hands in front of her, she laughed.

Something indefinable in that sweet tableau drew Elizabeth to it as to a flaming fire on a winter's day, and after exchanging brief pleasantries with Lafitt, she went to them. As she mounted the steps to the forecastle, for the moment yet unnoticed, Caledonne straightened and turned to Tess, and the look they exchanged assured Elizabeth that she was not mistaken in her suspicions. That, too, brought a measure of joy to her aching heart.

When she joined them Caledonne drew her close to point out the dolphins playfully leaping alongside and ahead of the ship.

"It's as if they're leading us on," she murmured.

He looked down at her, and she caught an indefinable emotion in his eyes. "Perhaps *le bon Dieu* has sent them to do so."

"Perhaps," she conceded, returning his smile with an effort.

Just then she both heard and felt *Aventure's* sails snap taut as the harbor's last islands fell behind. The deck heaved and fell, freezing sea spray crashing over the bow to wet them. The ship surged forward, the ocean's winds and waves taking her, the rest of the squadron fanning out behind.

Caledonne released her, and including Tess and Abby in his glance, said briskly, "Now I fear it's time for all of you to go below."

But his words escaped Elizabeth, nor was she aware when her aunt and sister left her. The psalm she had read early that morning flooded into her mind like the surge of the sea, and stepping to the railing, she clasped it and leaned out, straining for a last glimpse of the receding shore.

The voice of the Lord is upon the waters:
The God of glory thundereth:
The Lord is upon many waters . . .
The Lord sitteth upon the flood;
Yea, the Lord sitteth King for ever.
The Lord will give strength unto His People;
The Lord will bless His People with peace.

Peace.

She took a shaky breath and with resolution wiped tears and salt spray from her cheek with the back of her hand. *I'll not weep, for in your hand, Lord, you hold all my days. Every one of them is written in your book. And I thank you for every blessing you send in your mercy until I come home to you.*

She was only dimly aware that Caledonne still waited nearby. As though he sensed her grief and the plea of her soul, he said nothing and made no move toward her. Patiently he waited, standing like a sentinel between her and the ship's crew as they pursued their duties.

She did not know how long she watched, motionless, while the shores of her homeland fell away until all that lay behind was a misty cloudbank of purpled blue on the western horizon. And then the vast, heaving breast of the grey-green ocean blotted even that from her view.

Chapter Seven

THE NEXT MORNING White Eagle awakened to a world of pure, icy white.
The thin line of the first silver light edged the eastern horizon beneath
the lip of leaden clouds, with no breath of wind disturbing the early-
morning stillness.

During the long night he had come to a decision, knowing that it was
not possible for him to endure any longer the ceaseless, aching longing
that tormented him. He had made the decision on the bank of the Dela-
ware that he would choose to trust God with an undivided heart, to believe
that the gifts that came from his Creator's hand were the very best for him.
That even if he never saw Elizabeth's face again, he would put his trust in
Christ alone.

God had closed the door to any relationship with Elizabeth and brought
him back to this people of his heart. Yet his deep longing for a home and
family had not been assuaged, thus it must be the Father's will, after all, that
he choose a Shawnee wife and make a home and family among them as
his clan desired.

The realization brought with it both relief and numbing sorrow, but
he determined take up in obedience the life that had been given him. And
thrusting away the night's lingering shadows, he wrapped himself against
the piercing cold alongside Little Running Heron, while Sweetgrass prepared the morning meal.

Grabbing shovels and axes brought along to clear the trail as needed, they ventured outside. They joined the other men and youths in laughing camaraderie, knocking sleet-frozen snow from porches and rooftops with long poles and clearing narrow pathways between chest high drifts.

He took comfort in laughing and playing with the children who soon gathered in exuberant flocks. And by the time they returned inside, coated liberally with snow and red-faced from cold and exertion, to warm themselves and break their fast, the heavy cloud cover was streaming away to the northeast, and the sun had lifted above the horizon.

When they gathered outside again a little while later, the pale golden orb hung halfway up in a cloudless, cerulean sky, and the snowmelt dripping from the cabins' eaves was freezing into razor-sharp icicles. In a short time the messenger sent to Black Snake returned, all but frozen from his long, cold run, with face and hands chapped by the wind and ice crystals stiffening his hair below the layers of wool wrappings around his head. He brought word that the Kispokotha's principal war chief was on his way and expected to reach the town by midday.

After praying for wisdom and strength to obey God's leading, whatever it might be, White Eagle took Blue Sky, held in high esteem among the women, and went to visit the most influential matrons, beginning with their peace chief, Blue Crane, and their war chief, Cat's Eye. More than once their path crossed Raging Bear's as he also presented his cause to the women. To add to White Eagle's frustration, although each of the matrons received him and Blue Sky warmly and responded favorably to their reasoning, not one made any commitment one way or the other.

"Do not be concerned, my brother," Blue Sky assured him on the way back to her cabin. "The Great Father holds this decision in his hands, and it will be the right one."

OVER THE COURSE of the morning large delegations arrived from Blue Jacket's town five miles to the northwest, and from Dunquat's Town a mile north, although, significantly, the Wyandot half king did not accompany them. Smaller parties also filtered in from nearby towns inhabited by other Shawnee divisions and by allied tribes.

Clearly the severe weather had not hindered word of White Eagle's return from spreading quickly. His conversations with the men drove home the keen interest of not only the Shawnee, but also the surrounding nations in his mission. And he knew that the response of Black Hawk's clan to Washington's message and his own counsel would be a critical consideration for the tribes along the *Hathennithiipi* who favored allying with the British.

Black Snake arrived shortly after midday, bringing with him a number of Kispokotha chiefs and subchiefs. When they had greeted Grey Cloud and the town's other headmen, Black Snake turned to White Eagle, who clasped his hand and drew him into a hearty embrace.

"It's good to see you, my brother!" he said, meaning it. "Your wise counsel is always welcome at our clan's fire."

"I've longed to speak with you for many moons, brother," Black Snake returned warmly. "I rejoice that you've returned to us in good health."

Two winters older than White Eagle, the Kispokotha war chief was equally lean and muscular, a couple of inches shorter but imposing in appearance. His head was shaven to a scalp lock decorated with silver ornaments and turkey feathers, and like White Eagle's his face was painted with vermillion stripes.

Grey Cloud wasted no time in calling the council to gather in the *msikahmiqui*. While the building filled, Black Snake drew White Eagle aside, his gaze piercing.

"Red Fox told us of your great victories over the British."

Although his voice and expression remained noncommittal, White Eagle was well aware that he stood with Black Fish. The account Red Fox had shared privately of his meetings with the leading sachems over the winter bolstered White Eagle's confidence, however. Their victories in battle had greatly enhanced his reputation, his cousin had assured him, not only within the clan, but also within their division and the nation. White Eagle hoped this would give him enough respect and influence that the nation's headmen would take his counsel to heart despite their opposition to the Long Knives.

Black Snake released him. "Our brother Blue Jacket is eager to counsel with you, but several sleeps ago he went to our brothers and uncles in the north. I do not know when he will return."

White Eagle considered him thoughtfully. "Sandusky? Detroit?"

Black Snake shrugged, his expression revealing nothing. "I know only that he has gone north."

White Eagle greatly doubted that that was all Black Snake knew of Blue Jacket's movements and intentions, but he kept his opinions to himself. All in all, he liked Black Snake a great deal. The Kispokotha war chief had given him excellent counsel and unstinting support in the war against the white settlers that had resulted from Black Hawk's murder, and he felt himself greatly in his debt.

Outwardly he showed Black Snake every mark of deference and respect, but inwardly he remained wary. For life had taught him that liking and trust were two separate things.

The council house was packed, the townspeople crowded around the fires burning brightly all down its length. White Eagle sat facing a low table that stood at the building's front. Grey Cloud and the rest of the clan's council members were seated to his left, Black Snake in a position of honor among them, with Red Fox, Spotted Pony, Golden Elk, and several others of his leading warriors on his right.

For a long period they smoked their pipes without speaking, listening to the wind's whisper around the exterior walls, content in one another's company. White Eagle patiently bided his time, staring into the fire as he pondered how to present his case most effectively.

At length Grey Cloud rose and welcomed Black Snake to their council fire before continuing, "As you know, our brother White Eagle has brought a message to us from the Long Knives' war chief, Washington. Let everyone give careful attention his words that we may determine the wisest course for our people to follow." Nodding respectfully to White Eagle, he resumed his seat.

White Eagle rose and went to stand behind the table, facing the assembly. For a long moment he looked from one upturned face to another, in their expressions and the tension of their bodies reading worry, anger, defiance, uncertainty. A deep love filled him for this people, and again he wondered who he was to offer wisdom when he so often felt woefully lacking in it. Silently he asked for the Great Father's guidance.

At last he turned and nodded to Golden Elk. He stood and brought to the table the pouch containing the strings and belts of wampum they had brought with them to serve as a record of each part of Washington's message.

"My brothers and sisters," White Eagle began, "I have come a great way and through many storms to return to our fire that I may smoke this tobacco with you. Our Father Washington has sent me to offer you his deep respect and his warmest greetings."

Golden Elk drew out a string of wampum and gave it to White Eagle. He held it up so all could see before placing it on the table.

"I bring words of great consequence from our Father Washington, at whose right hand I stand to represent our people," he continued, "and through him from the Americans' Thirteen Council Fires. I know Washington to be a wise and good man, and I ask that you take these words to heart. By this string of wampum—" he took another string of wampum from Golden Elk and lifted it up before them "—I heal all the grief and hurt our people have suffered, unstop your ears, and clear your eyes of tears and of the dust of deception that you may hear these words without obstruction or misunderstanding and know that I would lead you by a good road."

He laid the second string on the table and took Washington's letter from Golden Elk, holding it up so everyone could see the writing on the page. "These are the words our Father Washington speaks to our people." He lowered the page and, translating into the Shawnee tongue as he spoke, read in a slow, measured voice loud enough for even those at the back of the council house to hear.

" 'My brothers of the Shawnee nation, I send gifts to you in gratitude for the many valiant warriors you sent me, foremost among them White Eagle, Golden Elk, Red Fox, and Spotted Pony. By their great deeds they have brought you honor in the war between these thirteen United States and the British, an enemy that over a number of years and through many cruel acts has oppressed our nation and yours. Because of these men's courage and faithfulness in our fight for justice and freedom, we offer you our thanks and friendship.' "

A murmur of approval rose among the listeners as White Eagle presented a long, richly beaded belt of purple wampum and laid it on the table.

" 'Now my heart is heavy because of the murder of our most loyal ally and friend, Cornstalk, and his companions—your brothers and ours—at the hands of a few evil men. Along with the sachems of our Great Council, I was sickened to learn of this vile deed and repudiate it in the strongest terms, as they do. I assure you that Governor Patrick Henry of Virginia even now seeks justice against the men who are responsible.' " White Eagle presented the corresponding wampum belt, noting that frowns furrowed some of the council members' faces.

" 'Earnestly I ask that you hold fast to the chain of friendship that has long existed between us, while this matter is investigated and a just resolution brought about. I know it is much to ask of a proud and honorable people such as your great nation, but I also know that you, as I, have seen how the taking of vengeance never ends and results only in deadly wounds on both sides. It is my very great desire, one shared by our Great Council, that we together choose to live in peace with one another. We look upon you as brothers born under the same sky, living on the same land, and having the same interests. For the good of our women, children, and elders, therefore, let us make common cause. Let our people on both sides bury the bones of our dead and our weapons of war and never dig them up again so that they may pass out of memory and our friendship remain forever unbroken.' "

He saw that the matrons listened gravely and a few nodded, though their expressions remained unreadable. But as he laid the long, richly beaded white peace belt on the table, open suspicion darkened the faces of many of the men, both Shawnee and from the surrounding nations.

Washington next pled for the Shawnee to ally with the Americans and send to him as many warriors as were willing and able to fight with them against the British. If they rejected this course, however, he admonished them to hold back their hands from the war altogether. As long as they did so, he pledged to personally hear their complaints whenever they arose and to ensure that their people were treated always with the friendliness and justice due to brothers. White Eagle now laid before them the wide red war belt.

He read the next portion of the letter in a steady voice, expression masked, bracing himself for the furious response he was certain it would touch off. For now Washington's tone turned cold.

" 'We have heard, however, that many of your chiefs and captains wish to ally with the British, while a few among you have already done so and have taken up the war hatchet against us. To choose this course can only bring you great harm. We have prevailed against the British in battle, killed many of their soldiers, and captured many others, and we will cast them out of this land. If you ally with them, my brothers, you make yourselves enemies to these United States, and you can be sure that severe reprisals will result.' "

Stony silence hung over the council house as White Eagle presented a long belt of gleaming black wampum. He surveyed the throng, meeting each hard gaze with an unflinching one before reading the letter's conclusion. It had surprised him when he consulted with the General on the letter's wording, but Washington had insisted it stay as dictated.

" 'I charge you to carry White Eagle in your bosom so that he suffers no interference from our enemies, whether British or any others. He is as close to me as a brother, and if he suffers harm, I will consider it an injury to my own flesh and act accordingly. Indeed I would have your answer back by his hand alone so that I may hear your words clearly and take them to heart.' "

No sooner had he laid the second black belt on the table than, on the far side of the assembly, Raging Bear sprang to his feet. "Will we give ear to these threats and lie down like dogs under the Long Knives' feet while the murders of Cornstalk and those with him cry to the heavens? Does anyone believe that they will ever punish those who did this thing?"

At this breach of etiquette a loud murmur rose across the assembly. Hot color flooded into Black Snake's face, while the Wyandots looked from one to another in disbelief. The council members all turned to direct scowls at Raging Bear, who stubbornly ignored them.

Containing his anger, White Eagle placed the letter on the table beside the belts and strings of wampum. Golden Elk met his gaze with an outraged one, but before either could respond, Grey Cloud sprang to his feet with an agility that belied his age.

"White Eagle speaks as the emissary of our Father Washington," he reminded the throng, his tone taut with fury. "Before anyone brings foolish accusations against him, let him advise us on this matter, and let us open our ears to what he has to say."

Undaunted, Raging Bear cried, "Can it be any clearer that White Eagle is the tool of the Long Knives? Is it not plain that his intent is to lead us on a path favorable to the interests of the Long Knives and ruinous to our own people?"

Refusing to acknowledge Raging Bear's outcry or look in his direction, White Eagle kept his steady gaze on the council members. "Our Father Washington's words are his, not mine. Indeed many times I have spoken our concerns to him without restraint to clear his eyes and open his ears."

As the onlookers' murmurs stilled, he continued, "I have brought this message to you that together we may consider it and choose the course we will follow from this day on. I've seen what you have not: how numerous a people the Long Knives are, how well established they are in their towns, what weapons they possess, and how they will fight for their homes and families even as we fight for ours—"

"This is our land, not theirs! They've robbed us and our brothers and uncles and grandfathers of much of it already, and they will not stop until they drive us out and take everything from here to the Great Western Waters!"

Hearing the fury and despair in Raging Bear's voice, White Eagle met his gaze and inclined his head in acknowledgement. "Indeed it is so. My brother speaks truth. But I speak equal truth.

"You know how four winters ago Cornstalk counseled our people to accept favorable terms of peace while they would be granted. Yet because our people demanded war, he took up the tomahawk against Lord Dunmore. When the British and the Long Knife militias defeated us and their army swarmed over our lands, devouring our towns like locusts, we were forced to accept highly unfavorable terms to end the destruction, even giving up our hunting grounds beyond the *Spelewathiipi* in Cantuckee."

"Your own father was killed by Long Knife settlers!" Loud Thunder protested.

"I've not forgotten it, nor will I ever. But all of you know how after my father's burial Cornstalk and I stood before you together and advised strongly that we make peace instead of again entering upon a futile war with the Whites. Even as he had done, however, at your demand I also took up the tomahawk."

Brown Bear rose. "Although Cornstalk and his men fought with great skill and courage, their numbers were too small to prevail over the Long Knife army. But you and your warriors drove the Whites from our lands. You proved yourself to be *psaiwi nenothtu,* a great warrior, and they fled before you."

It was all White Eagle could do to not throw up his hands in frustration. He swung to face the warrior, his face sternly set.

"All we accomplished was to spur the Long Knives on even more, my brother. Is this not what I warned our people would happen? Have you forgotten the destruction of Chillicothe and others of our towns and the deaths of so many of our men, women, and children?" Fighting back tears, he struck his breast. "Each one is a fire in my heart!"

Directing a burning gaze across the assembly, he demanded, "Have we learned nothing? Again settlers and soldiers enter our lands, and they will continue to come in numbers too large for our people alone to hold back. Already they are driving us farther and farther west toward the setting sun. I ask only that we consider our Father Washington's message carefully, that we remember the course we have taken before and where it led, and that with wisdom and discernment we choose a better one."

"Cornstalk counseled that we give in to them," Raging Bear shouted, "and the result was that without cause and without pity the Long Knife soldiers killed him and the others they held with him as hostages—"

"A small number of militia soldiers at Fort Randolph did this to avenge the slaying of two of their own by some of our people," White Eagle cut him off. "If we exact vengeance on those who had no hand in the murders, we act as unjustly as these Long Knife soldiers did. And where will be the end of it?

"Indeed our Father Washington speaks hard words, but he speaks truth in order to spare us, and we must attend to it. Vengeance accomplishes nothing but to breed more vengeance. We must keep our eyes fixed on a greater goal, my brothers."

"White Eagle is right that we cannot prevail if we fight alone," Loud Thunder said. "But the British are eager to supply us with weapons and aid us in fighting the Long Knives. What choice have we but to ally with them if we are to preserve our people?"

White Eagle held up his hand for silence, and gradually the clamor quieted. Feeling as though he stood upon a precipice, for a long moment he looked earnestly from one face to another. It struck him that should his nation turn against him on this matter—should even the Kispokotha do so—he could bear it. But if his clan rejected him and chose to ally with the British, he would lose his very identity. Yet even worse would be the consequences his people would suffer for making the wrong decision.

Quietly he said, "You all know there is unalterable enmity between me and the British. They seek my life, and will pay dearly for it. If our clan chooses to ally with them, then I must leave here and never come back among you again if I am to live."

Vehement objections filled the council house. Calls for him to stay and lead them as their war chief drowned out the party in opposition. But Raging Bear's shouts rose above the tumult.

"I say let the British have him! It is because of this false white man's religion he brought among us that Moneto has turned his back on our people. By restoring the ways of our ancestors and appeasing the good and bad spirits with sacrifices as we have always done, we will win back his favor and drive out the white faces forever!"

Before White Eagle could speak, Red Fox sprang to his feet. "Why should we return to the vain beliefs and practices of our ancestors? What have their gods ever done for us? We lived in darkness until the true Moneto, the Great Father in Heaven, sent White Eagle to bring to us the good news of his love. Indeed we saw how he affirmed his favor to our brother by many signs."

Many of the believers called out in agreement, Walks Far's among them. White Eagle returned Red Fox's look with a grateful one as he sat down.

"In truth, our people have always sought to worship Moneto, but our ancestors did so in ignorance," he said, scanning the faces that crowded the council house. "They did not know the one true God who has now revealed himself to us in this day through his Son Jesus. It is only by hearing his voice and following his ways that we may walk in his light so that his good purpose will be accomplished in our clan and in our nation."

Raging Bear gave him and Red Fox a venomous look. As he opened his mouth to speak, however, his voice came out strangled. Blinking, unable to speak, he abruptly sat down among his stony-faced adherents.

Here and there one of the elders shifted on his haunches and exchanged a sober glance with his neighbors, while the women, sitting at the building's, rear regarded White Eagle, some with frowns, others with open interest. Grey Cloud kept his face averted and his eyes downcast. Seated next to him, Black Snake met White Eagle's gaze directly, though with his expression masked. White Eagle had a distinct impression that he was drawn, but after a suspended moment he also looked away.

"These are matters to speak more of at another time," White Eagle said. "Our concern here is to decide the path our clan will walk between the Americans and the British."

Grey Cloud cleared his throat. "What is your counsel, brother?"

"It is that we live in peace for now. An ancient people called Romans once said, *Si vis pacem, para bellum:* If you wish peace, prepare war. Let us ally with the Long Knives against the British and make ourselves their trusted friends that we may gain reputation and influence among them. At the same time let us join with Blue Jacket and others of our sachems and seek to forge strong alliances with the Lenape, Mingo, Wyandot, Miami, Ottawa, Illinois, and others so that after the Long Knives cast the British out, we may speak to them with one loud voice. Then if they refuse to listen, we will have strength to oppose them with greater hope of success."

Grey Cloud pushed to his feet. Drawing his blanket around his shoulders, he raised his hand to still the crowd's murmurs.

"Are we not one people? Do we not belong to the clan of Black Hawk and the division of the Kispokotha? Our nation's Great Council will take careful account of the decision we make here, whether it is to ally with the Long Knives or with the British or to hold back our hands from their war. Let our clan's will be known."

White Eagle followed Golden Elk back to their seats and watched with outward calm as each member of the council strode forward in turn, first stopping before the low table to stare hard at the strings and belts of wampum before laying his stick on the ground to the right for allying with the Americans, in the center for maintaining neutrality, or on the left for allying with the British. But his gut churned as it had on the day two winters earlier when they had chosen him as their war chief.

The entire nation had supported him then in the war he had unleashed against both the Americans and the British. Now, however? How many would stand against Black Fish's party and the lure of the plunder and scalps his raids against the Long Knives might yield?

He cast a veiled glance toward Blue Crane and Cat's Eye, who watched the proceedings with unreadable expressions. Neither gave any indication of which side they favored.

When the votes were tallied, only those few who adhered to Raging Bear supported an alliance with the British, while the majority rejected it outright. A small faction voted for staying out of the war entirely, but the greater number affirmed White Eagle's advice.

By then it was mid afternoon. Dismissed by Grey Cloud, all the men rose and went outside, while the women held their own council. They did not wait long. As the women emerged, led by Blue Crane, White Eagle scanned the council members' faces. Blue Sky, Laughing Otter, and Rain Woman met his gaze with satisfied smiles, and he let out his breath, the tightness of his chest releasing in visceral relief.

As Blue Crane announced their decision in favor of his counsel, he managed to keep his expression neutral, but silently he exulted, *Thank you for this answer, Great Spirit! I praise you!*

Golden Elk, Red Fox, and Spotted Pony gathered around him, their smiles broad, while the majority of the men came to clasp his hand before walking off with their wives. Among them, to his surprise and gratification, were three of the older married members of Raging Bear's party, who now firmly declared their friendship.

Raging Bear stood apart, however, glaring at him, eyes narrowed with unconcealed hatred.

Chapter Eight

THAT EVENING, WHILE the rest of the clan gathered at the *msikah-miqui* for the nightly dances and to play games of chance, the fellowship of believers in Jesus met in the spacious lodge Red Fox had built for their worship next to Laughing Otter's cabin. Well bundled against the cold, they crowded close together on the benches he had fashioned, sitting as near as possible to the fire at the building's front.

White Eagle noted with sadness that in addition to Grey Cloud several other once faithful members were absent. His heart lifted to see that new members had been added, however, among them Blue Sky's friend Mary Douglas, Walks Far and her children, and John Walk on Water and his family. Especially he rejoiced as he embraced his warriors Brown Bear and Crooked Oak, who along with the young widow Falling Leaf and several other townspeople expressed interest in this Jesus he and Red Fox had proclaimed at the council meeting.

The following hour restored his energy and peace. After Red Fox invoked the presence of the Great Spirit, they entered into a time of individual prayer for shared needs. The lodge filled with the soft chanting of praise and supplication, while the sense of an unseen, but mighty power hovered over the members.

At length Spotted Pony led them all in specific prayers for Grey Cloud and others of the fellowship who had fallen away and for wisdom and guidance for their nation in the important decisions that lay before them. He concluded by imploring protection, discretion, and wisdom for White Eagle as he stood before the tribal council and sought to follow the course to which the Great Father called him.

Red Fox then rose, holding the opened Bible White Eagle had given him on his return to the clan the previous fall. As everyone listened intently, he read from the book of Isaiah, translating into the Shawnee tongue as he spoke.

" 'You, my people, will dwell in God's city, and you will weep no more! He will surely be gracious to you at the sound of your cry. When he hears, he will answer you. And though he has given you bread of adversity and water of affliction, your Teacher will no longer be hidden, but your eyes will behold him. And your ears will hear a word behind you saying, 'This is the way, walk in it!' when you turn to the right hand or to the left.' "

The words shook White Eagle. He was only dimly aware that Golden Elk gripped his knee, and that Stowe's hand rested on his shoulder.

Red Fox sat down. For some moments silence held sway, then Walk on Water quietly rose and fixed the upturned faces before him in an intent gaze.

"Most of you have heard my family's story, but for these who have not—" he nodded to White Eagle, Golden Elk, and Spotted Pony "—I would share this as a word from our Heavenly Father. My people live in the valley of the Mohawk River, in the land the Whites call New York. There has been much fighting between the Haudenosaunee and the white settlers—between those who support the British and those who oppose them as do the Oneida and the Tuscarora alone among the Haudenosaunee. Many on both sides have been killed.

"Our town, Oriska, lay near an American fort called Stanwix, which the British attacked last summer as they marched on the place called Saratoga. While they laid siege to it, the Mohawk warriors of Thayendanegea who allied with them raided and burned Oriska, putting a great number of our people to death. Rising Moon and I . . . we could not rescue our two sons and small daughter from the fire . . . or remain behind to bury them."

He stopped, unable to go on, as murmurs of horror and sympathy filled the lodge. Directing a glance at his wife and older daughter, who sat, heads bowed, tears trickling down their cheeks, he continued raggedly, "Of our little ones, only Rebekah remained to comfort us, and for that we give thanks to the Great Father. We fled from there first to White Eyes at Goshochking, seeking a place where we could live in peace with other believers in Jesus, then settled in the Moravians' town called Lichtenau, where we met our sister." He indicated Walks Far, who responded with a nod and a sad smile.

"When she returned to your clan last fall, we accompanied her," he continued. "But we arrived just as you were preparing to abandon the town and move here with those who ally with the British. We had great misgivings and thought to turn back, but we heard behind us a strong voice saying, 'Go!'"

Looking from one to another, he quoted from the gospel of John: "'Truly I say to you, the one who hears my word and believes in him who sent me has unending life and will not be condemned, but passes from death into life. The hour comes and is now, when the dead will hear the voice of the Father's Son, and those who hear will live.' All of us are dead in our sins and grief," he continued, "but Jesus reaches out his hand to save us and to restore all we have lost."

For a long moment he stood motionless, looking into the air as though he saw what they could not see, tears shimmering in his eyes. At last he said, "I was once named Stand in Water, but I have taken a new name: Walk on Water. For through all these sorrows I do so by the power of the Great Spirit who lives in me. And I testify to you that if you will grasp onto him, as we have done, though you may walk through deep waters, you will live."

His words struck deeply into White Eagle's heart, and unashamedly he brushed away tears. Those around him did the same, moisture shining in the visitors' eyes as well, while across the cabin voices called out softly in agreement.

Rising, he went to stand beside Walk on Water and beckoned Rising Moon and Rebekah to stand with them. Taking the Bible from Red Fox, he turned to the thirty-seventh chapter of Ezekiel.

"The Great Father brought the prophet to the Valley of Bones and spoke this word to him." He then read from the book, translating: " 'Thus saith the Lord God: "Come from the four winds, O breath, and breathe upon these slain that they may live." So I prophesied as He commanded me, and the breath came into them, and they lived, and stood up upon their feet, an exceedingly great army. Then he said unto me, "Son of man, these bones are the whole house of Israel: behold, they say, 'Our bones are dried and our hope is lost: we are cut off from our parts.' Therefore prophesy and say unto them, 'Thus saith the Lord God: "Behold, O my people, I will open your graves and cause you to come up out of your graves, and bring you into the land of Israel. . . . And I shall put my spirit in you, and you shall live, and I shall place you in your own land." ' "

A chorus of praise and amens followed the reading, and Walk on Water and his wife and daughter embraced him tearfully.

By the time Red Fox dismissed everyone after a final prayer, White Eagle was deeply moved at the evidence of how the members' faith had deepened and gained strength in his absence. Seeming reluctant to leave, everyone at first clustered around him to discuss the night's teachings. Soon the women drifted apart into their own group, with those older in the faith counseling the younger ones and the newcomers, while Red Fox and Walk on Water along with Spotted Pony and Golden Elk took the lead in answering the visiting men's questions.

Unless directly addressed, White Eagle held back, knowing that he could not always be with them, at least not until the war with England ended. If this small congregation was to remain faithful and to grow and spread the good news of Jesus to all their people, it was necessary that new leaders be raised up.

He was deeply glad to feel the movement of the Holy Spirit in this direction, and yet to see this role being given to others was bittersweet as well. As much as he wanted it, he found it hard to let go of what he had begun with such humility and dedication.

Your will, Lord, he prayed silently in release. *Your will, not mine, be done for your glory alone.*

A few at a time, those gathered dispersed into the freezing night to return to their homes. At last only Walk on Water and his family remained with him, Red Fox, Spotted Pony, and Golden Elk.

He clasped Walk on Water's hand. "Your words pierced my heart, brother."

"And yours, ours," Walk on Water returned.

"White Eagle and I remember your town from when we passed through there two winters ago hoping to negotiate an alliance between the Haudenosaunee and the Americans," Golden Elk said. "Our hearts are broken by what you've endured and what has befallen your people."

Walk on Water reached to clasp his hand, then turned back to White Eagle, his brow furrowed. "We heard that you were captured by our brothers the Seneca and suffered much among them."

"It is so," White Eagle allowed. "We also heard of Thayendanegea's raids when my Rangers were at Bemis Heights opposing Burgoyne. We grieve with you for those of your family and nation who've died in this war. It seems that all of us are being torn asunder."

"The Haudenosaunee have never before warred against one another. But now we wonder whether this rift can ever be mended."

"We fear that the great council fire at Onondaga will never burn again," Rising Moon said, her voice desolate.

White Eagle took her hand. "There's been bad blood between our people and the Haudenosaunee for a long time. But in Jesus there's no division between us."

"You speak truth, my brother," Walk on Water said, "and we're glad of it."

Feeling someone's scrutiny, White Eagle glanced at Rebekah and saw that she studied him intently. She had about sixteen winters, he reckoned, with a slender form, delicate features, and lustrous eyes and hair.

Her smile held tentative invitation, and sighing internally he returned it with one he hoped communicated nothing but good will. The gossips had clearly been at work spreading the news of his breach with Healer

Woman, and he had no doubt that more invitations were in store. Invitations he must somehow force himself to consider seriously.

Tomorrow. Another day. In time to come.

There were too many pressing matters to deal with for him to concern himself with this now. As the events of the following day proved.

Early the next morning he watched Raging Bear and his warriors ride out of the town, their horses loaded with weapons and packs. They spoke to no one and did not look back.

"No doubt they go to join Black Fish," he said grimly.

"It is better they do so than remain to sow dissention among us," Spotted Pony answered as Red Fox nodded his agreement.

Golden Elk scowled. "I fear they'll seek to influence the decision of the great council."

"That's as certain as the sun's rising," White Eagle answered. "We must do all we can to prevent them from succeeding."

"But if the tribal council refuses to listen to you and chooses to ally with the British, what will happen to our clan since we stand in opposition and indeed fight on the side of the Long Knives?"

Walk on Water returned Golden Elk's despairing gaze with a penetrating one. "In that case it may be better for your clan to remove far from here. For if the league of the Haudenosaunee can be broken over this war, what will become of your nation?"

"This matter can wait until the great council makes its decision," White Eagle cut them off brusquely. "But now our people need meat for the coming weeks, and I go hunting." Looking from one face to another of those surrounding him, he motioned for them to come with him and led them away.

Chapter Nine

ELIZABETH FOLLOWED the others to the magnificently proportioned grand *salle's* huge fireplace, where a crackling blaze held the air's chill at bay. Her awed gaze was drawn to the dark, hewn beams that crossed the enormous turret just beneath the conical, red-tiled roof of the château's ancient keep. A short distance below, windows spaced all the way around its circumference admitted mote-dappled streams of light that cast the reception hall in a mellow glow, warming the plastered stone walls and ornate furnishings.

"The château's original structure dates to the thirteenth century," explained Cécile Bettár, la marquise de Martieu-Broussard, in softly modulated, musical tones very pleasing to Elizabeth's ears. She indicated two wide, curving stairways of dressed limestone visible through broad openings to the right and left opposite the building's spacious foyer. "It was composed of this central turret and the two that housed the stairs, with just beyond them the solar on that side and the kitchens on the other."

"Those rooms were altered to become the galleries of the wings that were added later," broke in le marquis, Eugène Sevier. "You may have recognized the newer portions by their more smoothly dressed stone, the different style and smaller size of their turrets, and the dormers, which my ancestors added in the fifteenth and sixteenth centuries."

"We've certainly nothing to equal this in America." Tess turned to

Caledonne, her eyes sparkling. "I assume your estate at Marseille is equally grand, Alexandre."

The smile he turned on her caused her to hastily drop her gaze. "I hope to take you there this fall when my fleet returns to port again."

"I look forward to seeing it," she murmured.

Abby tugged on Elizabeth's hand and when she looked down confided in an excited whisper, "I've always wanted to live in a castle!"

Chuckling, Lucien bent over her. "Now you shall, *ma petit*—for as long as you please."

"And I promise we'll do all we can to make your stay a very pleasant one," Eugène assured the three of them.

Elizabeth noted with amusement that Abby and Charlotte were eying each other shyly. Fourteen to Abby's thirteen, Charlotte was slightly shorter, her light olive complexion; dark brown eyes and brunette hair; and slight, graceful form reflecting her mother's. Both gave promise of growing into beautiful women, she reflected.

"Maman, may I show Abigail my dolls?" she pleaded.

Cécile gave her an affectionate look before turning to Elizabeth and Tess. "Charlotte has a lovely collection of porcelain dolls upstairs in her chamber that Abigail might enjoy seeing—if it meets with your approval. Her governess, Madame Verignay, will supervise them."

At Abby's imploring look, Elizabeth exchanged a smiling glance with Tess, who quickly said, "By all means. I suspect they'll enjoy playing a great deal more than listening to our dull conversation."

Beaming, Charlotte reached for Abby's hand. She took it without hesitation, and the two girls hurried together up the stairway to their right, chattering as though they had been friends all their lives.

"It appears they're going to get on quite well together," Elizabeth said as she watched them disappear upstairs.

"I believe you're right," Eugène agreed dryly. "Charlotte's been in a state of rapture ever since she heard Abigail was coming to stay with us. We've hardly had a moment's peace."

"Perhaps I oughtn't to have told her in advance and spared you the drama." Caledonne's rueful comment elicited everyone's chuckles.

His fleet had put into harbor at Bordeaux, and after several days of rest, during which they indulged in the entertainments and shopping the city had to offer, they had spent ten days on the road to Paris. They had made quite an impressive retinue, with a mounted troop of Marines escorting their elegant berlines, one carrying Elizabeth, Tess, Abby, and the two men, with a guard seated beside the coachman in front and a duo of footmen perched at the rear. Their maids and the men's valets rode in another coach, and two more were burdened with overflow luggage and additional servants.

A short time earlier on that sunny afternoon of Monday, April 20, they had passed through the picturesque village of Passy on the lower slopes of the hill of Chaillot, a mile west of Paris and seven from Versailles. Soon they began to ascend the bluff's steep incline. Château Broussard overlooked the Seine River from the heights in front of them, Caledonne had told them, adding that the fields and woods below belonged to the estate as well.

Within minutes they turned into the broad, walled courtyard with its espaliered trees and topiaries that fronted the sprawling château. Servants and baggage were whisked away to the rear service entrance, while the butler and two footmen ushered them into the grand *salle,* where le marquis, la marquise, and their daughter welcomed them with embraces and every sign of genuine pleasure.

Any anxiety the three of them had harbored about their reception immediately vanished, for their hosts proved as amiable as Caledonne and no more prone to stand on ceremony. They quickly set their guests at ease, and within minutes they were all addressing one another with warm familiarity.

When the girls had gone, Cécile waved her hand to indicate their surroundings. "As you see, our home is a mélange of different times and tastes," she said with a merry laugh, "though we've done our very best to meld them all together."

"Quite successfully, I'd say." Tess admired her surroundings, her hand on Caledonne's arm. As had become his practice since their landing at Bordeaux, he had possessed himself of it the instant they alighted from the coach.

"We just finished a complete redecoration—much needed in this old building. My sweet husband indulged my whims." Cécile directed a smiling glance at Eugène, which he returned with undisguised affection.

"You know I wholeheartedly approve of everything you do, *ma chère.*"

"Indeed, my sister is the very paragon of fashion."

Cécile dimpled at Lucien's teasing tone. "I can't claim to be the originator of the new taste. The homage belongs entirely to our young queen."

When Eugène led the way across the *salle* to the salon's wide doorway, Lucien casually encircled Elizabeth's shoulders with his arm to usher her after the others. His manner toward was becoming increasingly protective, almost possessive, she thought uneasily, as she had more than once during the long weeks of their necessary confinement together. Although he never overstepped any bounds and his solicitousness seemed natural and unassuming, it left her feeling vaguely uncomfortable. It was just that her nerves were on edge, she assured herself, and she simply misread him.

These concerns vanished from her consciousness the moment she stepped over the salon's threshold. Coming to a halt, she clasped her hands before her in delight.

"C'est très charmante!"

"I love how delightfully airy and fresh it is!" Tess echoed, looking around her as Caledonne escorted her into the room.

Afternoon sunlight filtered through sunny silk draperies pulled back from the salon's tall floor-length windows and double, glass-paned doors, which revealed a sweeping a vista of terrace and gardens. The Martieu-Broussards' impressive coat of arms emblazoned the mantel above a low fire, and over it hung a large tapestry depicting a lush landscape. Large mirrors in gilded frames graced walls covered with exquisite murals depicting the Garden of Eden and other scenes from the Bible.

The furnishings were in the latest French style, set off by accents of pale cream and gold echoed in the elaborate *boiserie,* or moldings, as well as the coffered ceiling. Beneath the main seating area beautifully woven rugs covered the stone floor, adding another touch of color. Sprays of fragrant flowers and greenery that must have come from a conservatory, Elizabeth guessed due to the early season, spilled from large vases on tables and on the hearth's mantel. The entire aspect was light, airy, and lovely.

"Since the old king's death, her *Majesté* has begun replacing Versailles' somber colors with much more appealing ones according to her own taste. And like everyone of our acquaintance, I've been quite taken by it, as you can see," Cécile admitted with a soft laugh.

Eugène waved them to seats before the fire and sat beside Cécile. Hovering protectively over Elizabeth, Lucien settled her in a chair opposite them and drew his own next to it, while Caledonne claimed the seat next to Tess on the sofa.

"Was I not entirely right about this *magnifique* creature, Cécile?" Caledonne demanded, looking down at Tess with unconcealed affection.

"Are you ever wrong, Papa?" Cécile teased.

A becoming blush rose to Tess's cheeks. "Magnificent creature indeed!"

Elizabeth gave only part of her attention to the ensuing talk, which soon turned to the château's environs and the family's involvements. Instead she studied her hosts with interest.

According to Caledonne, monsieur le marquis worked as an assistant to France's finance minister, Jacques Necker, at the ministry offices at Versailles. He was of middling height, lean, and darkly handsome. In contrast, madame la marquise was small and all softness. Elizabeth guessed that in appearance she took after her own mother, for Elizabeth saw in her hostess but little likeness to Caledonne. To judge from his daughter, his late wife must have been Italian or Spanish and certainly quite beautiful.

She suspected that her aunt must be thinking the same thing. The Martieu-Broussards wore dishabille, informal at-home attire that was nevertheless quite elegant. Tess's cheerful responses seemed forced as though she was somewhat daunted by their hosts' splendor. But dressed in a becoming traveling gown of the latest French fashion acquired at Bordeaux, she had never appeared more youthful and vital.

"We were delighted to hear that Jonathan was finally to wed, and even more so when we learned of the opportunity to make your acquaintance Elizabeth, as well as yours, Thérèsa." Cécile turned a smiling gaze from one to the other. "Papa has praised both of you to the heavens, and we couldn't be more pleased to have you stay with us. I only wish your visit was under happier circumstances."

"On my return here last winter I told them everything you'd endured and what happened between Jonathan and your parents," Caledonne said apologetically. "I thought it best for them to know."

Relieved that she would be spared a painful explanation and the discussion that would inevitably follow, Elizabeth responded gratefully, *"Tant mieux."* So much the better.

Gently Cécile continued, "We were quite anxious for Jonathan when he disappeared before. I can't imagine what you must have felt then. And now again, so soon after your terrible ordeal—" She broke off in evident distress.

"We had much occasion to talk during our voyage, and Elizabeth confided everything to me. I know that our cousin has always good reason for what he does, but it grieves my heart to see the pain and uncertainty she suffers on his behalf."

There was an emotion in Lucien's eyes and an edge to his tone that caused Elizabeth to hastily avert her gaze from his. To say that she had confided everything to him was a considerable overstatement. Yet, as he had shown every kindness to her and her aunt and sister over the past weeks, she made no effort to correct him, which would have been awkward in any case. Indeed his lively conversation and warm interest in her and her family had done much to ease the anxiety that continually threatened to overwhelm her at being again confined below deck on a ship, no matter that *Néréide*'s accommodations bore no comparison to the horrors aboard *Erebus*.

She saw that Caledonne's jaw had hardened, and that he fixed his son in an unreadable look, which Lucien met with one that seemed to her to hold defiance. She often sensed a subtle tension spanning the air between them. On the surface their relations always appeared to be cordial, however, and having come to consider Lucien a friend, she again repressed a vaguely unsettled feeling.

Cécile's quiet voice interrupted her thoughts. "I pray Jonathan will think better of his decision. My dearest wish is that the two of you find the joy Eugène and I have in our marriage."

Elizabeth groped for words, finally managed, "It's in God's hands."

"Where it belongs," Caledonne agreed gruffly.

Eugène briskly redirected the conversation. "It appears you bore the voyage and the journey from Bordeaux reasonably well, Elizabeth. We were quite concerned that it would be too much of a strain after all you'd suffered."

"She tired more easily than we hoped," Tess fussed, turning a worried look on Elizabeth. "Dr. Lemaire feels there's still some weakness in her lungs."

Elizabeth forced a smile. "Believe me, I was very well taken care of."

"Just to make sure there's been no setback, I've arranged for my physician to attend you tomorrow," Cécile returned firmly. "Such a long sea voyage is hard to bear for even one in the best of health, and it's wise to take precautions."

As Elizabeth opened her mouth to protest, Eugène intervened smoothly, "Bordeaux is one of our favorite places to visit. What did you think of it?"

Tess embarked on a humorous description of their arrival and stay in the city. They had discovered that their countryman, John Adams, had landed there the previous week on his way to Paris to replace Silas Deane, one of the three American commissioners to France who had been recalled by Congress on charges of wrongful conduct. By all accounts Adams had been enthusiastically welcomed and much feted before leaving for Paris, and following all the excitement, their party had passed through almost unnoticed.

"I'm not surprised as your Monsieur Franklin has become all the rage throughout the country and at court for his republican manners and rustic dress," Eugène observed. "An amazing man. *Sans doute,* Monsieur Adams will bask in his reflection."

"From what I've heard of Adams, he's a man of the sternest Puritan principles, rather lacking in *savoir faire, n'est-ce pas?*" Lucien observed dismissively.

"He is plain spoken," Tess conceded. She went on to recount their attendance at Bordeaux's theatres and forays to restaurants and shops before leaving for Paris.

"The countryside is so beautiful, with all the fields and woodlands just now turning the most lovely hues of green," Elizabeth broke in, glad for the change of subject. "And, oh, those romantic châteaux on the mountain-sides overlooking the rivers! Of course, the cuisine is beyond compare even in the small inns we stopped at. If we're not careful, we'll soon be unable to fit into our new gowns!"

"And the colors, the fashions, the gaiety—and everywhere carriages and wagons and crowds!" Tess chimed in, laughing.

"Alas, these are the drawbacks of our modern way of life," Caledonne said, placing his arm across the sofa back behind her, "and the reason I love the sound of waves and wind on the open sea."

She met his look with a warm smile. "You've persuaded me that the seafaring life does hold its attractions, Alexandre." Returning her attention to the others, she went on, "We Americans tend to think ourselves such an advanced people in our 'new world'. But judging from what we've seen and experienced so far, I fear it's not only our waistlines that are in danger of seduction, but also our stern republican principles."

Elizabeth joined the others' laughter, then sobered. "Truly the beauty of this country is beyond words. Yet everywhere we saw so many beggars—men, women, and children who appeared entirely destitute. I apologize for bringing up an unhappy subject—"

"Please don't," Cécile broke in. "It's distressing to us as well, more so that this is the result of our government's policies."

"Nobles and clergy are exempt from taxes, maintaining the public roads, and serving in our military, you see," Eugène put in, his face darkening. "Thus we of the higher classes benefit from the taxes those below us must pay and the labor they're forced to provide. And our king, who holds absolute power, appears to be unable to arrest our government's extravagant expenditures, and hence our inevitable slide into bankruptcy."

"Don't misunderstand," Cécile hurried to say. "We love our king and queen, but the cost of the monarchy has become too high. France cannot go on this way forever."

"We both fear that our people will reap the consequences—and not far in the future." Seeing Tess cover a yawn with her hand, Eugène added quickly, "But forgive us. You've come a long way and perhaps would like to rest before supper."

"Mais, bien sûr," Cécile rose, and they all followed. "I'm forgetting my duties as hostess. Let us speak of this again later. When you feel yourselves refreshed, you might like to walk in the gardens for a while, and then we can talk further."

Chapter Ten

"I'M NOT SURPRISED she's fallen sleep after our long trip and all the excitement of finally meeting Charlotte." Seated at the delicate rosewood toilette table in her bedchamber, Elizabeth spoke softly as she directed a cautious glance through the open door into their suite's salon, which connected their three adjoining chambers.

"Miss Tess, too," replied her maid, statuesque, eighteen-year-old Jemma Moghrab, as she briskly brushed out Elizabeth's hair. "She was asleep almost before her head touched the pillow. And if you don't lie down a while yourself, Miss Beth, you won't be able to keep your eyes open by dinnertime."

Elizabeth relaxed, reveling in the feel of the soft bristles sliding through her hair. "I know I should, but I feel too restless to settle."

At their inn that morning the maid had, as usual, done the best that was possible with Elizabeth's barely shoulder-length hair, and she had been pleased at her reflection in the mirror. Now, eyes half closed, she watched Jemma deftly rearrange and pin her curls atop her head in a modified pouf, smoothing and intertwining the unruly mass with ribbons and giving it as much volume as possible.

She was grateful that their hosts knew why her hair had been cropped and had not brought up the subject. But she couldn't help reflecting ruefully that, although Cécile's coiffure did not tower as high nor was as ornately dressed as the ones she had seen at Bordeaux, she had abundant tresses that for formal occasions were surely dressed in Paris's most fashionable style.

Fingering the lace at the neck of her silk négligée, she transferred her attention to Jemma's reflection behind her in the mirror. They had always been more friend than merely maid and employer, but Elizabeth's struggles during the voyage had drawn them even closer. It pleased her to read the same frank affection in the younger woman's gaze.

"I trust you and Mariah are comfortably settled."

Jemma smiled. "We share a room in the servants' wing below. It's airy and light and has a lovely view of the front lawn and gardens."

"I wouldn't expect any less from the Martieu-Broussards."

Glancing at the clock, Jemma went to the bed where she had laid out a fashionable *robe à la polonaise* of soft cream silk dotted with delicate sprigs of spring flowers. The petticoat would be drawn up to hang in graceful swags over the under-petticoat striped in the same colors.

"Time's getting away," she said. "If you're going to walk out in the garden, I'd better get you dressed."

AFTER JEMMA HAD GONE, Elizabeth wandered to the nearest window, thrown open to allow the late-afternoon breeze to waft inside. Pushing back the damask draperies, she looked out across the gardens below her, where beds of tulips and daffodils rioted in glorious hues between formal plantings of sculptured shrubbery. To one side behind a stone wall she could see a picturesque row of stables, a carriage house, and other service buildings, all built of stone and roofed with red tiles. Eugène had told them that beyond these the cliff's verge afforded a broad view of the Seine at its foot, the plains opposite, and Paris's distant spires.

She turned and took in her immediate surroundings. They had been comfortably installed in a charming suite on the first floor of the north wing, separated from the family's suites in the south wing by a large circular library that occupied a turret between the two stairways. As in the rest of the château, lovely antique tapestries adorned the walls throughout the suite, along with mirrors and romantic landscapes painted by renowned French, Italian, and British artists, while thick rugs woven in designs of graceful arabesques and florals cushioned their feet.

Tess had chosen a chamber with celadon walls and accents of rose and cerulean. Abby's which lay opposite, was bathed in sunny tints of straw, orchid, and citron that suited her perfectly.

Elizabeth occupied the suite's central bedchamber. Located in one of the château's smaller rear turrets, its high ceilings and tall windows lent the space a serene aspect emphasized by the plastered walls' soft blush, the cream and gilt of the furnishings, and scattered accents of amethyst, emerald, and lapis lazuli. The rich damask curtains gathered at the four tall posters of the large bed pooled on the floor. And opposite, hanging above the fireplace, a large tapestry depicted a delightful garden scene of maidens romping with fanciful beasts.

The very strangeness and magnificence of her surroundings reminded her of what each passing day impressed more deeply on her heart: that she was a stranger in a strange land. Indeed she was grateful that God had brought her to such a lovely haven and to kind new friends. But it felt as though her exposure and capture by the British had stripped away her entire identity. And increasingly the question of what purpose her life held now, of what she was to do—and of *who* she was—tormented her.

It occurred to her that from birth she had been wrapped up in being a dutiful daughter to her parents, then in earning her father's pride as his assistant. Later it had been as the fiancée of the unstable David Hutchins, which had resulted in disaster; then as spy and courier for the Sons of Liberty, striving not only to do all the things a man could do, but to do them better.

And then her life had become tied to Carleton.

Was the trouble that she had never really discerned her life's true calling? The thought brought into sharp focus questions that had nagged at the back of her mind for a long time, but that she had thrust away because she had been so occupied in running after her own impulsive desires.

Had it been necessary for God to bring her so far from home to strangers in a strange land in order to teach her who he had designed her to be?

"Dear Father, help me to make sense of all this," she whispered. But it felt as though her plea fell into a void.

It was her earthly father she ached for right then—to gather him and her mother into her arms, to look into their dear faces and seek their wisdom! How much time would pass until it would be safe for her to return home? Would it ever? For all guarantees had been ripped away. Had not Tess and Abby been with her, the fear and aching loneliness that refused to relinquish its hold would have been unbearable.

Through her mind tumbled wrenching images of those who had gone from her into darkness. Will Stern, her dearly loved cousin, dead on Breed's Hill. And with him their great leader, Joseph Warren, who had also held a large share of her heart. The older of Jemma's two brothers, Sammy, lost at Brooklyn Heights. And Pieter Vander Groot, beloved friend and fellow doctor who had given up his life to save hers.

The memory of those still in harm's way followed. Her uncle and Will's father, Joshua Stern, with his younger son, Levi. Jemma's second brother, Pete, serving aboard Carleton's privateer *Destiny*. Another cherished friend and the one closest to Carleton, Charles Andrews, far away with him among the Shawnee.

At least Charles had Blue Sky and their baby—and how she missed them! She wondered whether they were well and the Shawnee women she had grown close to: Laughing Otter, Rain Woman, Autumn Wind, and others. A pang went through her at the thought that she might never see them again

And most of all, Carleton . . .

The silent months and long miles that stretched between them since he had vanished threatened to crush her. Panic welled up, constricting her chest and making it difficult to breathe.

How quickly those lost faded from memory—the contours of face and tilt of mouth, the angle of cheekbones, the precise color of eyes and hair—

until all that was left was a fleeting impression of the one who had gone beyond the reach of one's arms. The thought that even that would eventually recede into nothingness came near to bringing her to her knees.

She found her way to the toilette table and sat, fighting back the tears that threatened to overflow. Fingers fumbling, she opened the small cask that held her jewelry and from it took the miniature portrait that had been so precious to her when all other hope had fled.

She studied it hungrily, grateful that it had so unexpectedly been given back to her as though a gift from an unseen hand. As long as she had this, at least, Carleton would remain forever suspended in time and love, a young man of about twenty, whose smiling gaze tore at her heart as nothing else could.

She pressed the small oval to her lips and forced herself to release him into God's care again as she did daily, though with an anguish that would not yield. After tucking it back into the cask, she rose and crossed to the dresser where Jemma had tidily arranged her clothing, opened the bottom drawer, and lifted out Carleton's violin case.

She had found it impossible to leave it behind at Roxbury, knowing its full significance to him and how much of his heart it held. In addition to the miniature and his letter, it was all she had of him now. So she had brought it with her, painstakingly wrapped and packed with his music scores.

She opened the case now and removed violin and bow. Cradling them to her bosom, she carried them to the bedside table where they would be a comforting presence while she slept.

As she caressed the instrument, she remembered what solace Carleton had found in it. He also had endured the loss of those dearest to him, imprisonment and abuse at the hands of the British, brutal slavery among the Seneca, and the violence of war.

Her heart overflowed at the realization that he must constantly battle emotions very like the ones that had bedeviled her since her ordeal. To find solace he had painstakingly composed and memorized a score while held by the Seneca and lacking an instrument to play it on. Several measures filtered into her mind as they had from time to time ever since that night not long after her rescue when he had played it for her and her family, its haunting strains evoking misty Scottish moors, seething sea, distant forests and native peoples.

Inspiration struck her. Cécile also played the violin.

She might be willing to teach me, she thought, bending to kiss the violin's darkly gleaming wood *Surely he wouldn't mind if I played it. And perhaps I might find such comfort in it as he has.*

Her heart grew lighter at the thought. And with renewed resolution she dried her tears and went to find Cécile.

Chapter Eleven

A N HOUR LATER she and Tess stood with their hostess at the head of the rear terrace's wide stairway, wrapped in shawls against the cooling air. By now the sun had descended to the tops of the taller trees, slanting long bars of golden light and deep shadow across the expansive gardens below.

She could not help smiling as she admired the lovely vista of sweeping lawns and broad gravel *allées* edged with topiaries and statues. Between the walkways lay symmetrical parterres bordered with boxwood hedges sheared into geometric patterns or filled with early spring blooms in jewel hues, with ponds, fountains, and cascades interspersed among them. Graceful *bosquets,* ornamental groves, defined the grounds' farthest extent. Cécile had told them that additional acres on the far side of a stone wall behind the north wing were devoted to vegetables, herbs, grapevines, and fruit trees that supplied the kitchens.

Charlotte and Abby were already skipping down the central *allée*. The three women descended the stairs after them as the children turned off onto a cross-path, passed over a bridge across a small stream, and disappeared from view behind a bank of cypress trees.

Strolling along the path, they passed a number of men, women, and older children who appeared to be finishing their day's work of pruning hedges, repairing paths, and preparing flowerbeds for planting. Some carried shovels or pushed wheelbarrows filled with earth or clippings. All were clad in sturdy, colorful garments and greeted them cheerfully.

When Tess enquired about the rest of their family, Cécile told them that their older daughter, Aline, lived with her husband and baby daughter at his Normandy estate. Their son, Eugène-Philippe, was a student at the Université d'Aix in Marseille near the Bettárs' estate, where Cécile's younger sister, Julianne, and her family resided.

Engrossed in pleasant conversation, they stopped to sit on a fountain's broad stone ledge and dip their fingers into the water, soothed by its gentle rush and the misty rainbows the late afternoon sunlight cast above its cascade. "You spoke of the many beggars you encountered on your way here," Cécile said after a moment, returning to their earlier conversation. "Unfortunately our country is divided between the few of great privilege and wealth, the middling bourgeoisie, and the great masses of peasants who live hardly better than animals. Yet the latter must pay the taxes, while the nobles, the wealthy bourgeois, and the clergy are exempt.

"Maman was quite involved in ministries to the poor, and although Papa was often gone, he supported her work in every way. So I grew up with a good example before me. And when Eugène and I married we agreed that our lives would account for something more than our own pleasures. How could we close our eyes to the misery around us when God had blessed us with so much?"

Elizabeth indicated the people moving purposefully through the garden. "You employ many servants."

"An estate this size requires a large work force, as you can imagine. We hire as many of the local poor as we can and teach them useful skills."

"As we passed along the road coming here, your father pointed out how much of the land around us belongs to your estate," Tess noted.

Cécile nodded, smiling. "We have a farm and diary on the plain below. Our cattle and poultry, grain fields, vegetable gardens, orchards, and vineyards supply not only our own table, but also those of the people we employ and needy families around Passy."

Elizabeth frowned. "It's a shame that instead of following your example so many of the nobility turn a blind eye to the people's suffering and even lay greater burdens on them."

"The abuses inherent in a monarchy are the very reason we cast off our king," Tess interjected, shaking her head. She stopped abruptly and pressed her hand to her mouth.

Her face clouding, Cécile looked from one to the other. "A great many of our countrymen admire your Revolution—in theory at least. Eugene and I are among those who desire our government to institute more just policies. But there are others who've begun to advocate radical changes to the point that our sovereigns, particularly the queen, are growing quite concerned about our country's support for your cause."

"I spoke out of turn. We know our situation is different from that of France, and I promise we'll guard our tongues. We've no wish to stir up a hornet's nest while we're guests here."

Cécile placed her hand over Tess's. "You only spoke the truth. Eugène and I welcome that, but not everyone does." Dismissing the subject, she beamed at them. "I also work with a ministry to the poor overseen by Father Raulett, a priest in Paris. We supply spiritual counsel, of course, but also food, medical care, education, and any other practical help that's needed."

Tess brightened. "My brother, who's an excellent doctor, trained Beth as a physician and surgeon. She also has experience in midwifery. Perhaps she could be of use in your ministry."

"I'd love to help in any way I can." Noting Cécile's hesitation, Elizabeth said, "I promised Papa I'd endeavor to learn the latest medical methods and treatments while we're here. But when I mentioned this to Dr. Lemaire, he was . . . discouraging. To say the least."

Cécile gave her a sympathetic look. "A university medical degree is required by our Academy of Surgery to practice medicine in France. And our doctors are quite opposed to accepting women in their art, other than as nurses at their beck and call. It's the same in most other professions."

Tess rolled her eyes. "It's no different in America. Apparently we women are incapable of endeavors apart from the home."

Cécile considered them thoughtfully. "Many of those we minister to suffer from illnesses or injury. The hospitals are overcrowded, and often the poor won't or can't leave their families for treatment except in the most dire need, especially the women, who also may have to give birth alone. We never have enough doctors willing to work with us, and we'd be quite grateful for any help you're able to provide, Elizabeth. If you'd like, why don't both of you come along later this week when we make our rounds?"

Elizabeth and Tess exchanged smiling glances. "We'd love to!"

Cécile rose and beckoned them to accompany her to the nearby orangerie they had glimpsed through the trees along a path leading to the garden's outer wall. The head gardener met them at the main door to usher them inside, where the building's warmth dispelled the chill.

An abundance of orange, lemon, lime, pomegranate, and palm trees planted in huge pots filled the broad, high space. The gardener explained that these had been imported from Portugal, Spain, and Italy and were stored inside during the winter. The building's thick, stone and brick walls absorbed and reflected the abundance of sunlight its south-facing windows admitted. Charcoal-fired stoves supplemented its warmth, maintaining an interior temperature well above freezing. Once the danger of frost was past, the plants would be moved to their summer locations throughout the gardens.

"How delightful!" Tess exclaimed as they returned outside. "We have orangeries in our country, of course, but we've never seen one so extensive or such beautiful grounds."

"We're proud of our gardens, to be sure, but you must see the palace grounds! Ours are nothing to Versailles. The orangerie is much larger there as well and contains many more exotic plants. We must take a tour!"

Elizabeth laughed. "It seems we've enough to see and do to keep us occupied for months."

Cécile linked her arm through both Elizabeth's and Tess's in an affectionate manner. "I already have a feeling that when you must leave us—

which I pray will not be soon—we shall miss you beyond measure. But that's well in the future, I hope, and we won't talk of it until we must."

Elizabeth's emotions overflowed at thought of the new places and experiences that lay in store. She had always longed to travel in Europe, and it seemed almost unbelievable that she was in France at last. But it was the opportunity to be of service that to a greater measure eased the painful separation from home.

When they returned to the main *allée,* they saw the marquis with Caledonne and Lucien ahead of them down an intersecting lane, standing in front of a vine-bedecked summerhouse that faced a long pool. They appeared to be engaged in passionate debate, and Elizabeth noted that her aunt's gaze went immediately to Caledonne.

"Your father's absences must have been hard on your mother and you children growing up," Tess ventured.

"It was. When Papa was home, he was also often preoccupied with naval and governmental affairs and other concerns. He's an ambitious man when it comes to his career, as most men are, and after our elder brother, Frédéric, died, he buried himself in work even more." Looking away, as though speaking to herself, she murmured, "It was natural, I suppose, that he blamed himself . . . " Her voice trailed off.

Directing a concerned look at Tess, Elizabeth saw that she also wondered about what had happened to Cécile's older brother but hesitated to ask about something that clearly was still quite painful. And private.

After a moment Cécile turned back to them, her smile returning. "But we adored Papa and always knew certainly that he loved us. We were never in want, and Maman never complained during the times she was left to manage her household and children alone. She taught us to respect and honor him in all things."

Tentatively Elizabeth asked, "Do you ever know what his assignments are or where he's going?"

Cécile gave a careless laugh at odds with the emotion Elizabeth sensed beneath the surface. "Papa never speaks of his work in the future tense, only in the present or past, and then in the most general terms."

Elizabeth understood quite well the necessity for secrecy in military affairs. But she also knew that it had a cost. At times a high one.

She saw that her aunt noted it, too, in the piercing glance Tess directed at Cécile, then quickly away. "I know he loved your maman very much."

Cécile dimpled. "Theirs was a true love story."

Briefly she described how her parents had met in Italy when he was a junior lieutenant in the French navy. He fell at once madly in love with the lovely dark-haired, sloe-eyed Luciana Verdigi and swept her away. Theirs was a love that had never faded.

"He was entirely devoted to her. One of the officers closest to him told me once that he never formed any casual alliances or took a mistress, though this is something that is not only common but also expected in men of his rank. His faithfulness inspired me to seek such a man for my own life, one I found in Eugène. When Maman died Papa was so deeply stricken that I feared for him. Yet I've also seen how tragedy can change our hearts for the better. It was in this new grief that I think he began to realize how important family is. Little by little he's let go of unnecessary involvements and drawn closer to his children and grandchildren."

With a quick glance at Tess, who appeared to be absorbed in the ornate pattern of the nearest parterre, Elizabeth said, "He's never considered marrying again?"

Cécile shook her head and sighed. "I confess that until recently I worried how it would be for us if he did. But the Scriptures say that it's not good for a man to be alone, and gradually I've come to wish for him a loving companion for his latter years. Papa's always been an excellent judge of character, and if he should marry again, I know that he'll choose wisely."

She turned to Tess. "But you've remained unmarried, Thérèsa. Have you never wished for a husband to share your life?"

Tess's cheeks colored But she briefly related the story of her secret-betrothal in her youth to a sea captain whom her parents opposed, and of his death at sea.

"It must have been *tres* difficult to wait so long only to learn that he died on his way back to you!" Cécile burst out. "How admirable that all these years you've remained faithful to his memory."

Tears glimmered in her eyes, the emotion so genuine Elizabeth could not doubt it came from the marquise's heart. Already she felt herself increasingly drawn to Cécile as to a dear elder sister.

"It was hard indeed for many years," Tess admitted, glancing toward the men who were approaching. "But I never found another man like him."

Perhaps not until now, Elizabeth thought, amused.

Caledonne strode to Tess's side and took her hand. "Ah, but there comes a time, my dear Thérèsa, when we must finally set aside what was not to be and open our hearts to the new work *le bon Dieu* would do in us now—and for the future," he murmured.

Tess's color heightened, but she did not drop her gaze from his steady one. "I've always believed in keeping one's heart open to our Lord's will," she said earnestly. "He brings new blessings every day."

SHORTLY AFTER NIGHTFALL they gathered in the soft candlelight of the elegant *petit* dining room's crystal chandeliers, across from the grand formal one. Abby, Charlotte, and the governess joined them in feasting on a hearty ragout accompanied by fragrant, crusty bread; creamy cheese; and stewed dried fruit, all washed down with a fine red wine.

Elizabeth was relieved and pleased to see how happily her little sister engaged in the conversation and activities of her new friend and governess. Already her accent and phrasing were taking on the characteristics of their hosts' Parisian ones—as were hers and Tess's, Elizabeth noted with a smile.

"You didn't say anything about your voyage, Papa, but I assume it was a pleasant one," Cécile said, leading the way out to the terrace after the

girls had retired upstairs with Madame Verignay for a quiet time of reading until bedtime.

A cool breeze stirred the trees. The men wearing light coats and the
women with shawls wrapped around their shoulders settled on chairs
close to the château's walls, where the sun's warmth still radiated from the
stones.

"It was for the most part, though we did weather a few stiff gales,"
Caledonne answered.

Eugène regarded his father-in-law with raised eyebrows. "You didn't
run afoul of any British patrols now that our nations are formally at war?"

"British warships came hull up on the horizon a couple of times,"
Lucien answered, "but considering the size of our fleet, they didn't seem to
be exceptionally eager to engage us."

"Since we were necessarily confined below deck except for a very
brief airing in the morning and evening," Tess retorted, regarding Caledonne with mock reproach, "a sea battle or two might have provided a
welcome diversion."

She clearly meant to tease. But Elizabeth's stomach clenched, and
she suddenly found it hard to breathe.

Lucien's countenance darkened. *"Pardon,"* he said stiffly, "but having
experienced several naval engagements myself, I'd not advise anyone to
take such an experience lightly. Our elder brother, Frédéric, a naval lieutenant, died in the Bataille des Cardinaux in Quiberon Bay." He referred to
the decisive naval battle of the Seven Years' War twenty years earlier that
had broken the back of French naval power and made Britain the world's
dominant sea power. "I was serving as a cadet aboard his ship and held him
as he—my confidante and childhood hero—choked to death on his own
blood."

Fearful images of her experiences in battle while serving as a spy and
courier for the rebels tumbled through Elizabeth's mind, mixed with even
more terrifying ones of the night Carleton had wrested her from the horrors of the *Erebus*. Her voice trembling, she said, "There's no romance in

battle, whether on sea or land. There's only . . . chaos and desperation, blood and death . . . " Her voice choked.

A strained hush fell over the company. Lucian captured her hand and clasped it tightly. She lifted her gaze to his, tears starting, his grief unaccountably offering comfort for her own.

She became aware that Tess stared at them, her hand pressed to her mouth in dismay. Seated beside her, Caledonne stared into space, a muscle working in his jaw.

"Such is the tragedy of war," he said after a suspended moment, an uncharacteristic tremor in his voice.

"And as we all know, *mon père,* men must have war."

Bitter resentment and angry reproach lanced across the air between the two men. Although Caledonne held his tongue, Elizabeth could feel the anguish beneath his carefully controlled exterior.

So this is what stands between them, she thought, unsettled to see his heretofore unassailable composure shaken.

"Please forgive me for speaking so lightly!" Tess gasped. "I didn't intend—I only meant to tease—"

His brow furrowed with concern, Caledonne encircled her shoulders with his arm before directing a cold glance at Lucien. "*Mais, bien sûr,* Thérèsa. That was understood."

"No one blames you for what you could not have known," Cécile agreed.

Tears welled into Tess's eyes. "I can't imagine how painful it must be to lose a son—" she looked from Caledonne to Cécile and Lucien "— and a brother."

Cécile stared down at her folded hands. "Did not God's comfort and time's passing soften grief, it would be impossible to go on."

"One goes on indeed—and me to amusements other than a naval career," Lucien drawled.

His sardonic tone caused Elizabeth to wince inwardly. She was tempted to ask him what amusements he referred to, but he had avoided sharing any except the most commonplace details of his private life and volunteered nothing further now. So she held her silence.

EXHAUSTED BY THE LONG DAY of traveling and visiting, they retired early that evening. After Jemma had readied her for bed and gone, Elizabeth settled in a chair by the window to read a book she had found in Eugène's library. After the revelations of the past hour, however, she found it impossible to focus on the text.

The moon cast long silver beams onto the rug, beckoning her. At last she laid the book aside and blew out the lamp. Wrapping her shawl around her shoulders, she sank to her knees before the window and pushed the casement open a little way to let in a breath of the chill night air. Arms folded on the deep sill, her head laid on them, she took in the spring night. The garden's lush plantings spread below her to the distant groves, darkly shadowed and mysterious, their foliage edged with moonlight.

Just when she had begun to hope that she was at last free of the nightmares and sudden attacks of panic that had plagued her since her rescue, the long hours confined in their cramped cabin aboard Caledonne's flagship had reawakened the fearful memories of the prison ship's horrors and the men who suffered aboard it. Had it not been for Tess's and Jemma's loving care during the voyage, bolstered by much prayer and God's grace, she could not have endured. The renewed nightmares had subsided to a manageable level since their landing at Bordeaux, but she had come to believe that they would never entirely leave her and dreaded the nighttime hours.

Her capture and following ordeal had completely shattered all sense of safety, robbing her of the self-confidence and sense of supernatural protection that had carried her through the most dangerous situations she had faced in the patriots' cause. That Lucien still grieved for his older brother offered some measure of reassurance that her sorrow for those lost was not unusual.

The conversation she and Tess had had with Cécile before parting for the night drifted into her thoughts. "How terrible that Lucien witnessed his brother's death," Tess had said. "Clearly they were very close."

Elizabeth noted that Cécile hesitated before answering, "Lucien was always trying to follow in Frédéric's footsteps, to be sure. Even after all these years, he can't seem to accept comfort for his loss."

Though her aunt seemed not to note it, Elizabeth had been struck by her phrasing. And by what she didn't say.

The muted click of a door opening and closing broke her reverie. After a moment Caledonne and Lucien came into view, walking slowly across the terrace directly below.

"You're not the only one who grieves," she heard Caledonne say gruffly.

She hastily pulled back behind the draperies.

"I'm well aware of that," Lucien replied, sarcasm heavy on his tongue. "Frédéric was your pride and joy, after all—never me. Not only had he the good fortune to be charming, intelligent, and an accomplished naval officer, while I've never been any of those things. But he was also tall, blond, and blue eyed, like you. And, of course, Jonathan."

She caught her breath and edged carefully forward just far enough to glimpse the two men.

"You think appearance makes a difference to a father's heart? Well, you take after your mother, whom I loved above all women." Caledonne's back was to her so she could not see his face, but something in his look caused Lucien to clamp his mouth shut, lips pressed together as heat rose to his face.

"But Jonathan is the son of your angel sister, which places him above everyone. Even Frédéric couldn't compare to him in your eyes though everything he did was to win your favor—"

"That's absurd! He always knew he had it. You speak as though it's impossible to love more than one person, but love is greater than that. If only you'd understand that to truly love is to open your heart to all those around you. I loved Frédéric and I love you because you're my sons! Yes, I love Jonathan, too, but only partly because he's Julianne's son. Much more because of who he is: a truly kind, generous, and admirable man—"

"Which I obviously am not in your estimation."

"Will you forever make everything about you, Lucien?" Caledonne demanded impatiently. "You're not the center of the universe. None of us is. What I feel for another has nothing to do with what I feel for you. But you always insist on justifying your jealousy and envy. Rather than blaming others for your faults, you might, perhaps, try mending them instead."

Turning on his heel, he strode out of sight into the shadows along the side of the house, while Lucien glared after him.

Again Elizabeth heard a door open. A shaft of candlelight slanted across the terrace, and Eugène came outside.

He took Lucien's arm and bade him walk with him. Lucien did so with obvious reluctance, and the two men descended the terrace stairs into the garden. Turning onto one of the intersecting *allées,* they moved into the darkness and out of her sight.

Chapter Twelve

H EAD BOWED, ELIZABETH listened with aching heart as Father Raulett concluded the final rites in a muted voice. When he made the sign of the cross, she gently released the man's lifeless hand onto his chest. The oldest of the three white-robed nuns who accompanied them bent to draw a tattered blanket over the unnaturally still, twisted form.

It was the last day of April. On their arrival an hour earlier, a quick examination had told her that the middle-aged wagoner's crushed chest, added to his broken limbs and other wounds, were beyond any treatment. She had given him a strong dose of laudanum to ease his pain and done everything possible to make him comfortable on the single dirty straw pallet in one corner of the cramped room, while his wife and children wept.

With a muted sigh she closed her leather-bound medical case, grasped it by the handle, and rose. The two ragged men who had been waiting respectfully with Cécile just inside the door crossed themselves, heads bowed, then brought forward a litter and lifted the swathed body onto it.

The nuns silently followed the men outside as they carried their burden to the waiting cart, passing Tess, who ducked in through the low doorway. Short, plump, Father Raulett gathered the squalling infant from the new widow's arms into his own, compassion and sorrow vying on his round face, and handed the child to her.

Tess wiped dirt and tears from the tiny face with the edge of her shawl.

Settling the little one against her shoulder, she patted her back and bounced her gently to quiet her, while the priest explained to the widow that the nuns would prepare the body for burial in the parish cemetery for the poor. The men would return to fetch her and the children for the mass the following day.

As he spoke, Elizabeth discreetly pressed her lavender-scented handkerchief to her nose and glanced around her. An overwhelming stench pervaded the filthy one-room apartment. The cluttered space that housed the family of six faced onto a garbage-choked alleyway on the first floor of a decaying tenement, one of countless others crowding the maze of streets east of Les Halles, Paris's central market district.

"What'll we do now, Father?" the woman asked hoarsely, drawing Elizabeth's gaze back to her and her children. "We got no money but what my Pierre could make driving wagons. And that weren't enough to keep body and soul together for all these." She motioned to the children who crowded against her threadbare petticoats, bewilderment etched on their dirty, upturned faces.

The family included one less now, Elizabeth reflected, but no means to provide for their needs. And the widow's bulging belly testified to another life on the way. She guessed the woman to be no more than thirty years old though her careworn face and wrinkled, reddened hands belonged to someone much older.

"Have no fear, Jeanne-Marie. You're not alone," Cécile assured her, clasping the woman's hand. "We'll help you in any way we can."

"It's not for you to take care of me and my children," Jeanne-Marie protested gruffly.

Father Raulett patted her slumped shoulder. *"Tout au contraire."* On the contrary. *"Notre bon Dieu* commands us to care for the least of these for they are beloved by him. We're privileged to serve you."

Jeanne-Marie harrumphed and wiped her red eyes, then reached out to take her youngest back from Tess. "You know I'm grateful, Father. But where was our good God when my Pierre slipped and fell beneath that cart and when the horse trampled him? Where will our good God be when my children cry for their father?"

"He'll be right here as always, bearing your sorrow," the priest said gently. "Did he not himself suffer the grief of losing his only Son? Did he not bring us to you? In this world we will have trouble, but our Savior tells us not to fear for he has overcome the world."

Cécile embraced the woman, then set on the table one of the bulging baskets they had packed that morning at the church's parish hall before setting out on their morning's round, not knowing how badly it would be needed that day. "We brought new blankets and enough food to supply you and the children for several days."

Jeanne-Marie nodded disconsolately. But as Cécile explained the program the parish offered to teach women fine sewing and place them as seamstresses, a degree of hope returned to her tear-stained face.

"They provide child care and will transport you to the parish hall and home again. There will be a place for you, if you're willing," she concluded.

After promising to return to check on the family's needs early the next week, they took their leave.

Elizabeth settled into her seat in the waiting coach and carefully placed her new medical case beside her feet. Eugène had unexpectedly presented it to her a few days after their arrival—most likely at Cécile's insistence. She suspected he only condescended to what he considered a whim of theirs.

Nevertheless, she was immensely pleased with the gift and had already spent considerable time poring over the latest French medical text that accompanied it—all of which she had put to good use on their first venture into the slums of Paris the previous week and again that morning. Although she had not been able help the poor wagon driver, gratitude flooded over her to feel again the deep sense of healing power that flowed through her hands when she placed them on those she attended and prayed over them.

While Cécile, Tess, and Father Raulett talked companionably as their coach rattled across the cobbled streets' ruts, she stared thoughtfully out the window, taking in the neighborhoods through which they passed. On their first visit to the city, she and Tess had been astounded to discover that Paris, second only to London as Europe's largest city, still evoked to a great degree the medieval town from which it had grown and offered many scenes far from the splendor they had imagined.

According to Cécile the teeming working and poor classes, their numbers augmented by thousands of unskilled migrants from France's poorest regions, were increasingly concentrated in the central market district and the city's eastern side, with its thousands of small workshops and businesses, and on the Left Bank, near the tanners and dyers along the Bièvre River. At the same time the wealthy classes and nobility were steadily moving to outlying districts, where they built even grander houses with larger courtyards and more elaborate gardens.

The divide between rich and poor was rapidly expanding, and along with it ever greater discontent. Elizabeth could see the evidence on every side, her senses assaulted by a welter of constantly changing odors, sights, and sounds.

Decaying, multi-storied stone tenements; tall, turreted buildings with half-timbered facades and conical red-tiled roofs; and magnificent, steepled churches and cathedrals shouldered against each other along the streets and on the bridges across the boat-clogged Seine. Many towered so high they blocked sunlight from the narrow, winding warrens below. The smoke coiling from multiplied chimneys darkened the gloom, their soot blackening every structure, while the mingled fumes of sewers and tanneries cast a pall over the entire area.

They drove through several narrow, arched passageways connecting buildings. At intervals public markets spilled into the narrow streets, impeding traffic as the noisy multitude scurried about their business. For want of sidewalks, people thronged the roadway, jostling around and past their coach.

A dense cacophony filled the air: church bells clanging the hour; the splash of fountains; the clatter of horses, wagons, and carriages across the cobbles; tools banging and thumping in small workshops; animals lowing, baaing, squealing, and squawking as they were driven to market; the babble of men, women, and children garbed in the simple clothing of the middle and lower classes and the filthy rags of the poorest laborers and the destitute. And, vying for attention, prostitutes in dirty, gaudy clothing calling out their services.

They took leave of Father Raulett at the parish hall. As their coach turned west onto the Rue St. Honoré, she caught a brief glimpse of the magnificent spire, towers, and flying buttresses of Notre-Dame Cathedral looming above the buildings on the eastern point of the Île de la Cité, the largest of three small islands clustered in the Seine.

One of their first visits to the city had been to attend mass there with their hosts the previous Sunday. She, Tess, and Abby had marveled at the ornate high altar, the soaring pillars in the nave and transepts, the statues, the astonishing beauty of the staineed-glass windows, and the building's rich ornamentation both inside and out. Yet the imposing twelfth-century gothic cathedral showed disappointing signs of neglect and deterioration as well.

Narrow cobbled streets had now given way to wider, paved avenues and boulevards lined with graceful linden trees. Here mounds of rubble, stone, and lumber gave evidence of new construction. Fashionable hôtels of neo-classical design, châteaux, and grand marble palaces flanked the streets on either side and massive monuments and fountains dominated broad plazas, reminding Elizabeth of illustrated scenes of ancient Greece and Rome she had seen.

Here wealthy bourgeoisie clad in rich, dark fabrics and nobles in more elaborate and brilliantly colored dress bustled along on foot, astride horses, or riding in coaches or chairs carried by servants. They rolled past the beautiful Louvre, the Palais-Royal, and then the Tuileries Palais with its lovely gardens, yet at many intersections she caught glimpses down filth-piled side streets hardly more than lanes. Finally they turned south at the Champs Élysées, passing the Place de Louis XV with its magnificent statue of the young king's grandfather, and turned west onto the Cours de la Reine, following the bank of the Seine.

Woods, parks, and a number of grand estates stretched the rest of the way. Off to the west she caught a glimpse of the forest called the Bois de Boulogne where they had ridden with the Martieu-Broussards earlier that week. The forest offered entertainments from hunting to picnicking and horse racing as well.

Renowned for its mineral spring, Passy consisted mainly of clustered cottages beyond which picturesque vineyards and pastureland sloped gently south toward the nearby town of Auteuil. Wooded cliffs of middling height overlooked the Seine along its eastern side, with steep, unevenly paved roads like the one they ascended winding upward to turreted châteaux and hôtels on the heights.

The coach pulled to a halt in the château's courtyard, and Tess leaned forward to look out the window, breaking Elizabeth's reverie. "There's Alexandre's coach. He was afraid his meetings with Sartine and Vergennes might last until mid afternoon."

She and Tess had met the two men and their wives at a dinner hosted by the Martieu-Broussards the previous week. Antoine de Sartine was France's secretary of state for the navy. France's foreign minister, the dignified, sixty-nine-year-old Charles Gravier, le comte de Vergennes, was one of the first French officials to advocate allying with the Americans.

Noting the anticipation in her aunt's voice, Elizabeth met Cécile's meaningful glance with raised eyebrows and a smile. A footman let down the coach's step and assisted them to alight. As the three women started up the wide stone stairway to the château's front door, it burst open and Caledonne came rapidly down to meet them.

Scowling, he tucked Tess's hand into the crook of his arm and led her up the steps after Elizabeth and Cécile. "Where've you been?" he growled. "Your rounds can't have taken so long. Dinner's almost to be served."

"But we're here in time, aren't we?" Tess returned tartly as they ascended the steps and trailed after Cécile past the butler into the *salle*. "Are you so hungry you couldn't wait a little longer?"

"For your company, yes," he returned brusquely as footmen relieved the three women of gloves, shawls, and hats.

Elizabeth handed over her medical case, schooling her countenance to an innocent look. She almost gave way to a giggle when Cécile directed a quelling look at her father.

"It's but a quarter of one, Papa." Briefly she related the wagon driver's death. "We had his unfortunate widow and children to attend to. I know you'd not have had us neglect them in order to spare your anxiety, especially as you did mention that your meeting might run late."

"Bah! I was imagining all the disasters that might have befallen you in those slums."

He was interrupted by Charlotte and Abby, who hurried down the south stairway with Eugène following more slowly. Cécile swung to regard the children with a stern look.

"Are these the manners Madame Verignay has taught you?"

Both girls immediately adopted a gracefully sedate gait. *"Pardon, Maman,"* Charlotte said meekly as she stopped beside her mother, while Abby slipped demurely between Elizabeth and Tess.

"I see my daughter has everything well in hand," Caledonne observed dryly. "Including, it would seem, me."

Eugène laughed good-naturedly as he came to encircle Cécile's shoulders with his arm. "My good wife rules her household with every grace and sweetness."

Laughter twinkled in Cécile's eyes, but although her lips twitched she said only, "Where's Lucien? Is he not to join us for dinner."

"It appears he's off on some business with his friends."

"Sans doute this business includes Louis-Philippe, le duc de Chartres," Caledonne said curtly, referring to the son of the duc d'Orleans, the king's cousin and First Prince of the Blood, who was closest to the throne after the king's direct descendents.

"What is Lucien's business?" Tess enquired. "He did mention a change of careers."

Caledonne dismissed the subject with an airy wave of his hand. "What is it that courtiers do?"

Elizabeth noted that Cécile frowned and turned abruptly away. Eugène cut off any response by ushering them smoothly across the grand *salle* and into the *petit* dining room.

THE GOVERNESS, Madame Verignay, joined them for dinner as usual. While the servants passed in and out, serving the various courses, they carried on a casual discussion about the day's events and the children's progress at their studies.

A strikingly lovely woman named Anne-Louise d'Hardancourt Brillon de Jouy, who lived nearby, had called on them with her young daughters the previous week. They had made arrangements for Charlotte and Abby to spend the afternoon at her home, Moulin Joli, with her children and several of their friends from the neighborhood. As they rose from the table, the butler announced the arrival of her coach, and they saw the girls off, then Madame Verignay withdrew.

Talking lazily, they drifted outside onto the terrace and from there down into the garden and to the delightful summerhouse entwined with rose vines that were just beginning to bud. It had become a favorite retreat, and while the others found seats Elizabeth paused at one of the wide, open windows to breathe in the perfume of spring blooms planted below.

The day was fine and warm with a scattering of fluffy, white clouds sailing serenely across the sky's deep blue. Again gratitude welled up for the Lord's mercy in guiding them here and for their hosts, who made them feel very much at home and were quickly becoming dear friends. It had indeed been the right decision to come.

Her heart swelled with happiness to see how well Abby was adapting to this new land and culture. Her little sister occasionally gave way to tears of homesickness and longing for their parents when Elizabeth and Tess tucked her into bed at night, which was to be expected given her age. Indeed Elizabeth also suffered such moments. But Abby obeyed Madame

Verignay and the Martieu-Broussards without hesitation and eagerly joined in outings and visits with the neighbors' children. Under the tutelage of her governess, augmented by Charlotte's happy companionship, she was gaining in maturity and grace.

Gratefully Elizabeth reflected that their hosts' company provided not only a pleasant distraction, but also an excellent tonic for the anxious thoughts that continued to nag at her. Since Cécile's physician had pronounced her fit enough for most activities, needing only plentiful, wholesome nourishment and a period of rest each afternoon to fully regain her strength, every day had been filled to the brim.

She was especially pleased that a period each day was devoted to music, with Cécile introducing her, Abby, and Charlotte to new works that challenged and delighted them. And in addition to helping Elizabeth develop greater skill on the pianoforte, Cécile had also eagerly agreed to teach her to play the violin.

Madame Brillon had also invited Elizabeth and Tess to come to the salon she hosted at Moulin Joli. Cécile regularly attended and assured them that the most distinguished French philosophes were guests at these fashionable gatherings. She insisted they must attend both Madame Brillon's salon and the one held by Madame Helvétius, widow of the acclaimed philosophe Claud-Adrien Helvétius, at her nearby estate in Auteuil.

During the long hours of their voyage to France and since their arrival, Lucien had drawn Elizabeth into discussions of the works of Rousseau, Voltaire, and other foremost philosophes. The discovery that they shared the same ideals of government and human advancement increasingly drew her to him. That she might actually meet the men and women who developed these concepts and hear them speak thrilled her.

Suddenly becoming aware that the others' conversation had taken a more serious tone, she turned when Tess mentioned the talk they had overheard in Paris about the lack of an heir to the French throne though the king and queen had been married for eight years. Tight lipped, Eugène described the venomous charges being leveled against the queen by the *libellistes,* publishers of sensational pamphlets called *libelles,* which at times ran to book length or even multi-volume series. Labeling Marie Antoinette with scandalous epithets, they protested her personal extravagance and her attempts to influence France's policies to favor her Austrian homeland. The most recent criticism concerned her brother, Emperor Joseph II's, claim to the throne of Bavaria, which threatened war with Prussia and Saxony—and potentially France.

To Cécile's protest that the queen was caught between the interests of France and pressure from her brother, Caledonne shrugged. "Marie Antoinette is the queen of France, not Austria," he countered. "Besides, no French queen is allowed to hold any influence in the government."

Eugène waved the matter away. "These charges are nothing compared to the *libellistes'* obscene speculations about the queen's well-known attachments to a number of her courtiers, and especially to le comte d'Artois," he said, his voice heavy with disgust as he referred to Louis XVI's youngest brother, an avid gambler and frequent participant in the queen's card parties. "They contrast Artois' handsome appearance and virility with the king's impotence, and describe in detail the imagined pleasures she finds in his arms, while accusing her of endless other sexual intrigues as well."

"The queen wouldn't actually be unfaithful to the king, would she?" Tess asked doubtfully.

Caledonne snorted. "How could she engage in illicit liaisons without the entire court knowing every detail? She's not allowed to so much as dress herself and is accompanied everywhere she goes. If the king cannot visit her chamber at night undetected, how could someone else? Believe me, if she were ever to be so foolhardy, official charges would immediately be brought against her."

"From what I've personally observed, the queen is quite modest in manner and engages only in the most harmless flirtations. She appears to be genuinely affectionate toward the king, and he toward her. They were quite young when they married," Cécile explained, "she only fourteen and he fifteen. It's common knowledge that not only is the king shy in these matters, but there's also apparently some physical problem that affects his ability to fulfill his marital duty."

Elizabeth took a seat next to her aunt. "Who could be behind such scandalous publications? Does anyone know?"

Cécile's eyes narrowed. "We've wondered about Monsieur—Louis-Stanislas, le comte de Provence—the elder of *le roi's* brothers. He's second in line to the throne, and clearly he and la comtesse have no trouble producing children as their second son is already three months old. He's a schemer if there ever was one, and has the most to gain from the king's lack of an heir. And the relations between him and the king are notoriously contentious."

"Don't forget that d'Orleans and Chartres have much to gain as well," Caledonne pointed out. "They hold the greatest wealth in France and wield considerable power. I personally consider them the *libelles'* most likely source."

Frowning, Eugène said, "In the past, when the *libellistes* attacked our leaders, especially the king, they did so with a sense of respect, even of deference. But now they center on our government itself and on the monarchy as a whole with complete lack of restraint that I find most troubling."

"At a time when your sovereigns are being taken to task for their extravagance, what of France's support for our war against England?" Tess asked. "I'd think the queen's personal expenditures would pale in comparison to the cost of another war."

Caledonne gave her a wry look. "Indeed they do, *ma chère,* especially since our coffers are still depleted from the last war. But we French are by history and tradition hostile to England, and in the end it came down to what hurts our enemy helps us."

"This war is bound to plunge France deeper into this spiral of deficit that's already dragging us under," Eugène said grimly. "We're doing all we can in the finance ministry direction to reform the state budget and keep that from happening. In fact, Necker just transferred a huge sum from his own pocket to the royal treasury."

Preoccupied, Elizabeth gave only part of her attention to the others' discussion. For at Caledonne's comment about the Orleans' possible involvement with the *libelles,* questions had begun to spin in her head.

If they were indeed involved with these attacks, was it possible that Lucien was also? It was common gossip that le duc de Chartres wished to see France's absolute monarchy abolished and its monarchs overthrown in favor of a constitutional monarchy like England's.

Lucien had made it no secret that he and Chartres were very close friends. Or that he agreed with the duc about the monarchy. And she had to bite her tongue to keep the questions from springing to her lips.

Chapter Thirteen

"WELL, YOU SEE, my hair had to be cut when I was ill last fall," Elizabeth explained.

Feeling warmth rise to her cheeks, she could almost hear Aunt Tess chiding her for being self-consciousness about her short tresses, but it was hard not to when her coiffure so often became a topic of conversation.

"*Mon Dieu,* from your confinement aboard a British prison ship, we heard," crowed their hostess, the flamboyant Madame Helvétius. "What perfect horrors you must have endured!"

Hoping to cut off any further discussion of the subject, Elizabeth said quickly, "I was spared the worst, thank God. And my stay in your fair country has entirely restored my health."

Ignoring the assessing looks of the others who lingered with them around the dining room table, she returned the older woman's bold stare with a curious one, unsure of what she thought of her. She appeared to be in her mid fifties, and her clothing, though intriguingly exotic, was carelessly worn and needed laundering and mending. Her hair and makeup had also been done haphazardly and only served to emphasize the loss of the youthful beauty she had clearly once possessed.

Caledonne had swept Aunt Tess off for a ride and picnic in the Bois de Boulogne that morning, taking the girls and Madame Verignay with them, while Elizabeth had accompanied Cécile and Lucien to Madame Helvétius's modest estate a short drive away in Auteuil. On their arrival she had run outside before they were half out of the coach and welcomed each of them with an embrace and a kiss on the neck—the custom in France to avoid smearing the women's makeup.

It had quickly become apparent that the mansion and grounds were overrun by a veritable menagerie. They had braved a gauntlet of barking dogs, slinking cats, tame deer, cackling poultry, and caged birds, while dodging the muddy footprints and other deposits left liberally in the animals' wake both outside on the graveled walk and inside on the rugs and furnishings. Elizabeth had been taken aback by the contrast with the cleanliness and order she was used to at the Martieu-Broussards' château and the homes of their other acquaintances.

Despite their hostess's eccentricities—or perhaps because of them—her salon was as well attended as Madame Brillon's had been the previous week, attracting a wide range of the notable philosophes and high-ranking nobles who flocked to these weekly gatherings to discuss literature, science, philosophy, and politics. At dinner Madame Helvétius had seated herself between Chartres and the renowned philosophe Louis-Alexandre, duc de la Rochefoucauld, a staunch advocate for the American cause. Also at table had been Rochefoucauld's handsome cousin, the social reformer François Alexandre Frédéric, duc de la Rochefoucauld-Liancourt; and the brilliant philosopher and mathematician Marie-Jean Antoine Nicolas de Caritat, le marquis de Condorcet. The effort to remember all the long names and titles had Elizabeth's head spinning.

The men were in their thirties, around Lucien's age, and they all seemed to count him a close friend. That he joined in their discussion of a wide range of philosophies with a knowledge and comprehension equal to theirs genuinely impressed her, and she was eager to hear more.

To her disappointment, however, their hostess had carried on most of the conversation at dinner while feeding bites from her plate to her favorite lapdog. From time to time, in an apparent excess of emotion, she had thrown her arm across Rochefoucauld's or Chartres' shoulders or encircled their necks with a casual familiarity. No one else seemed to consider this in the least extraordinary, but Elizabeth could not consider it seemly.

When madame rose from the table, her guests did the same. On Lucien's arm, Elizabeth followed Cécile and the others through the *salle* and into the salon, the heavy fragrance of the courtiers' expensive perfumes wafting after them. Except for the clutter that filled the rooms and the noticeable traces left by madame's pets, the scene could not have been more beguiling. Here and there small clusters of guests either sang, played a variety of instruments, danced, or were engrossed in conversation, the severe, dark fashions of the philosophes mingling freely with the high-ranking nobles' brilliant plumage.

In a corner across the room she saw Madame Brillon's elderly husband conversing flirtatiously with their children's governess, a very plain woman everyone recognized as the old man's mistress. It was a situation that continued to astonish Elizabeth and her aunt, although it seemed unremarkable to the French. And apparently to Madame Brillon as well, who appeared to be entirely unconcerned.

Chartres, Rochefoucauld, and Condorcet clustered by the open terrace door, and Elizabeth strained to hear their animated discussion of a daring raid on England's shores that had become a sensation in Paris a few days earlier. Commanding a sloop of war, an American captain named John Paul Jones had captured a British sloop of war, *Drake,* and several smaller prizes the previous month, along with 200 men and the family silver plate of a British lord.

Lucien ushered her and Cécile to a divan, while Madame Helvétius sprawled across a chaise longue in an ungainly manner, displaying more of her underclothing than one could think proper. Madame Brillon and Rose Bertin, the stout, coarse-featured owner of Paris's most fashionable dress shop, Le Grand Mogul, who dressed the queen, settled in chairs along with several others, the women's voluminous petticoats billowing around them.

All through dinner Elizabeth tried hard not to stare at the courtiers, but found the temptation hard to resist. Most of them, both men and women, wore the heavy court *maquillage,* their faces whitened with a thick cream called *blanc,* on which thin blue lines were drawn to simulate veins. A large circle of brilliant rouge was painted on each cheek and more dabbed on the lips to form a cupid's bow. Their eyes were lined with kohl, the women's eyebrows either plucked into a half-moon shape and darkened with paint or enhanced with delicate strips of mouse fur.

Added to their fantastically ornate, jewel-bedecked dress and elaborate coiffures called poufs that were embellished with fanciful objects, the effect reminded her curiously of her first encounter with the Shawnee. She had thought their adornments bizarre and fearsome, but now found herself admiring their art a great deal more than the courtiers' artifice.

"But you know a good hairdresser has many means of adding the fashionable height," Bertin observed in a commanding voice. Her towering pouf, bedecked with tiny replicas of French and American warships engaged in battle with British ones, tipped at an alarming angle as she eyed Elizabeth critically.

Elizabeth gave Cécile a mischievous smile. "Ah, but madame la marquise made an experiment on me by having her *friseur* add many pads and tow and even a wire form to build up my hair. And then her maid covered my face with blanc and rouge as is required at court. When I looked in the mirror, I was astonished!"

When the delighted laughter subsided, Madame Helvétius marveled, "Yet none of it you wear today! You've come in your natural state!"

"Well, you see . . . I was unable to recognize myself. And if I couldn't recognize myself, how would any of you?"

Another gust of mirth rippled through the company. Stretching his arm casually across the divan's back behind her, Lucien said, "Your natural self is entirely sufficient, *ma chère.* Such beauty needs no enhancement."

Again she felt the color climb to her cheeks, but his look and tone were so earnest and unaffected that she couldn't help smiling up at him. He returned it with a fervent look that deepened her blush.

"I must say that I find our American friends' republican simplicity tremendously appealing," chirped Madame Brillon. "*La mode Américaine* has swept all of France since the arrival of our dear Sieur Frankleen. He admitted to me that his face has become as familiar in our country as that of the man in the moon."

As the titters subsided, Madame Helvétius looked Elizabeth up and down. "I confess can't see the appeal of such a plain style. Why a lovely young woman would prefer to dress like a little nun instead of displaying her charms for admiration escapes me."

Elizabeth felt as though her eyebrows were in danger of flying off her forehead. She considered her gown to be even more daring than those she'd worn while charming intelligence from British officers. But considering the décolletage of the women surrounding her, she was clearly a novice at seduction.

Looking down at her neckline in alarm, she said faintly, "But . . . this is more than I usually allow to show."

"How charming! How innocent!" rhapsodized Madame Brillon.

Cécile, who also was garbed modestly compared to the rest of the company, gave Elizabeth an approving look. "Here in France we've lived so long with artifice that 'displaying our charms', as you say, has become stale," she said firmly to Madame Helvétius. "The fresh, natural fashion of our American friends is what's needed to enliven our society."

"I couldn't agree more!" Madame Brillon trilled. "Many women I know are abandoning the pouf and going so far as to wear fur *chapeaux* like that of our *très sage* Sieur Frankleen. I confess I recently acquired one myself! Even her majesty is giving in to the style despite her former resistance. It's so much more comfortable, and, well, natural!"

"Speaking of the queen, she's recently stopped powdering her hair and hardly puts on rouge anymore—if you can imagine!" sputtered middle-aged la marquise de Masillon. "Why, she's almost entirely abandoned court dress in favor of *la polonaise,* which has now become acceptable even at the less formal court balls."

Elizabeth winced. Standing before her mirror a few hours earlier, she had thought the fashionable *polonaise* she was wearing exceptionally fine. A particularly fetching shade of aqua, it was beautifully fitted, the bodice sewn to an over-petticoat drawn up by tapes into elegant swags in the back, while the front remained open to reveal the ruffled white gauze under-petticoat.

Cécile's gown was equally frilled, and they exchanged amused, and rueful, smiles as the woman continued with a loud harrumph, "Such fashions are not only scandalous, but also totally impossible for us older women—which perhaps is the point since the queen seems to have no regard for age and experience. I needn't tell you that the arbiters of what is *de rigueur* and *the marchands de mode* are in an uproar. And where's it all to end? How can anyone know your rank and quality if you dress like a peasant girl? It's the paint for our faces and our panniers, stays, and silk *robes à la française* that distinguish us from the rabble."

"Not all *marchands* are against the new style," Bertin huffed. "After all, one must change with the times. I, for one, find it good for business, which is good for France."

"As to fashion, I'll wear whatever I want," Madame Helvétius interrupted with a sniff. "I'll not be a slave to the *marchands* nor to public opinion."

No one could possibly imagine that you would, Elizabeth thought, biting her lip. She met Lucien's laughing gaze, grateful that the safer topic of fashion held sway rather than the more personal questions she continually had to fend off with his and Cécile's deft aid.

"I've observed that the ladies of your fair country have incomparable complexions and a natural beauty that's unsurpassed," Liancourt observed nodding to Elizabeth before turning his gaze to the others. "The paints you employ to enhance your charms, *chère mesdames,* cannot compare to the natural blush of such a fine creature as this. *Certainement* they do your health no good, laced as they are with lead. How many of your sex have died as a result?"

"Blanc made with bismuth or vinegar and rouge lacking mercury are freely available," Cecile pointed out. "I use them myself."

As the ladies in their circle variously pouted, laughed, or scoffed, Chartres and his companions came over to rejoin them.

"I've never seen you at court barefaced," Chartres remarked, smirking as he nudged Lucien.

Lucien looked up and grinned. "If our dear queen sees fit to change the fashion, Philippe, I won't protest."

Chartres snickered. "Our dear queen indeed."

Elizabeth caught the look that darted between the two men. It was charged with malice, and although quickly erased from both countenances, brought back to her mind comments she had overheard about the Orleans family and their enmity to their cousin-king and his queen.

When Lucien had introduced her to Chartres, an imperious-looking man with undistinguished features, the duc had been all charm and attentiveness. Too much so, in fact. By all accounts he professed the high ideals of a moral and democratic government she held dear. But his effusive manner and reputation as a womanizer who had begotten several illegitimate children put her off and caused her to question Lucien's relationship with him.

"All this talk of fashion, *mesdames!*" Condorcet cried, a faint flush tingeing the arresting pallor of his face. "For mankind to progress, it is philosophy that must rule. As long as vanity holds such prominence, our society will never rise to its height."

"Vanity!" cried Rose Bertin. "*La mode* is our whole world!"

"And that, madame, is the trouble. Our society needs fewer *marchands de mode* and more philosophs, men such as Dr. Franklin."

"Now there's a man who's a friend of all humankind," Rochefoucauld put in. "All of France is in love with him."

"And the ladies in particular, who make free to kiss him and sit on his lap," Lucien observed dryly with a meaningful look at Madame Brillon.

She laughed merrily. "I consider him my very own *cher* Papa!"

Condorcet pulled a chair close to the divan and sat down, his bulging forehead and the unnatural paleness of his complexion giving strange force to his piercing gaze. "I assume you've met Franklin, Mademoiselle Howard," he said in a low, breathless voice. "An amazing man with an understanding of science and government second to none. We've had the most enlightening discussions. I'm persuaded he'll raise our civilization to a golden age!"

"I'm afraid I haven't had the honor. I have, however, seen his likeness everywhere I've gone on every conceivable object."

She joined in her audience's mirth. She knew that the famous doctor was close friends with Madame Helvétius as well as with Madame Brillon and regularly dined with them, had even invited the latter to become his mistress—an offer tactfully declined. She had attended both ladies' salons with some trepidation and was secretly relieved that he had not appeared.

Chartres frowned. "But you've met Monsieur Adams?"

"Unfortunately no," Elizabeth said with regret. *Not that he would know, at least,* she thought guiltily.

At that moment a cock wandered through the open terrace doors and stopped on the threshold, his brilliantly colored feathers flaming in the dappled May sunshine that slanted inside. After looking about he crowed harshly and deposited a slimy offering on the rug already soiled by their hostesses' other pets.

One of the courtiers advanced and stamped his foot at the fowl, driving it back outside with a great flapping of wings and outraged cackling. Madame Helvétius protested volubly. In high dudgeon she gathered up her barking lapdog and with the hem of her petticoat dabbed away the small puddle it had left on the floor, while a young housemaid hurried to scrape up the cock's mess.

Elizabeth was both repelled and amused. She joined in the others' hearty laughter, but her relief at the distraction was short lived. Chartres resumed their conversation, undeterred by the interruption.

"I met your fiancé, General Carleton, some years ago and was much impressed with him even then."

"All of France has heard of his exploits, mademoiselle," Madame Helvé-tius crowed, "how he boldly plucked you out of the very heart of the British stronghold at New York, thus covering himself with even more glory than he has on the battlefield!"

Beside her Lucien stiffened, his face hardening. Elizabeth tried to find the words to deny that Carleton was any longer her fiancé, but they choked in her throat.

"How exceedingly romantic!" exclaimed Madame Brillon, dramati-cally clasping her hands to her bosom.

Hardly able to breathe, Elizabeth stammered, "But it—no, he . . . " It was impossible for her to continue, and Cécile reached for her hand and squeezed it.

"By all accounts his fleet of privateers is wreaking havoc on the British at sea as well," Chartres drawled.

With an elaborate wave of her hand, Madame Helvétius again inter-rupted loudly. "One would expect nothing less, Philippe! He's half French, you know. His mother was a Bettár."

As Elizabeth glanced at Lucien she saw a look of cold rage cross his features. But it was quickly extinguished, and before she could speak, Chartres fixed her in a languid look that caused her heart to race.

"I meant to question you when we left the table, but you were dis-tracted with all that silly talk of fashion. It's unbelievable to me that the British would have such a beautiful and accomplished lady as yourself arrested and confined in such outrageous circumstances simply because of your relationship with General Carleton."

"They intended to use her to force Jonathan's surrender," Cécile inter-vened stiffly. "Clearly they misjudged him."

The duke appeared unconvinced. "One can't help wondering if there might have been more to it," he returned with smooth carelessness. "We've all heard of female spies, and it seems to me that a lovely one would be the most effective of all."

Elizabeth slanted an alarmed glance at Lucien. Had he confided her clandestine role to Chartres? To others?

He met her gaze directly, however, and gave his head a barely perceptible shake before turning a cool gaze on his friend. "*Sans doute,* a trollop would be quite effective in picking the pockets of the British, Philippe. But surely you don't mean to imply that Mademoiselle Howard belongs in that category."

Disapproving murmurs rose from the others. His face reddening, Chartres spread his hands in denial.

"Bah! You mistake me, my friend. Of course not." He swept Elizabeth an elaborate bow. "I assure you, I'd never think such a thing of a lady of your obvious delicacy and grace. I was merely speaking theoretically. Please forgive me if I've offended you in any way."

"No offense taken, seigneur." Still breathless, she forced a smile and inclined her head, not quite sure that his apology was entirely sincere.

Anxious to leave, Elizabeth followed Cécile and Madame Brillon, who had gone outside to the waiting coaches ahead of her while Lucien lingered to speak with Chartres. As she neared the dining room doorway, she heard the languid voice of one of the courtiers from inside.

"How I'd love to pluck the flowers in that garden," he drawled.

As she hesitated, not wanting the room's occupants to see her pass, a woman answered, her voice laden with boredom. "She certainly looks ripe for the plucking."

"She'd make a most delectable bouquet."

"Remember, she's taken," cautioned another woman, younger judging by her voice.

"Bah! And what does that signify? He's not here. The rumor is he's made himself one of the American savages."

Elizabeth's mouth fell open. *They're talking about Jonathan—and me!*

"You mean he prefers their barbaric pleasures to hers?"

Barbaric pleasures? Elizabeth thought, instantly furious.

From the moment of her arrival in the country, she had been impressed by the exquisite manners of the French. Everyone seemed so genuinely polite and eager to please, toward Americans most of all. But with Chartres's remarks added to these, it occurred to her that such courtesy might cloak darker motives.

How are the Indians' customs any worse than your own court rituals with your fantastic paint, absurd poufs, and outlandish dress? she fumed. *And instead of scalping your victims with knives, you do so with your tongues!*

"I can just imagine the assignations they've enjoyed."

Laughter followed the first woman's suggestive comment. Elizabeth seethed as she continued, "I remember him well from his visits with Caledonne in my younger days. He was the handsomest and most virile of youths, endowed with every wicked masculine charm. I suffered an excess of heat from our first meeting. Several years ago on his way to America from England he stopped to visit the Martieu-Broussards, and I employed all my wiles in the effort to breach his defenses."

"And your wiles, *ma chère,* are considerable," the man purred.

Elizabeth heard a sigh. "Alas, as all those years ago he was more than willing to tease but quite impervious to seduction."

"Perhaps you aren't to his taste," the man returned archly. "Or perhaps he prefers men."

With supreme effort, Elizabeth mastered the impulse to stalk into the room and slap all three of them.

Hearing footfalls, she turned to see Lucien striding through the salon doorway. He came to her side. Stomach knotted but chin uptilted, she took his arm and allowed him to lead her, with deliberate slowness, past the doorway in full sight of the gossipers.

Chapter Fourteen

THE THREE OF THEM had no sooner walked into the château's *salle* than Caledonne's coach rolled into the courtyard. He, Tess, Madame Verignay, and the two girls—by now dubbed *les petits mademoiselles* since they were constantly together—were in high good humor from their outing in the Bois de Boulogne. With a pang of pleasure Elizabeth noted that Caledonne's attentions were evoking a new sweetness and contentment in her aunt.

Eugène had not yet returned from Versailles, and after the girls went upstairs with their governess, she followed the others out onto the terrace. They found seats where the late afternoon sun still warmed the stones. Caledonne opened a letter that had arrived while he was gone, scanned it, then directed a pleased glance at Elizabeth and Tess.

"Several days ago I sent a message to your commissioners proposing a meeting. Monsieur Adams writes that he and Dr. Franklin will be delighted to receive us Tuesday morning if that's convenient." With a wry smile he added, "It's not certain that Lee will attend. From what Adams has told me, he and Franklin are continually at each other's throats. Which doesn't surprise me, considering that Lee's thoroughly made himself persona non grata with everyone in the government who's had to deal with him."

"Whether he attends or not, we're honored that Adams and Franklin, at least, are willing to make time for us in their busy schedules," Tess responded cheerfully.

Elizabeth stomach clenched. "But why should they wish to meet with the two of us? We're of no consequence as far as the commission is concerned."

Tess regarded her with surprise. "They're our fellow countrymen. They're just down the road, and back at home Adams is practically a neighbor of ours."

"But we've never met. At least . . . not officially."

Tess smirked, while the others gave Elizabeth questioning looks.

"Unofficially, then," Lucien teased. "Do tell. We won't give you a minute's peace until you spill all the details."

Giggling in spite of herself, she described how she had met John and Samuel Adams and John Hancock at Philadelphia's State House when she petitioned Congress's Marine Committee for letters of marque authorizing Carleton's privateers to attack British ships.

Engulfed in laughter, Caledonne managed to gasp, "In disguise as one of my agents, a man named Tesseré? Ah, how I wish I could have witnessed this scene!" He gave her a wicked grin. "I'm sure you were brilliant, *ma petit.*"

She conceded a mischievous smile. "I rather think I was, if I do say so myself. But then, Jonathan outfitted me so beautifully that no one questioned my nationality—or masculinity. Of course, the credentials you provided were impressive, to say the least."

Caledonne's mouth quirked. "Strangely I don't recall signing any such papers."

"Jonathan thought you wouldn't mind if he signed for you."

Everyone joined in delighted chuckles.

"Then, *sans doute,* all was in perfect order." Sobering, Caledonne wiped the tears from his eyes and cleared his throat. "Adams is most eager to learn about Jonathan's attack on New York Harbor. He particularly wishes to hear about the the exact situation of the Americans held prisoner by the British as he's quite involved in efforts to gain their release."

Elizabeth felt suddenly and unaccountably overwhelmed. "I hope . . . he won't draw any connection between me and . . . and Tesseré."

Lucien pulled a chair next to Elizabeth's and possessed himself of her hand. "Would it be such a bad thing if he did?"

"I don't want anyone here to know of my . . . my involvements—" Abruptly she broke off, avoiding the others' concerned gazes.

She heard Tess sigh. "The ghosts of that wretched prison ship still haunt her. When we were confined to our cabin during our voyage, she was often overcome by panic, especially at night. Marie, Jemma, and I had much to do to calm her."

Elizabeth looked up to see that Caledonne had stilled and was watching her intently. After a moment he asked quietly, "Beth, why did you not confide in me?"

"She refused to let us tell Dr. Lemaire, much less you," Tess explained. "She became distraught when we even brought up the subject."

"You've been too kind already, Uncle Alexandre," Elizabeth broke in anxiously. "Your duties and concerns with the fleet occupied so much of your time, and I didn't want to add more troubles. I should be stronger—" Head bowed, she felt Lucien's arm go around her shoulders, while the others murmured reassurances.

Caledonne rose and came to stoop before her. Taking her free hand, he said, "Never think that, *ma chère*. You see my shoulders? They're strong enough to bear your troubles as well as mine."

Unable to speak, she clutched his hand and gave him a shaky smile.

"I wasn't wrong, then, when I felt that something was distressing you," Lucien said, frowning. "But every time I tried to draw you out, I could feel you pull back from me. I hesitated to press you, fearing it would only cause you more pain. Now I wish I had."

She gave him a grateful look. "But you did help a great deal. You seemed to know just how to distract me from . . . from this darkness."

"I enjoyed our talks, too, very much. I'm glad I was able to help if only a little." Hesitating, he added, "You're truly a heroine. You know that, don't you?"

"But I'm not!" She pulled her hands free, tears of shame stinging her eyes as the words tumbled out. "I'm nothing less than I am a heroine. I'm weak and cowardly and—"

"How can you believe that?" he protested. "Elizabeth, you're very brave. How many women—or men—have risked for their country what you have? You may not think it, but you are a hero!"

As the others echoed his words, Elizabeth looked from one face to another, their faith in her distressing her even more. "Those who fight for our country's freedom or suffer in shameful conditions because they refuse to change their allegiance are the true heroes. I was held for hardly more than three weeks, while they endure inconceivable abuse daily, sometimes for years, and die without hope." She stopped, then covered her face with her hands. "Why was I rescued when even their names and graves are lost?"

Tess came to sit at her side and put her arms around her.

"How do you think I felt when Frédéric died?" Caledonne asked softly.

Bending her head, Elizabeth whispered, "Responsible."

He nodded. "He always wanted to follow in my footsteps, and I encouraged him to do so even though the dangers worried Luciana. I oversaw his training. I urged him to continue when he struggled. And when I learned he'd been killed in battle, I accused myself for his death and for the grief of my wife and children.

"It took years before I could recognize that he'd wanted a career in the navy for himself. He loved the sea, loved sailing, hoped someday to be the captain of his own ship. I did nothing more than to help him accomplish what he was made for. His death was an accident of war, one of many. None of us, you see, is exempt from loss and sorrow."

Looking up, she caught the penetrating glance that Lucien turned on his father. His expression softened, and for a fleeting moment she thought he was about to speak. But then he averted his gaze.

She turned back to Caledonne. In his focus on her, he had missed the brief change in his son, so quickly lost.

"Clinton and Howe are responsible for the suffering of those held aboard their prison ships," he said firmly. "You're not to blame that you were rescued—indeed you're the reason so many were saved! Would Jonathan have risked taking on the British Navy in its own lair if you hadn't been held captive there? God used both of you to accomplish his own inscrutable designs."

She swallowed with an effort, nodded, tears blurring her eyes. For the first time she could believe it, and gratitude washed over her. It felt as though a heavy burden had been lifted from her shoulders and she could finally breathe again.

Seeing it, he smiled. "God isn't finished with you yet, *ma chère*. Trust him, follow his guidance, and he'll give you the deepest desires of your heart."

Chapter Fifteen

H IS EXPRESSION GUARDED, White Eagle studied the statuesque woman who walked with him along the bank of the churning Mad River.

Dubbed by the British The Grenadier, she matched her brother Cornstalk's height, standing near a hand's breadth taller than White Eagle so that he had to look up to meet her equally frank gaze. Indeed, if the legendary Amazons did exist, he thought, she was certainly one of them.

Her name in the Shawnee tongue was Nonhelema. In English: Not a Man.

Indeed she was not.

Time's passing had only lightly marked her renowned beauty. Her long, flowing hair had gone white. That and the fine lines at the corners of her eyes and across her brow alone testified to the sixty years since her birth. Her vigor appeared undiminished from when he had briefly met her at Black Hawk's death rites two winters earlier, where she had accompanied Cornstalk, now dead himself at the hands of white men.

In his grief White Eagle had taken little note of her then. He'd had no opportunity to speak with her, nor any desire in the shattering of his adoptive father's death, followed by the wrenching council that had driven him to war with the Whites. But both before and since he had heard much of this female sachem of the Shawnee, daughter of the great Maquachake sachem Paxinosa.

In her youth she had fought as a warrior, her well-formed body naked and painted black like the men's. Yet later, like her mother before her, she had been baptized by the Moravian missionary David Zeisberger, a mark of her true faith since the Moravians refused to baptize anyone whose life did not reflect firm allegiance to Christ. She had taken the name Catherine then, and had become a peace chief among the women. Her influence had also swayed Cornstalk to seek peace with the Long Knives after the debacle of Lord Dunmore's War four winters ago.

It was now early May, *Hotehimini kiishthwa,* the Strawberry Moon, with the Corn Planting Ceremony and Bread Dance just past. White Eagle had spent much of *Shkipiye kwiitha,* the Sap Moon, with the men in the hunting camps to supply the clan with much-needed game. Afterward, during *Pooshkwiitha,* the Half Moon, he had traveled throughout the region with the captains of his warriors to counsel with the clan and division sachems of the surrounding towns. He had presented his case with careful deliberation, seeking to build alliances ahead of the nation's great council—a quest that had largely proven as unfruitful as he had feared though for the most part he had been received with the courtesy and respect his reputation as a warrior commanded.

He and his party had returned early that afternoon to find Nonhelema and her adopted middle-aged white daughter just preparing to leave. She had immediately requested this private meeting, and he had accompanied her out of the town to pace along the riverbank, with Little Running Heron shadowing him at a short distance as was his wont.

Bitterness tingeing his voice, White Eagle finally said, "I am grieved at the murder of my brother and yours. His death is a great wound to our people. The Long Knife sachems protest that they abhor this crime, but that no one will testify against his murderers and they can do nothing to punish them."

"Is not everything in the hand of the Great Father?" she returned.

Although her voice remained steady, he read deep sorrow in her gaze. And resignation tempered with determination.

"You still stay at Fort Randolph?"

She nodded. "Captain Arbuckle and many of his men were as grieved as I at the deaths of my brother and nephew and those with them, so I stayed. I serve as interpreter for the new commander, Captain McKee, now."

As though the subject pained her too greatly, she turned abruptly away. They came to a halt in the cool shade beneath the overhanging branches of the towering sycamores just above the ford. Here the stream's turbulent course flowed across shallows embedded with smooth, flat stones before again boiling up in white spray over the large rocks below.

She studied him silently before saying, "Grey Cloud told us that our Father Washington sent you as his emissary."

At the hoofbeats of approaching riders, he directed an assessing look toward the town's steep height. Another small party of warriors rode up the bluff's slope to the gates—Lenape, by their appearance. The ranks of his warriors continued to swell as the weather warmed. Those who had wintered in towns to the east had already all gathered, bringing more men with them, and to his gratification, a small but significant number of those he had counseled with during his visits to the region's towns were filtering in as well.

He returned his attention to Nonhelema, who had followed his glance to the newly arrived riders and was watching them thoughtfully. "I agreed to do it only because I know the British will not win this war. If we make ourselves the Long Knives' enemy, when they prevail they'll sweep us away as well. But I fear they'll do so in any case."

A frown creased her brow. "I hear our people's talk on every hand. Whatever their views on this matter of our alliances, they hold you in high respect, my brother. They take pride in your victories, even against the British."

White Eagle gave a short laugh. "That may be so, but although they listen to me with courtesy, they do not heed my counsel."

He leaned back against a sycamore's broad trunk and stared across the river to the west. All around them gently rolling meadowland bordered by trees and studded with wildflowers undulated gradually upward from the secluded river valley, finally stretching into the distance in rising folds cloaked with the forest's deep, impenetrable green.

Towns belonging to the Miami, Lenape, and Mingo spread throughout the region. Dunquat's Wyandot town was close at hand to the north, and a short ride to the west lay Blue Jacket's Town. Not far south were Maquachake Town, Piqua Town, Black Snake's Kispokotha Town, and Black Fish's Chillicothe on the *Cakimiyamithiipi,* the Little Miami River, little over a day's ride away.

The hills surrounded them like a rampart against the outlying world, offering an illusion of isolation. Of safety. But it *was* an illusion.

Her quiet voice broke into his thoughts. "You know that Dunquat plans to attack Fort Randolph and that many of our people's warriors have joined him?"

He gritted his teeth at the memory of his meetings in the surrounding towns during the previous weeks. "I've argued against it with all our sachems, but they say they cannot stop the young men. The truth is that they don't wish to intervene because many of them also intend to fight with Dunquat." He glanced at her. "Will you warn McKee?"

She nodded. "We're on our way back." After a brief hesitation, she added, "I went down to Chillicothe to see my brothers Nimwha and Silverheels. The rest of our headmen don't welcome me, but Nimwha warned that the decision is already made to ally with the British. They'll stop their ears against the arguments of any who oppose it. You'll gain nothing if you go."

"This doesn't surprise me. Nevertheless, our Father Washington sent me to present his message and gifts to our nation, and I must do it whatever the result."

"The man Boone is there, and no matter what Black Fish promised him, he plans to attack Boonesborough this summer. My brother refuses to warn Boone, and he'd not let me. Will you do it?"

"If Nimwha will not, neither will I," he answered sharply. "If the settlers continue to ignore our warnings and trespass on our hunting grounds, they must suffer the consequences."

"We gave up those lands after Pontiac's War," she reminded him.

"They're no less our lands."

She looked away, then after a moment returned a penetrating gaze to him. "You persuaded your clan to ally with the Long Knives, but when our nation's sachems choose the British, what will you do then? What will your clan do?"

"If we're to live in peace, we must either join your division and the others who live under White Eyes' protection in hope that the Long Knives honor their treaties with us or seek refuge with the Spanish beyond the Great River among the Thawekila division."

She shook her head slowly. "My brother, you speak peace, but you fight. Does your heart not thirst for revenge? When your father, Black Hawk, was murdered by white men, you agreed with my brother and counseled our people against this course, but you followed it nonetheless. In my life I've seen that vengeance has less to do with justice than with the darkness in one's own soul. I saw in a vision many winters ago that war will never settle the conflict between our people and the Whites. What does it lead to but more violence—and thus more vengeance?"

"I seek not vengeance, but justice!" White Eagle returned. "I took up the tomahawk against the *shemanese* even as Cornstalk did before in order to stop them from killing our people and robbing us of our lands. How could I stand back and do nothing? I'll not watch our people go to their destruction when I know how the white men fight and how to oppose them most effectively."

She remained silent for a long moment, finally conceded, "By making yourself one of the Long Knives' great warriors, you will gain much influence in their councils."

He dismissed her words with a frustrated gesture. "In the end it will not matter. They also stop their ears. We are too few to hold them back for long even had we all the weapons they possess. But to fight on the side of the British is sure destruction for all the native peoples, and I do not know what other course to follow."

"You and I have been called to this course, and we must follow even if in the end our people turn us away." She gave him a keen look. "We must see this matter as the Great Father sees it, for we are not of this world but of his. For this time, you are our people's best hope for peace. Never doubt this, and never forget it."

"I'll not forget," he said, his voice hard. "But doubt is another matter."

He turned away, and his gaze fell on the distant figures of women and maidens hoeing weeds in the fields partially visible between the bluff and the stream's sweeping southwest curve. Nearer at hand two maidens approached along the riverbank with several small boys and girls trailing after in a dancing cluster, all laughing and calling out to him and Nonhelema. The oldest, the animated, bright-eyed maiden named Nettle Flower, carried a squirming, yipping bundle of honey-brown fur.

She ran forward and reached them first, with Walk on Water's daughter, Rebekah, at her heels. In moments the little ones pressed around them, smiling faces upturned. Squatting, he teased the children to giggles, while Nonhelema bent to catch a tiny girl up in her arms.

As he rose, Nettle Flower held out the puppy to him. "My dog weaned her pups, and I give this one to you, my brother. He is the largest and healthiest of the litter, and both his mother and father are brave hunters. I've not named him so that you can do it."

He took the pup from her and cuddled him against his chest, laughing as the small animal gave a sharp yip, then licked his hand and eagerly wriggled upward to lick his face. "I thank you for this gift, little sister."

He held him up to look him over approvingly, then gave him back to her. "He is yet too small to go with me when I return to our Father Washington. Will you care for him until I return in the winter?"

Accepting the pup back, she agreed eagerly, but then with a pout demanded, "Why must you leave us again? I wish you would stay!"

He sobered, pretending not to see the coy look she cast him. "Indeed I'm eager for the day when I never need leave our clan again. But while this war lasts, I must fight on behalf of our nation."

Rebekah pressed forward, "My father told me you asked him to stay and lead our fellowship in your absence, but I wish I could go with you!"

White Eagle returned her smile but shook his head, ignoring the jealous look Nettle Flower turned on her. "Only the wives and children of our clan's warriors go with us. But we'll return by the new year if all goes well."

Nonhelema set down the little girl she held, her movements communicating a subtle dismissal that the two maidens reluctantly acknowledged. They respectfully bade her farewell, and with sidelong smiles at White Eagle, led the little ones off toward the river bottoms. When they had gone, Nonhelema studied him for some moments.

"There's another war in your heart, my brother."

Her piercing gaze evoked the image of Elizabeth, more vivid than it had been for some weeks. Each day he determinedly focused all his attention on immediate concerns, doing all he could to bury the thought of her. He tried to do so now, but she read the change in his face.

"I heard that you love a white woman who was taken as sister by Golden Elk's wife," she said slowly. "You've not married her nor brought her back with you."

Hesitantly, unwillingly, he explained that both the clan's council and Washington had forbidden them to marry for the time. And that, at any rate, as a result of her ordeal aboard a British prison ship she had been too ill to travel so far or ever live among their people again.

"So you've left her."

He focused his gaze across the river. When he remained silent, she sighed and murmured as though to herself, "It is this love I've longed for all my life."

After a moment she said, "Why do you not then take a wife from among our people? I see the way the young women look at you. They make no secret that they desire such a man as you to give them strong sons and daughters."

"I've resolved to do so," he returned gruffly, thinking of Falling Leaf and her children.

While hunting he had come to the painful decision to take her as his wife when he returned to the clan in the winter. He had spoken of it to no one and would not until her year of mourning was over.

She watched him shrewdly. "Have you? I think your heart yet holds the white woman."

"That door is closed to me. The two of us have no choice but to walk forward. For now I'm called to war."

"I can see you long for children, nevertheless, and they'd comfort you for the losses you've suffered. Does not the Great Father call us to be fruitful? War is no impediment. I've made children in war or peace by my husbands, by some who were not, and also by adopting Fawney as my daughter. In these I find joy. They'll carry my life when I'm gone." She stopped and looked him up and down with a meaningful smile, eyebrows raised. "But if I were younger and could still bear . . . "

He faced her, hands on hips, deliberately returning her suggestive gaze with one equally bold. She had indeed borne children to several men, he knew, both Shawnee and White, before marrying her current husband, the Shawnee sachem Moluntha. An Indian agent from Congress named Richard Butler had been among them, with whom she had acquired large herds of cattle. Before him, however, she'd had a liaison with Alexander McKee, another agent whose many ties to the Shawnee—and to the British—held a powerful influence among the tribe.

It was she who broke off their gaze. Turning from him with a regretful expression, she beckoned him to accompany her back to the town and led the way without speaking, her stride long and graceful.

When they stepped inside the gates, she turned abruptly and took hold of his arm. "If you must go to Chillicothe, my brother, be very careful. Do not trust the sachems of our people. Nimwha also warned me that Black Fish and his allies mean to hand you over to the British."

He stiffened. "Surely Black Snake would never allow this."

"I don't know about him or Blue Jacket, but Black Hoof agrees to it. He and Black Fish hold you as their enemy, and they'll do you great harm if you fall into their hands."

He held his silence for some moments, finally said in a hard voice, "I've no choice but to meet with them."

"Then I pray the Great Father's protection over you, my brother. And I tell you clearly, go softly but take all your warriors with you arrayed for war."

"Enough, Blue Sky—"

She rounded on Golden Elk, eyes narrowed and fists on hips. "Healer Woman is my sister, and White Eagle belongs to her! I'm sick of watching Sour Plum try to ensnare him into taking Nettle Flower to wife. And she's not the only one who—"

"It is a matter for him to decide, not you," Golden Elk pointed out gently, slanting an apologetic look at Nettle Flower, who stood beside her mother, both clearly outraged.

Sour Plum grabbed her daughter by the arm. "We do nothing wrong! Did not White Eagle himself make it clear that he'll never marry Healer Woman? A great warrior such as he needs a wife to bear him many children. Who better than Nettle Flower?" she declared proudly, indicating her daughter's curvaceous form and comely appearance.

Both women turned up their chins and swung on their heels. Glancing back, Nettle Flower said smugly, "White Eagle shows me every sign of favor. I'll not turn him away if he chooses me as his wife tonight when we dance." With a triumphant smile she flounced off with her mother.

Blue Sky's mouth fell open, and she stared indignantly after their retreating backs. "You see, my husband? The young women shower him with so much attention that he begins to give in to them!"

Golden Elk rolled his eyes. "He's kind to all the women. And men. And children and elders. He makes no distinction between one and another that I can see."

She regarded him suspiciously. "You're a man. What do you understand about these matters?"

With a broad grin he took her by the shoulders and pulled her to him. "Perhaps I should show you."

Blushing, she nestled against him and let out a sigh. "I'm sorry I spoke so harshly to them, but should I not be worried for my sister? Even Red Crow's widow, Falling Leaf, turns her eyes on him now."

"And should he not take her and her children under his protection, as is expected?"

She looked up to meet his gaze with an anxious one. "Has he stopped loving my sister? Will he indeed choose a wife at the dance tonight?"

"I do not believe it."

He gently turned her toward their cabin. And found White Eagle standing several feet away.

He met Golden Elk's gaze with an unreadable one. "Our sister Nonhelema has gone. Grey Cloud and Loud Thunder wait for us in the *msikah-miqui* with Red Fox and Spotted Pony. An urgent matter has arisen that we must consider."

Heat rose to Golden Elk's face, and he hastily released Blue Sky. "I come at once."

White Eagle began to swing away, then stopped as though in afterthought and glanced back, looking from Golden Elk to Blue Sky. "I do not dance tonight," he said in an even voice, "if this is a matter that concerns you." Turning abruptly, he stalked off.

Chapter Sixteen

IT WAS LATE MORNING on Saturday, May 9, when Caledonne's coach climbed the steep road leading to a height above Passy not far from the one Château Broussard occupied. Bypassing a line of carriages waiting for entrance to the Hôtel de Valentinois, it came to a halt in the crowded courtyard of the château's twin pavilions.

The lavish, turreted buildings nestled amid an encircling terrace bordered by lush gardens in the full bloom of a glorious spring. Elizabeth, Tess, and Caledonne were admitted without delay into the spacious *salle,* where a crush of women and children, both noble and bourgeois, milled among academics, philosophes, and government officials. All had come to meet with the renowned American doctor, Caledonne told them as he shepherded them through the crowd to the major domo.

The man welcomed them with a deep bow and ushered them with dispatch into the apartment where Benjamin Franklin and John Adams lived and worked as guests of its wealthy owner. A contractor for the French government and former slave trader, Jacques Donatien Le Ray, le Comte de Chaumont, was deeply involved in the once covert and now open supply of war materiel to the United States.

Elizabeth took in her surroundings with heightened interest and not a little trepidation as they entered the salon of the elaborately appointed apartment. All around them the detritus of politics, invention, and science littered the corners, the fireplace mantel, every bookshelf, and most of the chairs and tables—except for one of the latter occupied by a chess set displaying a game in progress.

Elizabeth recognized Franklin instantly from his portraits. He sprawled at leisure on a chaise longue across the room, dressed in a rumpled, plain brown suit, the balding pate above his high, square forehead fringed with thinning shoulder-length grey hair. His head rested against the chaise's back and his eyes were closed, his round, wire-framed spectacles sitting on the end of his nose and his hands were clasped across his portly middle. She exchanged an amused glance with Tess as a soft snore emanated from his partially open mouth.

His back to them, John Adams perched on the edge of his chair at a small desk by a window, perusing a document and scribbling notes. Unlike at their previous meeting in Philadelphia, he was clad in the latest French mode, though quite modest compared to Caledonne's exquisitely embroidered blue velvet suit and hers and Tess's fashionable gowns.

The sound of the door's quiet opening brought him around. He jumped to his feet and came forward as the major domo announced them, then silently withdrew.

After they exchanged courtesies, Adams exclaimed, "I was delighted to learn that you were here and that you'd agreed to meet with us! I can't tell you how good it is to visit with fellow countrymen—or women—so far from home. I confess, though I've been in France for barely a month, I already miss my dear wife and our quiet, plain life at home immensely.

"Do you know that no news has arrived here from Congress for months?" he demanded, hardly pausing to take a breath. "Dr. Franklin tells me it can take half a year to receive an answer to a single letter, even though an express can reach any capital on this continent in ten to fifteen days, with a response returning in the same amount of time. The delay places us at a complete disadvantage when it comes to negotiations."

Somewhat taken aback at his volubility, Elizabeth searched Adams' face, to her relief finding no shadow of recognition in the penetrating blue eyes that met hers from beneath arched brows. Forty-two-years old, the newest American commissioner stood a couple of inches taller than she, of average height for a man. In the absence of a wig, his high forehead and receding light brown hair emphasized the roundness of his clean-shaven face, punctuated by a nose so sharply pointed it reminded her of a bird's beak.

"I was told you landed in Bordeaux, as did I. What do you think of the country so far? And Paris? I'm sure you must be familiar with the city by now."

"Indeed we are," Tess returned with a smile. "Boston, New York, and Philadelphia appear as rustic hamlets compared to Paris and Bordeaux." As the others chuckled, she smiled up at Caledonne. "And I need say nothing of French fashion, culture, and society."

"Bah! We've had centuries to establish ourselves, while you Americans are yet an infant as a nation," he responded, giving her a fond look.

"Infants we may be," Elizabeth said, turning to Adams, "but we must resolve to cling wholeheartedly to our cherished republican virtues if we're not to be seduced into abandoning them."

"You hit too close to the mark," Adams conceded with a short laugh. "I've been thinking the same thing ever since my arrival. Reality has swept away all my preconceptions."

Ushering them to seats, he indicated his clothing with a sweep of his hand. "You see me garbed in French style, though nothing to what I was required to wear yesterday when Vergennes presented me to the king at his *grand lever,* along with Lee and Dr. Franklin. I even had to wear wig and sword!"

With a smile, Caledonne asked, "And what did you think of our young king?"

"He appears to have a robust constitution, and there's goodness and innocence in his face," Adams returned thoughtfully. "I'd guess him to be a kindhearted man."

"I'm surprised you think so since you Americans have thrown off your own sovereign."

Adams settled onto a chair next to Caledonne. "If we had a king as forward thinking as Louis the Sixteenth appears to be, we might not have been inclined to do so." After a moment he sighed. "I find very much about this country immensely appealing, I confess. I love the way you French approach life. Were it possible to make us humans happy by the things that please the eye, the ear, the taste, or any other sense, passion, or fancy, then this country is indeed the region for it. But I'm enough of an old republican to value the Roman concept of simplicity and honor. I believe as they did that decadence inevitably follows luxury."

"I'm also a student of the Roman classics, Monsieur Adams, and unfortunately you make an observation I can't dispute. Our society has sunk into corruption, and I've only to look about me to fear that we French are destined to reap the consequences of not only our blindness, but also our indifference to it."

By now their conversation had roused Franklin, who slowly sat up, swung his legs around to place his feet on the floor, then pushed his portly figure erect. After pulling onto his head the bearskin hat Elizabeth had noted on numerous likenesses of him, he came ponderously to join them. They rose to return his bow with their own courtesies.

Slightly shorter than Caledonne, the seventy-one-year-old inventor, scientist, and diplomat stood a shade under six feet. Elizabeth noted that, although his hazel eyes peered from beneath drooping lids, they appeared to digest everything around him at a glance. It was also immediately apparent by the compliments he paid to her and Tess that he was a master of what on the surface seemed to be guileless flattery. He quickly had them both blushing, beguiled by his easy charm despite themselves.

"We apologize profusely for disturbing your nap, Dr. Franklin," Caledonne said with a smile when they resumed their seats.

Adams snorted. "My esteemed colleague rose little more than an hour ago—early for him—while I've been up since five."

"I'll have you know I didn't get to bed until well after midnight," Franklin grumbled. Depositing the papers piled on a nearby chair onto the floor, he sat down.

"What kept you out this time? Chess? Checquers? Or another *tête-à-tête* with one of your numerous lady friends?" Adams enquired mildly, his mouth quirking with amusement.

Franklin pursed his lips. "As I keep reminding you, my dear Adams, diplomacy is a seduction of sorts."

"And I'm sure I needn't remind you that 'early to bed, early to rise . . .' "

"Certainly not, considering that I'm the one who wrote it," Franklin returned with pleasant equanimity. "Although I can't say I'm wealthy, I do believe I have some claim on being healthy and wise."

Elizabeth detected genuine affection and liking in the two men's banter. But there was also a degree of exasperation on Adams' part that made it difficult for her to maintain a straight face.

Franklin rang for the major domo, who quickly appeared and was sent to bring wine. "We've been given freedom of our host's vast wine cellar so we might as well take advantage of it," he told them expansively as the man reappeared and unobtrusively supplied each of them with full goblets before again withdrawing. Franklin went on to explain that Chaumont also provided them servants and meals and had his staff care for his coach and pair, while his wife managed Franklin's dinner parties.

"We are indeed fortunate in our situation," Adams conceded, "though it worries me continually that the piper will eventually have to be paid. But I'm very happy that my son, John Quincy, who accompanied me here, could be enrolled in an excellent boarding school close by, where Dr. Franklin's grandson also attends."

After they exchanged a few more pleasantries, Caledonne enquired whether Lee would join them.

Adams consulted his pocket watch. "He planned to, but he rarely arrives before eleven even though he's only ten minutes away at Chaillot. I assume he'll be here shortly."

Just then a grave-faced man with a long nose, whom Elizabeth judged to be in his mid thirties, entered the salon from an inner room. Franklin beckoned him to join them and introduced Dr. Edward Bancroft, a Massachusetts-born physician and chemist he had met in England. Among Bancroft's many accomplishments, Franklin told them, was that of writer, inventor, and fellow member of the British Royal Society.

"As soon as I was appointed to the commission I recruited him to serve as our secretary. He speaks French like a native, and he's made himself indispensable to our business here." As the younger man took a seat at his side. Franklin patted him affectionately on the shoulder. "We couldn't get along without him."

"I'm the one who benefits from our association, sir," Bancroft protested with easy affability.

Elizabeth noted that Adams regarded the man through narrowed eyes, lips pressed into a thin line. That he clearly did not share Franklin's affection for Bancroft aroused her curiosity, but Adams turned to her, leaving her no time to puzzle over the matter.

"I'm sure you know that the news of General Carleton's attack on New York Harbor to rescue you caused quite a sensation here in France as well as in our own country." When she nodded reluctantly, he continued, "In fact, added to our victory at Saratoga—in which I understand he was also involved—the damage he inflicted on the British fleet was a deciding factor in persuading the king to finalize the alliance with our country. Because of my work in Congress, I'm greatly concerned for our prisoners of war, and though I'm making every effort to gain their release, I've made little headway. It would be quite helpful to know the realities of their situation, and Caledonne assured me that you're willing to share your personal experience with us."

It was the moment Elizabeth had dreaded. A wave of panic threatened to undo her, but with everyone looking at her expectantly, she took a breath, staring down at her hands clenched in her lap. Voice faltering, she described the horrors of her imprisonment: the stench and filth; the putrid, insufficient rations and water; the lack of sanitation, medical care, clothing, blankets, and fire for cooking or warmth in the coldest weather; and the daily toll of the dead.

When she finished she saw that Tess's mouth was pressed in a tight line; that Caledonne regarded her with a face hard as marble; that Adams and Franklin stared at her, livid; while Bancroft frowned, gaze averted. Raising her goblet with a shaking hand, she emptied it and set it down.

"Many would be allowed to enter the British service if they but renounced our cause," she managed to say. "But they refuse. And suffer."

Adams cleared his throat. "Miss Howard . . . I can't express my feelings at learning that our enemies sink so low as to subject even a woman to such abuse. Your fortitude in service of our country is admirable in the extreme. Thank God General Carleton was able to rescue you and the men held with you!"

"Dieu Merci, en effet," Caledonne murmured. Thank God indeed.

Bancroft turned a penetrating gaze on her. "It remains a puzzle to me, Miss Howard, why the British had you arrested. It seems rather heavy handed for no more than a rumored association with General Carleton . . . unless you'd also been involved with our cause on a higher level."

Elizabeth's mouth went dry and her mind blank. To her relief, Tess quickly intervened.

"I must heartily disagree, doctor. The British consider General Carleton the worst of traitors. While serving as aide-de-camp to General Gage in Boston, he delivered the most sensitive military intelligence to the Sons of Liberty, escaped from arrest and hanging, and joined General Washington's staff. He fought against them in a number of critical battles, Saratoga among them as Mister Adams pointed out. That's to say nothing of the damage his privateers are inflicting on Britain's ships. Wouldn't you agree that holding the woman he loves hostage in the worst conditions would be the surest way to force him to surrender?"

Bancroft stiffly inclined his head as the others murmured their agreement. "Most eloquently put, madam. Thank you for the clarification." He rose, and looking from Tess to Elizabeth, suggested smoothly, "It's an extraordinarily fine day. Perhaps you'd like to walk out in the gardens."

Adams sprang to his feet. "Excellent suggestion! I much prefer the outdoors to sitting inside all day, which I've been forced to do too much since coming here."

They all got up, Franklin uttering a low groan as he levered to his feet. Bancroft ushered them through double, glass-paned doors onto a small terrace from which a graveled path wound among a profusion of vegetation. For some minutes they wandered along *allées* lined with graceful linden trees and interspersed with fragrant lilacs and other flowers. Franklin genially pointed out different species of plants and described in detail the plumbing that supplied the fountains.

At length they paused at on overlook that presented a magnificent view of the Seine's serene blue ribbon far below and the misty towers and spires of Paris a mile away. Leaning back against the wall, Adams turned to Caledonne.

"You know, of course, that our Congress's Marine Committee provided the letters of marque for General Carleton's privateers. I don't mind telling you I was doubtful when your man Tesseré approached me . . . "

Glancing uncertainly at Elizabeth, he let the words trail off. She pretended not to hear, focusing her attention on the view, and after a brief hesitation he gave his head a slight shake, his expression clearing.

"Thankfully he was most convincing. I hope you'll convey our appreciation for the good turn he did us."

Caledonne bent in a half bow. "I'll be sure to do so. I've always thought highly of Tesseré's abilities. It's most gratifying to have them affirmed."

He allowed his gaze to rest on Elizabeth only long enough for her to see the laughter dancing in his eyes. Biting her lip, she turned quickly away.

They resumed their leisurely walk. When they returned to the terrace outside the commissioners' apartment, Bancroft ushered them back inside.

"I wonder that, although our alliance with France has been in effect for three months now and England has declared war on your country, she's yet to attack your navy," he said to Caledonne.

"It is, *certainement,* the calm before the storm," Caledonne replied, giving him a level look.

"Well, they've certainly laid about our privateers," Franklin broke in. "From the accounts I've heard, General Carleton has until now enjoyed singular success because your fleet, my dear sir, is protecting his ships. We'd appreciate your intervention with your government to give the same protection to our other privateers and to our navy, as a matter of fact. We're losing badly needed ships, men, and materiel, and I needn't point out that much of it is supplied by France."

To this Caledonne replied indifferently, "I'm not the one to make these decisions, Dr. Franklin. I'm afraid you must take up the matter with Vergennes."

"I've already done so on multiple occasions, but he's been less than forthcoming."

Adams frowned. "We've had some reports lately indicating that General Carleton's privateers have become the target of Admiral Howe's particular vengeance and that the number of his merchantmen as well as his privateers is undergoing a rather dreadful reduction."

Elizabeth managed to suppress a gasp though her hand flew to her bosom. She searched Caledonne's face.

Beside her, Tess murmured in distress, "You've said nothing of this, Alexandre."

"The matter's well in hand, *ma chère.* I didn't want to distress you unnecessarily," he responded in a low tone. Transferring a grim glance to Elizabeth, he added, "We'll speak of it later."

He had stopped beside Franklin's paper-strewn desk, now casually picked up a document. "My dear doctor, have I not advised you countless times to secure your correspondence from eyes that should not see it?" he chided as he replaced the papers on the desk, laying them upside down.

Franklin waved his warning away, his expression reflecting mild annoyance. "And I've told you before that it's impossible to discover everyone who pretends friendship in order to spy on us—"

"On that point I have to disagree."

Ignoring Caledonne's interruption, Franklin continued, "—and as a consequence I make it my invariable policy to be concerned in no affairs that might cause me to blush if made public and to do nothing but what anyone is welcome to see. For example, my *valet de place* is most likely a spy—as you doubtless know—but I like him, and so I wouldn't discharge him even were I certain of it."

Caledonne allowed a faint smile. "Although that may be a reasonable policy in your provincial politics, surely you recognize how disastrous it can be in time of war."

"You need to heed his warnings, my friend, and not leave your papers lying about," Dr. Bancroft broke in. "You're far too casual about security."

"I can't agree more," Adams interjected, though the look he turned on Bancroft indicated to Elizabeth that he both disliked and distrusted the man. "If you ask me, we're most certainly living in a houseful of spies."

Franklin waved his hand dismissively. "No doubt you're right, but, you see, I have my own sources of intelligence to counter theirs."

"I doubt they're a match for Eden's operation," Caledonne returned, referring to William Eden, the head of Britain's Secret Intelligence Service. "Would you not agree, Dr. Bancroft?"

There was something in the gaze Caledonne fixed on the doctor that set Elizabeth on guard.

Bancroft readily agreed. If he sensed any undercurrent in Caledonne's challenge, he gave no evidence of it.

Before anyone could make a rejoinder, the door to the apartment swung open and a tall, erect man with a prominent nose strode inside, clutching a packet of papers.

"How condescending of you to join us before—" Franklin consulted his pocket watch "—noon, Mister Lee."

Arthur Lee flushed and his high forehead furrowed, making his long, thin face appear even more morose. "I arrived half an hour ago and found no one here," he answered querulously.

A Virginian, he had been a doctor before turning to the law, Elizabeth knew, had then become an accomplished writer in support of the American cause and a diplomat, first to England and now to France. That he was distrusted and disliked by the government's officials did not make him an asset to negotiations.

"The weather's so pleasant we decided to take a turn through the gardens," Adams said hastily. "I should have left a note for you to join us."

Lee brusquely dismissed his apology and the requisite courtesies and introductions. Unfolding the papers he held, he turned to Caledonne and gave him a perfunctory bow.

"While we were speaking, an express arrived from Vergennes with this letter from London—from Lord North himself—directed to your government, our commission, and specifically to your immediate attention, Admiral. It's dated May 5, four days ago."

He turned a gaze on Elizabeth that caused her heart to lurch. "The prime minister claims that you, Miss Howard, were arrested and imprisoned for your treasonous activities as the rebel spy, courier, and smuggler commonly known as Oriole, and as an agent for General Washington."

Unable to speak, she became aware that both Adams and Franklin regard-ed her openmouthed. "Oriole—a woman!" Adams exclaimed. "No wonder you operated so successfully for so long—" He broke off abruptly.

Franklin came to capture her hand and kiss it. "My dear, it's a high honor to meet the famed Oriole at last," he said, beaming as he straightened. "Who would have imagined our infamous spy would turn out to be a woman of such beauty and grace?"

Before she could protest, Adams said, "I keep thinking we've met before. Obviously you're exceptionally skilled in disguising yourself as a man, and it occurs to me to wonder whether . . . you might have been Monsieur Tesseré."

She could only stare at him in stunned dismay. When Tess began to intervene, Adams cut her off.

"But you were!" he crowed, clapping his hands together. "Astounding disguise! I never suspected for a moment. We're greatly in your debt, Miss Howard. You've done our cause a tremendous service."

Lee cleared his throat loudly. "To the point, Lord North says that it was to rescue you that General Jonathan Carleton breached New York Harbor and inflicted damage to several British ships of the line—"

"Inflicted damage!" Tess exclaimed. "He *sank* four of them!"

Lee glanced assessingly at her, then back at Elizabeth. "It's known to Lord North—thus to the king—that you're now in Paris under the protection of le comte de Caledonne and le marquis de Martieu-Broussard. He demands that the French government hand you over to the British Ministry on the instant. Should that be denied, he offers a reward of £500 sterling to anyone who delivers you up to any British official."

Elizabeth's mouth fell open. It was an astronomical sum.

Her legs had lost the ability to hold her up. There was a roaring in her ears, and she felt as though her head was wrapped in a thick layer of wool.

As from a great distance she heard Caledonne say sharply, "Vergennes will suppress this—"

"It's too late," Lee cut him off. "It's already been made public in London. And in Paris by Eden's secret agents. It'll be common knowledge within hours—if it isn't already."

As Tess guided Elizabeth to a seat, Lee continued grimly, "That's not all. Lord North also issued a new reward for General Carleton's capture: £1,000, with an additional £300 if General Charles Andrews is also brought in."

Stunned, Elizabeth looked up by instinct to Tess, read the horrified dismay in her eyes. Feeling sick, she transferred her gaze to Caledonne, who bent protectively over them. At sight of his ashen face the bottom dropped out of her stomach.

It was Bancroft, hovering off to one side, who captured her attention then. There was a cold calculation in his steady gaze that sent a chill through her.

Chapter Seventeen

THREE SLEEPS AFTER Nonhelema's visit, her warning still rang in White Eagle's ears as the detachment emerged from behind the imposing *msikahmiqui* to intercept his path. He drew hard on the reins, bringing his stallion to an abrupt halt. On either hand Grey Cloud and the clan women's peace sachem, Blue Crane, did the same. Trailing behind, Stowe, Golden Elk, Red Fox, and Little Running Heron urged their mounts forward to flank them.

The soldiers carried bayoneted muskets. Tomahawks and knives hung from their belts, and rawhide cartridge pouches and blanket rolls were strapped across their shoulders. Their sleeved waistcoats and breeches of worn, faded blue wool; cloth leggings; knit caps; and moccasins identified them as *Canadien* militia.

A lean, swarthy man with black hair and several days' growth of beard who appeared to be the company's commander swaggered forward, a triumphant smile spreading across his weathered face. Sweeping a mocking bow, he purred in French, "Ah, if it is not the infamous White Eagle I've been expecting. Or should I address you as Major General Jonathan Carleton, commander of Carleton's Rangers—and of the recent privateer attack on New York Harbor?"

Malevolence glittered in his dark eyes as he dismissed the question with a careless wave of his hand. "Captain Antoine Dagneaux de Quindre at your service, *mon Général.* I assure you that Gov'nor Hamilton will be quite pleased to entertain you at his headquarters. He's waited for this honor for a very long time though I doubt your anticipation of the meeting has been quite as acute."

The day was pleasant and warm, with a light breeze, the sun not quite at its zenith. White Eagle's gaze flickered briefly over de Quindre before settling on the Shawnee headmen gathered outside the enormous council house. It stretched the full length of the new town of Chillicothe, recently moved there from the Scioto. Less than two day's ride south of Grey Cloud's Town, Black Fish's home and the capital of the Chillicothe sept as well as of the Shawnee nation topped a long, low hill that dominated newly planted cornfields on the southeastern bank of the *Cakimiyamithiipi,* the Little Miami River.

The Chillicothe war chief, middle-aged but still wiry and lean, stood at the forefront of the tribal leaders, both male and female. At his side was the Maquachake war chief, Black Hoof, a small man a few years older than White Eagle who was renowned for both his ferocity in battle and his eloquence as an orator. At the far edge of the crowd he caught a glimpse of Raging Bear and his warriors. They watched the unfolding scene with unreadable expressions, making no move to draw closer.

Tightening his grip on the reins, he returned his attention to the council house doorway, through which Nimwha now emerged. His younger brother, Silverheels, stepped out behind him but kept to the background. Both were as tall and imposing in appearance as Cornstalk and Nonhelema, and they met White Eagle's challenging gaze with veiled ones. Nimwha, however, deliberately inclined his head.

His suspicions had been correct, he concluded. The Shawnee's principal sachem had intentionally told his sister of the trap, knowing she would warn him.

He had taken her advice to heart. Everyone in his party was fully armed, and he carried his feathered war spear in his hand.

He directed a questioning glance at Black Snake and the Piqua war chief, Blue Jacket, who sat their horses amid their own retinues to one side of his small party. They had met up a short distance outside the town and entered together, the last to arrive for the meeting of the council on the morrow. He was reassured to see that the two men appeared taken aback, their expressions conveying that they had known nothing of the detachment's presence in the town.

It came as no surprise to him, however. His scouts had brought the news to their camp the previous night, and it required a stern effort to contain the outrage that roiled through him.

Keeping his expression impassive and his voice steady, he jerked his head in the direction of the officer and said, "What does this mean, my brothers?"

Black Fish and Black Hoof refused to meet his gaze, instead darting glances at Blue Crane, who faced them with a narrow-eyed scowl. With satisfaction he noted that they appeared less confident than when he and his companions had first ridden into the town, festively painted and garbed in their finest ceremonial regalia as were those already gathered there—and to all appearances unaware of the trap that awaited them.

Black Fish shrugged, his expression sullen. "These men arrived yesterday. We knew nothing of their coming."

"We heard you returned from treating with Governor Hamilton at Detroit some sleeps ago," Red Fox returned evenly. "How is it that you did not know he was sending soldiers after you?"

Black Fish pursed his lips. "Our Father Hamilton does not tell us everything he means to do."

White Eagle forced himself to choke back a sarcastic retort. "Then send them away," he countered as calmly as though he discussed the weather. "You know that I bring our Father Washington's message to our nation, and these men have no place at our council fire."

Before either Black Fish or Black Hoof could respond, de Quindre cut in, "Not so quick, my friends. We've business here that holds precedence. I've orders to take General Carleton into custody and deliver him to the gov'nor at Detroit. According to our agreement," he added with emphasis, fixing Black Fish and Black Hoof in a pointed look. This time he spoke fluently in the Shawnee tongue so everyone could understand.

The mood on both sides changed in a breath. Black Fish and Black Hoof retreated a step as de Quindre moved forward. He reached for the bridle of White Eagle's stallion, who snorted and jerked his head up, half rearing, ears flattened and eyes rolling. At the same instant Blue Crane drew her horse back, while the rest of his companions spurred their mounts forward between him and the officer, forcing him to stumble awkwardly out of the way to keep from being trampled.

He rounded on Black Snake. "Did you also agree to this, my brother? Will the Kispokotha betray me as well?"

Black Snake leaped out of the saddle, glaring at Black Fish and Black Hoof as uneasy murmurs passed through the crowd. "White Eagle is Kispokotha. If you hand the war chief of Black Hawk's clan over to the British, then our division will turn their backs on you."

"To do such a thing is unjust and dishonorable," Blue Jacket agreed angrily, also dismounting.

With satisfaction White Eagle noted the narrowed eyes and nods of agreement from many of the sachems he had personally counseled with over the past weeks. Clearly he had been wise in making every effort to marshal support well ahead of the council.

Before he could speak, Golden Elk drew his horse around to face the tribe's leaders. "Would you begin a war within our nation that will ruin us?"

De Quindre gaze became calculating. "Ah, and then there's you, Gen'l Andrews. The gov'nor'll be pleased to see you as well, and my purse'll be considerably heavier for delivering two traitors 'stead o' one." Turning back to Black Fish, he added, "And your people will receive an even greater reward."

Murmurs of eager anticipation and angry opposition rippled through the crowd. One of the Chillicothe warriors posted at the town gates ran up, and at the same moment a low rumble of approaching hoofbeats caught everyone's attention.

"A large, heavily armed party of warriors approaches from the forest," he panted. "They drive two of our scouts before them."

The babble of voices rose in volume, and everyone swung anxiously to look in the direction he indicated. The rest of the guards scattered from their posts as the party cantered through the gate, two crestfallen Chillicothe scouts in the lead with Spotted Pony and the rest of White Eagle's warriors on their heels. In moments they flowed around White Eagle and his companions and drew to a halt.

He had brought with him all his warriors who had gathered at Grey Cloud's Town, and they outnumbered de Quindre's detachment, an apprehension that quickly dawned on the *Canadien*. A furious scowl creased his brow as he rounded on Black Fish and Black Hoof.

"You gave your word there'd be no trouble!"

Spotted Pony indicated the *Canadiens* with a jerk of his chin. "I see these men have come to disturb our council. We'll be glad to escort them out of our lands for you."

Heads bent together, Black Hoof and Black Fish conferred, their words unintelligible. But it was clear from their expressions that both had been taken unaware and were furious.

"If you harbor this criminal, then you're no friend to England! Will you forfeit the reward your people will receive for this Long Knife and break your alliance with the British for a man who is not of your people? Look at him!" de Quindre sneered. "His skin's as white as mine."

Heat darkened Grey Cloud's face. "White Eagle is the son of Black Hawk, and Golden Elk is my son, a great warrior of the Kispokotha and the father of my grandson! Dare any man dispute that they belong to our nation?"

"Indeed it is so! Did not my brother Pathfinder's spirit rise as he died and enter me?" White Eagle cried out fiercely. Touching the three white feathers secured in his hair, he continued in a steely voice, "Moneto gave me this *opawaka* as a sign of his favor. Both Golden Elk and I have made ourselves odious to all the Whites in our nation's defense—both Long Knife and British. Neither of us has any other people."

"By our ancient traditions, those adopted into our nation are fully equal to those born among us," Red Fox reminded them. "Would you now cast this custom aside?"

De Quindre cut him off with a contemptuous snort. "Then why does the Long Knife Washington hold them so close to his bosom?"

Golden Elk leaned toward him from his saddle, eyes narrowed. "We win battles for him."

De Quindre turned to the others. "*Oui,* they fight for your enemies—for Cornstalk's murderers!"

Spotted Pony brandished his rifle above his head. "Have the British not also broken every one of their treaties with us? Have they not killed many of our people? We are fools if we trust them!"

Angry shouts of agreement and opposition drowned him out, along with the heated replies of White Eagle's warriors.

De Quindre raised his voice to be heard over the tumult. "Your Father Hamilton is graciously willing to erase your brother Golden Elk from his memory!" he shouted, deliberately using Golden Elk's Shawnee name. "It's General Carleton he wants, and he'll pay the full ransom for him alone."

Livid, Golden Elk raised his fist. "Is it any less a betrayal, my brothers, to *graciously* allow me to live among you, but give White Eagle up?"

Black Snake stalked into the center, his face contorted with fury. "How can we do this thing? Our brother, Black Hawk's son, has won many victories for our people and stands at Washington's right hand as our mouth to the Long Knives!"

Raging Bear roughly shoved through the crowd to the forefront. "Do you not see that the reward the British offer for this man is enough to feed and clothe all our people for many winters to come? We gain nothing by protecting him!"

Nimwha fixed him in a cold gaze. "Black Snake is right. Are we then to sell our brother for money and our honor for his blood? If so, we make the name of our people worthless."

Sensing that the moment hung on a thread, White Eagle hastily dismounted, Little Running Heron sliding from his saddle at the same instant. He motioned to the rest of his party to do the same, then handed his spear to Golden Elk and advanced toward the tribal leaders, striking aside de Quindre's hand as the *Canadien* reached out to grab his arm. Clinging like a burr to his side, Little Running Heron roughly thrust the man out of the way, and the glint in his eye and knife in his hand warned him and his men to keep their distance. By now Black Snake's and Blue Jacket's retinues had dismounted as well and hurried forward to join the two war chiefs.

"Shall we indeed tear apart our nation?" White Eagle demanded, looking from one to the other. "We meet in council tomorrow. Let me speak our Father Washington's words, and then let the council decide our wisest course with calm deliberation."

His face darkening, Black Hoof raised one hand to quiet those who pressed in around them. When everyone stilled, he pointed to White Eagle's warriors and said mockingly, "You speak words of peace, but you bring a war party to the meeting of our council."

White Eagle swung around, searching for Blue Crane over the heads of those jostling around him. At his nod, she beckoned forward the clan matrons, until now unnoticed at the rear of White Eagle's warriors. As they pushed forward to surround her, all festively painted and wrapped in ceremonial robes, she fixed Black Fish and Black Hoof in a haughty stare.

"If our brother's intent was to make war on our nation, would he have brought us with him?"

An uncomfortable silence greeted her words. As though uncertain how to respond, Black Hoof and Black Fish exchanged brief glances. Each looked uneasily from de Quindre and his detachment to White Eagle and his warriors. Then to the women, who regarded them with narrowed eyes, raised chins, and arms crossed over their bosoms. The only voices that could be heard now came from the female sachems of the tribe, who voiced their agreement and called for the council to meet.

White Eagle carefully avoided Golden Elk's smug gaze, knowing that if he met it, he would not be able to contain his laughter. He had always admired and respected Blue Crane, and from that moment he loved her like his mother.

At length, as though recognizing his lack of further options, Black Fish conceded gruffly, "Our brother speaks with wisdom. We will hear our Father Washington's words about these matters tomorrow, and then carefully consider his counsel."

"Very well," De Quindre said coldly, his expression making it clear that he feared his hopes were about to go up in smoke. "Let this traitor speak the empty words of the Long Knives. Gov'nor Hamilton'll be quite interested to hear 'em when I escort the gen'l to Detroit for the just judgment he so richly deserves."

Nimwha shook his head, his gaze hard. "As our brother said, no white men, whether Long Knife or British, have a place at our nation's fire while we consider this matter. Go, then, and tell our Father Hamilton that after we hear Washington's words and White Eagle's counsel, we will send our decision to him. Tell him also that regardless of this matter we will never give our brother into his hand."

Chapter Eighteen

HEARING THE COACH return that afternoon, Elizabeth rushed from her private salon and down the stairs, Tess at her heels. They found Cécile already in the *salle,* and as the three men strode inside Lucien raised his hands to forestall the women's questions.

"There's no reason to be concerned. As we predicted, the king would never consider such demands."

"You're certain?" Tess demanded anxiously.

"We were given a private audience—with not only Vergennes, but also our naval minister, Sartine, present," Eugène replied. "We asked his majesty directly, and he made it clear he'll suffer no such interference on the part of a foreign power. Should anyone attempt to harm you, the consequences will be severe."

Impatiently Caledonne said, *"Mon Dieu,* even were our two countries not at war, to submit to such a demand would be a violation of our nation's sovereignty, to say nothing of our treaty with your government. It's laughable, and both George the Third and Lord North know it."

Eugène ushered them everyone into the salon. "It sends a message, however, especially backed up by the outrageous rewards they offer."

"Even I never expected this, and, believe me, there's little I don't anticipate," Caledonne growled. Capturing Tess's hand, he drew her down onto the divan beside him. "They mean not to pull their punches, as boxers say."

"They wouldn't in any event," Lucien scoffed, "but they're merely blowing hot air with this warrant. His majesty's quite sympathetic to your plight, Beth. He was delighted to hear of your daring and how you repeatedly tweaked the nose of the British lion in service to your country. He offered to provide any protection for you that we deem necessary, even to providing you an apartment at Versailles."

"What of your apartment, Alexandre?" Eugène asked.

"You rarely use it anymore, Papa," Cécile agreed. "Lucien's settled here since your return and is perfectly welcome to stay as long as he wishes."

Caledonne nodded. "*Certainement.* It's available to you and Thérèsa if you'd feel safer there."

Frowning, Lucien said, "Personally, I think we can keep Elizabeth just as safe here."

"I'd rather stay—as long as you'll let me, that is," Elizabeth said.

Cécile reached to clasp her hand reassuringly. "Then we won't give you up, *ma petit.* We'd much rather have you with us."

"I agree with Lucien," Caledonne said. "Most, if not all, the British agents in this country are known to us. We're well aware that ever since news of Saratoga reached Paris last December, increasing numbers have been quietly filtering into Paris hoping to discover what peace terms you Americans might consider."

"Full independence, nothing less!" Tess exclaimed.

Caledonne gave her an approving look before saying, "Sartine honed his skills in gathering intelligence as lieutenant general of the Paris police. He promised to make full use of his very considerable resources for your protection, Beth."

"There are many among our own nobles whose fortunes have sunk and who've relations with the British. Any of them might devise a plot to secure the reward, and themselves by fleeing to England—" Cécile stopped abruptly, then burst out. "We ought never to have allowed you to attend the salons or go into Paris—"

"How would it be better for Beth to be imprisoned here rather than in Boston and to never to experience all that France is?" Caledonne scoffed. "Our trip from Bordeaux could have been compromised or one of your servants might have dropped an unguarded word to the wrong person. No, we knew from the beginning that it was impossible to keep her location secret from the British for long."

Unable to sit still longer, Elizabeth sprang up and went to the open terrace doors, fighting to keep in check the fury that kept welling up. "The date on North's ultimatum was four days ago. How long will it take to reach Clinton? If Jonathan has no advance warning—"

Caledonne's mouth tightened. "An express is already on the way to Louis, but it'll be weeks before it can reach him out in Ohio Territory. It worries me that I've not heard from him since we left Boston."

"We haven't received any letters from Samuel and Anne yet either," Tess pointed out. "Who knows if ours have reached them? You heard what Adams said about how long it takes even for official mail to travel between our continents."

"But we've our own methods of transport—more reliable ones." He shook his head. "This silence is troubling."

"For Jonathan to act as Washington's emissary to the Shawnee puts him in the way of those who wish to ally with the British or have already done so. How better to eliminate him than by handing him over?" Elizabeth returned to her chair, her stomach churning. "And then there's Charles. What will become of Blue Sky and their little son if he's captured?"

"Surely the Shawnee would never betray either of them!"

Elizabeth turned to Tess in despair. "Can you believe that there wouldn't be at least one person who'd give up even his own brother for such a sum?"

❋ ❋ ❋

"THIS HAD TO HAVE been done with extraordinary secrecy or our agents at the British court would have alerted us before the warrant reached Vergennes."

It was Eugène who spoke in low tones. Elizabeth hastily withdrew her hand from the library door, which stood slightly ajar. By inclining her head cautiously forward, she could see him seated at ease in a chair, arms folded, while Caledonne paced back and forth, frowning, head lowered.

"*Sans doute,* the English know our agents as well as we do theirs."

"Not all of them, surely," Eugène protested. "Even Vergennes doesn't know how many men Sartine has embedded among George the Third's courtiers."

Caledonne made an impatient gesture. "Don't imagine that we know all of Eden's agents. We must keep our wits about us and assume nothing."

Elizabeth pushed the door farther open and stepped across the threshold. Caledonne looked around, a slow smile spreading over his face as he crossed the room to her.

"Come in, *ma chère.* Please join us."

Eugène pushed to his feet as she approached. "It's growing late. My dear wife will be impatient for my company by now, and I'm sure you've much to discuss. Please excuse me." Waving off their protestations, he withdrew.

She sank into the chair Caledonne guided her to. Blinking back angry tears she studied the shadowed library, its bookcases stretching to the ceiling filled with Eugène's extensive collection of books on every subject imaginable.

"What troubles you?"

She regarded Caledonne reproachfully. "Can you ask? To think that the king who was once my sovereign not only knows my name, but also desires my head is somewhat disquieting! I've some idea of . . . of what Anne Boleyn must have felt facing the Tower—and the block!"

"You knew what the consequences might be when you chose to become a spy."

"I suppose it never really sank in that I might actually be caught. Oh, the folly of youth!"

"And of old age. I'm well acquainted with both."

She regarded him with surprise. "I can't believe you've ever deceived yourself so."

"I've foibles like any other man."

"You don't consider Aunt Tess a foible, I hope."

The words were out before she could strangle them. She immediately clapped her hand over her mouth, her cheeks burning.

Far from taking offence, he chuckled as he sat in the chair beside her. "*Mais non!* Thérèsa is the best decision I've made since my dear Luciana." His gaze sharpened. "Don't tell her that, though. I don't want to scare her off."

"I put in a good word for you whenever opportunity arises," she allowed mischievously, "though it's hardly necessary. She's trying her best to fend you off, but there are signs it's a losing battle."

"I'm relieved to hear it. Now I've only to break down her last defenses." Smiling, he dismissed the subject with a wave of his hand. "But you've not come to discuss this."

"No, I—" She stopped, bit her lip, then cried, "You promised that I'd be safe here!"

"I'll keep you safe. However, *ma chère,* let me remind you that your actions until now have not been those of one whose concern is safety."

She stared down at her hands. "But . . . the thought that—" she took a shaky breath "—that I might be captured and returned to that dark place terrifies me."

"The bravest man in the world would be rightly frightened after suffering what you have. To have no fear when in danger is to be a fool. Believe me, I have my own scars and wrestle with my own demons, yet I've gone on. And so must you."

"But you're a—" She broke off abruptly.

"What? A man?" When she stiffened and raised her chin defiantly, he chuckled. "When the cause is great, courage must be all the greater, Beth. Courage compels us to stand fast in the face of our deepest fears. Ought not the injustice your countrymen suffer urge you even more strongly to work for their freedom? But to do it you must fix your eyes on the One who is greater than you and for whom nothing is impossible. Is he not the only one who can truly protect you, after all?"

His words cut deeply, but she could not dispute their truth. And to her surprise, her nerves steadied, determination unexpectedly energizing her.

He saw it and said approvingly, "There's the Beth I know."

Meeting his fierce gaze, she returned the firm pressure of his hand, then leaned to kiss his cheek. "Thank you, Uncle Alexandre. I don't know what role I can have now, but in whatever way the Lord calls me to be of service to my country, I'll trust in him to help me, come what may."

"You didn't need me to remind you of that. Your heart has always known it. And you'll find a new calling. Or rather, it will find you."

For a moment they regarded each other, smiling. At last she blurted out., "What are your responsibilities? Besides as an admiral in the Marine Royale."

To her surprise he answered frankly, "Naval intelligence."

"Officially. But not exclusively . . . naval," she hazarded.

He conceded a faint smile.

"I suspected as much, though I didn't think you'd be so forthcoming."

"Are we not both spies? A woman so young who endures the rigors of a British prison ship without giving up to her captors even a scrap of the intelligence they seek . . . " He spread his hands. "She knows how to keep her own counsel, I think."

She regarded him thoughtfully. "I keep wondering . . . what's Eugène's involvement in your . . . ah . . . involvements? And Lucien's, for that matter."

He made no response. Nor did he drop his steady gaze from hers.

"They *are* involved."

"Eugène has connections and influence that are very useful. And Lucien has his own skills."

"He told me something of Sartine's 'particular expertise'. And yours."

Caledonne's mouth twitched. "All military establishments have their sources of intelligence."

"In other words, all your captains are spies."

"Not formally. But it would be natural for them to keep their superiors abreast of developments at sea, would it not? Your naval captains do the same thing. The officers in your army, too, as you well know."

"*Oui.* But we have far fewer of them than you and the British. That puts my country at a distinct disadvantage."

"Not for long. Consider how effective you were as a spy."

"But no longer now that I've been exposed." Tipping her head, she narrowed her eyes. "Tell me, is anyone in this country what they appear on the surface?"

"We're all what we seem to be," he protested. "It's just that . . . there are depths."

"Speaking of depths, what about Dr. Bancroft?"

The question seemed to amuse him. "A spy will always know a spy."

He went on to explain that the previous year Arthur Lee had accused Bancroft of being a traitor, charges that were discounted because of the American commissioner's reputation for suspecting everyone of ill doings. And over the ensuing months Bancroft had forged a close relationship with the American naval captain John Paul Jones, who not only used him as an intermediary with Franklin in the effort to secure a ship, but also defended him vigorously against charges of spying. As there was nothing more than circumstantial evidence, the matter was dropped.

"I've repeatedly attempted to warn Franklin, but he refuses to believe ill of his friend, and I can't afford to make an enemy of the good doctor."

"Because you spy on him too?" she enquired sweetly. Suddenly trembling, she rose and moved away from him across the room. "If you suspected him of being a British spy, why did you deliberately place me in his way?"

She rounded on him, fighting to keep the rage out of her voice. "Was it to use me as bait in hopes of confirming your suspicions? In that case you succeeded. Franklin obviously knows that your fleet protects Jonathan's privateers, which means Bancroft does too. Doubtless he informed the British, with the result that Jonathan's losing ships, as Adams told us. And he certainly sent word of my whereabouts to Eden after you arranged our meeting."

Leaning back in his chair, he watched her with an unreadable expression, making no effort to interrupt her.

"Now I understand why Jonathan always seemed so guarded when you called on us last winter," she rushed on venomously, pacing the length of the room. "Did you use him like this too?"

To her surprise he immediately rose and came to capture her hands. "I'm sorry I've hurt you, *ma petit*," he said earnestly. "I assure you I didn't mean to. Have I lost your trust?"

She blinked back hot tears. "How could you treat me so?"

For a moment he said nothing, then gently asked, "Can you say you've never used others when necessary for the cause you serve?"

"I'd never—" Heat flooded into her face, and she dropped her gaze from his, conscience accusing her.

She winced to think how many people she had charmed for the purpose of uncovering intelligence. Even her own father! And before she had learned his true loyalties, Carleton, though his defenses had proven impenetrable.

He continued, "I am aware that Bancroft may indeed be the one who alerted Eden that we're protecting Jonathan's privateers, and we're keeping a close watch on him. But as to North's ultimatum, it would have required a considerably longer time for a measure of such gravity to be proposed to King George, considered by his ministers and approved, then signed and distributed. I proposed our meeting to Adams less than a week ago. It takes at best four days for an express to reach London from here and the same amount of time to return."

"But you didn't know about the warrant!"

"I was, however, certain that the British already knew where you were. And also that I have the power to protect you. I felt it important for you to meet your commissioners—or rather for them to meet you." He smiled down at her. "I don't blame you for feeling particularly vulnerable right now. None of us expected the British to go to such an extreme; however, we may be able to use it to our advantage if you'll continue to trust me."

She regarded him searchingly, shame staining her cheeks. She couldn't blame him for anything he'd done, for she had done no less.

"How could I not after how kind you've been? Please forgive me for my unwarranted suspicions. But if Bancroft isn't responsible for this, then who is?"

He released her and paced around the room, hands clasped behind his back, chin sunk on his chest. "Considering the amount of time needed to arrange it, I doubt the intelligence could have come from here."

Her stomach clenched. "Boston then? But who?"

"We took the utmost precautions to bring you away secretly and conceal your destination as long as possible."

She drew in a sharp breath. "Not someone in Aunt Tess's household surely?"

"Possible, though I doubt it. One of Jonathan's Marines might be the source, but that's also unlikely. I'll wager there's a mole in his import office. His manager's duties include more than just supervising the business. He's also one Louis' agents, responsible for passing along intelligence from there."

"And Louis works for you too," she guessed.

"On occasion."

"I suspect it's more than that. And wouldn't that be a conflict of interest?"

He turned to look at her, one eyebrow cocked. "I can't imagine why it would be."

Jonathan might feel otherwise, she thought, a shaft of pain piercing her at thought of him. But she held her tongue.

He waved the matter impatiently away. "As I said earlier, it troubles me that I've heard nothing from Louis since we left Boston. Of course, there are the vagaries of travel such a distance across the ocean, and especially now with Britain's warships patrolling the seas. But he's always sent his reports by more than one channel for that reason."

He shook his head. "No, I fear his network has been compromised from within. And since he's out in Ohio Territory, he may not yet know it."

Her mouth went dry as ashes. "Then Jonathan's in even greater danger than we thought. And Charles—and Louis as well."

He met her dismayed gaze, his mouth pressed in a hard line. "The agents I've sent out have to travel across an entire ocean now infested with a hostile navy, and then a wilderness where the British also operate. And until—or if—the three of them are found, they remain vulnerable to the schemes of the enemy."

Chapter Nineteen

T HE CANADIENS HAD NOT left quietly, but they had finally gone, forcibly escorted from the town and out of the vicinity by a substantial contingent of Black Snake's and White Eagle's Kispokotha warriors and warned not to return. Guards had been posted to ensure that they did not violate the admonition.

That evening at the banquet Black Snake drew White Eagle into a circle that included Black Hoof, Black Fish, Nimwha, Silverheels, and several other war chiefs and sachems. Seated between him and Blue Jacket, with Little Running Heron quietly taking his place at his back, White Eagle joined freely in sharing jokes and stories while they ate.

The betrayal burned in him like fire, but he set the matter aside, determined that no grudge would taint either his relations with the tribe's sachems nor the coming council. All men fail, he reminded himself resolutely, whether from human weakness or driven by evil intent. The Great Father alone never failed, and he required forgiveness from his followers.

By words and manner he endeavored to demonstrate that he held no ill will against anyone for the confrontation with de Quindre. And when the talk grew serious he made it clear that even though their opinions differed on important issues, he, as they, wished only to ensure the nation's security and welfare.

By degrees the tension between them eased, and others gathered to join their conversation. He was gratified that everyone listened to him thoughtfully and with respect. Indeed, he felt genuine liking on the part of a number with whom he had counseled during the past weeks even though the ones who disagreed with him on the matter of allying with the British did not hide it.

He found himself increasingly attracted to Blue Jacket. The Piqua war chief made an impressive figure in a scarlet, gold-laced frock coat with a multicolored sash tied at his waist and silver armlets on both arms; matching red leggings; and moccasins beaded and quilled in fine designs. Slightly shorter than White Eagle, he was equally muscular and finely proportioned, his large, piercing eyes; high forehead; aquiline nose; firm, generous mouth; and open countenance testifying to intelligence and decisiveness. White Eagle concluded that he would be a strong ally in forming alliances with the surrounding nations to oppose any further infringement of their territory by white settlers.

The one issue there seemed to be no way to overcome was Cornstalk's death. Word had filtered back from Virginia that the soldiers who had murdered him and his companions had been acquitted because no one would testify against them. As far as the tribe's headmen were concerned, this additional injustice deepened the offence past bearing.

No one brought up the planned attack on Fort Randolph, nor did he. But he could feel the anger simmering like live coals beneath the surface of their discussion.

AT NIGHTFALL THE PEOPLE gathered on the council house yard. As the first group strode into the circle to dance, Nimwha drew White Eagle aside.

"Perhaps it is better if you and your clan go back to Goshochking to live among those of us who have settled there under White Eyes' protection, my brother," he said. "The British offer a very high price for you. Although the agreement was made this day that we will not turn you over to them, the time may yet come when some change their minds and seek to do you harm. Then there will indeed be war among us."

Frowning, White Eagle stared into the shadows outside the fire's light. "I'll consider this and speak with Grey Cloud," he finally responded, clasping Nimwha's shoulder. "But I fear that White Eyes and his people are too vulnerable to attack if another provocation arises like the one that led to Cornstalk's murder."

"I fear the same thing, yet the division in our nation over the matter of our alliances concerns me even more. Would it not be better for you—for all of us—if you separated from the Long Knives and lived at peace among your clan?"

White Eagle's visage hardened. "I've committed to fight on the side of the Long Knives in this war. If I do not, I'll have no influence among them to speak on our people's behalf. And the truth is, my brother, that after my attack on the British at New York, they'll make it impossible for me to live in peace. I must either fight them or die."

Nimwha regarded him with sympathy, concern in his dark eyes. "What will become of our nation? Did not Jesus say that a house divided cannot stand?"

"It is so. We must seek wisdom and help from the Great Spirit if we are to preserve our people."

After Nimwha left him, White Eagle glanced around. As usual, Little Running Heron shadowed him, but Red Fox, Spotted Pony, and Golden Elk were nowhere to be seen. Nor were any of the warriors who had fought under his command from the beginning.

He had sensed a subtle excitement among the men that evening, but the rest of his party answered his questions with shrugs, barely suppressed grins, or the shake of their heads. Bemused, he went to take a seat near the fire next to Black Snake.

In the east the moon's glowing orb, just past the full, beamed from a cloudless sky, gilding in a pale patina the council house and yard, the surrounding palisade, and the tops of the darkly shadowed trees visible above it that ruffled in the cool wind. Chanting dancers moved with rhythmic steps in and out of the firelight to the seductive throb of drums and sibilant whisper of rattles, but sunk in concerns for the coming council meeting, he paid them scant attention.

The moon stood high in the sky, already on its decline, when his warriors suddenly emerged from the flickering shadows, wrenching him from his reverie. Arrayed in their most festive garb and painted in brilliant colors, they entered the circle's center on the heels of the departing dancers. As the drums' pulsing beat and the rattles' seethe resumed, they began to step gracefully in rhythm, forward and back, side to side, their silver brooches, earrings, and armlets glancing back the firelight.

Spotted Pony was the first to move to the dancers' forefront, chanting in a low voice that rose by degrees to a compelling cry as he recited White Eagle's great deeds in the war he led against the Whites to avenge Black Hawk's murder, while mimicking with his movements the frenzy of battle. His song ended, and he melted back among his companions.

While White Eagle watched, speechless, Red Fox took his brother's place. In powerful song and fierce movements he portrayed General Washington throwing the British out of the great harbor at Boston, the victorious battles of Trenton and Princeton, and the triumph at Saratoga. He recounted how White Eagle and his warriors stood at Washington's right hand to defeat the British, the scalps and loot they took, and how the Americans vanquished General Burgoyne's entire army, taking him and all his soldiers captive.

By the time he eased back into the line of warriors, the entire assembly was clustered closely around the fire, watching and listening as though spellbound. Only Raging Bear's faction kept their distance in the shadows of the cabins bordering the yard.

Golden Elk came forward now, emerging from the shadows to seamlessly take up dance and chant. In riveting detail he portrayed White Eagle's coup in breaching the British naval stronghold at New York to save Healer Woman, how he robbed General Clinton of all the prisoners aboard the prison ship where she was held, then sank several ships while fighting his way back to the open sea.

It was a gripping, mesmerizing performance that clearly left a deep impression on its audience. When the drums and rattles fell silent and his warriors left the circle with the fire falling to embers, the gathered crowd remained seated for some minutes, murmuring softly among themselves in the windswept darkness. Beyond words, White Eagle glanced toward where Raging Bear and his followers had been, saw that at some point they had silently withdrawn.

As though reluctant to leave, the assembly slowly rustled to their feet and began to disperse. The majority stopped to greet White Eagle with smiles and nods and clasp his hand as they filed past. Last came the nation's principal sachems and war chiefs, who also took his hand and nodded to him with respect, though he could tell that Black Fish and his adherents did so grudgingly. Several others, however, told him that they were eager to hear Washington's message and White Eagle's counsel on the morrow.

Gratitude filled him. And humility. He offered heartfelt thanks to each of his warriors, then the majority moved off exuberantly toward their camp in a grassy clearing to one side of the town's palisade, those assigned to stand guard heading to their posts in the surrounding forest.

At last only Red Fox, Golden Elk, Spotted Pony, and Little Running Heron remained with him on the council house yard, while the night deepened After laying more wood on the fire, they found seats on logs beside it, filled their pipes, and for some time smoked silently.

At length White Eagle laid aside his pipe and looked from one to the other. "I thank you, my brothers. You've encouraged my heart greatly for the council."

Before they could answer, a lean, stockily built white man about a head shorter than he eased out of the surrounding shadows into the firelight. He moved with the silent, lithe stride of a frontiersman, and White Eagle guessed him to be in his mid forties. His flaxen hair had been shaved to a scalp lock and adorned with feathers, and he wore a threadbare linen shirt over a breechcloth, leggings, and moccasins. Prominent cheekbones, a high brow, long nose, and pointed chin gave definition to a gaunt, narrow face striped with red and yellow paint.

White Eagle stiffened as the stranger squatted on the other side of the fire from him and his companions. Lighting his pipe with a coal from the fire, the man settled back to smoke. And to study him with bold curiosity.

He had noted the man at the edge of the crowd during the confrontation earlier that day, again at the banquet, and later at the dance, and had taken him to be the captive Daniel Boone. Accompanied by a fresh-faced white youth, he had kept to the edge of the crowd, appearing always to be on the alert, his keen blue eyes restlessly darting glances all around him.

When White Eagle's warriors had danced, he had noticed that the frontiersman watched and listened with intense concentration as though he strove to grasp the sense of the narrative. Now his gaze moved warily from him to each one of his companions in turn, finally back to him with an assessing look. Deliberately White Eagle returned his attention to the fire, while the wind's whisper, the creak of the trees' branches overhead, and the crackle of the fire filled the silence.

At length, speaking in a soft, melodious voice, the man said, "I be Daniel Boone—the one they call Sheltowee. I take it thou art White Eagle."

He gave Boone an indifferent glance and inclined his head.

"They say thou art a general under Washington. Yet the Shawnee claim thee as a great warrior among 'em."

"I am Shawnee."

Boone regarded him silently for a long moment before transferring his gaze to Golden Elk. "Thou also art a warrior and a general with the Continentals?"

"I am." Golden Elk allowed a faint smile.

Boone directed a sidelong glance at Red Fox and Spotted Pony, who regarded him with blank faces, before returning his attention to White Eagle and Golden Elk. "Black Fish captured me 'long with some o' my party and brought me here. He adopted me and the boy Ben Kelly into his family, even took us with him up to Detroit. Gov'nor Hamilton let the men taken with us go, but not us," he added, appearing somewhat crestfallen. After a moment he drew himself up and continued firmly, "We're Shawnee now, but I'm thinkin' that . . . since thy skin's white like mine, thou hast still some sympathy with thy white brethren."

White Eagle returned his gaze in stony silence for some moments before replying, "I've no sympathy with those who steal our lands and kill our people, whatever the color of their skin."

Boone shifted, frowning. "I was raised Quaker and am against killin', 'specially such as was done to Cornstalk and his men."

"I'll not help you escape if that's what you seek."

Smiling apologetically, Boone raised his hands in a peaceable gesture, palms outward. "That ain't what I mean—not a'tall. I find the Shawnee to be a good, admirable people, and I'm happy to stay amongst 'em."

"You have a wife and family among the Long Knives," Spotted Pony observed, giving him a level look.

"And you're an officer in the Long Knife army," Red Fox added.

Their fluency in English clearly made Boone uncomfortable. "All o' thee fight for 'em as well."

"For now," White Eagle said softly.

"And what does Washington think o' that?"

"We're useful to each other. But when this war's ended and the British are thrown out . . . " White Eagle shrugged. "We'll see what the Long Knives do then."

Boone slid his gaze to Golden Elk. "And thou?"

Golden Elk tipped his head toward White Eagle. "As he said."

Boone nodded thoughtfully. "Wal, thou hast a Shawnee wife and son, accordin' to Black Fish. Reckon that makes a difference." He considered both of them eyes narrowed. "As long as the British art thine enemies, don't make no difference to me. I ain't no friend o' theirs."

"Nor are you a friend of the Shawnee." White Eagle made no effort to conceal the hostility in his tone.

Boone concentrated on stirring the fire's embers with a stick. "Why dost thou fight fer the Continentals if thy people hate 'em?"

"Why did you seek us out?"

Boone cocked his head. "There's much talk about thee, and I jist wanted to make thy acquaintance."

"You trespass on our lands and bring others with you."

"Cantuckee is fertile, unsettled land," Boone responded gently. "Thy nation gave up rights to it after the war with Dunmore."

"Not all of us. You stole the hunting lands the Great Spirit gave to our nation. Remove from there and take your people with you, or all of you will suffer the consequences."

"I promised Black Fish I'd persuade my people to surrender to him in the spring." Defensiveness edged Boone's tone.

Golden Elk let out a snort. "You stay only to learn what Black Fish will do. Once you know it, you'll run to warn your people so they'll be prepared to fight when his warriors come against Boonesborough."

Boone's thin lips tightened. "He gave his word and I gave mine—"

"And we all know the value of the white man's word," White Eagle cut him off, his voice thick. "Heed my warning."

Chapter Twenty

WHITE EAGLE'S EYE caught movement overhead, and he looked up, hand raised to shade his eyes against the bright sunlight. High above, a great, pure white eagle took form as though emerging from the sky's clear azure. Wings outstretched, it circled gracefully on the windstream before melting into the sun's brilliant radiance and disappearing from his sight.

The slight breeze quickened at the same moment. Shifting from southwest to west, it cast up dust and rattled the trees, blowing strands of hair across his face and tugging at the eagle feathers secured in his headband. There was moisture on its breath. Hearing the low growl of thunder far off, he turned to look to the west, where a thin leading edge of dark clouds was steadily rising above the palisade wall.

Nonhelema's words came back to him then: *You and I have been called to this course, and where we are called, we must follow even if in the end our people turn us away. We must see this matter as the Great Father sees it, for we are not of this world but of his.*

He became aware that on either hand Red Fox, Golden Elk, and Spotted Pony regarded him questioningly. "Today will be a good day," he told them. "Come, let us seek the Great Spirit's will."

With a confidence he knew to not be his own, he stepped into the council house, his companions surrounding him like a bulwark. They took their places in the half circle of tribal headmen seated before the fire at the assembly's front. Little Running Heron crouched just inside the building's open door, and at White Eagle's orders several of his younger warriors loitered casually outside, where they could observe the meeting but were free to act on a moment's notice if necessary.

It was early afternoon, and everyone in the town packed the enormous *msikahmiqui* to its full length. For a long period the assembly smoked silently, while White Eagle pondered the message he would present. Outside gusts of wind buffeted the council house. Thunder rumbled close at hand now, and the darkness inside and out thickened, broken intermittently by slashes of lightning.

The first heavy drops of rain spattered across the roof, quickly gave way to a torrent. The warriors standing outside hurried in and closed the door, while some of the townspeople built up the fires along the council house's length to drive back the shadows.

At length Nimwha rose to ceremoniously greet White Eagle and call on him to speak. As he resumed his seat, White Eagle took his place behind the low table at the front, facing the gathered people, with Golden Elk at his side to hand him the strings and belts of wampum that accompanied each part of the message.

He spoke the same words of introduction he had at his clan's council fire, looking earnestly from one face to another and raising his voice so even those at the back of the council house could hear over the storm. He then took up Washington's letter and held it up for the assembly to see before reading it aloud word for word and presenting each belt of wampum in turn.

Complete silence reigned in the assembly while he read, keeping his gaze fixed on the page. He gave no outward evidence that he felt the subtle ripples of curiosity, suspicion, uncertainty, resentment, and outright anger that stirred the gathering. The message was no secret; he had already read it to the sachems with whom he had conferred over the previous weeks so that they could discuss it among their clans, and he knew each one's opinion.

His manner easy and measured, he continued through Washington's conclusion, warning of the bitter consequences if the Shawnee allied with the British or if he himself suffered any harm at their hands. The reading finished, he laid the second black wampum belt beside the first, in line with the red war belt and white peace belt. Straightening to his full height, he faced the assembly sternly.

"I come to you as the emissary of the Long Knives' great Father Washington, whose words these are. I ask that in our deliberations this day we set aside the injustices we've suffered at the hands of all white men—Long Knife and British—and keep our eyes fixed on a good future for our people."

As he had expected, a clamor of voices instantly arose. Predictably the objections and arguments followed the same lines as at his clan's council, and he countered each one as before, patiently but forcefully. Although the speakers' manner toward him made clear that the recital of his victories in battle the night before had made a deep impression, it was still as he had feared. Neither his reputation as a warrior nor any argument he could make could blot out the tribal leaders' deep distrust of the Americans or rouse any confidence that they would ever act justly toward the native peoples.

At length Red Fox rose. "Along with others of our grandfathers, uncles, and brothers, our people took the side of the French against the British in that great war," he reminded them. "And when the British won, the French abandoned us. We had no voice in the matter but were forced to accept the terms the British imposed. Have they proven more trustworthy than the Long Knives since then? They built their forts on our lands and brought in their soldiers when they swore not to do so. And on their heels came settlers and traders bringing rum. Do I need to speak of Pontiac and Guyasuta or of Cornstalk, all of whom rose against them because they broke the treaties they made with us—or of how they burned our towns and slaughtered our people for resisting them?"

Black Fish waved his arguments away dismissively. "That is in the past. Why should we listen to the words or this 'Father' Washington? The

Americans do not respect us and are stingy with their gifts, while British traders bring more and better trade goods than any the Long Knives' Great Council ever offered. The British promise that they will return the lands the Long Knives took from us—"

"The British conspired with the Iroquois to steal our hunting lands in Cantuckee and give it to settlers like this man Boone!" exclaimed Golden Elk, gesturing toward Boone, seated along the wall toward the back with the captive youth named Benjamin Kelly and two young Shawnee boys.

Black Fish's lips tightened, but he ignored his furious objection. "Our Father Hamilton at Detroit freely gives gifts of guns, ammunition, food, and clothing to any who will attack the Long Knives. We are fools if we turn against them!"

"We received many emissaries from the Thirteen Council Fires," Black Hoof sneered. "Formerly their fire blazed at the great city called Philadelphia, but the British threw them out of there, and now only a little flame flickers at a village called York. The British hold New York and other great Long Knife cities, while from all accounts the Long Knife army is poor and starving. They won a few small battles indeed, but they've not driven the British back across the Great Water."

White Eagle conceded a faint smile. "The Long Knives have not won every battle, but their victories were not small ones," he said mildly. "In fact, strong forces are gathering against the British because the Long Knives have proven that they can defeat them—as they did at Saratoga when my warriors and I helped them capture one of their greatest generals and his entire army."

The two men's faces darkened, but, nodding to Nimwha and Silverheels, he continued inexorably, "Black Hawk's clan and many from the Maquachake and Piqua divisions hold to the chain of friendship, as do the Lenape. Some have gone to White Eyes to become one people with them rather than continue this ruinous fight against the Long Knives."

The Cherokee, Oneida, Tuscarora, and other nations had sent warriors to fight with Washington, he added. The French had been sending the

Americans money, guns, and ammunition for some time and by now had undoubtedly concluded a formal alliance, with soldiers and ships to follow. The Spanish and Dutch were providing considerable aid as well, and even if they held back from the fighting, he assured the council, they would never fight on the side of the British.

Some time earlier he had become aware of the wind easing and thunder fading into the distance. Now, feeling the stir of cool air, he glanced idly toward the door. The rain had diminished to a light mist, and his guards had gone back outside, leaving the door open so the fresh breeze could clear the smoky air.

He turned back to the council. "No, the British stand alone against the Long Knives, and already their own people far across the great waters grow weary of this war. When the Long Knives prevail, which they will, the British will abandon us even as the French did before them. And then the Long Knives will turn their attention to the native peoples of this land who've made themselves their enemies."

"It's easy to speak strong words," Black Hoof snapped. "But do you claim to see into the future? Can anyone guarantee that it will be as you say?"

"I've lived both in England and in this land. I've sailed between the two shores many times and visited the large American towns along the Great Water. Have you done so, my brother? Have any of our people except Golden Elk and I?"

"Both White Eagle and I were born in England, and we know that they cannot sustain this war much longer," Golden Elk, agreed. "The people cry out against the taxes levied on them for a war that is not in their interests and that they see no reason to continue. At their Great Council Fire in London many voices are raised in opposition to the king's war and in support of the Long Knives' cause."

White Eagle nodded. "As long as the Americans can keep an army in the field—and we, Red Fox, Spotted Pony, and all our warriors have seen that they will—England is left only two choices: continue the war until they ruin their own country, or make peace. We fight on the side of the Long Knives that we may have a strong hand with them. For they are a people of long memory, and after they have driven the British from our lands, they will wipe away the towns of all those who opposed them as a man wipes the blood of battle from his knife. They will wrest this land from us forever."

Movement to his right caught his eye, and he again turned briefly toward the door. Little Running Heron had pushed to his feet as one of the guards ushered a man inside. The three stood darkly outlined against the bright sunlight that had broken through the clouds, but with his attention focused on the debate, he gave them only a passing glance.

"The British offer us the means to strike the Long Knives now, while they are weakened and distracted by this war, and should we not take it?" Blue Jacket cried out, ignoring Red Fox, who abruptly left his seat beside him and slipped over to the men at the door. "Now is the time to overcome them and drive them out!"

White Eagle raised his voice to be heard over the tumult Blue Jacket unleashed. "Brother, the British will not fight alongside us! They want us to force the Long Knives to send soldiers against us, thus weakening their army in the war with Britain. They will benefit from such an alliance, and it makes no difference to them that our people will suffer."

Golden Elk suddenly moved away from his side, but he took no notice of it, his attention on Black Snake, who fixed him in a hard stare.

"If you continue to fight on the side of the Long Knives," the Kispokotha war chief demanded, "will you not end up fighting against us—your own people?"

It was the impossible dilemma all of them had avoided voicing until now. They had already accepted weapons, supplies, and money that committed them to fight the Americans, rendering all of his arguments futile as Nonhelema had warned. But he had made himself a force the tribe's sachems could not ignore or set aside now that Washington's warning against doing any harm to him had to be taken into account. Coming on the heels of Black Fish and Black Hoof's attempt to hand him over to the British, the threat carried enormous weight.

The tribal council would not be dissuaded from approving a formal alliance with the British. Yet to do so they would have to solve the problem he, his warriors, and his clan posed—a solution that would not irretrievably tear asunder the nation, already fractured over the war, and immediately bring on themselves the full fury of the Long Knife army.

He could not even imagine what that resolution might be, and he could fairly hear Black Fish and Black Hoof grinding their teeth.

From the corner of his eye he noted that Nimwha pushed to his feet and went to join the men clustered just inside the door. A nagging unease caused him to glance toward them just as the newcomer turned so that he stood in profile against the sunlight.

Preoccupied, he started to turn back to Black Snake. And froze with a shock of recognition. He jerked his gaze back to that familiar, portly figure.

It was Teissèdre.

He wrenched his attention back to the rows of assembled sachems, war chiefs, and townspeople. Ignoring the chill that tightened his chest, he forced his mind to focus.

"I do not fight for the Long Knives!" he cried. "I fight for our nation, not against it! My brothers, in my heart is war against all the *shemanese* who would trespass on our lands, but in my mind is a warning: We cannot defeat them, whether English or American, as long as we fight alone! Our only course to avoid destruction is to act astutely now, while making alliances for the future that we may preserve our people."

"Would you have us believe that you'll not fight us if Washington commands it?" Black Hoof demanded angrily.

"He will not," White Eagle countered. "For he knows that the day he commands me to do so is the day he'll lose not only me, but also all my warriors. All of us will abandon the Long Knives before we will fight against our own people."

Looking from one face to another across the assembly, he pleaded, "My brothers, whatever may happen, do not make our nation an enemy of the Long Knives. It will be our destruction!"

By now the stir at the door had begun to filter into the consciousness of those seated in the foremost rows, who increasingly directed questioning looks at the stranger. After a brief consultation, Red Fox ushered Teissèdre to White Eagle's side with Nimwha and Golden Elk following.

The Frenchman wore a voluminous oilskin and his shoes were muddy. The wide brim of his hat, beaten down by the rain, dripped water. This he removed before bowing deeply to White Eagle, and then the assembly.

A babble of voices demanded his identity and the reason for his presence. "He is named Louis Teissèdre," Nimwha told them. "He is French, and he says he is White Eagle's agent."

Black Fish turned a frowning gaze on White Eagle. "Is this true?" When White Eagle reluctantly nodded, he demanded, "You consider him to be trustworthy?"

White Eagle regarded Teissèdre thoughtfully for a deliberate moment before acknowledging him with a slight inclination of his head. "I do," he said evenly. But the look he turned on his old friend clearly communicated: *Within limits.*

To his satisfaction he saw that Teissèdre received the message. A faint smile quirked his mouth, but he held his silence.

Suspicion darkened Black Fish's face as Nimwha returned to his seat. "What is this man's business here?"

Teissèdre glanced at White Eagle, eyebrows raised. He shrugged and motioned for the Frenchman to speak, then went to take his seat between Golden Elk and Red Fox as Little Running Heron came to crouch close behind him.

Teissèdre took his place before the assembly, drew his rotund body to its full height, and raised his chin to a lofty angle. "In the name of *sa majesté* Louis *Seize, le roi de* France, I bring greetings to your highly esteemed nation," he said with immense ceremony. "The renowned Admiral Alexandre Bettár, le comte de Caledonne, the uncle of your great war chief White Eagle, himself placed this message in my hand."

Well, that's uncommonly bold, White Eagle' thought, astounded. He turned an astonished gaze on Golden Elk, who carefully avoided it, to all appearances struggling to contain his mirth.

"With the deepest gratitude his majesty remembers the faithful service your nation rendered under his grandfather, Louis *Quinze,* and holds you in his closest affections even as his own beloved children," Teissèdre rolled dramatically on. Sweeping his arm toward the council house doorway, he proclaimed, "He sends many rich gifts to all those gathered here, which will be distributed at the end of this council."

The assembly was now entirely transfixed. Surprised smiles spread across each upturned face, and an approving murmur rippled through the council house. White Eagle looked around and saw that the women appeared especially pleased; indeed happy gratification radiated like the sun from the rows they occupied along the building's far side.

He watched in stunned disbelief while Teissèdre proceeded to relate how France's defeat in the former war with Britain had forced her to most unwillingly leave America, and rendered her unable to protect her native allies. This had long been a source of great distress to the king, and now that his government had concluded treaties of amity and commerce with the Ameri-can government, he concerned himself for his former allies' welfare.

Breathless silence reigned. The throng appeared to hang on every word.

Bending close to White Eagle's ear, Golden Elk hissed in English, "What the deuce is he playing at?"

"Only the Almighty and Teissèdre know," White Eagle muttered, scowling.

Deep in his oration, Teissèdre assured his audience that the king would warmly welcome an embassy should their nation decide to send one to counsel with him regarding their people's concerns and how he might be of assistance. Black Hoof was the first to grasp the possibilities the invitation offered and wasted no time springing to his feet to press his support for this idea. Turning a speculative gaze on White Eagle, he proposed in gracious terms that he was undoubtedly the most suited for the task.

From this point the council's response progressed as naturally as the passing of the seasons. White Eagle was shocked to appalled silence, mind reeling, as the succeeding speeches advocated that he be appointed the nation's delegate to France. Incapable of summoning a coherent protest, he was only vaguely conscious that on either side Golden Elk, Red Fox, and Spotted Pony observed the unfolding scene stoically, while Grey Cloud joined his voice to the others in obvious delight to have the war chief of his clan chosen for this high honor.

The vote was quickly called for, and the tally was unanimous. Even the factions of Cornstalk's Maquachake and the Piqua who advocated neutrality as well as a number from both divisions and the Kispokotha who supported allying with the Americans enthusiastically voted to send White Eagle to France.

A palpable sense of relief pervaded the council house when all was done. Uncertain whether to bless or curse his old friend, White Eagle reflected with dismay that it was a solution to the council's dilemma, all right. One he would never have thought of even in his wildest imaginings.

Feeling Little Running Heron's hand on his back, he glanced around. Brow furrowed, the older man appeared to be struggling to decipher what had happened.

In English White Eagle muttered, "Louis persuaded them to send me to France."

Little Running Heron considered this, then nodded, grinning. "Ah, well, that'll get ye out o' the way, won't it, sir?"

"Quite," White Eagle agreed through gritted teeth.

He turned his attention to Black Snake, who had risen to face the gathering. "It is wise to send more than one delegate to counsel with such a great king." He inclined his head to White Eagle. "What trusted man would you chose from among us?"

Mentally dismissing Golden Elk, who as brigadier of his Rangers would have to take command in his absence, he glanced to his left. And smiled.

"If it is the council's will, let Red Fox accompany me."

Barely suppressed hilarity spread across Golden Elk's and Spotted Pony's faces, while Red Fox stared at him as though he had lost his mind.

Grey Cloud nodded his approval. "Our brother stands among us as the most capable for this task," he called out.

When Red Fox opened his mouth to protest, White Eagle growled in an undertone, "If I have to go, so do you, my brother."

He did not believe for an instant that Red Fox would ever agree to cross the Great Ocean. But although the warrior paled and swallowed hard, he took a deep breath, then rose with great dignity and said firmly, "If it is the will of the council, I will go with our brother."

White Eagle regarded him with even greater astonishment than he had Teissèdre and watched dumbfounded as approval was quickly granted. After charging him and Red Fox to meet with the leading sachems after the banquet that evening to receive terms and instructions for their negotiations, Nimwha concluded the council.

A rustle of movement and the clamor of eager voices filled the council house as the crowd rushed outside after Teissèdre. Standing by the door, White Eagle, Golden Elk, Red Fox, and Spotted Pony watched the distribution of gifts from the Frenchman's heavily laden, mud-splattered pack train waiting on the yard.

"You'll truly go aboard a warship and cross the Great Water to the Frenchman's land, my brother?" Spotted Pony demanded incredulously after some moments.

White Eagle shook his head doubtfully. "You used to refuse even to cross a lake in a canoe. Has your aversion to large bodies of water changed?"

Arms crossed, Spotted Pony gave his brother an amused look. *"Mattah."*
No.

"You do know you'll be out of sight of land for weeks?" Golden Elk warned soberly. "And you might well face battle at sea."

Red Fox hesitated, looking from one to the other, but after a moment his expression cleared. "I heard in my soul a voice commanding me to do this thing."

White Eagle laughed and clasped his shoulder. "Then you'd best heed it, for you are the right man."

Chapter Twenty-one

"IS THERE NO PLACE ON EARTH where you cannot find me?" White Eagle demanded in French, pacing restlessly up and down, his steps constricted in the narrow room.

Twilight had fallen by the time all the gifts had been distributed. Patience at an end, he had extracted Teissèdre from the delighted recipients—and the Frenchman's Indian scouts, a small detail of black Rangers he had sweet-tongued Colonel Moghrab out of, and White Eagle's Marines brought along from Boston—and marched him off to Sweetgrass's small lodge.

Seated on a stool by the hearth, damp and rumpled, Teissèdre said expansively, "While it's harder at times than at others, it is, after all, my business since you do employ me."

"I flattered myself to think so. You speak for the king of France now, do you?"

"Bah. As to that, it's possible I overstated the case slightly," Teissèdre acknowledged with an elaborate shrug.

White Eagle came to a halt. "Possible! Slightly? Does my uncle know about this?"

"He will as soon as he receives my report."

"I see. And where, pray tell, did all these gifts come from? It was quite an impressive array."

Teissèdre's face assumed a pained expression. Stroking his chin, he ventured, "I may have made free with your accounts."

"Strangely I suspected that. Money well spent, no doubt. It would appear you've accomplished your mission. In spades."

"One of my more successful endeavors if I do say so myself." Looking inordinately pleased, the Frenchman cocked one eyebrow at him. "You do understand that the king will probably decline to intervene in this matter."

"I harbor no illusions on that score. I'm well aware that France has her own interests in this war and is unlikely to do the Americans' bidding, even less the Shawnee's. But it's a convenient excuse for Black Fish to get me out of the way."

Teissèdre nodded approvingly. "You've always been a realist."

"Not in all things," White Eagle muttered, averting his gaze.

Teissèdre fixed him in a sympathetic look. "Ah, but in the affairs of the heart, all of us are illusionists." Letting out a gusty sigh, he continued, "By the by, your General Washington had your colonels bring your Rangers back to Valley Forge. He insisted I impress upon you that he wants you and General Andrews back in command before the summer campaign begins."

White Eagle had resumed his pacing, but now stopped in his tracks. "I don't suppose you mentioned that your plan was to render that impossible."

"The subject didn't arise. It'll be best for you to tell him of the change in plans in person. And alone."

"Naturally you wouldn't want to be there. I'm sure we'll have an interesting conversation on my brief return," White Eagle added dryly, emphasizing the word brief.

"Knowing your persuasive powers, I'm confident you'll smooth every ruffled feather."

Ignoring his harsh laugh, Teissèdre pulled a handful of papers out of his pouch, looked them over, then began to read through a detailed report of White Eagle's business accounts.

Arms folded, he cut the Frenchman off. "These are matters of the completest indifference to me."

Teissèdre raised his gaze from the papers. "So you do not care that Admiral Howe is busily blowing your ships out of the water—at least the ones left after the depredations of those infernal Barbary pirates."

Stiffening, White Eagle envisioned through a bloody haze bags of pounds sterling along with the lives of his sailors winging their way out the council house door. Rage speared through him with the force of lightning.

"*Pardonne-moi.* I misspoke. As a matter of fact, I do care. Monstrously, to be precise."

"I thought you might."

White Eagle fumed silently while Teissèdre proceeded to detail the losses to his merchantmen, with a couple of fully loaded ships taken as prize. He concluded, "As to your privateers, *Columbia* and *Adventure* were sunk last fall, as you know, but according to the latest report I received, the replacements le comte procured were on the point of sailing after being completely refitted and furnished with crews. In the meantime, those cursed Barbary pirates put *Pursuit* and *Wasp* out of action with heavy damage—not before they sank the pirates, however—and are under repair at Marseille. Howe's fleet took *Patriot,* renamed her *Avenger,* and impressed her entire crew. *Destiny* and *Concord* are currently careened at L'Orient after fighting off another of Howe's attacks, which leaves *Black Swan* to guard what remains of your fleet."

"It would seem there's not much of it left to guard." Through gritted teeth White Eagle added, "I want *Patriot* recaptured, her name restored, and her crew freed. At the earliest instant."

"I'll forward your instructions to le comte as soon as I return to civilization."

"This *is* civilization. Just not yours." White Eagle eyed his agent suspiciously. "Knowing my uncle, I'm sure he has things well in hand. Why have you really come, Louis? I think it's for more than this."

"I hoped I might detach you from the Shawnee and send you to France."

"Which you've accomplished. Why?"

"Mmmm . . . well, you see. . . it became expedient for le comte to take your lady there. As you know, Clinton is not a man to forget an injury. His last attempt on her life almost succeeded, but luckily I arrived in time."

White Eagle briefly pressed his eyes closed, the pressure that had been building in his chest ever since his agent appeared at the council house door clenching like a steel band. He dragged in a slow breath and let it out, willing his nerves to steady.

"That possibility occurred to me," he admitted in a muffled voice. "Either that or . . . " He could not go on.

"No," Teissèdre responded softly. "Your Marines did an excellent job of guarding her. But it had become too dangerous for her to stay at Boston, and at any rate there was no longer any way to conceal the truth from her and her parents."

White Eagle nodded, said gruffly, "Well, it matters not. She's in my uncle's care. And no longer my lady. I'm sure by now she's gone on with her life and put all thought of me from her mind."

Teissèdre regarded him with outraged incredulity. "She's in love with you, man, if you hadn't noticed! Absence makes the heart grow fonder, not the reverse."

White Eagle's hand instinctively went to the pouch that hung around his neck by a thong. Therein lay Elizabeth's last letter to him. Still unanswered. He'd told himself countless times that he must destroy it, but it remained a thing impossible to do.

Teissèdre's voice jerked him back to the present. "You've clearly had occasion to learn that yourself by now. If you don't go to her, you're an obstinate fool."

For a long moment White Eagle stared into space, reason and doubt warring in his soul with a desire that refused to be quenched. "She's well?" he asked hoarsely.

"As well as she can be in your absence." Witih a gentler tone Teissèdre added, "Indeed, her body—if not her heart—has noticeably gained strength. Once she's safe in France, she'll have the best of care and will be back to full health in due course."

For some moments White Eagle remained silent, at last managed, "I'm bound for Paris, not Marseille." He tensed as Teissèdre's gaze shifted guiltily away from his.

"It . . . ah . . . well, your uncle took her to Passy instead."

White Eagle cursed violently under his breath, all other thoughts temporarily obliterated. "Caledonne is taking her directly into that viper's pit when I directed him to keep her from there?"

Teissèdre spread his hands. "He felt she'd be safer under the care of your cousin and the marquis. Château Broussard is considerably easier to secure than the Marseille estate."

White Eagle fought to contain his temper. "And—with Versailles just down the road—awash in the court intrigues in which my uncle and the marquis are both deeply mired!"

"Le comte would never allow Mademoiselle Howard to be endangered," Teissèdre protested, his expression pained. "He loves her as well as he loves you, but he's an admiral, you know. He'll have to go back to sea, especially now that we're at war with England, and he trusts the marquis—"

"I've no doubt he loves her," White Eagle snapped. "The trouble is that I've had occasion to learn very well how my uncle has no compunctions against employing in his webs those he loves the best."

"Bah! You never came to harm."

"No credit to him," White Eagle growled. "Mademoiselle Howard has no way of knowing what he's about—or protecting herself from his designs. My uncle could charm the very devil." He regarded Teissèdre through narrowed eyes. "Who's his target this time? The American commissioners?"

Teissèdre made a dismissive gesture. "That's hardly necessary."

"How could I have imagined it was? Your agents, *sans doute,* know even the content of their dreams by now."

His expression innocent as a new-born babe's, Teissèdre changed the subject. "The elder Madame Howard and Mademoiselle Abigail accompany her. Le comte thought it an excellent situation for all of them."

White Eagle's mouth dropped open. "There's one conversation I wish I'd been privy to!"

"It was quite entertaining. It is true that your uncle can charm the devil, but in this case it was the ladies who overcame Dr. Howard's objections."

"After he charmed them."

Teissèdre smiled like a wolf. "Since you'll be stopping by Valley Forge on the way to France, I'd better bring you up to date on what's been happening in the other war during your absence."

Briefly he related that colonels Matthew Farris and Isaiah Moghrab, for the time sharing command of the Rangers, had discipline under tight control and were shaping the brigade into an even more formidable fighting force than before. General William Howe was due to return to England imminently. General Henry Clinton, who replaced him as British commander in chief, had orders to evacuate Philadelphia and—according to Teissèdre's agents at Lord North's elbow—to force Washington to a decisive engagement in the process. In addition he was to mount naval attacks against every port along the coast from New York to Nova Scotia, seize or destroy every American ship, and destroy all wharfs, stores, and ship-building materials in reprisal for the depredations of privateers, including White Eagle's, against British shipping. Meanwhile, an American captain named John Paul Jones was carrying out successful raids along the British coast, setting the countryside in an uproar.

While at Valley Forge, Teissèdre had learned that Washington had handily displaced the cabal arrayed against him that winter. He had also taken on as inspector general of the army an officer newly arrived from Europe. Baron Friedrich von Steuben had served as aide-de-camp to

Frederick the Second of Prussia and was achieving encouraging results in reforming the army's administration and training.

"Thank God for that!" White Eagle exclaimed at the latter. "Now perhaps my insistence that we'll defeat England has some hope of success."

Teissèdre dismissed his comment with a wave of his hand. "But how could there be any question on that score when France was inevitably to enter the fray against her old enemy?"

"The treaties took long enough to conclude." White Eagle stretched himself across the sleeping platform, his frown fierce.

For some moments Teissèdre studied him earnestly. "I've never felt I truly knew you, my friend," he said at last. "Oh, I've watched you among your Rangers, and that tells me much. But now, seeing you stand before the council of this people with such confidence, such earnestness and grace—" When White Eagle turned a sardonic look on him, he broke off and said, "You may not recognize it, but it's there. And genuine passion. For the first time I feel I've seen into your heart."

"What good has this passion you speak of accomplished?" White Eagle questioned bitterly. "I've changed nothing, and now they're sending me away."

"Perhaps because your work here is finished—for now, at least," Teissèdre replied. "You've other work to do. And a dear lady who needs you with her more than you know."

⊛ ⊛ ⊛

THAT NIGHT, FOLLOWING the banquet and after the leading sachems had given him and Red Fox detailed instructions for negotiations with the French, White Eagle strode alone into the forest surrounding the town. After checking with the guards posted around his camp to make sure all was as it should be, he wandered to a wooded height overlooking the river. There he stood unmoving, leaning back against the trunk of an immense chestnut and looking up through its branches into the indigo bowl of the star-scattered heavens, while the drums of the dancers throbbed late into the night.

He had confided to Golden Elk, Red Fox, and Spotted Pony the bare facts of what Teissèdre had told him, keeping his expression masked and voice level. He had made no response to their astonishment, had not answered their eager questions or spoken of what his future might hold.

He had also gone to Crooked Oak, one of his warriors of the Maquachake division. His wife had sickened and died before his return, leaving their small daughter in the care of his elderly mother. Although he spoke little, White Eagle knew he mourned deeply. Choosing his words with care, he had asked Crooked Oak to take the young widow Falling Leaf and her two children under his protection, pleased when he agreed without hesitation.

The rest of that evening White Eagle had acted as though nothing was out of the ordinary. But he could no longer suppress the leap of emotion, the quickening of his heartbeat at the thought that surely this must be the sign he had pleaded for. How likely was it that such a wholly unforeseen, impossible turn of events could be mere chance?

For any way forward among his people was blocked to him now. To do their bidding he must leave them, and in that he had been given no choice.

It came to him with piercing force that for all his efforts to bridge these two worlds—the Shawnee and the White—he would always stand between them, a part of both yet separate from each. But unexpectedly, a quiet resignation, a soul-deep knowing strengthened him.

Now therefore ye are no more strangers and foreigners, but fellow citizens with the saints, and of the household of God . . .

The ancient words flooded into his mind, and peace fell over him. And bone-deep gratitude.

Fellow citizens of the household of God, he thought wonderingly. *It is enough—more than all else in all this world. Your will, oh Father, be done in me.*

Indeed, his work among this people was finished, he acknowledged with sadness. For now, as Teissèdre had said. He still had his clan. They would never turn him away, and someday he would return to them. Of that he was as sure as of the sun's rising. As sure as that he would always find Elizabeth again no matter how far their individual destinies might take them from each other.

The hope remained, too, that the Great Father would enable him to again take up his place in the nation when this war was done. Perhaps even Elizabeth, Healer Woman, would be strong enough to return with him then.

For if she would have him still, he would marry her as soon as the mission to France was completed. Regardless of whether her parents or Washington or his clan opposed it. He was doubly convinced now that his earthly home was to be with her, and with the children God would send to bless their union.

Yet somehow he felt that there would not be any opposition in the end. The heavenly Father had the power to work out his will as he chose. Just an hour earlier Blue Sky had urged him to do this, and Red Fox, Golden Elk, and Spotted Pony had agreed. Even Grey Cloud and Blue Crane had mentioned the matter in his hearing with implicit approval.

Beth!

Now that all was settled here, how his heart yearned for her! How his blood raged against the intolerable barricade of time that loomed between them until he could hold her in his arms again, kiss her wine-sweet lips, and never let her go!

If it had been possible, if there had not been so much that clamored to be done before he was free to leave, he would have leaped on his stallion that very moment and raced recklessly away to go to her. But Dunquat would soon lead his warriors to Fort Randolph if they had not gone already, and he had to know the consequences of their attack before leaving his people again.

He knew as well that once he returned to Valley Forge, it was unlikely that Washington would blithely send him off to France with his blessing. He did not relish the prospect of that interview or what his commander might require of him.

"But I *am* coming!" he murmured. "Dearest of my heart, do you not feel it? Do you not feel my love? I'll not fail you again—I swear to you. Don't despair, for a blessed future surely lies before us now no matter what trials may yet beset us."

He would write to her the moment he returned to Valley Forge. He would finally answer her letter, assuring her of his love, promising that he was on his way back to her. He breathed a prayer for her safety and that her love remained steadfast.

With one last glance toward the river's turbulent waters, glimmering darkly beneath moon- and starlight, he turned and strode with quick, light steps back toward the camp.

Chapter Twenty-two

A WAYWARD GUST of wind fluttered Elizabeth's apple-green petticoats and the sky-blue ribbons on Lucien's walking stick, and tugged at the wide brim of her flower bedecked straw hat. With a small shriek, she pressed her skirts down with both hands, while he righted the hat, which threatened to pull free of the bow securing it under her chin and sail off her head. Tess and Cécile fought to keep their own apparel from upending, and they all laughed together at the wind's sudden assault.

"What a fine day for flying kites!"

"A shame we don't have any," Lucien responded. "We must remember to bring one next time."

She forced a smile in answer to his. "We couldn't have a fairer day to enjoy Versailles' gardens. Nor a lovelier view."

The afternoon was unusually warm for mid May, with the sun beaming down from a clear blue sky. She turned to take in the graveled *allées,* manicured lawns, formal parterres outlined with sculpted boxwood hedges, and groves of tall, graceful trees that extended around the palace and its surrounding buildings as far as one could see. Pools, fountains, and cascades; steams spanned by picturesque bridges; classical-style statues on pedestals; balustrades and marble columns; trellises and ornamental gates enhanced the simple but elegant plantings. The effect was almost more than the mind could take in.

They had followed a lavish picnic on the bank of the Grand Canal with a gondola ride, Lucien good-humoredly poling the vessel. While Cécile and Tess chatted lazily and admired the swans gliding across the water, Elizabeth had trailed her hand disconsolately in the water, the outing doing little to lift her spirits.

It was only three days since the arrival of Lord North's warrant, though it seemed an eternity. Suddenly restrictions hedged every movement. Despairing at the prospect of weeks and months of the same to come, she had agreed to another foray to Versailles as a distraction. At least here the formidable Swiss Guards, striking in their ornate red coats faced in dark blue, patrolled the grounds, and the bodyguards who now shadowed her whenever she left her hosts' estate did not need to hover close at hand.

It seemed that all of Paris had heard of her role in the rebellion and clamored to learn every detail, whether true or not. Accordingly, fantastic, even scandalous, accounts abounded in the *libelles*. And in spite of Caledonne's and the Martieu-Broussards' efforts to shield her, increasing numbers of their acquaintances, all at high levels in the government and society, called at the château or issued invitations to dinners and other gatherings under thinly veiled pretexts. Invariably everyone pressed intrusive questions, including about her relationship with Carleton, a subject too painful to think of, much less speak to strangers about.

Even trips around the area had become a trial. On their first visit to Versailles three weeks earlier, they had toured the palace in relative anonymity. This time, however, many of the courtiers they encountered either recognized her from previous encounters or immediately realized who she must be because of her companions. Ignoring Cécile's and Lucien's efforts to fend them off, they had flocked around Elizabeth to offer compliments that didn't ring true, gush admiration for her daring that felt false, and demand an account of her adventures, especially any seductions. Others had simply stared down at her through their lorgnettes as though she were some alien insect. Finally she and her party had retreated to Le Petit Trianon, where entrance was restricted.

"At least today the wind carries off most of *le eau d'égouts*," Lucien said, humorously referring to the stench of sewage they had noticed a week and a half earlier.

On that first visit to Versailles, she, Tess, and Abby were awed by the imposing Royal Gate with its gilded spikes, the Ministers' Courtyard, and the Cour Royale, the latter crowded with the stalls of *marchands* selling all manner of goods or renting the swords and hats required for all men who entered. But the splendor of the grand halls and state chambers was truly stunning. Beyond peer was the Hall of Mirrors with its magnificent chandeliers and silver furnishings. The Salon de Mars was equally fabulous, its walls covered in blood red damask and the throne set on a dais draped in ermine embroidered with golden fleurs-de-lis, where the king held court, surrounded by his royal bodyguard in blue uniform.

In many areas of the palace and grounds, however, they had been forced to hold scented handkerchiefs over their noses to ward off unpleasant odors emanating from the estate's inadequate sewers. Cécile and Lucien had explained that the original modest brick and stone hunting lodge built by Louis XIII in the forest outside the village of Versailles had been expanded by his successors into one of the most extravagant and costly buildings in the world. They had also cleared the rest of the estate's 37,000 acres to create the magnificent gardens, all of which affected the land's drainage.

"There are around 5,000 nobles and servants living in the palace," Cécile had told them. Fourteen thousand soldiers and more servants are quartered throughout the estate and in the village, to say nothing of vast numbers of horses and other animals."

With a shrug, Lucian had added, "A great deal of money and effort has been spent to solve the problem. But the sources of water available in this area simply can't handle the needs of such an enormous population."

While touring the palace, they had been struck by what seemed extra-ordinarily lax security, in contrast to the numerous guards who patrolled the estate. Throngs of courtiers surrounded by attendants crowded the seemingly endless maze of halls and chambers. All were fantastically garbed, coiffed, and bejeweled, their faces painted lavishly with the court *maquillage* that attested to wealth, rank, and privilege. It appeared that everyone at Versailles vied to outdo their rivals by wearing their wealth on their persons.

At the same time, mobs of common people also roved the halls, a great many unwashed and in rags, appearing to have no other business than to gawk at the extravagance that surrounded them. With Aunt Tess she had watched in amazement while two Swiss Guards with leashed spaniels routed out vagrants who had actually taken up residence in several of the palace's innumerable nooks and crannies, brazenly relieving themselves in the corners. According to Lucien, this was not at all unusual, no more than the royals allowing their multitude of pampered dogs and cats to freely romp through the ornately furnished chambers, barking, yowling, and leaving their droppings for the army of maids to clear away.

To their astonished questions, Cecile had explained that every French subject possessed a traditional right of access to their sovereign. From the market women's right to address the queen on ceremonial occasions had developed a general right of access. This in turn had given way to the more recent custom of their accosting her and railing to her face at her perceived faults.

They had reached the main gate of the romantic English-style *jardin anglais* belonging to the small, square, Greek-style palace called Le Petit Trianon. According to Cécile Louis XV had built the charming château for his mistress Madame de Pompadour, though after her death her successor, Madame du Barry, had been the first to live in it.

After his ascension to the throne, Louis XVI had given it to Marie Antoinette, who was transforming it into her private domain, a refuge from the court's rigid routines and the public's scrutiny. Only her inner circle was admitted to its grounds, which understandably drew the ire of those who were excluded.

As Cécile began to lead the way past the two Swiss Guards posted at the gate, Tess asked nervously, "I assume you've permission to enter. But does that include your guests?"

"*Oui, bien sûr!*" Yes, of course, she answered, nodding to the guards, who opened the gate and stepped aside. "I spoke to her this morning at her *lever.* She's most eager to meet both of you, and this is the time she walks in her gardens."

Elizabeth exchanged an alarmed glance with Tess. "You don't mean that her majesty—"

"And here she is right now!" Lucien broke in, flourishing his walking stick in one hand as he placed his other on Elizabeth's back to urge her gently forward.

She swung to face the queen, who indeed approached, attended by two ladies in waiting and three footmen arrayed in the queen's own red and silver livery. With them was the king's handsome, dark-haired, dark-eyed youngest brother, Charles, le comte d'Artois, a somewhat pudgy youth, who bounded forward to greet Lucien.

"We've been playing at *écarté* all afternoon," he exclaimed, adding with a laugh, "I do hope you've come to join the fun."

Lucien turned partly away from Elizabeth, but not before she caught a glimpse of his knowing smile. "Not today, I'm afraid," she heard him say in an undertone as he moved a short distance away with the prince. "As you can see, I've more a valuable prize at stake."

"*Peste!*" Grinning, Artois directed a bold glance at Elizabeth. "But what a lucky dog you are, you scoundrel!"

By now the queen had reached them, giving Elizabeth no time to bristle at Lucien's remark. He bowed, while she sank into a deep curtsey with Cécile and Tess. When they rose, the queen came to clasp Cécile to her bosom and kiss her neck, her movements elegantly graceful.

Elizabeth tried not to gawk, but she could not keep her eyes from being repeatedly drawn to the young queen. She appeared to be near her own age, with clear blue eyes and a delicately luminous complexion lacking any need for *blanc,* which she clearly was not wearing. Nor were her cheeks stained with the great circles of rouge the other ladies affected, but held a soft, natural blush. Her light red-blonde hair showed no hint of powder and was swept up into a relatively modest pouf decorated with sweet little clusters of pink and blue flowers and feathers.

Everything about Marie Antoinette was exquisite, from her simple but elegantly fashioned *polonaise* of delicate violet satin embroidered with tiny flower clusters and accented with fine white lace; to the bows on her matching high-heeled slippers; to the sparkling diamonds and other gems that richly adorned her neck, ears, and hands. Set against the splendor all around her, she radiated an impression of incalculable wealth.

Releasing Cécile, she took Lucien's hands and gave him a reproachful look. "You've neglected to attend me of late, monsieur. I've begun to fear I've lost your love to another."

"Never, *votre Majesté*," he protested fervently, giving her his most charming smile. "Can you doubt that you'll always be my first love?"

"Men always promise to be true, but so few are in the end," she chided with a low, musical laugh. "Don't deny it—you'll inevitably fall hopelessly in love with some wayward young thing, and I'll be forgotten!" She waved away his good-natured protests as she turned to Elizabeth and Tess.

Cécile introduced them, and they curtsied again to the queen, and then to her ladies: la princesse de Lamballe, a gentle, morose-looking blonde; and la comtesse de Polignac, a striking chestnut-haired beauty. From the stiffness of the two ladies' manner and the distance they kept between them, Elizabeth quickly gained the impression that they were rivals for the queen's favor and neither liked nor trusted each other.

"How beautiful both of you are!" the queen exclaimed as she clasped Tess's hands, then Elizabeth's.

"You're most kind, *Majesté*," Tess murmured.

"We've all heard rumors of your *affaire de coeur* with my dear Caledonne," she replied mischievously. "I see he has chosen well. And I assure you a lady could make no better choice in a lover."

Elizabeth had to bite her lip hard to stifle a giggle as Tess turned scarlet. But to her surprise her aunt replied quietly, *"Merci.* I think most highly of le comte."

"And, of course, we've heard of the cruel confinement you suffered aboard a British prison ship, Mademoiselle Howard," the queen continued, giving Elizabeth a sympathetic look. "And now it's revealed that you served as a spy for your General Washington and even dared to engage in battle. But you're so lovely to have disguised yourself as a man and faced such danger!"

Elizabeth met the queen's curious gaze with an admiring one. "Coming from one so beautiful herself, *Majesté,* this is a great compliment."

The queen dimpled. "You're as charming as you are pretty, I see. It was your cousin, General Carleton, who plucked Mademoiselle Howard out of the very center of the British stronghold, was it not, Cécile?"

When Cécile inclined her head, the queen let out an ecstatic sigh. "I'm told that he's your fiancé, mademoiselle. Yours is a romance that all of Paris is swooning over!"

A pang went through Elizabeth, but before she could respond, Lucien said, "My cousin was adopted by the American natives some time ago and claims to be an Indian war chief—"

Guffawing, Artois broke in, "A white man an Indian warrior? Surely you jest!"

The queen pressed one hand to her bosom, wide-eyed. "How very curious—yet even more romantic!"

Lucien shrugged. "Some may think it to be so, but sadly last winter when General Washington sent him back to the Indians to negotiate an alliance against the British, he broke their engagement and made it clear he'd no intention of ever returning."

Elizabeth felt as though he'd struck her. The mouths of the princesse and comtesse dropped open in astonishment. Tess slipped her arm around Elizabeth's shoulders, while Cécile frowned and gave Lucien a disapproving shake of her head.

The queen appeared to take no notice of their by-play, instead regarding Elizabeth with genuine concern. "I'm so sorry, *ma chère*. Your heart must be broken!"

Avoiding Lucien's gaze and wishing mightily that he had held his tongue, Elizabeth murmured, "I'm very grateful that I've been offered sanctuary here, and that the king so kindly extended his protection to me after receiving Lord North's warrant."

The queen placed her hand on Elizabeth's arm. "You've no need to worry! The presumption of the British is outrageous, and no harm will be allowed to come to you as long as you're in France."

The others murmured their agreement, and Lucien bent over her. "Didn't I tell you how kind and good our sovereigns are?"

Forcing a smile, she nodded. But she avoided his gaze.

"Your bravery is most admirable," the queen said with a pensive look. "But I confess it troubles me that a people such as yours would rebel against their lawful sovereign."

"We suffered many abuses over a number of years before taking this drastic step, *Majesté*," Tess ventured. "I assure you the decision was not lightly made."

"Our situation is quite different from that of France," Elizabeth put in, choosing her words with care. "English law grants all Englishmen certain inviolable rights, as you may know. But in the American colonies a great many of those rights were trampled. For many years we appealed, petitioned, and finally protested to our king, only to have him refuse us justice. At last we were left no other course."

Sensing the others' tension, Elizabeth waited on tenterhooks while the queen regarded both of them thoughtfully. At last she smiled and said, "Well, it's a matter for the men to determine, *n'est-ce pas?*"

"As to foreign relations you must always remember, Madame," Artois drawled lazily, "that as they say, 'The enemy of my enemy is my friend.' "

Lucien smirked. "Indeed so."

The queen gave a light laugh. *"Tout à fait."* Quite.

Everyone relaxed into smiles and chuckles. Beckoning them to follow, the queen led the way into the gardens. With infectious enthusiasm she pointed out favorite flowers and trees she had just planted and outlined her plans for additional improvements. Her ladies trailed behind, looking daggers at each other when they acknowledged the other's presence at all.

They meandered along a picturesque stream until they came to the framework of a partially completed footbridge. There they paused to take in a charming Greek-style folly set on the island at the bridge's far end amid a profusion of trees and shrubs. A graceful circle of Corinthian columns poised on a marble floor atop several steps, supporting a curved, coffered roof with an entablature embossed with rosettes and arabesques. Mirrored in the stream's glassy waters, it offered an exquisitely romantic vista in spite of the signs of construction on the lawn around it and its empty central pedestal.

"It's to be a monument to love!" the queen cried, clasping her hands in delight. "When complete, it will have as its centerpiece a copy of Bouchardon's *Cupid Fashioning His Bow from Hercules' Club.*"

She turned quickly to Elizabeth, and seeing the pain that crossed her face in spite of her efforts to conceal it, said, "Do not grieve, mademoiselle! How could General Carleton not return to you? That he endangered himself so greatly to rescue you surely testifies to the depth of his love."

Before Elizabeth could think of a reply, she added, smiling. "I know— the king must send Caledonne to persuade him to come to France. Once he sees you again, Cupid's arrow will strike his heart, and he'll be powerless to deny you." Turning to the others, she exclaimed, "We must have him at court, and in Indian dress! It would make quite the sensation, would it not?"

The queen's ladies dutifully agreed, while Elizabeth remained at a loss for words.

"I'd not miss that sensation for the world," Artois snickered.

Scowling, Lucien turned away, but said nothing.

When they resumed their walk the queen linked her arm with Elizabeth's. Cécile, Tess, and the queen's ladies followed at a short distance, while Lucien and Artois lingered behind, talking in low tones.

"I believe we share a birth year," Elizabeth ventured. "I turned twenty-three in March."

"I thought we were close to the same age. You are only a few months older than I," the queen responded with a smile.

Tentatively Elizabeth asked, "You're the queen of a great country but . . . do you ever wonder about the purpose of your life?"

"Why, it's to support my husband, to bear his heir, and to render godly service to others," the queen answered. "As women, we find our life's meaning in this, do we not?"

Elizabeth bit her lip, frowning. "God has given me the gift of healing. Now that I can no longer assist in her ministry to the poor in Paris, madame la marquise arranged for me to take over the medical care of those who work for her. I find great fulfillment in such service, but . . . I do so long for a husband and children . . . " The last words were whispered.

"Only God will decide this matter, mademoiselle," the queen reminded her kindly. "In submitting to him, you will find true love if this one is not to be. Be assured that there are many men worthy of your affections. I've learned that to brood over one, even if he's your most particular love, will only keep you from the blessings God would bestow."

Elizabeth sighed. "I know you're right. The trouble is that hearts can be stubborn."

"I've some experience of that," the queen replied with a tinkling laugh. She slowly sobered. "Have you spoken with your priest? He can offer you comfort and guidance."

Cécile and Tess had come up to them, and Cécile said, "I confided something of your plight to Father Raulett. He'd be very glad to counsel with you."

Elizabeth exchanged a glance with Tess, who hesitated, then nodded.

"Let me arrange it," Cécile said briskly.

The others had caught up with them by now, and Cécile began to describe the places they had taken their guests and the salons, ballets, and operas they had attended.

"But you've attended no balls?" the queen enquired. When Tess and Elizabeth admitted they had not, she said, "We hold two balls at the palace every month. One is a *bal masque* in the Hall of Mirrors."

"I've never been to a masked ball," Elizabeth admitted, "but the Hall of Mirrors would certainly be an extraordinary setting for one."

"The next one is Monday." The queen turned to Lucien. "You must escort her!"

He immediately swept Elizabeth a low bow, straightened, and took her hand with an eagerness that unsettled her. "I'd be most honored if you'd consent to accompany me. Do say you will!"

She hesitated, in a quandary. Following the past days' upheaval, the prospect of a ball, and a masked one at that, was well nigh too great a temptation to resist.

Before she could answer, Tess said brusquely, "You've no ball gown, and it's impossible to have one made up in two days." Turning back to the queen, she quickly changed the subject. "Does the king also attend these balls?"

"He does not enjoy such entertainments and much prefers to spend his time in hunting and studying his favorite sciences. And I fear that I shall soon have to forego such strenuous activities, even including carriage rides," the queen added, sighing.

Cécile regarded her in surprise. "But I've never seen you so blooming. You're positively radiant. And can it be that your cheeks have grown more round?"

The queen beamed. "It may be so. Indeed I asked the king for 12,000 francs for the relief of those in the Paris debtors' prison who owe payment to their children's wet nurses, and 4,000 for the poor of Versailles. To my delight he kindly gave it to me."

For a moment all of them regarded her, puzzled, then Cécile's face brightened. "*Votre Majesté!* Have you and the king happy news to announce at last?"

Her cheeks warmed with becoming color as she looked from one to the other, tears shimmering in her eyes. "Soon, I pray. The donation will be announced tomorrow, but for now, say nothing to anyone outside this company."

"Not a word!" Cécile pledged fervently.

By now comprehension was dawning on Elizabeth, as it clearly was on Tess and Lucien. Cécile turned to them with her finger to her lips. "The queen may at last be *enceinte*—with child!"

They had arrived back at the gate. After offering their warmest congratulations and promising to speak not a word to anyone of the matter until the palace issued a formal announcement, they made their courtesies and took leave of the queen and her ladies.

Chapter Twenty-three

"C'EST TRES EXQUISE!" Elizabeth exclaimed in delight, trailing her fingers lightly across the tissue-thin *lustrine*. "I adore how the silk shimmers from silver to gold with every movement."

"It's perfect for your coloring and will make up into a lovely ball gown." With a satisfied nod, Tess handed the swatch of cloth back to Madame Bertin. Picking up two samples of finely woven lace from the table, one narrow and one wide, she said, "With this finishing off the edges of the bodice and petticoat front, and this for the sleeves?"

The *marchand* regarded Elizabeth assessingly. "It's a shame the balls at Versailles have been suspended for now due to the queen's delicate condition. However, one hosted by Chartres at the Palais-Royal is hardly of less consequence. In the queen's absence a lady of such renown as yourself must put all others to shame. May I suggest that in keeping with the ball's theme you portray the goddess Diana, mademoiselle, as in this design? It's quite daring and will display your figure to the best advantage."

Elizabeth tore her gaze away from the rolls of lush fabrics, fashionable hats, and accessories that filled the shelves and displays of Le Grand Mogul, their vibrant colors and flamboyant styles making her head swim. Jemma and Mariah crowded around them as she and her aunt bent to scrutinize the illustration in the pattern book Bertin laid before them.

"Ah . . . this is perhaps a bit too daring," Elizabeth gasped.

The two maids' eyes had rounded and their mouths formed perfect o's. "Scandalous!" squeaked Mariah, a slight, brown-haired mouse of a woman.

"A pagan fertility goddess?" Tess protested in alarm.

"She's also the goddess of the hunt," Bertin pointed out. "Quite appropriate, *non?*"

"*Non, non, non!* The gown is far too short. And as it'll be impossible to wear stays and panniers beneath it, the *lustrine* will cling to every curve." Tess shook her head adamantly. "Such styles may be acceptable in Paris, but neither my niece nor myself choose to show so much skin."

Bertin laughed. "Ah, *oui—la mode Americaine!* How sad that with such charms to display you must be such proper republicans. But perhaps if we bring the hem to the floor and drape the décolletage in this way." She indicated a curved line at a more modest distance below Elizabeth's shoulders.

"It fits the ball's theme of deities and sovereigns perfectly," Elizabeth murmured with longing.

Tess considered her, then the design with a frown, but finally conceded reluctantly, "I suppose one's only young once. That will do—but with more fullness to accommodate stays and a shift and to keep the fabric from clinging quite so intimately."

Bertin rolled her eyes. "As you wish."

Jemma returned Elizabeth's calculating look with a knowing smile, mischief dancing in her eyes. Even with the changes, the design was more daring than any she had ever worn, Elizabeth reflected. Some internal deviltry tempted her, however, whispering that the golden sash cinched the gown's waist so attractively. Stays could be left off without anyone's knowing, a silk shift substituted for linen . . . . and she would be wearing a domino cloak and mask, after all . . .

Bertin's voice interrupted her speculations. "And what of you, madame? You'll attend with le comte?"

Tess waved the matter away. "He's otherwise occupied that evening. Besides, masked balls are for the young."

"There are many ladies of more mature years who love to dance and are looking for agreeable assignations," Bertin scoffed. "In the absence of le comte—"

Eyebrows raised, Tess cut her off. "Although I love to dance, I've no interest in secret rendezvous."

"You *Americaines!* But the emerald damask is perfect for you. Shall I have it made up *à la française* for evening wear?"

Tess hesitated. "I do love it." At Elizabeth's urging, she agreed, then asked, "Now what of our bill?"

Bertin raised her hands. "It's of no concern, madame. Le comte has established a very generous account for the purchases of both you ladies."

Tightlipped, Tess said to Elizabeth, "Didn't we have a discussion over this very thing at Bordeaux? I thought the matter settled! Alexandre knows very well I'm able to pay for anything we buy—within reason, at least."

At Bertin's questioning look, Elizabeth explained, "In our country it's considered scandalous for a man to give intimate articles to a woman to whom he isn't married or, at the very least, engaged."

"Bah! In France it's unremarkable for men to give intimate gifts to their lovers—or those they wish to be." Both their mouths fell open, but she continued firmly, "Le comte was quite adamant that all your purchases are to be charged to his account."

She remained unmovable, and at last Tess reluctantly gave in. After arranging for delivery of the gowns and accessories they had chosen, they thanked the *marchand* and left the shop, trailed by their maids.

"It appears Alexandre and I are going to have another discussion on this matter," Tess snapped as they marched along the teeming Rue Saint-Honoré, their ears assaulted by the city's clamor.

Elizabeth laughed and tucked her arm through her aunt's. "And you know it'll do no good at all. I'm afraid you've met your match."

From the corner of her eye she noted that two of the guards assigned to attend them whenever they left the château's grounds drifted casually in their wake, while two more strolled a short distance ahead of them.

The men blended easily into the shifting throng, their weapons concealed, unobtrusively on the alert for any sign of danger. Although Elizabeth did her best to ignore them, she found it hard to get used to having every movement under surveillance.

The Tuileries gardens had quickly become one of their favorite places in the city. They detoured into it to stroll between the beautifully planted parterres, the guards casually lingering nearby as though merely enjoying the fine day.

Giving her aunt an amused sidelong look, Elizabeth ventured, "I suspect there's more the two of you need to talk about. He's making no secret of his intentions."

"I'm more concerned about the situation you're getting into with Lucien," Tess cut her off, giving her a reproachful look.

"Lucien?" Elizabeth exclaimed with a laugh. "I enjoy his company, that's all. He's like a brother, and——"

"You're blind if you think that's all he feels for you. I see the way he looks at you, and it isn't with brotherly affection. You're very different from the women he's known all his life, and that can be very appealing to a man. Whatever possessed you to agree to accompany him to a masked ball?"

Elizabeth bristled. "Why shouldn't I? I've never attended one. It'll be fun, and the Palais-Royal will be perfectly safe——"

"There's more than one kind of danger. The Opera, the Comedie Français, picnics and riding and even races at the Bois de Boulogne—and now a masked ball! There's a charged situation, if attending races together wasn't enough. Do you think it wise to spend so much time alone with him?"

Elizabeth met Tess's searching gaze with a frown. "You, Uncle Alexandre, and the Martieu-Broussards are almost always with us."

"Not of late. From my vantage it appears that he's falling in love with you."

Elizabeth felt heat climb to her cheeks. "I've never given Lucien any impression that there's more between us than friendship."

"Then he isn't getting the message."

Elizabeth came to a halt the shade of a bank of trees, while the two maids settled on a nearby bench. May had turned unusually warm, and she fanned her face while surveying the lush plantings awash in warm sunshine from beneath the wide brim of her straw hat.

"You know very well that Uncle Alexandre asked him to accompany me for my protection whenever I leave the estate. He doesn't seem to have any concerns about our relationship."

"When it concerns their children, fathers don't always see what's under their noses."

"In this case there's nothing to see." Elizabeth bent over the carmine roses that edged the parterre beside her, breathing in their heady perfume. "I enjoy his company and the places he takes me, that's all. Just as I love caring for the estate's servants."

"That's another matter that concerns me. You spend hours in the kitchen office tending to them, not to mention down on the plain visiting them in the fields and barns and in their homes. I'm afraid you'll wear yourself out again after you've just regained your strength."

"I've never felt stronger, and both Cécile and Jemma help." Smiling, Elizabeth added, "Besides, I love getting to know the servants and workers at the farm better and ministering to their hearts as well as treating their bodies. The children and elderly are especially dear. And I count it a great privilege to pray with the women for their families, their work, and other daily concerns."

"But it weighs on you too." Tess shook her head. "You're too concientious. I know you need diversions from time to time, but—"

"I've made up my mind to enjoy our lives here," Elizabeth said firmly. "And I've been frank with Lucien about … about not wanting any attachments. He invited me to this ball with that understanding. Behind a mask I'll be anonymous. It'll be a relief to simply enjoy dancing and laughing and talking without being smothered by the attention my notoriety always brings."

Tess sighed. "I don't blame you for that, but it bothers me how Lucien responds whenever Jon's name comes up."

Elizabeth dropped her gaze, the acrimonious scene she had witnessed between Caledonne and Lucien from her window the night of their arrival at Château de Broussard suddenly convicting her. She had never confided it to Tess, feeling that to do so would be to violate the two men's privacy.

"I've noticed it too," she admitted reluctantly. "He begins as though he's defending him, but then he twists what he's saying so that Jonathan's actions appear dishonorable."

Tess drew her forward along the path. "And then there's the tension between him and Alexandre, particularly when the subject of Frédéric's death arises."

Elizabeth chewed her lip. "I can't help thinking that there's more to it than simply Lucien's grief for his brother."

"I've been tempted to question Alexandre, but I hesitate to intrude on his relationship with his son. Most of the time they seem to be quiet cordial."

"And Lucien couldn't be kinder or more attentive to all of us."

"To you most of all. And overly protective in my view."

Elizabeth shrugged. "Considering my situation and the fact that his family has offered us their protection, that seems only natural, doesn't it? Besides, he and Jonathan are cousins."

"Men will vie with one another for control—and conquest—even when they're family."

Elizabeth frowned. "I've never seen Jonathan act in such a way."

"Wielding authority is as natural to him as breathing," Tess pointed out. "That kind of man has no need to prove himself, and consequently he arouses insecurities in those who feel their own lack. To them he's a rival, one they must put in his place to prove their own quality. Especially if it involves a woman."

She hesitated before adding thoughtfully, "It isn't that I dislike Lucien. I see much to admire in him, but I keep wondering what his motives are. Whatever his relationship with Jon really is, beware that he doesn't make you part of his game."

"Aren't you being a bit harsh, Aunt Tess? As things stand between me and Jonathan, it's unlikely to ever come to that," Elizabeth said dismissively.

"Perhaps. But you'd do well to be on your guard."

Just then Lucien appeared around a corner behind Tess and strode toward them. Evidently noting the change in Elizabeth's expression, Tess moderated her own as she turned.

"Here you are!" Elizabeth said gaily.

He came to her side and bent over her hand. Straightening, he tucked it into the crook of his arm and offered the other to Tess, who placed her hand on it with a smile.

Directing a warm look from her to Elizabeth, he exclaimed, "What *bonne chance* to have the company of the two most beautiful ladies in Paris! Forgive me for being tardy. My business took longer than I intended."

He led their party back to the street, the guards unobtrusively trailing to each side and behind. "Cécile and *les petit mademoiselles* are already waiting for us at that little café I told you about."

Pretending she hadn't a care in the world, Elizabeth pulled him and Tess to a faster pace. "Let's hurry then," she said, laughing. "All this shopping leaves me ravenous!"

AFTER THE EVENING MEAL Tess drew Elizabeth outside to walk with her in the château's gardens. As they wandered along the *allées,* with the light slowly fading in the west and a cooling breeze stirring the trees, she fixed Elizabeth in a keen look.

"Beth, regardless of your protestations, I know you're hurting—"

"Actually I'm doing quite well," Elizabeth said abruptly, avoiding her gaze.

For a long moment Tess said nothing, then, slowly, "Have you given up on Jon altogether then?"

"There's been no communication from him since he left. It's been six months, Aunt Tess!"

"He disappeared before, and for more than a year we didn't know whether he was alive or dead."

"He was captured. He wasn't given a choice. This time he left me of his own volition, and I can't blame him after what Mama and Papa said to him."

"In the letter he left you he said he'd always love you."

"And I'll always love him," Elizabeth returned with a steadiness she didn't feel. "But he also said it was better for me if he went away. What if that's true for him? I've wondered ever since he came back from the Shawnee whether I only made things worse by finding him and persuading him to return."

"He did so willingly."

"Because of me, not because he wanted to leave them. He's been torn between these two worlds ever since. Perhaps it's time for me to let him go."

Tess regarded her sadly. "All I'm saying is that you had the same struggles then, but you didn't give up hope. And you shouldn't now."

"Am I supposed to wait forever? You told me back then that I have a life to live and I must live it. You said the pain will lessen in time, and it will. It has to," she concluded, fighting to keep the desolation out of her voice.

"It's possible he's written to you and the letter went astray, you know. We've only received one letter from your parents, and they wrote that they hadn't received any of ours, though we've written every week. Why, he might not even know we're in France."

"Surely Louis has found him by now." Elizabeth turned away, throat so tight she could hardly speak. "Or perhaps he's been captured, even executed. We may never learn his fate."

Swinging to face her aunt, she burst out, "I can't live paralyzed like this! I'm still young, but I won't be forever. I want to enjoy all France has to offer while we're here—all life has to offer! I want to put aside despair, have some fun. I want—"

She broke off abruptly. Pressing her fist hard to her lips, she looked away, her vision too blurred to see clearly.

"If I had any hope that he'd ever return, things would be different." She lifted her chin and concluded firmly, "But I don't. And I must find a way forward."

"What's past is past, and by bringing you here the Lord is guiding you to a new course. Why, look at all the good you're already doing with the servants."

"I am beginning to think this is the path I'm to follow now," Elizabeth said wistfully.

Tess enfolded her in her arms. "Time will tell. But one thing I know is that you weren't made to be an ordinary woman living an ordinary life. And I'm confident that whether Jon ever returns or not, God will fulfill his promises to you."

"I believe it here—" Elizabeth touched her head, then laid her hand over her heart "—but here the sorrow and longing never lessens despite my brave denials."

Tess chuckled ruefully. "I've much experience with that very thing."

Elizabeth drew her closer. "I can't imagine the heartache you suffered for so many years after your dear love's death until grief finally gave way to resignation. I imagine you felt then as I do now that it'll never happen and your heart will always bleed."

"I did. But through that pain I learned that the most sorrowful times of our lives will lead to something better and purer and higher if we only allow the Lord to work all things for our good. You know, there's a reason for this period of separation," she continued, regarding Elizabeth earnestly. "It may be that God meant to use Jon for a greater purpose, for something only he could do, something he was made to do, and he's leading him surely in it just as he's leading you. Whatever the case, if he brings you back together again, then all doubt and fear will finally be removed."

Later that evening after Jemma had prepared her for bed and withdrawn, Elizabeth knelt at the window as had become her habit each night. But as she looked out across the luxuriant, gardens wrapped in shadow below, the startling impression of the Garden of Eden came to her.

It was followed by the troubling thought that a serpent might lie therein as well.

Clearly Lucien had inherited the charm of the Bettárs as thoroughly as had Carleton. And like him Lucien employed it far too effectively whenever it pleased him.

She was still unsure what she felt toward him. Gratitude for his kindness in watching over her, certainly. Her fame had already made her the object of more subtle and frank attempts at seduction than she could number. But never in Lucien's presence. Whenever the matter concerned her he was like a guard dog. No one dared presume on her when she was in his company.

Their frequent long, private conversations proved him to be intelligent and insightful, delightfully witty, and good-humored. And increasingly she felt herself drawn to his company.

Still, the acrimonious confrontation between him and his father that she had accidentally overheard from this very window weighed on her mind, causing her to question whether it might have been wise to confide it to her aunt after all. For she had caught snatches of another angry encounter the previous week just before Lucien took her to the races at the Bois de Boulogne to watch Artois' stable of horses run.

It was an outing both Tess and Caledonne had opposed as too dangerous. She had laughingly dismissed their concerns, however, desperate for escape, if only for a little while, from restrictions that were coming to feel more like a cage than protection. And a few days later she had accompanied him again.

But the morning of that first time, while quietly walking through the passageway from the servants' quarters, she heard Caledonne and Lucien speaking in low tones as they ascended the stairs ahead of her.

"At least you could have the decency to restrain yourself where she's concerned until we learn if he . . . "

Caledonne's voice faded as they reached the upper landing, and she had been unable to make out the rest of what he said. But although Lucien's response had also been indecipherable, his tone was heated, Caledonne's answer sharp. Then they moved out of her hearing altogether, leaving her with the uncomfortable certainty that she was the subject of their dispute.

And Carleton. For it was increasingly apparent that he was the continuing point of contention between the two men.

Chapter Twenty-four

T HE SUN STOOD HIGH overhead in a cloudless sky when Carleton's party rode into the Valley Forge encampment on Wednesday, June 17, liberally coated with the sweat and dust of the journey.

A sweltering, humid heat had hung over the land for days, disturbed only by an occasional vagrant, desultory breeze. Like the rest of the warriors, both Carleton and Andrews endured the heat garbed only in breech-cloth, leggings, and moccasins, with hair roached and feathered, silver armlets encircling both arms, and sheathed knives hanging around their necks by rawhide thongs. Their bare torsos were burnt to bronze, their hair bleached almost white by the sun, while their warriors' swarthy skin had darkened almost to black. Even Carleton's Marines and Rangers had stuffed wool uniform coats and waistcoats into their knapsacks after only a couple of days on the trail and by now had also doffed their shirts.

Carleton noted the difference between the Marines' current easy relations with the warriors and the first few days after leaving Grey Cloud's Town. At first the Marines had kept their weapons close to hand and shifted uneasy, sidelong looks between their native companions, the shadowed forest through which their path wound, and the Indian parties they frequently encountered.

At thought of how disconcerting it must be to see their commander armed, painted, and garbed in the regalia of a Shawnee war chief, with his second in command similarly turned out, he suppressed a grin. They must wonder where their greatest danger lay, he reflected.

Privately he blessed Teissèdre for not only bringing the Marines with him from Boston, but also the detachment of his black Rangers, with difficulty pried away from their reluctant colonel. In spite of the strangeness of their present situation, both followed orders without question or protest. Added to his clan's warriors, a substantial number of Piqua and Maquachake loyal to Cornstalk and Nonhelema, plus a contingent of warriors from other tribes and Teissèdre's native scouts, they constituted a formidable force.

He had armed the entire company to the teeth for the attacks he knew would come. And whenever his scouts reported the approach of a hostile party of Indian warriors mixed with *Canadien* militia or an ambush waiting ahead of them, he immediately sent the Marines forward with a mixed detachment of warriors and Rangers under Spotted Pony to drive them off. More than one firefight had ensued, but each time they beat the enemy back handily, inflicting casualties while suffering none.

To Andrews' and Blue Sky's unconcealed happiness, Carleton allowed their clan's warriors to bring their families if they chose, judging it to be safer than leaving them with the rest of the townspeople amid the British-allied factions on the Mad River. He had armed the women, too, and they made good use of their weapons, while mothers with infants and young children, like Blue Sky and Mary Douglas, rode in the warriors' midst directly behind him and Andrews.

Clearly their attackers had not reckoned with a force the size he commanded. Persistent in spite of being repeatedly chastened, they had followed all the way to the vicinity of the Beaver River just west of Fort Pitt, looking for an opportunity he refused to give them. At last free of harassers, he took great satisfaction in imagining the unhappy report they were carrying back to Detroit.

What he did not take satisfaction in was news of the attack on Fort Randolph that runners had brought while he and his warriors prepared for the journey. He had spent much of the three weeks following his return from Chillicothe in calling on neighboring tribes throughout the region, accompanied by an imposingly accoutered retinue. His party had traveled as far as the *Myaamiaki,* the Miami tribe, on the *Waapaahšiiki,* the Wabash River, to spread Washington's appeal, although with little success, as he had expected. Already fighting an excess of frustration and impatience only held in check by a raveled thread, he had not been gladdened to learn that Dunquat had carried out his planned attack. Or its result.

Ten days after the council at Chillicothe, a mixed force of between 200 and 300 Wyandot, Mingo, and Shawnee warriors led by the Wyandot's half king had surrounded the fort at Point Pleasant at the confluence of the Kanawha and Ohio rivers, only to discover that Nonhelema had warned the fort's commander. Captain William McKee had been well prepared to fend them off, and after a week-long siege, Dunquat had broken off the attack and turned his attention upriver to Fort Donnally, hoping for better success.

Again Nonhelema outmaneuvered them. More runners had reached Grey Cloud's Town the following day with news that this attack had also been beaten off. Learning of Dunquat's plan, she garbed two militia soldiers as Indians and sent them 160 miles upriver to the fort. Forewarned, the garrison held out until relieved by a force from Lewisburg. The warriors had been so enraged by what they viewed as her perfidy that they entirely destroyed her large herd of cattle in retribution.

All this was far from being Carleton's only concern. It was well nigh all he could do to hold at bay the beguiling thoughts of Elizabeth that wove incessantly through his brain, the swelling desire that urged him to throw over the demands of duty and sail for France without further delay to repair all he had upended between them. Repeatedly he assured himself that the end was in sight, and that he would soon be on his way to her arms.

Teissèdre had been almost as anxious as he for assurance that Caledonne had brought her away to France safely. But during his absence in Ohio Territory, the Frenchman had received no news from his agent at

Boston. Equally unsettling, neither did the runners he sent out from his scouts bring back any news from his extensive web of Indian and French contacts.

When no messengers awaited him at Fort Pitt, Teissèdre had delayed no longer than necessary to replenish his supplies before riding off with his scouts. Something was wrong, he had told Carleton grimly. And he meant to find out what it was and set it to rights.

CARLETON'S RANGERS were encamped inside the main camp's inner works, just beyond the western ford across Valley Creek and within sight of the mansion serving as Washington's headquarters. As his party rode in, the off-duty troops came at a run to jubilantly welcome them back, with colonels Moghrab and Farris at their forefront.

While the riders dismounted, the brigade's chaplain, sturdily built, red-haired Scot, Major James McLeod, pressed through the crowd to clasp Carleton's hand, then Andrews'. Raising his voice to be heard over the exuberant voices of the jostling men, he said, " 'Tis grand to see ye back! The colonels did a superb job o' keepin' us shipshape, but ye've been missed."

Carleton took in the neat rows of tents. "I didn't expect any less," he said approvingly as he returned the colonels' salutes.

Tall, rugged Captain Josiah Hutchinson and sandy-haired Tom Spencer, two of the prisoners rescued from the *Erebus,* who had joined the Rangers, stepped forward. Carleton surrendered his stallion's reins to Stowe and reached to shake their hands. Learning that Hutchinson had been made captain of a mounted troop under Farris's command, while Spencer had joined a dismounted troop at the rank of sergeant, he congratulated both.

Blue Sky hurried to Andrews' side, Leads the Way squirming in her arms and reaching out for him. Chuckling, Andrews turned his mount over to his servant, Corporal Henry Briggs, and claimed the infant.

Mary Douglas hovered nearby, holding her own small son against her shoulder, and looking from one to the other, McLeod crooned, "Ooch, now, what a wealth o' fine, braw lads." He laid his hand gently on Leads the Way's downy head, smiling down at him, before turning to Mary. "And how's wee Jimmy doin'?"

"Growin' like a weed," she answered with a shy laugh.

"And ye, Mary?" McLeod murmured, holding out his hands for the boy, who went happily to him.

Carleton noted the blush that rose to the young widow's cheeks and the light in McLeod's eyes as the two turned aside, their heads bent together. *Absence does indeed make the heart grow fonder,* he thought with amusement, followed by a sharp stab of loneliness.

The colonels directed the new arrivals to the area set aside for them along one side of the brigade's camp. They had hardly begun to move off when one of Washington's aides, handsome young John Laurens, the son of Henry Laurens, president of Congress, galloped up in a cloud of dust. He reined to a halt so abruptly in front of Carleton that he had to take a hasty step back.

Laurens saluted briskly. "Oh, good, sir, you're here—sorry for almost trampling you!" He paused, appearing nonplussed as though for the first time registering their Indian garb, then rushed on, "His Excellency has been waiting anxiously for your return, as you might imagine. He's had me on the lookout for weeks, with standing orders for you and General Andrews to present yourselves to him immediately on your arrival.

"General Clinton has taken command at Philadelphia, with orders to withdraw from the city, and we expect them to move out at any time," he continued breathlessly. "His Excellency is currently holding a council of war, and you and General Andrews are wanted on the instant. Please follow me if you will."

Indicating their Indian dress, Carleton said dryly, "As you can see, we're in some dishabille. Are we allowed time to wash up and change into uniform?"

Laurens squeezed his eyes shut, his expression pained, before meeting Carleton's challenging gaze apologetically. "I'm afraid not." His voice came out in almost a croak, drawing a short laugh from Andrews.

Carleton sighed. At the moment he wanted nothing more than to fol-low several men who were drifting off in the direction of Valley Creek, shedding clothing as they went. But shaking his head in weary resignation, he motioned Red Fox to join them.

When Laurens frowned, he said coldly, "Red Fox is the commander of my warriors and will need to be briefed for any coming action."

Laurens began to answer, appeared to think better of it, then touched his fingers to the brim of his impeccably cocked and trimmed hat in salute. "As you wish, sir. Shall I tell His Excellency you'll wait on him directly?"

"I was just going to suggest that."

With no further ado, Laurens reined his mount around.

"It's good to see that Lauren's exuberance hasn't suffered deflation," Andrews said as he watched him gallop off. After returning his son to Blue Sky and urging her after the women, he added cheerily, "We enjoyed some highly entertaining discussions last fall."

Scowling, Carleton growled, "By what stroke of genius do we always manage to end up in a meeting with His Excellency and his entire staff in Indian dress?"

"There's something about their expressions when we enter the room that I find extremely gratifying. I'm especially glad you insisted on Red Fox attending," Andrews added, grinning at the warrior.

"Do you think we ought to put off our weapons?"

"I think we ought to have tomahawk and scalping knife in hand. Put them on notice."

Carleton gave him a quelling look. "Now, Charles, this is our other life. At least for now. Act like a proper Continental officer if you would."

"As my brother says, 'I do not speak to a Long Knife without a weapon in my hand,'" Red Fox noted, a glint in his eyes.

Carleton stifled a laugh. "Not you too! Let's try not to start a war on our first day back, shall we?"

As they took the reins of their horses back from their servants, Andrews muttered, "You're a fine one to talk, my friend. If anyone will start a war, it's you."

WHEN THEY ARRIVED at Deborah Potts Hughes' tidy stone house, Laurens was pacing outside the parlor that served as Washington's office. He immediately threw open the door. As they stepped inside, every head swiveled, and the gathered generals looked them up and down with raised eyebrows.

"Well, I see our Indians are back," said handsome General Anthony Wayne, peer down his long nose at them. "One wonders if it's as friends."

By main force Carleton wrestled down the impulse to respond that if his warriors had accompanied Wayne at Paoli the previous year, the general's detachment might not have been routed by a British surprise attack while they slept, thus dealing a lamentable blow to the fiery general's reputation. Beside him Red Fox returned Wayne's hostile gaze with an impassive one, but Andrews dropped his hand to his tomahawk, a hot flush rising to his face.

Carleton clamped his hand over his friend's shoulder and squeezed hard. His gaze fixed on Washington, he said peaceably, "We've only just arrived, Your Excellency. We would have washed and changed into uniform if Laurens hadn't insisted that we wait on you immediately."

Washington inclined his head. "I appreciate your coming at once in spite of the inconvenience." No one ventured to speak as he allowed his narrowed gaze to slide from one face to another. "I am glad to see you back with us after the no doubt successful embassy to the western Indians I sent you on. As I am certain all of us are."

Equally certain of it, Carleton bit back an unpolitic response.

"Personally, I consider the services of our Indian allies indispensable to our cause," General Charles Lee pontificated. "I myself, as you may know, was adopted by the Seneca and sired a son by the daughter of one of their notable chieftains."

Carleton resisted the urge to roll his eyes. *Lovely. Yet another of the multitude who've made the same claim. Pity it never seems to keep them from taking every advantage of their supposed kin for their own benefit.*

Lee's unkempt appearance added to a big head with a large nose on his small, withered body reminded Carleton of nothing so much as a scarecrow. He was convinced that Lee's ambition was to supplant Wash-ington as commander in chief. And here he sat unabashedly at their commander's right hand, no doubt again holding his ear, an inauspicious portent if there ever was one!

Formerly a British officer of some repute, Lee had come to America to enlist in the cause of rebellion, only to be captured by the British more than a year earlier due to his own negligence. *A shame he's been exchanged,* Carleton reflected sourly. *He must be devastated after being treated like royalty by the British and hobnobbing with their most important officers and officials.*

He became aware that a portly officer with a plain, stolid face stared at the three of them in apparent astonishment, muttering something in German. The Baron Frederick von Steuben whom Teissèdre had told him about, Carleton surmised. The major general's ornate dress uniform and erect bearing couldn't have offered greater contrast to Lee.

Next to him sat slender, twenty-year-old Major General Gilbert du Motier, le Marquis de Lafayette. "I couldn't agree more," he said earnestly. "My Oneida scouts acted admirably last month during the action at Barren Hill. I'm as proud to have been made a member of their renowned nation as I'm sure General Carleton and General Andrews are to have been adopted by the Shawnee."

Conceding a faint smile, Carleton inclined his head to the young French nobleman in acknowledgement, as did Andrews.

Happily the conversation returned to the looming campaign. The room was too crowded to accommodate more chairs. So for the next hour he leaned back against the wall just inside the door between Andrews and Red Fox, frustration rising while the generals dithered over what to do when the British abandoned Philadelphia. Of the generals present only Pennsylvania General John Cadwalader and Wayne favored attacking the withdrawing force. And although Red Fox listened with his usual stoic inscrutablilty, Carleton could feel Andrews simmering toward the boiling point

"We've only 13,000 effectives currently available," Lee cautioned in the querulous tone that invariably made Carleton long to slap him. "In my estimation, it's best to avoid taking such a risk now that France is coming into the war. We've learned that of their fleets recently put to sea, and it may well be on its way here. Our best course is to wait until it arrives, and then act in concert with the French."

Generals Nathaniel Greene and Henry Knox spoke up in agreement, only to be cut off by Cadwalader. "But Clinton's army is inferior to ours in numbers, and for once we're well supplied for a general engagement!" he exclaimed, waving his arms with a vehemence that endeared him to Carleton. "They've scoured New Jersey until there's nothing left by which they can sustain themselves. The present appears to me to be as good an opportunity to strike a decisive blow as we shall probably ever have during this contest. Even were we to suffer a defeat, it would be no essential disadvantage to us and cannot in the least serve their cause."

"I fully agree. No matter how an attack turns out, it'll appear to the public that we forced the enemy to retreat and succeeded in 'Burgoyning' Clinton, if you will." Wayne's staunch support for an attack did much to improve Carleton's opinion of him.

At last Washington sought his gaze and demanded, "What is your opinion, sir?"

By now there was no doubt in Carleton's mind that his commander was not only keen to confront Clinton on the field of battle, but that his regard for Lee was on the ebb. Casting caution to the wind, he said, "Your Excellency, if we wait for the French to arrive, organize, and act, we'll wait a very long time. Find the best ground possible and attack. Throw everything at Clinton you have. He won't expect such boldness, and in surprise lies victory—or at the very least a draw. As General Cadwalader pointed out, how could that possibly harm our cause? Would our initiative not instead encourage the French and urge them to greater efforts on our behalf?"

A clamor of voices opposed him, but he took satisfaction in the flash of eagerness he read in Washington's gaze.

"Your Excellency, perhaps it might be wise to wait for the British to move, and then follow at a small distance to see what opportunities arise," Brigadier General John Peter Gabriel Muhlenberg suggested.

Washington considered him thoughtfully for a moment, finally nodded. "Excellent suggestion, general." Surveying the gathered officers, he ordered, "Prepare your men for a move, and keep a careful watch on the city. I want to know the instant Clinton marches out. It's a long way to New York, and that should offer any number of possibilities that we might exploit."

When he dismissed the meeting, Carleton and his companions were the first through the parlor door. But before they could escape outside, another of Washington's aides, tall, thirty-three-year-old Tench Tilghman, blocked the path of their retreat. His Excellency wished Carleton to wait upon him immediately to brief him on the results of his mission to the Shawnee, he told him.

Carleton's stomach clenched. But there was nothing for it, and he drew Andrews and Red Fox aside as the other generals pushed past on their way to the outer door, several glowering at the three of them.

"Take a party and scout the roads leading out of Philadelphia," he told Red Fox in the Shawnee tongue. "Keep Golden Elk and me informed of every movement the British make. I want to know when they march out before Washington does."

An eager light came into the warrior's eyes. With a quick nod, he strode after the last of the generals exiting the house, with Andrews fairly treading on his heels.

Chapter Twenty-five

CARLETON SLOUCHED into a chair in front of the writing table as Washington settled into the one behind it.

"The only bright spot in this interminable winter was Mrs. Washington and the other officers' wives." The General shook his head, brow furrowed. "The fortitude they showed in the face of such adversity and their care for the men put us officers to shame."

"I'm impressed with the changes to the camp," Carleton observed, stalling for time.

Washington relaxed into a smile. "All due to Baron von Steuben. I admit I had doubts when Congress sent him along, but he has fully justified their recommendation. He reorganized the camp and personally drilled the men until I am confident that they will be able to stand up to the best troops the British can throw at us. And now that our alliance with France has finally been concluded, I am eager to open the campaign. Time is wasting."

Carleton opened his mouth to expand on the theme, but Washington cut him off. "And how, pray tell, was your winter?"

"Long. And cold," Carleton temporized.

"Thank God you are finally here. I had all but given up hope of your return."

"To be frank," Carleton said slowly, "I might not have if I hadn't been sent by my people's council."

Washington fixed him in a hard look. "You presented my message to all their headmen?"

"I did." Carefully avoiding mention of how near he had come to being captured by the British, Carleton described the negotiations he had undertaken.

"Despite my best arguments—and believe me, I used every persuasion I could think of—most of the Shawnee and the other tribes in the area have already allied with the British. That's an accomplished fact that will not be changed. Along with Black Hawk's clan, those from the Maquachake and other divisions who supported Cornstalk will either fight with us or remain neutral. I managed to assemble a substantial force that includes some warriors from the surrounding tribes along with the Marines I'd left at Boston. That was the best I could do."

Washington expelled a breath and slumped back in his chair, rubbing his jaw.

Feeling his way, Carleton continued, "The tribal council is sending me to France to negotiate with the king for his favor—"

"What?" Color rushing into his face, Washington sprang to his feet, Carleton hastily rising with him. The General's chair teetered backward, only saved from crashing to the floor by his quick grasp.

"I've waited patiently all this time for you to decide to return to your duties and—"

"As I recall, you delegated me to go—"

"It took you long enough to accomplish your mission!"

"You thought I'd just ride in after more than a year's absence, read your letter to them, and they'd happily fall in line to do your bidding?"

"I thought nothing of the sort," Washington snapped. "Nor did I expect you to delay your return until we're on the very point of battle only to tell me that you mean to abandon your duty for some fool's errand."

"Sir, I'll see through whatever action arises when the British withdraw from Philadelphia," Carleton offered, conscious that too much lay at stake for him to lose his temper. "But then I must go—"

"I do not give you leave for such a mission, sir," Washington said, biting off each word crisply.

Carleton stiffened. "Pardon, Your Excellency, but it's not a matter for you to decide. I serve as an officer of this army because you're my friend. I may even act as your emissary to my people because of that friendship. But the Shawnee are a nation worthy of respect who fight for their freedom just as you Americans fight for yours."

"And you mean to negotiate with Louis the Sixteenth to take their part when you have just acknowledged that they are our enemies!"

"I think you have that reversed."

"Jon, we are friends, and you are as American as I am!" Washington exploded.

Again Carleton wrestled his temper into submission. He'd said everything possible on the subject too many times and saw no reason to repeat it. All he wanted was to go to Elizabeth, claim her for his own forever, and be done with the rest.

But he knew that he would never be done with it.

Inclining his head, he said softly, "I am also Shawnee, and they're my first concern. In truth I've little hope the king will even give me an audience, but I'll do all I can for their sakes. There's nothing you can do to stop me. Except to arrest me."

"If that is your attitude, then friendship be cursed! I am perfectly willing to cashier you, if not court martial you for dereliction of duty, if you leave this camp without my leave." Shoving his fingers through his hair, Washington paced across the room and back, the perfect picture of outrage.

"As you wish, Your Excellency," Carleton returned icily. "You've threatened me with this often enough. If you'll excuse me, I'll go inform my Rangers and warriors that they're released to go home."

Washington glared at him for a long moment, finally turned away to stare out the window behind him. "Both of us know very well that if I try to stop you, I will be left in worse case than if I simply let you go. So we stand at checkmate."

"Sir, this is not the only reason for my going to France," Carleton said, striving for a conciliatory tone. "I've no choice if my ships, and thus my brigade, are to survive."

He related Teissèdre's report concerning the war Admiral Howe was waging on his privateers and merchantmen. His privateer fleet had been exceedingly effective in the naval war, while the small American navy was having little effect, he reminded Washington. His merchantmen, which transported war materiel from France for the army as well as goods that provided him an income, were also in danger of being destroyed.

"I'm bleeding men, ships, and money, sir. Without the revenue my privateers and merchantmen bring in, I'll be unable to maintain my brigade. It's urgent that I consult with my captains and my uncle on this matter and remedy the situation as quickly as possible."

Returning to his chair, Washington wearily scrubbed his hand over his face. "I know too well that our cause desperately needs the supplies and funds your ships bring in," he conceded. "And I also cannot do without your brigade. Even should they choose to remain with the army were you to leave it—which I have no illusions of—I could not afford to maintain them. It appears that, as usual, you have left me no choice."

Carleton resumed his seat. "Not I, Your Excellency. Circumstances."

Washington narrowed his eyes. "General Andrews will take full command of your Rangers, of course."

Carleton inclined his head. "I think you've had occasion to learn how capable he is as well as colonels Moghrab and Farris. Also Spotted Pony, who'll command the warriors since Red Fox accompanies me to France."

Washington's eyebrows rose. "I've heard Mr. Franklin is cutting a wide swath among the French with his rustic ways, so perhaps adding an Indian in war paint to our delegation will increase the effect."

Convicted that his tongue had gotten him into trouble more times than he cared to think about, Carleton wrestled temptation into submission. Settling on a peaceable response, he replied, "The army won't suffer in my absence, and I'll return as soon as I've everything in hand."

"While in France, you might as well call on our commissioners. Only the Almighty knows what machinations they're carrying on at the behest of one or another of Congress's factions. It would be useful for me to know since everything they do affects the army."

Carleton was highly tempted to retort that it would be easier and save everyone time to simply ask Caledonne for the details, but managed to refrain.

"Doubtless the French court is awash in its own intrigues, not to mention being overrun by British spies," Washington continued, oblivious. "Caledonne will certainly be a useful connection for you in that regard and perhaps will be able to persuade Vergennes to finally send us troops and a fleet or two."

Carleton gave him a bland smile. "So I'm to spy on our commissioners, the French court, and the British spies, and persuade my uncle to pressure Vergennes to send us an army and a navy."

"If I allow you to go on this wild goose chase, I expect you to make yourself useful to me," Washington growled. "There is much at stake, Jon, and we must all pay a price if we are to succeed in our aims."

Carleton regarded his commander for a long moment, contemplating what the war had already cost him personally and the price he was likely still to pay before all was done. *But my people and the other tribes will pay the highest price,* he thought bitterly. *And we'll lose everything in the end.*

He rose and gave a perfunctory bow. "I'll do everything possible to make myself useful to you, Your Excellency."

"I have every confidence you will. But until the current campaign is over, I cannot release you to attend to this matter, especially considering how long you are likely to be gone."

"If I'm delayed too long, sir, the winter storms will make the voyage practically impossible until the spring!"

Washington raised his hand to silence him. "You'll leave when I release you and not a moment before." He added a curt dismissal.

For a moment Carleton stood frozen, fury burning through him. As desperately as he wanted to go to Elizabeth, however, the reality bore heavily on him that to defy his commander now would be to cast aside the course he had pleaded with his clan and the tribal council to follow and to tacitly justify their alliance with the British. At last, recognizing the wisdom of not sending any more bridges up in smoke, he gave a brisk salute, turned on his heel, and strode out the door.

The sense that he groped through the dark toward a destination he did not know and over which he held no control overwhelmed him. But the Great Father did know and was in control of even this, he reminded himself bleakly.

He had sworn that he would trust with an undivided heart. And he determined to keep that promise even if it stretched him to the very core.

ON THE WAY BACK to camp, Carleton detoured to the Grand Parade Ground. He watched as several companies performed their drills with a speed and crispness almost equal to that of British troops, encouragement sorely needed after the strained meetings of the past two hours.

When he reached the brigade's camp he saw that his marquee had been set up at its center and all his gear and furnishings piled inside, with Stowe and Sweetgrass making speedy work of organizing the mass. Next to it, lounging with Isaiah and Farris in camp chairs under the overhang of his own marquee, Andrews beckoned him to join them.

"Well, Teissèdre's prediction that I'd be able to soothe His Excellency's ruffled feathers turned out to be extraordinarily prescient," Carleton drawled, dropping onto the vacant chair Andrews indicated.

The sarcasm in his tone wasn't lost on his companions. "I take it he wasn't overjoyed," Andrews noted wryly.

"That would be an understatement."

The sound of pounding hooves brought them around to see Teissèdre riding into the camp. He whipped his horse to where they sat, drew the

animal to a sliding halt, and leaped from the saddle with an agility belied
by his age and portly figure.

Dread clenching his chest, Carleton sprang to his feet with the others
following. "Surely you haven't been to Boston and back already, Louis."

Teissèdre pulled off his hat. After mopping the sweat and dust from
his face with a handkerchief, he explained grimly that while on the road
he had met a messenger from his agent in Boston who had warned him of
a breach of his network. A couple of hostile agents had been discovered
waylaying communications meant for him, which they redirected to their
own contacts in addition to other mischief. They had been quietly dispatched, and their contacts were being sought.

"What else has gone wrong?" Carleton asked, not reassured by the
Frenchman's expression.

"The messenger brought news from our agents in the British court
that I ought to have received weeks ago." Tersely Teissèdre related Lord
North's ultimatum to the French government that they hand Elizabeth
over. And the reward offered to anyone who would produce her.

Mind reeling, Carleton stared at him, feeling as though he had taken a
vicious punch in the gut. Andrews swore violently, and the two colonels
exchanged appalled glances.

"You've heard from le comte?" Carleton demanded when he could
speak.

Teissèdre shook his head. "It appears that network also has been
breached."

Carleton added his curses to Andrews'. "Surely your government will
never agree to such a demand, much less from a nation with whom they
are at war."

Teissèdre dismissed the question impatiently. "Unfortunately, however, there are those in high places with access and ability who are also
in desperate need of cash and for whom a reward of this magnitude will
be extremely difficult to resist." He clasped Carleton's arm in a painful
grip. "At the moment, however, there's an even more pressing concern."

He went on to describe the rewards also offered for Carleton and Andrews.

It took a long moment for Carleton to regain control of his emotions as he strode up and down in front of the marquee. At length, meeting Andrews' gaze with a hard one, he said, "I wonder if that has anything to do with de Quindre's showing up at Chillicothe. He did refer to the rewards."

"I assumed he referred to the ones we knew about." Andrews rubbed the back of his neck. "The *Canadiens* were devilishly persistent following us back here. Perhaps Governor Hamilton received advance warning so he could act before we learned of it."

Teissèdre looked from one to the other. "Washington knows nothing of this?" When Carleton shook his head, he narrowed his eyes. "How did your interview with him go regarding the matter of your leaving for France?"

Carleton wasted few words in describing the confrontation, then drawled, "Alas, the feathers that were ruffled remain so, along with a few more besides."

"He refuses to release you until the campaign is done?"

"And only the Almighty knows when that'll be, Charles. But I'm left no choice if I'm to be of any use to our people. All I can do for now is to pray that my uncle and le marquis can keep Beth safe," he added, failing in the effort to keep his tone and look steady.

"You know their abilities," Teissèdre reminded him. "And once le comte returns to sea, he and le marquis have the means and determination to protect her even if they must secure her at Versailles. Lucien also seemed more than willing to do whatever necessary—"

Carleton stared at him in disbelief. "He accompanied you to Boston?"

The Frenchman held up his hand to forestall his protests. "Your uncle brought him along because there's no one more skilled with pistol and rapier—as you know. He's quite capable of taking care of her."

"I'm sure he is," Carleton snapped. "And he's a good part of the reason I didn't want her taken to Passy."

"Le comte impressed on him most adamantly that she's affianced to you—"

"And when has such an obstacle ever stopped him before? It only makes the game more interesting and his determination more fixed."

"He's changed for the better since you last saw him. At the moment you've only to concern yourself for your own safety," Teissèdre insisted.

That was the least of Carleton's concerns, however. Not only would Elizabeth be worried about her safety, when she had believed herself out of British reach, but now his as well. Dismay filled him at the thought of the anguish she must suffer with no way of learning whether he had been captured or was even alive. But the thought that, if he stayed true to form, Lucien would certainly take advantage of her vulnerability caused his stomach to roil.

Teissèdre's voice brought him back to the present. "By the by, did you happen to mention that she's in France?"

Shaking off his anxious thoughts, Carleton narrowed his eyes. "The subject didn't arise."

Teissèdre frowned, clearly taking his point. "He'll need to know the details of Lord North's warrant now before the news reaches him through other channels. I'll go inform him—"

As he started to turn away, Carleton grasped him by the arm. "Let it lie."

"He has to know what danger you're in, at least," Andrews protested.

"He already knows there's a high price on both our heads, Charles. This changes nothing."

Isaiah and Farris joined their vehement objections to Andrews'. Finally Teissèdre exclaimed, "When your commander learns of this development and that you concealed it from him—which he inevitably will—he'll be furious."

"He already is. What difference will little more fury make?"

Teissèdre transferred his gaze to Andrews. "What of your wife? Should she not know of the danger to you and her adopted sister?"

Andrews opened his mouth to speak, then gulped. With a guilty sidelong glance at Carleton, he said gruffly, "There's nothing any of us can do about it. It would only upset her needlessly."

Carleton rounded on the colonels and in a steely voice said, "If either of you breathes a word of this to anyone, I'll court martial you for insubordination."

Isaiah raised his hands in a peaceable gesture, palms out. "You be the commander, sir. Though I think it be a fool thing to do."

Farris echoed the sentiment forcefully but added his reluctant agreement.

The Frenchman lifted his arms to the heavens. *"Mère de Dieu,* I've done my duty! What more can I do?" Fixing Carleton in an outraged gaze, he sputtered, "You're a stubborn man!"

"That comes as a surprise?"

"Bah!"

As Teissèdre climbed into the saddle, Carleton caught his horse's bridle. "Don't leave before I have a chance to write a letter to my lady. I'll need you to make sure it reaches her."

Teissèdre drew in a slow breath, let it out, forced a smile. Sketching a half bow from the saddle, mouth twitching, he said, *"Serviteur, mon Général,"* and rode off into the camp.

Chapter Twenty-six

S HE FELT AS THOUGH she had nothing on.

In the lack of stays, panniers, and petticoats and wearing only a sleeveless, tissue-thin silk shift and gown, with delicately wrought Roman-style sandals of silvery leather cradling her bare feet, she hardly did.

"You make the most exquisite Artemis I've ever encountered," Adrian-Louis Pennet, chavalier de Veillars, breathed in her ear.

"Diana. Roman, not Greek," she corrected him smilingly.

The chevalier laughed. "What matters one small detail after all?"

He was one of the small number attending the ball whose only disguise was the *de rigueur* domino mask and cloak, and she had quickly recognized him. Tall and well muscled, he was handsome in a decadent, corrupt sort of way that on closer acquaintance repelled her.

She knew little about him other than that he and Artois were acquainted. The prince had casually introduced them the previous week at the Bois de Boulogne while she and Lucien viewed his horses and chatted with the jockeys before the races. Veillars's manner had been aloof then, but she'd felt unaccountably unsettled every time his gaze rested on her. As it had this evening with disconcerting frequency.

He'd been even more annoyingly persistent in paying addresses to her than the rest of the fervent admirers who had hovered around her all evening

like a cloud of gnats. She was beginning to look for a means of permanently
discouraging all of them, and especially .

"Have you no regard for historical accuracy?" she drawled, fixing him
in a languidly dismissive look.

His hot gaze swept her from heat to toe. "Both, after all, are the goddess of the hunt, able to turn darkness into light. As you do so magnificently, mademoiselle."

She had the uncomfortable impression that he had guessed who she
was in spite of her domino disguise. The mask of golden silk embroidered
with Roman designs covered the upper half of her face, while the voluminous floor-length cloak draped over her shoulders. Constructed of lustrous
black silk embroidered with tiny golden bows and arrows, the latter swung
open with every movement to serve as the perfect backdrop for the bril-
liance of the costume beneath.

The modified ensemble Bertin had promised was not the one the
marchand had delivered, saving for the Roman stola's décolletage and length
and the loose drapery of the silver *lustrine*. Indeed the gown covered her.
But with only a thin silk chemise beneath, the fabric clung to the contours
of her body with every movement.

Two braided golden cords had been added. Held in place by the wide
golden sash cinching her waist, they passed over opposite shoulders, criss-
crossing the bodice in back and front. As far as she could determine, they
served no purpose other than to emphasize her bosom.

In another change, the skirt was composed of irregular, fluttering layers that alternated between the silvery silk that glimmered gold with every
movement and a golden *lustrine* shimmering to silver to give an effect of
constant motion. The gown fell to her feet, to be sure, but the fabric was
draped so that one side angled upward to reveal her calves, wrapped to the
knees with the thin thongs that secured her sandals.

By the time the gown had arrived early that hot Saturday afternoon,
June 20—more than a week later than promised—there was no time to
devise a substitution. And as Lucien was to meet her at the Palais, where he

had gone to dress in Chartres's apartments so they would not arrive together, she could not refuse to go. Or so she assured herself, while temptation whispered beguilingly in her ear.

Jemma, who was developing a genius for dressing hair, had woven Elizabeth's plaited tresses into a crown on the top of her head, studding it with fresh flowers. At the front she had pinned the small diamond-encrusted crescent moon, the goddess's symbol, that had accompanied the gown.

Taking in her reflection, wide-eyed, in the long mirror in her room, Elizabeth had to acknowledge that the effect was truly spectacular. At the same time she wondered guiltily how much the ensemble had set back Caledonne's account. And what reaction it would evoke.

He, Aunt Tess, and the Martieu-Broussards had appeared more shocked than pleased when she descended the stairs to the *salle,* but she had given them no time to object. Thanking Caledonne profusely, and with a quick kiss for each of them, she had run off to the waiting coach, escorted by her guards, all garbed in costumes and dominos to blend seamlessly into the crowd of revelers.

Veillars' fervent voice broke into her guilty reflections. "*Ma chère,* I must confess that I'm thoroughly besotted with you."

"Alas, I can't say I share your feelings," she countered with feigned regret and real boredom. Wishing mightily that he would go away, she stepped aside, widening the space between them.

The Palais Royal, with its colonnaded front and triangular gables adorned with ornate friezes, lay across the rue Saint-Honoré from the Tuileries and Louvre palaces. The imposing building was the main residence of the house of Orleans, where Chartres and his duchesse, Louise Marie Adélaïde de Bourbon, lived with their four young children in the splendor their immense fortune allowed. On descending from her coach, Elizabeth had been swept through the spacious entry court along with the arriving throngs, her guards invisible as they melted into the crowd.

By then second thoughts had begun to drain away her excited anticipation. There had been no time to ponder her doubts about the wisdom
of attending the event, however. Or to escape.

There was no denying that she had made an impression the moment
she set her sandaled foot in the magnificent ballroom. Her dance card filled
up at a speed that daunted her as much as the bold gazes that took her in
from head to foot. Gavottes, minuets, and polonaises followed one after
the other, played delightfully by members of the Académie Royale de
Musique housed in the Palais's beautiful Théâtre.

She had little time to enjoy the music, however. She had not sat down
since arriving except for the midnight dinner. And immediately afterward
she had been swept away by importunate suitors as contra dances began
to succeed the more formal ones. She calculated that it had to be at least
three in the morning by now.

A plump, rumpled Bacchus draped with leafy grape clusters and little
else interrupted Veillars' gushing flattery. Sweeping her an elaborate bow,
he pleaded for the dance just then starting. She regally extended her hand,
grateful for escape from the chevalier in spite of her rescuer's debauched
appearance.

However do I manage to get myself into such predicaments? she chastised herself silently. *Will I never learn?* Vexed, she allowed him to lead her tri-
umphantly into the line of dancers, though she wanted nothing more than
to flee.

The ball's promise of great fun had turned out to be quite the opposite. She had never seen such outrageous displays as those that surrounded
her on every side. Chartres and his beautiful and fashionable duchesse
were brilliantly but comparatively modestly dressed as Charlemagne and
his queen Hildegard, but they, along with very few others, were the exception. Disgusted, Elizabeth hoped never to see such sights again.

While gracefully navigating the steps of the dance she forced an occasional smile at her partner, but more often threw a discreet glance across the
crowd, seeking Lucien. Reassuringly, one or another of her guards who

filled the ranks of the disguised dancers regularly passed nearby. But so far, as they had agreed, he had kept his distance. He had only partnered with her twice and otherwise occupied himself with one or more of the scantily clad ladies in attendance.

Everywhere she turned all that night she heard whispered speculations as to her identity. One thing her costume accomplished was that no one had yet ventured to propose her name. Her reputation for dressing in what the French considered simple, republican attire was widely known, as well as that she went nowhere without Lucien and a flock of guards. And she was confident that none of them could be identified.

Also to that end, Lucien's costume bore no relation to hers. His, thankfully unseen by his family, was mouth dropping, so shockingly scandalous that she knew Bertin must have been the designer. Women young and old flocked around him as avidly as the men were drawn to her.

Garbed as an Egyptian pharaoh, he wore a belted and pleated kilt of the finest—and all but transparent—blue, red, and gold linen covering his loins, his waist cinched with a multi-colored sash, while his muscular torso, arms, and legs were bare and gleaming . . . with oil? she wondered, trying, but failing to avert her gaze. A stunning, wide, jeweled collar lay around his bare neck and blue and gold armlets encircled his arms and wrists.

The royal pleated, blue-and white striped head cloth with a rearing cobra at the center of the forehead was bound tightly around his hair, its lappets resting on his shoulders. From it hung a blue false beard that was secured beneath his chin. Leather sandals, the crook and flail of the god Osiris, henna-painted hands, lips reddened with ochre, kohl-rimmed eyes, and startlingly green malachite eye shadow completed a look so decadent she felt guilty for staring but found it hard look away.

The costume of a willowy young lady costumed as Nefertiti was as much the match to his as though it had been planned. Elizabeth had to wonder whether it was. She certainly was not shy about draping herself lasciviously on Lucien's arm, nor did he appear to object. Quite the opposite.

Even with doors and windows thrown wide to admit the sultry night air, the chamber had been stifling since her arrival. Now with the heat rising from perspiring revelers and musicians added to that radiating from the myriad candles in the chandeliers, the late hour, and the dances' exertions, she was beginning to feel lightheaded. At last the set ended, and before anyone could claim her for the next, she navigated her partner to the edge of the dance floor.

She directed a quick glance at the nearest of her guards, catching his eye. Then she laughingly pleaded an arranged tryst and slipped through a nearby door into a dimly lighted passageway, leaving her Baccus staring after her, mouth open in disappointment.

SHE FLED DOWN the passage to a door at its end and a short flight of stairs, her cloak gathered around her, its pointed bahoo hood pulled over her head in spite of the night's heat. Soft giggles and whispers reached her from clandestine meetings in the shadowed alcoves along one side, but she ignored them. All she wanted was fresh air, quiet, and concealment to ease her throbbing head and steady her nerves.

She had some acquaintance with the palace from attending the Opera and visiting the gallery that displayed the hundreds of paintings in the Orléans' collection. After navigating through several passages and antechambers, she found her way outside into the public gardens at the sprawling building's rear, confident that her guards must be following.

She pushed off her hood and threw back her cloak. Even though the air remained warm and heavy, the feel of the light breeze moving across her bare skin offered relief after the oppressive heat inside.

For some minutes she wandered along the *allées* between the elaborately designed parterres. All across the gardens tiny points of candlelight twinkled from the sculpted topiaries, and paper lanterns swaying overhead in the trees cast their radiance across the ground. Darkly shadowed forms moved here and there, met, then hurried away arm in arm. But none came near her, leaving her alone with her angry self-recriminations.

The contrast between her present surroundings and the simple, rustic lives of the peasants she ministered to at the estate came into sharp focus as she paced. They struggled daily just to live. But judging from what she had seen thus far, the majority of the nobles and wealthy upper classes devoted their lives to appearance and frivolity, pursuing the pleasures of the theater, concerts, public spectacles, and fashion to the exclusion of concern for their fellow man Apparently, in their estimation, one's splendor was the measure of one's worth. She wondered how many, besides Caledonne, the Martieu-Broussards, and a few others, ever did any productive work.

It was so easy to be seduced by that careless life. Yet the peasants' earthy labors, plain dress, hearty fare, and quiet faith seemed to her much sweeter and more satisfying than the lavish display of sensual indulgence evident all around her that night. The realization that she had chosen to play a part in such an affair pained her exceedingly.

Oh, if Mama and Papa were to see me now! She felt sick at the thought.

But one even worse assailed her: What would Carleton's opinion be if he saw her displaying her body so immodestly?

She cringed, the painful wound his absence had left in her breast aching like a raw gash. Angrily she thrust the accusing question away, her wounded heart unable to bear the thought of his disappointment in her.

He was not here. Had he not left her, she'd not be here either. If anyone was to blame, it was he.

It was a lie, and she knew it. Only she was to blame for the predicament she found herself in. As happened far too often.

And now the worst question of all: How did her Lord and Savior view yet another repetion of her reckless willfulness? She knew better than this! Surely by now she should have learned obedience.

Earnestly she prayed, *Oh, forgive me, Lord! I repent with all my heart. Help me never to act so foolishly again. Help me ever only to glorify you in all I do and think and say!*

She drew in a deep breath, at once feeling the burden lift from her shoulders. She was made of weak and sinful flesh, after all, but her Lord had paid the price for her failures and offered renewal each new day. Through his grace today she would do better, and each morrow thereafter.

She would find Lucien, she decided, relief sweeping through her. By wrapping her cloak around her, she could slip unobtrusively along the edge of the crowd, somehow capture his attention and beckon him to follow her outside. She felt certain he would take her home at once.

Distracted, she did not hear the muted crunch of footsteps approaching until a purring voice behind her caused her to start and swing around in alarm.

"*A votre plaisir, mademoiselle*." Veillars swept her an elaborate bow. "I wondered where you'd disappeared to, my Diana."

Annoyed no end, she drew herself stiffly up. "Sadly, monsieur, I'm not *your* Diana, and your presence does not please me. I came out here to find solitude."

He gave a light laugh. "I adore women of spirit! Ah, my sweet, I'm ravished by your beauty. Come close and I'll tell you a secret."

He was already standing far too close, and she stepped back. "What if you have no secrets I care to know?" She forced a laugh in return, hands clenched to prevent herself from slapping him.

He smiled—a cold twitch of his lips with something of calculation in it. "I assure you this one is worth knowing. You're in greater danger than you think, Mademoiselle Howard. The queen opposes you Americans for unlawfully putting off your sovereign, and—"

Her breath caught at the confirmation of her suspicions, but she refused to let him see its effect. "This is no news to me, monsieur," she broke in. "Her majesty made some mention of her concerns when my aunt and I discussed the issue with her frankly at Le Petit Trianon. She was most gracious to us."

He regarded her with a lazy smile that now held open malice. "*Sans doute* she is cognizant of the influence of Caledonne, the tool of Sartine and that impotent monkey who calls himself king. You are, I assume, le comte's confidante seeing that you live with him."

"Are you normally so insolent?" she returned, outraged by what he implied. "What would your 'important men' think of your indiscretion?"

He rasped a laugh. "You labor under an illusion if you think discretion a virtue at the court of France. But then, of course, you are *Americaine*. Such delusions arise from the republican virtues you revolutionaries espouse, *ma petit renarde*."

His use of the word *vixen*, the contemptuous term applied to prostitutes who were even rumored to wear foxtails attached to the back of their petticoats, enraged her. She slapped him hard across the cheek.

To her surprise, he hardly flinched. "Such revolutionary fervor only heats my blood," he said, eyes glittering.

His forward step followed the path of her retreat, and he possessed himself of her hand, the strength of his grip bruising as she attempted to snatch it back. She wished violently to apply her knee to his groin, but the voluminous folds of her heavy domino hindered her. As she tried to pull away she realized that he was standing on its hem. She endeavored to thrust him back, but he might as well have been a stone wall.

Failing to win her freedom, she withdrew to the length of her arm. "If your method of seduction is to insult the object of your lust into submission, I fear your hopes will be disappointed."

He jerked her to him, painfully wrenching her shoulder and causing her to stumble against his chest. "I wish only to protect you from your enemies."

"Don't make me laugh," she said through clenched teeth.

"You're the most delectable, ripest fruit I've ever encountered—one I must taste—and will," he panted.

She fought vainly to wrench out of his grip, gasped in revulsion when his hand cupped her breast. "I don't wish to be tasted by you, monsieur! Let me go!"

Desperate calculations flitted through her mind as she scanned the vicinity. The garden appeared to be completely deserted now, and it was unlikely that her voice would carry over the mingled strains of music and murmur of voices filtering from inside the Palais. But if someone did hear, the scandal would be broadcast to all corners of the court, exposing her identity and causing damage to Caledonne's reputation and influence—

Veillars bent over her, cutting off her racing thoughts. His moist, demanding mouth captured hers. Her stomach revolted at the heavy taste of wine on his tongue.

Wrenching her head to the side, scandalized and indignant, she cried, "Monsieur, this is not decent!"

He snickered. "Whenever was the throne of France decent? Come with me to safety, *ma petit fleur*, and let me induct you into the customs of the court. I promise I'll make the experience most pleasurable."

Rage lanced through her. She applied the heel of her shoe to his foot, bearing down hard with all her weight behind it. Instead of loosening his hold, however, he gripped her more tightly, cursing volubly as he kicked his foot free.

"You'll pay dearly for that when I turn you over to Lord North."

She sent a beseeching glance toward the nearest door into the building —too far away even if she could escape—earning his laugh. "If you're looking for your guard dogs, my men have taken care of them. Particularly your paramour, Monsieur Bettár."

"How dare—"

Behind her a drawling voice cut off her furious response. "Don't be absurd."

She felt Veillars stiffen. Straightening, he dragged her around, staggering, so that her back was pressed firmly against his chest, in the same movement swung to face Lucien, holding her between them.

He sauntered toward them from the shadows. The moon and lantern light that glimmered across his outlandish costume gave the illusion that she had somehow fallen into a bizarre fantasyland. As he drew nearer she made out the faint glint of the small pistol in his right hand, its barrel aimed, unwavering, at Veillars' head.

"You might wish to remember that I'm the one who takes care of matters. As I already have of your men," Lucien mocked.

As he was speaking, Veillars released her with one hand long enough to snatch a dagger from inside the opposite sleeve of his domino. Before she could tear free, he pressed it against her throat. Feeling the prick of the keen blade, she sucked in an involuntary breath, immediately stilling.

"Take your hands off her at once or I guarantee the consequences will not be pleasant," Lucien warned, his tone and look steely.

"Drop your pistol or I'll slit her throat," hissed Veillars.

"And what will that gain you? The British want her alive, and you'll lose the reward." Lucien laughed softly. "I'm afraid you've no way to win this game."

Elizabeth jerked hard at the sound of the pistol's report, felt the blade's sharp sting and Veillars falling away. She staggered forward, sobbing, and Lucien sprang to gather her into his arms.

"Don't look, *ma chère*. It's not a pretty sight."

Fighting to gather self-possession, she cast a quick glance toward Veillars, sprawled across the stones with a thick black stream winding slowly from a jagged wound at the center of his forehead, then quickly away. "I've s-seen worse in battle," she managed, suppressing a shudder.

He steadied her on one arm while shoving the pistol into the waistband of his kilt with the other. Shadowy figures emerged silently from the darkness. Several she recognized by their costumes as her guards, but the rest wore livery—Chartres's? They moved with silent swiftness to the body.

Lucien hurried her away, back through the door into the Palais, and she saw no more. Drawing her into a shadowed alcove, he bent over her.

"He didn't hurt you?"

She lifted her chin. "I'm . . . entirely well. But thank you." This last was uttered with a tremor in her voice. "Was it . . . was it really necessary to kill him?"

"You'd have had your jugular cut if I hadn't. I'm sorry you were frightened."

"He said . . . he was going to . . . "

"Turn you over to Lord North."

She nodded, mute, realized suddenly that the cut on her neck stung and a sticky fluid wound toward her shoulder. And that something wet had splattered onto her face.

He gently wiped her cheek with the edge of her domino, then pulled his sash free and wound it carefully around her neck to stanch the trickle of blood. When she glanced nervously down the passage toward the ballroom, he said, "The report of my pistol couldn't have been heard from inside. And my men made sure no one else followed you. Don't worry. He and his accomplices will be removed with the utmost discretion."

"What . . . how?"

He drew her tenderly into his arms. "Your heart's beating so hard I can feel it."

"Where were you? You disappeared!"

He chuckled. "Nefertiti was trying her best to seduce me, and it took some doing to extricate myself. My men never lost sight of you, however, and would have intervened if necessary. But I came as soon as they alerted me that you'd slipped away into the gardens and that Veillars had also disappeared."

Her eyes widened. "You knew he was dangerous!"

Smiling down at her, he murmured reassuringly, "Philippe posted guards at every entrance. It would have been impossible for Veillars to smuggle you out of the building."

"Then why did he try?"

"He was a fool."

Although she made no protest, she found that hard to believe. Veillars, she was certain, had had a plan and the accomplices to carry it out.

Realizing she was in shock, she took a shaky breath. "If you hadn't come, I'd have screamed—in spite of the scandal it would cause."

Merriment danced in his eyes. "Actually, I'd have intervened sooner had I not been laughing so hard. You were doing an admirable job of defending yourself until you infuriated him by stamping on his foot."

Now that he was there holding her and she was safe, she laughed in return, feeling on the verge of hysteria. "You were watching!"

"Of course. But only briefly, I assure you." He sobered. "I'd never allow you to come to harm. You know that?"

She nodded absently, looking toward the ballroom door. "Whose man is—was—he?"

"Let me worry about that." He kissed her on the forehead, murmured, "It's late, and everyone will be worrying about you. I'd better take you home."

She pulled back to regard him searchingly, finally allowed him to escort her back through the ballroom. Four of her guards had vanished, she noted, leaving only two to attend them.

While they waited at the building's entrance for the coach to be brought around, and then all the way back to Passy, her mind raced. In spite of the fact that they had been on the point of abducting her, she felt sick at the thought that Veillars had been killed because of her, perhaps his men as well. It all felt far too personal.

She had the sinking sense that this was not the first time Lucien had quietly removed an enemy. Everything about the incident seemed so . . . planned. Efficient.

It occurred to her that he might have learned of a conspiracy against her and deliberately brought her to the ball to flush out its members. Chartres was certainly involved in it, had posted guards at all the entrances, had his men help remove Veillars . . . and who else?

For if Veillars' intent really had been to kidnap her and carry her across the channel to England, he had to have had a widespread network of contacts. And if Lucien knew of the plot, she thought slowly, stomach clenching, then his most likely source was his father.

Before now she would have been angered by that. But in this uncertain environment of dangerous intrigues and shifting alliances that she could not fully penetrate, she found herself grateful, though unwillingly, to both men for their protection.

Sitting beside her, Lucien gently nestled her against him, one arm encircling her shoulders. He cupped her cheek with his free hand, tipped her head up, and kissed her lightly on the temple.

"I'll always keep you safe, Beth," he murmured huskily against her cheek. "You've nothing to fear. Ever. Not as long as I'm with you."

She sat frozen, not knowing what to say, unable to pull away. He had never before called her by her pet name instead of Elizabeth.

Chapter Twenty-seven

THE FOLLOWING FRIDAY evening a messenger arrived from Sartine while the footmen were clearing the dishes from the supper table. The girls and their governess had excused themselves to take a cooling walk in the garden after another hot day, while Elizabeth lingered with the others as they finished their cups of bittersweet chocolate.

Caledonne followed the butler into the *salle*. When he returned some moments later he carried a thick packet, its seal already broken.

Elizabeth noted that Eugene's gaze sharpened. He inclined his head to the footmen, who immediately left the room.

Resuming his seat, Caledonne deliberately laid open the packet and spread its contents on the table in front of him. All of them followed his movements with surprise, and Elizabeth exchanged a questioning glance with Tess. Eugène leaned back in his chair, eyes hooded. Lucien's expression remained unreadable, and Cécile watched her father, frowning.

"Sartine's sent a number of highly confidential reports obtained by our contacts inside the British court," Caledonne told them.

"You don't mean to share intelligence with us, do you, Papa?" Cécile said, clearly taken aback. "You've never done so."

He turned his gaze to Elizabeth. "There is much I cannot share, but several details are included that might allay some of our concerns about Jonathan."

Her breath caught, and she leaned forward. "Please tell us as much as you can."

Frowning, he pulled out a page. Scanning it, he said, "As I feared, Louis's network was breached at Boston. Communications directed to me were stolen by British agents and came into the hands of Eden, the head of their secret intelligence. Luckily our agents got a look at them without anyone being the wiser. According to this, all communications from Boston ended abruptly and without explanation. I'm guessing that the manager of Jonathan's Boston office discovered the leak and put an end to it."

"That's why we've heard nothing," Tess said.

Caledonne nodded. "If Jonathan's manager did what he should, he alerted Louis at once so he could investigate whether hostile agents still lurk in his networks beyond Boston."

He laid the page with a couple more aside face down and took up another. "The information in this one verifies that Lord North's warrant reached Governor Hamilton at Detroit, perhaps also General Clinton, well before it was sent to Vergennes. At the end of April Hamilton dispatched *Canadien* militia to capture Jonathan. Several weeks later they found him at a tribal council at Chillicothe—a new location farther west, where the tribes allied with Britain are gathering." He looked up. "The tribe's headmen refused to turn him over and sent the *Canadiens* packing."

"Praise God!" Tess exclaimed. "I wouldn't have expected that considering their opposition to us."

"Does it say anything more?" Elizabeth pleaded. She could feel Lucien watching her, but kept her gaze fixed on Caledonne.

"There's a brief report added at the end," Caledonne answered. "It's dated the first day of this month, so it must have traveled by a very fast ship. It states that he'd just left Grey Cloud's Town with his warriors, traveling east."

Eugène shifted in his chair. "It appears they're following his movements very closely."

"A *Canadien* force went after him." Caledonne's face hardened. "Clearly Jonathan's intent is to rejoin Washington. And theirs, to stop him."

"With Howe relieved of command, Clinton's been ordered to withdraw his former corps from Philadelphia to New York," Eugène put in.

Caledonne nodded. "They'll soon be moving out if they haven't already. But knowing the British, they're far from light on their feet." Stroking his chin, he leaned back in his chair, eyes narrowed. "Washington's army suffered considerably from supply issues over the winter, but that's been corrected. Their training has also vastly improved."

He turned to Elizabeth and Tess. "Clinton has a long march ahead of him, and if I were in command of your army, I'd attack before they reach their stronghold at New York. My impression of Washington is that he's of like temperament."

"He's hampered by a number of older generals who are averse to risk and oppose him," Elizabeth responded. "But his aides and the younger officers like Jonathan are on his side when it comes to battle."

"Once a warrior, always a warrior," Lucien drawled. "I'm astonished that even my cousin could manage to ingratiate himself with this General Washington despite his reputation for laying waste to white settlements on behalf of the native savages. I fully understand why your parents forbade him any further contact with you, Beth. I can't imagine your life being squandered on a man who's more devoted to the destruction of his own people than he is to you."

Utter stillness lay over the room, conversation and movement suspended. Speechless, Elizabeth stared across the table at him. His expression showed only sympathy and concern for her, but she read an emotion in his eyes that sounded a warning in her mind.

Caledonne rose deliberately, a level gaze fixed on his son. "That was grossly unwarranted, and I demand your apology. Are there no depths to which you refuse to sink?"

Lucien sprang to his feet, the legs of his chair scraping loudly across the stone floor. "I wouldn't have expected any less of you, *mon père*. You're so predictable when it comes to your nephew."

With a harsh laugh, he strode from the room, and after a moment Elizabeth heard his footfalls retreating up the stairs.

ALL THE PREVIOUS WEEK she had felt the tension building between the two men. When she and Lucien arrived home from the ball at dawn's breaking, Caledonne was already awake, perhaps had not slept. He stepped out of the library to intercept them as they climbed the stairs. And after one glance at her ashen face, he turned his gaze to his son and took in his costume with an unconcealed scorn that caused her breath to catch but seemed to daunt Lucien not at all.

Bidding the two men a hasty good night, she had fled to her suite. And to Tess's arms, there to sob out the story of the night's events, her humiliation, her apologies. To her gratitude, her aunt supplied gentle consolation with no reproach.

Over the succeeding days she had focused her energies on her medical duties among the servants. Plainly dressed in a blue linen gown and white pinner apron, her hair gathered into a simple cap, she visited kitchen and garden and barn. As usual, she regularly encountered Eugène overseeing the farmers in company with his steward when he was not at Versailles as well as Cecile making her weekly rounds among the workers, and was freely welcomed to accompany them. And as often as Madame Verignay would release Abby and Charlotte, they eagerly joined her to visit with the children and elderly while she tended to the sick and injured.

She cherished their company and the opportunity to linger with the servants young and old, to hear their troubles, share their joys and play with the children with abandon. She found renewal in the bountiful pleasures of peaceful, sunny days and star-spangled nights in thir simple, rustic environment.

To her surprise, and some unease, Lucien also began to accompany her whenever he was not away at Versailles or in Paris. He carried her supplies, seemed delighted to visit with her patients, and teased the children into happy laughter as naturally as though it was his habit.

It seemed impossible to reconcile this gentle, tender, attentive man with the one who had with nerveless calculation pulled the trigger while her head was so close to Veillars' and his knife was poised against her throat. The dark shadow of that moment left her weak kneed. And terrified all over again.

The stiffness of his and Caledonne's manner toward each other made it all too clear that they had quarreled bitterly over the matter, but she carefully avoided becoming embroiled in their dispute. Not only did her conscience accuse her of her part in it, but her own relationship with Lucien was becoming increasingly strained.

At least as far as she was concerned. He gave no evidence that he was aware of any tension between them.

She did not question the necessity for him to discuss the attack with Caledonne and Eugène. She herself had told Aunt Tess. But on the way home in the coach, she had pleaded with him not to disclose the attack to anyone else, instinctively knowing that neither Caledonne nor Eugène would involve even Cécile in it.

But when she had risen at noon that day, eyes and heart heavy, Cécile had come to her in deep distress. *"Ma chère,* I'm so sorry you experienced such horror!" she exclaimed, wringing her hands. "Oh, to think what would have happened had Lucien not been there to protect you!"

Even more dismaying was the discovery that Abby and Charlotte also had learned of the attack. They clung to her in terror, and it took much reassurance and persuasion for them to leave her side. The news even spread to the servants throughout the estate. And although Elizabeth was touched by and grateful for their concern and obvious love for her, she had to fight back her anger and keep telling herself that it was only because of his concern for her that he mentioned the matter to others.

The wound had broken open now, however, and she could no longer pretend to ignore it. The hours stretched out endlessly that evening, awkward and tense. Their conversation revolved around the expanding naval war, the likelihood of battle between the American and British armies, and Carleton's possible role in it. But beneath the outward calm, the scene at the supper table hovered at the back of everyone's thoughts.

Also carefully avoided was the continuing lack of any communication from Carleton. His and Elizabeth's relationship—or the ending of it—seemed a subject impossible to broach.

When they finally retreated to their suites for the night and until silence fell over the château, she pondered what, if anything, she should do about the scene at table earlier. At length, worried that she might make things worse rather than better but unable to sleep, she hesitantly traversed the darkened passage to Lucien's suite, her slippers silent on the soft runner.

She knocked lightly on the door, with trepidation laid her cheek against it and called softly, "Lucien?"

For a long moment there was only silence within, and she almost retreated. Then she heard his soft tread, and the door swung slowly open. He regarded her searchingly for a moment before gently drawing her inside.

He settled her on a small divan. Sitting beside her, he took her hand and regarded her earnestly while she distractedly took in her surroundings.

She had never been inside his salon, which was lavishly furnished as all the others. A comfortable chair had been drawn next to one of the windows flung wide to the night, and an open book lay facedown on its seat. The lazy breeze wafting inside disturbed the gauzy draperies and flickered the soft candle flame that illuminated the space. Other than that, all was orderly, even severely so, with no possessions personal to him anywhere that she could see.

"I hoped you'd come."

She returned her troubled gaze to him. "I . . . it grieves me that you and your father are quarreling. If I'm to blame because of what happened at the ball—"

"Of course you aren't," he said gruffly.

Feeling entirely foolish, she bent her head, unable to meet his probing gaze. "I know the two of you differ in your opinion of Jonathan." She looked up, rushed on, "But you misunderstand him, Lucien. He isn't at all as you keep portraying him. And my parents—"

His face darkened for an instant, but quickly smoothed. "If you'll remember, I've met your parents, and I think I understand their concerns very well. I was quite impressed with their love for you and how your good-ness justifies that love. Understandably they want only your best."

"I'm not ignorant of my parents' love or their concerns. But I'm a grown woman and capable, I think, of determining the best course for my life."

His expression softened. "Of course you are, *ma chère*. But I'm a little older than you and well remember decisions I made at your age that I thought for my best, but which proved over time to miss the mark."

When she started to protest, he continued, "I don't mean to say that you're wrong in loving my cousin. I don't dispute that in many ways he's an admirable man, and I apologize if anything I said was unfair. But when we were younger, I saw him do things that, well . . . " He let the words trail off.

Staring at him, she shook her head. "What things?"

He shrugged. "Undoubtedly he's changed now. It's just that there are things about him—as about all men—that a woman can't know like a man can, things that raise serious questions in my mind."

Stiffening, she said coldly, "I assure you, he confided everything to me."

"Can one truly know everything about oneself or bare one's heart completely to another?"

Conviction pierced her, but she shook it off. "You know I referred to his past."

He pressed her hand to his lips, then drew back to regard her with concern. "He goes so far as to call himself an Indian. When you found him among them, what did you find—a civilized man . . . or a barbarian?"

His question evoked the memory of the horrifying rumors that had swirled around the warrior White Eagle before she found him. The fear that had overwhelmed her when she finally did. The vast gulf she had felt between them then.

"If he returned or if you could find him again," he continued, "would he not this time be even more the thing you found that day? He chose freely to go back to them, and he always will. What does a beautiful, civilized young woman with all the world at her feet have in common with such a man? Would your heart not be broken over and over again?"

She could not stop a flinch, and he saw it. "It was his decision to leave you," he said softly. "And knowing my cousin as I do, it's unlike him to change his mind."

His words were like the sharp point of an arrow, piercing her heart with agonizing effect. He didn't mean to be cruel, she assured herself. But what he said felt cruel indeed.

She swallowed a sob, fought to blink back tears. Before she could pull away, he gathered her into his arms and kissed her lightly on the brow.

"Forgive me, Beth. I've become inordinately fond of you, I confess. Your goodness has caused me to see my own life in a different light and to repent dearly of my failings. I've done too many things I'm not proud of, but you make me want to be a better man. With you beside me I know I can be."

"Lucien, I . . . I can't . . . I still . . . It wouldn't be fair for me to entertain the addresses of another while my heart is so . . . uncertain," she blurted, groping for words to convey the impossible.

"I completely understand. But do you blame me for worrying about your attachment to a man who claims to love you, but who's left you for months on end without a single word? No response at all to your letter assuring him of your love. Not one word to let you know that he's well and misses you and loves you still. No concern about how you're getting on!"

Tears stung her eyes. And dismay. She couldn't deny that what he said was true. Almost seven months had passed since Carleton had left her. Did her anguish over his leaving not concern him at all? Could it be that he no longer loved her?

"I don't blame you. You've been the very soul of kindness and a great comfort," she said hesitantly, overcome by the unaccountable feeling that she needed to reassure him.

That she had was immediately apparent in his smile. He drew her closer, and for fear of hurting him she didn't pull away.

"I'm glad you decided to come home with us. It's been good for us—and for you too, I think."

The word *home* warmed her, and the vulnerability she read in his eyes melted her defenses in spite of her doubts. Forcing a smile, she murmured, "So it has."

"I feel I have an ally in you," he said huskily, capturing her hand and pressing it to his cheek, "the first I've had since Frédéric was taken from me. You can't know how much you mean to me."

Afterward she couldn't remember her response, but she took her leave as quickly as possible. Pleading the lateness of the hour, she bade Lucien good night, and retreated to her own suite. Unsettled by a strange impression that the ground shook beneath her feet, she found no rest and tossed and turned until dawn, regretting mightily that she had gone to him.

She couldn't deny that there was much in him that attracted her: his attentiveness; how sensitive he seemed to her innermost emotions; his ability to comfort her; his charming, witty liveliness; his quick intelligence. He was knowledgeable about so many things, and she took delight in their long discussions of culture and the arts, philosophy, politics, and government that helped to fill the hollow place left by Carleton's absence.

But their relationship was becoming increasingly fraught. There was no denying now that he wanted a much closer relationship than friendship, and her efforts to make clear that her feelings for him were only a sisterly affection seemed to make no impression.

Beneath his outwardly amiable exterior she sensed dark emotions she could not penetrate and that stood as a shadowy barrier between them. But he was their hostess's brother and Caledonne's son.

Which made it impossible to seek their counsel and intervention. And unthinkable to break off her relationship with him.

Chapter Twenty-eight

"I MISS MY WIFE and younger children intolerably," John Adams confided to Elizabeth the following afternoon with a sigh. "Were it not for John Quincy, I don't know how I'd bear this separation. The worst is that there seems no end in sight."

"I miss Mama and Papa terribly too," she admitted. "But it's more than that. I miss our homeland and particularly Boston and my family's own dear little nest."

His face brightened. "Exactly so! I'm simply too much of a homebody. As much as I love France and all it has to offer, it isn't home."

Their laughter, tinged with longing, was almost drowned out by the murmur of voices that echoed in the château's crowded *salle*. Footmen circulated, offering flutes of champagne while the guests waited for the call to dinner.

With the naval war heating up, a combined fleet under Vice Admiral le Comte d'Orvilliers was preparing to sail. It included one of Caledonne's squadrons, and Eugène and Cécile were hosting a dinner for high-ranking naval and government officials before he left for the port at Brest.

He stood across the *salle* from Elizabeth and Adams, conversing earnestly with Vergennes and Sartine, while Cécile and Tess entertained their wives nearby. In apparent good humor unshadowed by the conflict of the evening before, Lucien mingled with officials adorned with sashes and honors and resplendently uniformed admirals who spilled into the salon. Among them was Chartres, an infrequent guest as Caledonne and the Martieu-Broussards kept their distance from the House of Orleans.

Jacques Necker and his very plain wife stood virtually unnoticed by the unlighted fireplace with only Eugène attending them. The fifty-six-year-old director general of finance looked the banker that he was: plain, dark suit, oval face, high forehead beneath powdered hair, small mouth pursed above an under-slung jaw with sagging chins. Popular with the common people for reforming the government's finances, he was the focus of many of the nobles' growing opposition to those very reforms. It didn't help that his fabulous wealth was a source of envy or that he was a Protestant and from Geneva, thus an outsider.

"I can't tell you what a delight it is to converse in my native language with a fellow patriot who isn't named Franklin or Lee," Adams said with a chuckle, drawing her attention back to him.

"Speaking French has become so natural to me since our arrival here," she responded lightly, "that I fear I'm going to forget English altogether if I don't speak it more often. So you're doing me a good service, sir."

She suppressed a smile as she glanced at Benjamin Franklin, who commanded the *salle's* center, surrounded, as usual, by women, many of whom adopted *la mode Americaine*. He was regaling them with an amusing story, made more so by his blundering French. In spite or perhaps because of it, they tittered and simpered and hung on every word.

On weekly outings to the opera and theater with Abby, Tess, Caledonne, and his family, she had often encountered the American commissioners, though rarely Lee, who had characteristically tendered his regrets for today's dinner. Franklin was also a fixture at the dinners and other social engagements they attended, unlike the other two men. Every-where he went he flattered the ladies whether young or old, attractive or plain, and they fluttered around him like colorful butterflies. To her amusement he had even made it quite apparent that he was inclined to expand his acquaintance with her beyond mere sociability—an offer she had tactfully deflected.

Adams, though less social, she found more congenial. Feeling him to be in many ways a kindred spirit, she had sought him out among the other guests. Although he mingled easily enough, when not engaged in conversation he appeared forlorn, giving her the impression that he greatly preferred to be alone in the commission's apartment working. And today she also felt social demands to be more a burden than a pleasure.

His gaze turned sober. "Monsieur Bettár told us about the recent attack against you. Thank God he was able to save your life! I hope anyone else who might be tempted to claim the reward will take the incident as a cautionary tale."

It took considerable effort for her to conceal her dismay. In spite of Caledonne's warning to speak to no one outside the family of what had happened at the ball, Lucien had obviously confided everything to the American commissioners, too, with himself featured as the hero.

Whom else had he told? And Chartres, whom Lucien had involved— was he spreading his own account?

The one saving grace was that she and Lucien had escaped before the traditional unmasking at night's end. She had heard no rumors linking her to the mysterious Diana who caused such a stir. So far, at least. The thought that she might yet be thus linked caused her chest to tighten.

She excused herself and crossed the *salle* toward Caledonne. She was repeatedly intercepted, each time gracefully curtseying and answering the questions pressed on her about the attack at the ball with as much restraint as possible before she extricated herself tactfully.

Vergennes drifted away as she approached, but Vice Admiral le comte d'Orvilliers immediately joined Sartine and Caledonne. Disappointed in her hope to speak to him privately, she paused at a discreet distance.

"Chartres is to command our rear squadron?" she heard Caledonne demand in an undertone as he glanced toward the duc, who appeared to be engrossed in conversation just inside the salon. "For what reason is this? He's never so much as commanded a ship before."

D'Orvilliers shrugged. "Philippe has formal training, if you'll remember, and he persuaded us that he's equal to the task. Besides, it'll provide him good experience."

Caledonne stared at him, incredulous. "He trained in his youth, years ago. The time for a squadron commander to gain experience is not in the midst of a war against a highly experienced enemy who'll exploit every weakness! Let Chartres command a ship, if you will, but not an entire squadron."

"That's impossible. He's an admiral. Besides, your orders are to avoid action if at all possible," Sartine responded firmly, glancing from him to d'Orvilliers. "Keep to that, and there'll be no trouble."

"*Certainement!* Now that we finally have the advantage over the British, we squander it," Caledonne fumed. "If it were up to me, we'd attack them wherever we find them and drive them off the sea."

Sartine shook his head indulgently. "But it isn't up to you, Alexandre. You know the king's position on the matter. D'Orvilliers' orders are to protect our merchant shipping—"

"But the British pursuit of d'Estaing weakened their Channel fleet," Caledonne began to protest, referring to le comte d'Estaing, commander of a French fleet sent that spring to aid the Americans.

"They still outnumber mine," d'Orvilliers pointed out.

"Yes, and you know they'll pursue us. If we're forced into an engagement, having an inexperienced commander in the fleet is to court disaster!"

Elizabeth's breath caught. Lucien had approached unnoticed while they were speaking. Caledonne became aware of him at the same moment, and they exchanged challenging glances.

Lucien's face darkened, and his mouth tightened into a hard line. But the announcement of dinner cut off any further discussion.

Turning on his heel, he skirted around the men and came to claim Elizabeth's hand.

❋ ❋ ❋

"Poor Cécile."

"I think she feels even worse about this conflict than we do," Tess agreed with a sigh. "She told me that Eugène's almost at the end of his patience, and you know how restrained he is. If Lucien continues this much longer, he'll likely insist he return to Alexandre's apartment at Versailles."

Elizabeth wandered to the nearest window of Tess's chamber, partially open to admit the moist breeze that cooled the stale, heavy air. She stared through the rain-spattered panes into the darkness.

Their solitude was an immense relief. Carrying on conversations with their dinner guests for hours had finally become too much to bear. She had repeatedly answered the same questions and responded graciously to exclamations of horror for what she had endured, accompanied by admiration for her fortitude and especially for Lucien's heroism. The recital she, Cécile, Abby, and Charlotte had presented in the music room afterward had provided a welcome reprieve and received great applause. But the performance had also been exhausting.

"I hate to be dragged into the middle of their dispute, but I do understand," she said. "What family doesn't have its disagreements, after all? Ours certainly has had a considerable share of drama."

"I assured her of that," Tess responded, "and it did offer some consolation. But the worst of it is how it wears on Alexandre to be constantly at odds with his son on top of his burdens in this war."

Elizabeth came to sit beside her. "Has he said anything to you—about your relationship, I mean?"

Tess picked at the lace on her négligée, avoiding her gaze. "Not directly. But I'd be a fool to mistake his interest. And intentions."

"And what do you intend to do when he does broach the subject? You know he will."

"Heaven help me, I'm half afraid of him.!" Tess responded, throwing up her hands. "He can be so charming that he makes you forget how powerful a man he is—and, I suspect, how dangerous a foe he can be."

"He's never peremptory with his family. Remember what Cécile told us the day we arrived? Clearly he's very protective of those he loves, but also very patient. Lucien's repeatedly provoked him, and although Uncle Alexandre gets angry, he's never cast him out, even though he could. Even though Eugène's on the point of it."

Tess sprang up and began to pace.

"Does the memory of Captain Scott stand in the way? I know how much you loved him."

Tess made a dismissive gesture. "Over the years grief inevitably softens. One must release the past in order to live life, and I have."

"It appears Lucien wants to cling to it," Elizabeth said softly.

"It's harder for some than for others. But I'm a realist. I finally let go of what might have been because I had to. It's just that I never met another man like Daniel who could tempt me to give up my single estate—"

"Until now?" Elizabeth teased.

Tess gave her a wry look. "Alexandre is definitely a force of nature."

"It seems to run in the family."

"Both the Bettárs and the Carletons, I'd say," Tess returned dryly.

Elizabeth studied her, frowning. "Does it bother you that he's a seafaring man?"

"Having lost one love to the sea does make it hard to let down my guard even after all these years," Tess admitted. "I feel Alexandre's eagerness for the fight. On the voyage here, that time British sails came up on the horizon, he'd have gone after them without hesitation, like a wolf after prey. He didn't only because we were aboard and he wouldn't endanger us. That's what haunts me: Alexandre out on a hostile sea in the midst of a war, fearlessly and relentlessly seeking the enemy."

Involuntarily images of Carleton rose to Elizabeth's mind. In brutal hand-to-hand contest with Wolfslayer. Riding out to war at the head of his brigade. Whether warrior or Ranger, when he faced battle a nerveless, coldly calculating recklessness possessed him as well.

Pain so sharp that it sucked the breath from her lungs lanced through her. But she quickly thrust the memories back into the deepest recesses of her consciousness.

"You wouldn't want a man who was less than that, would you?"

"No," Tess murmured, then with a short laugh added, "But I don't know whether I can live with it either."

"Are you in love with him?"

Tess regarded her with an expression so despairing that Elizabeth had to laugh. "The truth is that's what I'm afraid of most. After I lost Daniel I swore I'd never love another man so engaged, and now here he is—a French admiral whose entire life is the sea and war! You heard Cécile. He's constantly leaving for somewhere unknown with no idea of when he'll return, and now that France is at war with England—" She broke off, finally said tremulously, "I'm afraid to open my heart again, only to lose him too."

When Elizabeth looked down, tears blurring her eyes, she came quickly to sit at her side, clasped her hands in her own. "Oh Beth, I understand how you must feel, and it tears at my heart."

"We're in the same muddle, aren't we? But there's nothing to be done about my situation." Elizabeth took a breath and steadied. "Alexandre's sixty years old. How many more years can it be before he retires?"

"He's in excellent health. I doubt he'd retire before the war ends, and who knows how long that will be. But you're young. To marry, with all that entails, is your natural course, while I've lived all my life alone. I've never been with a man in that way, and . . . " Color rising to her face, she let the words trail off.

Elizabeth squeezed Tess's hands. "If he's as he seems and what Cécile told us is true, then he'll be kind and patient and tender, and the marriage bed will be sweet indeed. Surely you're not so old that you've lost all youthful passions."

Tess laughed softly and gave her a mischievous look. "I'm still a woman."

Elizabeth drew her into an embrace. "Then open your heart, dear aunt! If it's our Father will, he'll work out everything for your good."

Pulling back, Tess regarded her with concern, brow furrowed. "But how would you feel if we were to marry? Truly? I don't want to cause you any more pain than you already suffer."

"If you were to be given such joy, how could I not fully share in it?" Elizabeth demanded. "I trust the Lord to have his best in store for me as well, and I choose to be content whatever my future holds. If he gives you such felicity, then rejoice in it, as I shall, without reservation!"

How bravely she had spoken! And she had meant every word.

Yet when she returned to her own chamber, she gave way to a storm of tears—for Carleton, for herself, for all they had lost and the uncertainty of their future. That they had entered upon the dangerous game they had played, not knowing how far it would take them from the safe world they had once known . . . and from the surety of each other's arms.

In her dreams that night, as on every night, he was so vitally present with her that her heart melted with joy. Only, on awakening, to have his absence and the impossibly vast, insurmountable distance that stretched between them shatter her once more.

Patiently, heart aching, with each new sunrise she schooled herself to take up her life as it was now, striving to find peace and even a measure of delight in it. And she did find enough to ease her sorrow for that day and enable her to go on.

But, oh, if only the nights did not inevitably return! For then, lying in the thrall of sweet slumber, she sheltered in his arms for another brief, evanescent moment before morning's light again awoke her to intractable reality.

Chapter Twenty-nine

CARLETON BRACED AGAINST a scrub pine in the concealment of the stunted trees and brush that cloaked the bank of the winding East Ravine directly north of Monmouth Court House. Carbine poised, he cast a swift glance to each side to make sure his men were in position. They were, every man intent on the field before him.

On his right Stowe held a post on the other side of the tree's trunk, beyond him Major Josiah Hutchinson, whom Carleton had promoted and made his aide. Then the line of Isaiah's black troops. And stretching off to his left, his warriors.

Another British volley rent the air, and a musket ball whined through the branches directly above his head, clipping off a leafy twig and jerking his attention back to the wavering red-clad battle line. It had drawn within range, and at Isaiah's command, he chose his target and pulled the trigger, the sharp, multiplied report of his detachment's gunfire crashing around him. The officer in his sights staggered and fell.

He jerked a cartridge from his cartouche box and reloaded with deft speed, movements honed by long practice, again brought the smoothly worn stock to his shoulder. Blinking back the stinging sweat that trickled from under his woven headband into his eyes, he squinted down the barrel's length, waiting for a fickle breath of air to fragment the billowing gunsmoke that shrouded the oncoming enemy.

As always when in battle it seemed to him that the world had shrunk to the boundaries of the field of conflict. The savage passion of battle possessed him, causing each detail to stand out with an intense clarity, while the consciousness of all else faded into a distant haze.

It was mid morning on Sunday, June 28. A week and a half had passed since the council of war at Valley Forge and Clinton's march out of Philadelphia early the following morning. Yet Washington's army had tracked the withdrawing force fewer than fifty miles across New Jersey, while a steaming miasma settled over the land.

Nor would there be any relief today, Carleton reckoned.

Over the past week almost daily thunderstorms had turned New Jersey's roads, fields, and woodlands into sucking bogs, and streams like McGelliard Brook at the ravine's bottom into torrents. By the time he and his detachment had slogged along its rushing course all the way from the bridge on South Amboy Road and scaled its steep bank, they had been liberally bedaubed with mud.

All in all, he was glad of the disguise the greasy, stinking muck afforded as well as of its cooling insulation against the merciless sun that was turning yet another breathlessly hot day into a furnace. A heavy layer of sultry air blanketed the two forces, and hanging halfway above the eastern trees behind a shimmer of rising humidity, the incandescent crimson orb already baked the misty, wooded hills, its fiery heat sapping the energy and strength of man, beast, and vegetation alike.

Why is it, he wondered with exasperation, *that when it comes to battle we're invariably either freezing or frying?*

The previous evening Clinton had settled his army into a well-fortified position south of the small village amid a landscape cleft by ravines, where only a few narrow causeways afforded constricted passage to a pursuing army. Or a retreating one. Carleton had passed through the Monmouth area a number of times when traveling between Virginia and Boston years earlier, and most recently the previous November on his way to rescue Elizabeth. A stealthy reconnoiter with his warriors under cover of darkness had assured him that his memory of the area's daunting terrain was accurate.

His detachment had been on the move since first light, when the main British column of 6,000 men had resumed their march, following in the wake of their twelve-mile long baggage train and trailed by General Lord Charles Cornwallis's elite 2,000 man rear guard. Middletown lay only a day's march ahead of them and, not far beyond it, the British-occupied shore of Sandy Hook Bay below New York City.

Carleton couldn't help commiserating with the sweltering, purple-faced British soldiers advancing in neat rows across the sandy ground in their heavy red woolen coats, burdened with weapons, cartouche boxes, canteens, and heavy haversacks. He remembered the misery all too well from his own service in the 17th Light Dragoons, surely a lifetime ago.

Despite the Continentals' and militias' relatively lightweight hunting shirts and breeches, they were suffering almost as badly from the stifling weather. At his orders his Rangers had stripped to their breeches, while he and his warriors wore only breechcloths, leggings, and moccasins. Even so, men moved sluggishly on both sides, the oppressive heat rendering any swift, sustained movement virtually unsupportable.

Their horses were another serious concern. He had dismounted most of his brigade, holding their mounts well to the rear with the baggage train and camp followers. Riders had orders to stay in the trees' shade when not on attack and to keep both their mounts and themselves well watered—a challenge when many of the wells in the vicinity had been stopped up by Washington's advanced corps and streams and ponds were either muddy or brackish.

With Andrews holding the rest of the brigade in reserve at the West Ravine two miles to the west, Carleton's detachment had inched its way along the left flank of Lafayette's division until they lay slightly ahead and to the right of General Wayne's brigade. The first to make contact with the enemy, Wayne was currently engaged in a heated exchange with Cornwallis's rear guard.

General Lee held overall command of the advanced corps. He had first turned the assignment down as beneath the dignity of his exalted rank. But when Washington assigned the corps to Lafayette, increasing its size to three divisions totaling over 5,300 men, Lee had suddenly seen the matter in a different light. And to Carleton's thorough disgust, Washington had handed the corps to him after all.

Then, to turn the command into a complete muddle, Washington had added two additional brigades, including Carleton's Rangers, and assigned Lafayette to command the division that threatened Clinton's left flank. As a sop to the young marquis, he was allowed to retain overall command until making contact with the enemy, at which point Lee would take precedence.

When he learned of it, Carleton had stifled a groan. Too often he had seen how quickly confusion on the battlefield could rob a commander of victory, and his gut churned at thought of the unhappy possibilities in the offing. To make things worse, since around eight o'clock when the advanced corps first engaged the British rear guard a short distance north of Monmouth Court House, Lee had sent no orders at all to his divisions—as sure a recipe for disaster as Carleton could imagine. But as it appeared they were now on their own, he determined to make the most of any opportunity luck or divine providence afforded.

As though to confirm his grim reflections, Spotted Pony called out a warning that a sizeable body of troops had turned back from the withdrawing British main force and was flooding onto the battlefield, more than doubling their beleaguered rear guard. Carleton wrenched his spyglass from its pouch, while Spotted Pony dropped from his perch overhead in the scrub pine. Red Fox and Isaiah ducked through the brush to join them.

For some moments Carleton studied the rapid movement to the British right flank of a large contingent of Regulars accompanied by the 16th Light Dragoons and bolstered with artillery. Obviously feeling the increasing sting of his detachment's bullets, they meant to turn their full attention to their tormentors.

An officer rode up behind the newly arrived battalions and halted. He also held a spyglass to his eye, and a shock of recognition went through Carleton.

It was Cornwallis.

By the way he intently surveyed their line, Carleton couldn't help wondering whether the news had reached Clinton's command that in spite of Governor Hamilton's efforts to capture him he had safely returned to Washington's army, bringing along a substantial party of warriors. And the sight of his blond hair among them was all Cornwallis would need to make the identification.

He collapsed the spyglass and returned it to the pouch, silently blessing the mud that splattered him from head to foot. "We'll have a stronger position there," he told his companions abruptly, indicating a thick hedgerow several yards ahead of them to the left.

He wasted no time setting a small detail to guard the surgeon's mates and their wounded charges, with orders to keep to their sheltered position on the ravine's bank. Then with the crash of redoubled gunfire and thunder of artillery all but drowning out his voice, he shouted for the rest of the detachment to advance. At a run he led the way to the shelter of the new position, Stowe and Hutchinson on his heels, warriors and Rangers pressing close behind.

Breathless from the heat, he grabbed the wooden canteen that hung on a strap across his chest, uncorked it, and tipped the last drops of water into his mouth. As he replaced the cork, he noted with concern that all of his sweat-slicked men gulped water greedily, too many of them emptying their canteens. There was no time to send a detail down to the creek to refill them, however, and he quickly returned his attention to the field in front of them.

Their new position behind the densely woven, head-high overgrowth lay oblique to their original line, providing a wider view of the maneuvers of both Continental and British units. His detachment's shift to the left had not gone undetected, however, and the bolstered British right front wheeled in their direction.

He shoved the barrel of his carbine through the interlaced branches of bushes, saplings, and thorny vines. Spreading out to each side of him, his men did the same. The tips of the Rangers' rifled carbines and the warriors' muskets bristled through the hedgerow.

Beneath the clamor of battle, he could faintly hear shouted commands. Then the red line surged in their direction.

He squinted down the length of his carbine and squeezed off a shot, its report echoed by a volley from the rest of the detachment as sharp points of fire blasted from the hedgerow. The day was windless, and the gunsmoke obscured his view for some moments. When it finally fragment-ed, he made out that the orderly red line had staggered backward. Bodies littered the foreground, and those in the back ranks had dropped to one knee to return fire.

He reloaded with feverish speed, keeping one eye on the hastily re-forming enemy. No sooner had he rammed home the charge than Stowe wrenched him to the ground as a blazing cannonball tore a hole through the tangled brush to his left, plowing a deep furrow along the soft ground at their back and spewing up a geyser of black mud that splattered every-one in the vicinity. Giving Stowe a grateful glance, he levered onto his knees.

"A little closer, sir, and it would've taken off yer head."

He returned Hutchinson's grin, both of them wiping their dripping faces clear. Before he could answer, Isaiah hurried over to them.

"Looks to me like some o' our brigades be movin' back," he growled.

Carleton sprang to his feet. Pulling out his spyglass, he scanned the field for the regimental flags of the Continental units visible above the drifting gunsmoke. He quickly determined that Wayne's brigade held their position against rapidly intensifying pressure. On their far side Lafayette's brigade indeed appeared to be giving way before the British advance, but as he watched anxiously, they reformed in good order and drove back their pursuers with a massed volley.

He expelled a breath. "They simply moved to a better position."

The words were hardly out of his mouth when Isaiah directed his attention to the Continental artillery detail, which was not only pulling back, but proceeded to abandon the field altogether as they watched. In moments the units holding the American right flank began a rapid withdrawal south toward the village in the face of ferocious enemy artillery fire.

He swore and shifted the spyglass back to the British line in their own front. It had reformed as well, and at the van an officer shouted an order, brandishing his sword. The clamor of artillery drowned out his words, but there was no mistaking their import, and the enemy line boiled forward.

Hastily putting away the spyglass, he commanded, "Prepare for a bayonet charge!"

Isaiah and Red Fox wasted no time, moving in opposite directions down the line of their men, calling our orders and encouragement. Warriors and Rangers together serviced their weapons at nerveless speed, Carleton taking grim note that fewer than half of his cartridges remained.

"Ready!" Isaiah's deep voice boomed.

Again gun barrels pushed through the hedgerow, while the enemy spread out, hurtling toward them at a flat-out run, screaming hoarsely, bayonets glinting fiery shards of light beneath the relentless sun. Carleton steadied his carbine between Stowe's and Hutchinson's, the calculation of distance and elevation instinctive and instant.

Without warning the image of Elizabeth formed in his mind as it did often at unaccountable moments. He sought to banish it, but for a fleeting moment it was as vivid and real as though she stood before him, summoning an intensity of desire that weakened his limbs and robbed him of breath.

On its heels came an emotion foreign to him, a sharp lancepoint of fear, not of battle or even of his own capture or death, but of the dangers hovering over her, the terror that he might never see her again and she never know how very much he loved her. And that he grieved with every heartbeat for having left her.

For the blink of an eye he froze, deeply shaken. The words of the psalmist floated through his mind then: *Surely he shall deliver thee from the snare of the fowler . . . Thou shalt not be afraid for the terror by night; nor for the arrow that flieth by day . . .*

"Aim!"

The image evaporated, and in high relief the closing bloody line took its place. Teeth clenched, he tightened his grip on his carbine, mentally drew an invisible line at forty feet.

In seconds the stampeding enemy crossed it.

"Fire!"

He squeezed the trigger in same instant, felt the immediate recoil, heard the deafening explosions of gunfire rippling outward to either side, erupting a sheet of flame and smoke through the dense growth. And as though punched through by a massive, invisible fist, gaping holes appeared instantly in the front ranks of the approaching enemy line.

Chapter Thirty

"Lee ordered a retreat? Why the devil—"

"Your guess is as good as mine." The expression of Washington's slight, sandy-haired, blue-eyed young aide, Lieutenant Colonel Alexander Hamilton, reflected Carleton's own stunned fury.

From the shelter of the trees and underbrush along the ravine's verge, Carleton glanced back toward the hedgerow, where his detachment had just driven back another assault. "His corps could destroy Clinton's rear guard if he'd only attack!" he shouted over the crashing din of gunfire. "The men have more than proved their mettle."

Hamilton tightened his grip on the reins of his agitated mount. "That's irrelevant at the moment," he said, biting the words savagely off. "If you don't withdraw, your position will shortly become untenable and retreat impossible."

"I can see that," Carleton snapped.

"If you'll excuse me, sir," Hamilton responded through gritted teeth, "I have to alert the General to this debacle."

Carleton returned his salute and watched in helpless frustration as the aide urged his horse to a gallop westward ahead of Lee's retreating corps. Then he dodged back to the battle line and motioned Isaiah, Red Fox, and Hutchinson to him.

"Lee's ordered a retreat," he told them as they crouched shoulder to shoulder. "He's maintained from the first that our men can't stand against a British assault, and it appears he's determined to prove it."

Isaiah ripped off his slouch hat and slapped it hard against his thigh. Directing a dark look through the tangle of branches at the retreating brigades, he reluctantly allowed, "Can't hold out much longer 'thout reinforcement. Got no water left and ammunition be runnin' low."

There was no time to consider options. In glum resignation Carleton commanded Isaiah and Red Fox to hold off the British advance while the surgeon's mates lowered the wounded back down into the ravine, then to follow, while covering their retreat with heavy fire. The thick overgrowth and the creek's winding course would provide concealment for points of ambush, making it difficult and dangerous for the enemy to pursue. And as they pulled back to the bridge at South Amboy Road to meet Andrews with the rest of the brigade, the men could cool themselves in the water and refill their canteens.

Taking Stowe and Hutchinson with him, he led the way into the ravine, and then on a breathless, heart-pounding rush back in the direction from which they had come, their weapons slung over shoulders, ducking under overhanging branches, clambering over rocks, and splashing through muddy bogs and swirling water at a punishing pace. When they emerged below the bridge, where their horses were tethered by the water in the shade of a copse of trees, he sent Hutchinson off to Freehold Meeting House with orders for Andrews to bring a large supply of ammunition with him, collect his detachment at the bridge, and then provide immediate support to Lee's retreating advance corps.

By the time he and Stowe spurred their horses out of the trees and onto the plain, Carleton saw that Lee's fragmented corps was pushing southwest toward the causeway over the Middle Ravine. Many of the companies were maintaining good order and laying down a punishing fire to hold off pursing enemy infantry. Among them, however, milled growing mobs of individual stragglers and scrambled units.

Their horses were sluggish from the heat, already heavily lathered. But Devil flicked his ear to Carleton's voice when he bent to stroke the stallion's neck and whisper an apology, and he obeyed the urging to a canter. With Stowe pressing his mount close behind, he kept to the woods' concealment and shade as much as possible.

They covered the two miles to the bridge over the West Ravine on Monmouth Court House Road in good time, pacing along the battle's perimeter, fairly lying on their mounts' necks while dodging bullets and cannon shot. Chest constricted, counting every yard as they nursed their horses along, Carleton fought to contain his raging impatience to find Washington and the blinding fury that he'd risked his men's lives only to have their efforts come to nothing.

During the previous week unfamiliar terrain, a lack of solid intelligence, a divided staff; and the sweltering weather had resulted in countless missed opportunities to waylay Clinton's column. The small advance corps of General William Maxwell's Continentals and General Philemon Dickinson's New Jersey militia that Washington dispatched ahead of the main army had done their best to make life miserable for the enemy, while gathering up British deserters along the way.

They had stopped up wells, torn down bridges, and felled trees across the roads ahead of Clinton's route, while their snipers steadily picked away at his soldiers. Stung by the unrelenting harassment the Regulars had finally rioted through the towns and farms they passed in a spree of indiscriminate killing and plundering that enraged patriot and Tory alike.

All the while Washington's army lumbered through the Jersey countryside trying to find their meandering enemy, only to have another council of war yield the same frustrating result as the first when they finally did. The only concession had been to send out additional units to harry the British rear.

When Clinton altered his route for a shorter one to Sandy Hook, however, a number of the generals had thought better of their earlier timidity. On the outskirts of Monmouth, with time slipping through their fingers like sand through an hourglass, they had suddenly advocated an attack, and Washington had seized the opportunity he had been itching for all along.

He hungered for a victory equal to the one at Trenton, Carleton suspected. Perhaps even one as great as Saratoga. Indeed, if their luck held, triumph lay temptingly within reach.

For once the Continentals were well trained and equipped and they outnumbered the enemy, though not by much. If they could drive Clinton into full retreat, both his column and any reinforcements he might summon from Sandy Hook would find that huge, slow-moving baggage train blocking them on opposite sides of the narrow, sandy passage into Middletown. Clinton would be vulnerable to a rout.

But with one stroke it appeared that a decisive victory might be snatched away. All due to the incompetence—or the deliberate subversion—of Washington's second in command.

The thought was intolerable.

THEY WOVE THEIR WAY across the West Ravine causeway through a crush of pushing, shoving men to find Washington approaching at a fast canter toward the loudest clamor of battle, flanked by his mulatto slave, Will Lee, and Tench Tilghman, with another of his aides and his Life Guard ranging around them. It was clear that the General was in a froth.

"I expected to come upon a British rout, not to find my entire advanced corps fleeing the field!" he shouted to Carleton over the roar of artillery fire. "Lee's last message claimed that Cornwallis's rear guard was his."

Just then a young boy came running by, a fife clenched in his hand. He was gasping for breath, his sweaty face beet red. Before he could dodge past, Stowe was out of the saddle and had him by his shirt collar.

Washington leaned down to fix the boy in a stern look. "What's happening, boy?"

"Lee's retreating, sir," the child squeaked, voice quavering as he tried to squirm out of Stowe's grip.

"Retreating! Why is that?"

"I don't know, sir," the boy yelped. Twisting free, he dodged away and disappeared in the disorderly flood of retreating men.

Hastily Carleton explained that Clinton had sent back a large detachment to reinforce Cornwallis's troops. Now outnumbering the Continentals' advanced corps, they were pressing a ferocious counterattack.

"Lee knew I was bringing up the main army and should have held his ground!"

"I fully agree, sir. My detachment and Wayne's Pennsylvanians were holding out against a superior force but in danger of being flanked when Hamilton came by to alert us to the retreat. I've ordered General Andrews to immediately bring up the rest of my brigade. I only came to alert you to what's happening and to get your direct orders."

"I dispatched a couple of my aides to determine what the exact situation is, and they returned a few minutes ago to report that the British are on the verge of overrunning Lee's corps," Washington responded with a scowl. "On top of it, my horse collapsed from the heat, and I had to commander this mare," he added, disgruntled, indicating the heaving chestnut he was astride.

Just then Hamilton pushed his way through the melee on foot, red-faced. "I apologize for taking so long to return. My horse was shot out from under me," he gasped breathlessly. "Laurens and Fitzgerald have both been wounded, but they're not in mortal danger," he added, referring to two more of Washington's aides.

"Find a mount at once!" Washington barked. "There's no time to spare."

Hamilton dodged off toward several mounted infantrymen.

His jaw hard, chin jutted, Washington motioned to Carleton to follow and urged his horse forward against the retreating flow. By main force they pushed across the causeway. Closing on the Middle Ravine, they came upon an entire division of Lee's corps streaming toward the rear.

At Washington's demand for an explanation, one of the men shouted, " 'Twas Lee ordered us t' withdraw. 'E's flyin' from a shadow, that 'e is, sir"

"Called fer us t' pull back after firin' a single volley!" added one of his mates.

Seeing rage wash over Washington's features, Carleton protested, "Sir, whatever the case, I know that to be patently false."

But his commander wasn't listening. "This is rank treachery!" he muttered under his breath, adding curses Carleton had never heard him utter even in his worst temper.

By now Hamilton had joined them astride a lathered, wild-eyed bay. Again Washington spurred his mount and led them along the road through a hail of bullets, weaving at breakneck speed through a growing crush. They had just passed another of the dense hedgerows that crossed the fields, with a modest house a short distance off to their left when they intercepted Lee leading a broken column back across the Middle Ravine causeway.

"What is the meaning of this, you cursed poltroon?" Washington shouted above the crash of artillery and gunfire.

The color drained out of Lee's face. Clearly nonplussed, he sputtered, "S-sir? Sir?"

"What is all this confusion and retreat?'

"The only confusion I see is the result of my orders not being properly obeyed."

"And instead of marshalling your corps, you turned tail and ran."

"W-we had a variety of contrary intelligence," Lee stammered. "My men were outnumbered—"

"I have certain information that the enemy before you is no more than a strong covering party," growled Washington.

Lee drew his emaciated form stiffly erect in the saddle. "That may be so, but they were stronger than my corps, and I thought it imprudent to press the engagement."

"You should have undertaken it, sir!"

"The British charged with bayonets, and my men took flight," Lee countered hotly. "They would have been destroyed had I not saved them. You know I opposed an attack from the beginning—"

"So you did, and I herewith relieve you of that unwelcome command," Washington returned icily. "In the devil's name, sir, go to the front or go to hell. I care little which."

He spurred his horse past Lee. Carleton followed with the others, and glancing back, saw that Lee watched them go, mouth agape.

IGNORING FLYING MUSKET BALLS and blazing cannon shot, Washington guided his horse into the shoving crowd bunched up at the middle causeway with as much exuberance as though on a fox hunt. "Stand fast, my boys, and receive your enemy," he called out above the clamor of battle. "The Southern troops are advancing to support you."

The horde of pushing, shoving men began to stagger to a halt, every head turning to his commanding figure. Suddenly caps and hats flew into the air and hoarse cheers erupted.

"It's the Gen'l!"

"Now we'll drive them buggers off!"

Fiery cannonballs were exploding geysers of earth all around them, and bullets peppered the air with the approach of the British van. As though oblivious to danger, Washington rode among the men, Carleton close behind him with Stowe, Will Lee, and the General's aides, helping to sweep up the scattered companies of two retreating brigades.

In the next half hour, the fleeing troops, who had held against the enemy for hours, exhausted and fainting with thirst from the sapping heat, confused by conflicting orders or no orders at all, discovered new energy. The most fatigued were sent to the rear to rest and regroup for a new advance. Washington then directed Wayne to form up the rest at the crest of a nearby rise, there to stall the British advance until he could establish the main army in a strong position behind the West Ravine.

Ordered to bring up his Rangers on the double, Carleton rode off to find Andrews and his brigade with all possible dispatch, Stowe keeping pace at his side.

Chapter Thirty-one

ANDREWS LOOKED AROUND as Blue Sky slipped along the battle line to his side behind the embankment. Like the other women she was clad only in a shift from which the sleeves had been cut, and carried a loaded musket and cartouche pouch slung across her shoulders, with a pistol thrust into the sash at her slender waist. Beneath a sheen of sweat, her face was as deeply flushed as his.

She held out a dripping canteen. "Drink, my husband!" she commanded, shouting to be heard over the deafening thunder of artillery.

Holding his carbine in his right hand, the canteen in the other, he emptied it in two long gulps, not minding its brackishness. He could have drunk twice as much.

At the same time he kept one eye on the redcoats forty yards away on the other side of the deep morass in their front. In spite of their blistering fire the brigade's women, both native and white, passed along the line, handing out filled canteens to the wilting troops and collecting empty ones as though oblivious to the hail of bullets and cannon and mortar shot that streaked the air.

All that seemingly endless afternoon, while the sun declined by agonizing degrees, the two armies had grappled in ferocious assault and equally ferocious repulse across fields and woods that had become an inferno of scorching heat. Wayne's command had held the hill and woods between the middle and western ravines as long as possible, putting up a stiff resistance. But at last they were dislodged, pushed back to a hedge-row and orchard by the fierce attacks of the British grenadiers and 16th Light Dragoons with Clinton himself at their head. Outnumbered, Wayne's men had nevertheless contested each inch of ground step by hard-fought step until finally pushed across the West Ravine causeway.

By then the main army lay entrenched along a formidable battle line spanning the ridge behind the ravine along Monmouth Courthouse- Freehold Meeting House Road. Greene commanded the right division and Lord Stirling, the left, anchored by Carleton's Rangers. Washington personally commanded the center, with Wayne in his front and Lafayette holding the majority of Lee's broken corps in reserve at the army's rear.

Andrews handed the canteen back to Blue Sky, scrubbed the sweat from his filthy face with his free hand, and cast an anxious glance behind her toward the corps' rear.

"Do not worry," Blue Sky assured him. "Rain Woman and the older maidens care for the children. Leads the Way and the others are safe."

Straightening, he took aim and pulled off a shot. "It's too dangerous for you here! Please stay with Rain Woman and the children."

She gave an adamant shake of her head. "Then the other women will have to work harder."

"They're not with child!"

"How do you know?" she retorted, softening her words with a smile that melted his heart.

He caught a flash from the corner of his eye. Dropping his carbine, he dragged her to the ground with him. Her head pressed to his shoulder, he sheltered her with his body, while a cluster of fiery balls arced through the air low overhead. They tore through the relief detail just then coming up behind them, adding the screams of men and horses to the tumult. Both shaking, they clung to each other.

They drew apart and scrambled upright as a number of women and surgeon's mates swarmed to the dead and injured men. McLeod ran up, one arm protectively around Mary's waist, his musket clenched in the other hand. They crouched beside Andrews and Blue Sky. Releasing Mary, McLeod propped his musket barrel on the weed-topped embankment and fired.

She immediately exchanged his weapon with her loaded one. "The rear guard's bringin' up more ammunition," she said as she swiftly reloaded the discharged musket. "But our supply's runnin' low."

Feeling lightheaded, Andrews swiped the sweat from his brow with the back of his arm before straightening cautiously to observe the enemy's movements. Clouded by fragmented gunsmoke, shimmering waves of heat rose from the baking earth, distorting and rendering insubstantial everything in his field of vision. He blinked and rubbed his eyes until the plain ahead of him came into clearer focus.

The sun's red-orange ball had finally sunk below the western ridge behind them. But when he checked his pocket watch, its hands had not quite reached four o'clock. He gave an inward groan.

Across the battlefield he saw that the British were bringing up yet more artillery. Understandable since Greene's and Knox's artillery had taken possession of the high ground on opposite sides of the road and were laying down a deadly enfilading fire that mowed through Clinton's neat regimental rows like scythes through ripe wheat.

He cast a quick glance to either side. Gaps in his battle line indicated where casualties had been carried away. But although the rest appeared ready to faint with the heat, each man blazed away at the enemy as fast as he could fire and reload.

"We've thrown back every assault they've made, and even broke their attempt to flank us!" he shouted as Laughing Otter scrambled over to them. "They can't keep this up much longer!"

"Nor can we," McLeod returned grimly, squinting down his musket barrel.

"We brought many men back to the rear with heat sickness," Laughing Otter told them. "Two died, and the horses are sickening as well. The surgeons are too few. If only Healer Women were here to help us!"

Andrews winced, glad Carleton wasn't present to hear her remark. It was certain Washington wouldn't be releasing him anytime soon to go to France, not with the campaign likely to last into the fall. Although Carleton remained silent on the matter, it was clear to Andrews that he chafed mightily at being thus bound when his heart yearned for Elizabeth.

"Go back to the rear where you'll be safe!" he ordered the three women with a scowl.

Blue Sky handed him his carbine, which she had loaded. "It's dangerous for you here too," she protested, touching the trickle of drying blood from a raw graze on his brow. Like the others, he was covered with scrapes and scratches from pushing heedlessly pell-mell through brambles and thorny vines. "Our children need their fathers."

"Who will care for them if they lose both parents?"

That silenced her, and when Mary began to protest, Laughing Otter gave both of them a stern look. "Come, my sisters. We will have much to do to care for the injured. We only get in the way of the men here."

She had no sooner spoken than a couple of surgeon's mates hurried by, supporting Spotted Pony between them. His face was tensed with pain and dripping sweat, his thigh wrapped with a bloody bandage. But he clutched his musket, protesting vigorously that he could still fight.

Exchanging glances with Mary and Laughing Otter, Blue Sky gave a reluctant nod. The three women immediately scrambled over to them. Casting a look back at Andrews that brimmed with love and concern, she retreated with the small party toward the surgeons' tents at the brigade's rear.

His chest clenched painfully with love for her, their little son, and the child to come. Following her every step with a prayer for her safety and that of their babes, he kept anxious watch until the three women disappeared through the trees and into the welter of men, horses, and wagons at the brigade's rear.

Suddenly he became aware that the thunder of artillery had increased. As he started to turn around, his gaze caught Hutchinson emerging from the line of trees at the base of the hill behind them. He dodged bullets and shot, racing to Andrews' side.

Isaiah and Red Fox ran over to join them. Every one of their purpled faces were masks of dust and gunpowder streaked with trickling sweat and blood, their bodies caked with dried mud, giving them the appearance of unnatural spirits from the bowels of hell. He undoubtedly presented the same appearance, Andrews reckoned ruefully.

As soon as Carleton had his Rangers disposed behind the ravine to his satisfaction, he had left Andrews in command and, taking Hutchinson and Stowe, climbed to the top of the wooded height that loomed at their backs. From there, above drifting dust and gunsmoke, he kept watch on the movements of both armies through his spyglass, with his aide and servant relaying urgent information to Andrews, Washington, and the division commanders and bringing messages back.

Andrews cocked his head, noting that the crack of gunfire from the British units ahead of them had begun to diminish. Hutchinson met his questioning gaze with a grin.

"The gen'l's concluded that since Clinton can't dislodge us by frontal assault, he's goin' to give it a go at poundin' us into submission with his artillery," he said dryly.

"On that score we're giving as good as we're getting—better even."

Hutchinson's grin widened. "They're gettin' the message. From up top looks like Cornwallis is pullin' his other regiments back."

BENT OVER, ELBOWS PROPPED on knees and knife in hand, Carleton savagely sliced curling strips from a stout stick, letting them fall to the growing pile between his feet.

He never whittled. He had no idea why he was doing so now. But, jaw clenched, he continued stripping the stick's end to a sharp point, fighting the mental and physical fatigue that came near to leveling him.

Unable to rest, from time to time he looked up to survey what he could make out of his brigade in the rapidly deepening dusk. Exhausted, sleeping men mantled the lower portion of the ridge's flanks and the verge of the morass as far as he could see.

For two hours, while the ground shook with the cannon and mortar shot the opposing artillery hurled through the air, Clinton had slowly withdrawn his command, with difficulty repulsing the Continentals who harried him. Finally, with night coming on, the British had settled in a strong defensive position east of the Middle Ravine on the outskirts of Monmouth Court House, where they now lay bivouacked.

Washington had champed at the bit to send fresh troops to attack the British flanks. Praise God, darkness had engulfed the field too quickly. The sliver of the waxing moon had already sunk below the ridge behind them, leaving no choice but to put off pursuit until morning. The men could not have borne another assault.

Carleton studied the battlefield in front of them, hills and woods cloaked in deep purple shadows. Welcome silence reigned, though the pounding of artillery fire still pulsed in his ears. Here and there he could make out the dark forms of details from both sides picking their way among the bloated bodies of horses and men to carry those still living back behind their respective lines. The rank stench of gunpowder, sweat, blood, and flesh rotting in the heat, and the guttural groans of the wounded clogged the sultry, motionless air.

He felt entirely sapped. His troops and warriors certainly were. With no desire to light even small cook fires, the women and the brigade's cooks had distributed water and cold rations, which the men devoured like wolves, himself included. With the women sent back to the rear, the men had stripped to shirt or breechcloth and, like the rest of the army, simply dropped to the ground where they sat, weapons in hand, unconscious almost before they swallowed their last bite.

Isaiah and Farris stayed among their men, but Andrews lolled nearby, sleeping like the dead, propped half upright against a log. Stowe hunched next to him, dozing. Hutchinson lay unmoving at their feet.

Spotted Pony stretched across the ground to one side, insensible but restless under Red Fox's alert gaze, wound dressed, face slicked with sweat. Thankfully the bullet had passed cleanly through his thigh, the injury not life threatening as long as infection could be avoided. To that end the surgeon had doused the raw flesh with brandy, which Spotted Pony endured stoically though Carleton knew from experience that it scorched like fire.

Red Fox looked up to meet his gaze with an understanding one. Carleton turned abruptly back again to scrutinize the motionless men spread out around him.

His heart was bound to them. And to her. Thus this intractable dilemma.

Looking down, he stared at the stick in his hand. Reduced to half its original length, it was keen enough to serve as a spear. He cast it and the knife to the ground.

How long would this campaign last? How long until he was finally free to go to her? For the door so briefly cracked open, only to again slam shut in his face, remained locked.

Bedeviled unrelentingly by the pressing concerns of the past months, he had persuaded himself that where Elizabeth was concerned he could forever hold thoughts of her at bay, bury emotion so deep it could not be dredged up. It was a deception.

The reality of her was all that kept him sane. Behind every thought, every action lay the determination to survive that he might finally go to claim her for his own. And now, as always when he sat idle, she came to him as a hunger and a thirst that could not be satisfied by mere memory any more than that evening's meager rations could satisfy physical need.

That interminable day had breached the barricades he continually fought to shore up, and now a flood tide of vivid, beguiling images of her tore them utterly away. This night he welcomed them, longed fiercely to draw her out of thought and into his arms so he could sate this aching hunger and slake this endless thirst before he died of it.

But at the same time, the thought of Lucien seethed at the back of his mind like a storm-beset sea.

HE ROUSED AT FIRST LIGHT. With the other division's scouts just beginning to stir, he sent a small detail of warriors to reconnoiter Clinton's camp. They were back before dawn's breaking to report that during the night their enemy had slipped away.

All that remained in their abandoned camp was a litter of castoff possessions and weapons, a number of dead bodies, and the most grievously wounded of their injured.

Chapter Thirty-two

T ESS HAD MANAGED to avoid Caledonne all during the previous evening, had retreated early to her chamber with the excuse that she was exhausted. That morning, the last Monday in June, she intended to escape upstairs after breakfast while the servants loaded his baggage into the coach. But as she tried to slip through the door of the *petit* dining room after the others, he intercepted her.

Drawing her insistently into the *grand* dining room opposite, he imprisoned her gently against the wall, one hand propped on each side of her, his head bent far too close to her own. The light in his eyes caused her to drop her gaze hastily, feeling heat rush to her cheeks.

"Thérèsa."

Her name on his tongue was so tender that tears unexpectedly stung her eyes.

"I think you know what my heart holds."

She drew herself erect, met his steady gaze with a toss of her head. "Now, Alexandre, we're well past our youth and thoughts of romance."

A smile tugged at his expressive mouth, and she fought back the urge to taste his kiss.

"Ah, but are not mature adults who know their own minds and have the courage to speak it the most capable of true romance? I've known from our first meeting that I want to spend the rest of my life with you—"

"You go too quickly!" she cut him off with an emotion very near to panic.

"I go only as quickly as my heart tells me to, and I hope that my feelings are shared. Are they?"

Her heart was fluttering far too like that of the young woman she had thought long left behind. "I . . . I won't deny that . . . I feel a great deal for you, but—"

"Bah! Always there is a *but*." He chuckled. "Indeed, dearest lady, we're no longer young, yet we've many good years ahead of us. Why delay in settling our future? For many years after my Luciana died, my heart was so deeply grieved that I felt I could never love again. You told me of the captain you lost before your love could even be consummated, and I wonder if you've felt this too. Is it not so?"

When she nodded, head downcast, he continued earnestly, "During the past year it began to seem as if God was opening my heart again. I found myself asking that, if he had a new love for me, he'd bring her to my arms. Have you not felt this also, *ma chère?*"

"You're a powerful man," she said quickly, "and I'm nothing more than a simple provincial woman."

"We both fight for our countries with any weapon at hand. In that and much else we're alike, you and I, Thérèsa. I can conceive of no one as suited to be by my side as you. But that's not why I propose our union. It is because I've grown to love you with all my heart and soul, and I feel an answering passion on your part. It's why I wanted so much to bring you here —to see you in my environment as you've seen me in yours—so that both of us could feel free in our minds that we can share in every aspect of our lives."

"Alexandre, I've seen only a very small part of your involvements, and already I have to wonder how I could possibly share in any of them!" she protested.

He straightened and possessed himself of her hand. "I'm at the station of my life where I've accomplished all I set out to. I've been alone these ten years, and lonely. And I've come to realize that before all else I need the love of one who completes me. And that is you.

"Don't mistake me," he hurried on before she could speak. "I loved my dear Luciana deeply. She was the wife of my youth, the mother of my children, and I cherished her. What I feel for you is different—the communion of two settled individuals who know themselves, who've accomplished much and who come to each other as equals, as true partners. I promise that you'll rule me second only to God. If that means I withdraw from service to the king, then I'll freely do what makes you happy, for it will give me joy to please you."

She shook her head, alarmed. "You know I could never—would never —demand that of you!"

"You see, I've chosen well. We're of the same mind, are we not?"

"It appears we are." She took a shaky breath and continued, voice muffled, "To be completely truthful, you drew me into your spell from our first meeting. And when you asked me to come here, I worried that your family would be cold and unwelcoming. I confess that part of me hoped they would be. I feared the most that they'd be as they are—kind and good and generous, that they'd receive me with open arms and I'd love them. And I was concerned that I'd hate your country, that it would feel strange and uncomfortable compared to mine. But I feared even more that I'd find it beautiful and appealing and that I'd come to love it and feel at home in it."

As she spoke, a twinkle came into his eyes, and she could not hold back a laugh. "As you know, no doubt, my worst fears have been realized. But I'm an old New Englander stuck in my ways, and—"

"It seems to me that you've adapted remarkably well to this land and family of mine and to all the changes your life has undergone so far," he scoffed, his smile irresistible.

She sighed. "I've no title, no position, and although I'm well provided, I've certainly no fortune to compare to yours."

"It's no secret that in my youth I was a very ambitious man," he said, giving her a wry look. "But with age comes wisdom. I've learned what's truly important in life. Titles and position are the very least of it, and as to fortune, I've more than enough for both of us even had you no other provision. All that matters to me now is those I love."

"Can you say that your career in the navy isn't important to you, that you don't have to go into danger when and where duty calls? That, in fact, you seek it? I lost my first love to the sea—"

"You'll not lose me, dearest lady. I promise you that. I already plan to retire after this war ends. And wherever you wish to live, be it here or in your own land, it makes no difference to me as long as we're together." Gazing deeply into her eyes, he pled, "Can you love me? Will you love me as I love you, Thérèsa?"

For a long moment she hesitated, face downcast, finally looked up. "I do already. But there's another concern that worries me. I'm Anglican and you're Catholic. We worship the same God, but there are differences in our faiths that are difficult to bridge. If you married in my church, would yours recognize it? If I married in yours, would mine?"

He enclosed her in his arms, gathered her against his breast, and kissed her temple so tenderly that the last of her defenses were undone. "Leave that to me. You're not to worry over this. Believe me, there's no impediment that cannot be overcome."

She found herself nestling against him, molding perfectly into that space above his heart, nor could she find the will to pull away. At last he released her, his reluctance perceptible. Stepping back regretfully, he took her hands in his and raised them to his lips.

"I'll be gone for some months. When I return we'll talk again, and I'll want your answer then. Promise me that you'll consider my suit carefully and follow your heart."

She took a deep breath, let it out, and nodded. "I'll think and pray about it until your return."

He drew her back into his embrace, and the emotion she read in his eyes sent a thrill through her beyond anything she had ever felt before. All resistance fled.

As he bent to her, she instinctively slipped her arms around his neck. Qualms forgotten, she returned his kiss hungrily, finding in it the promise of everything her heart had longed for, and more.

Chapter Thirty-three

TUESDAY MORNING, August 4, Elizabeth hurried outside into the hot August sun after Tess and the others to surround Caledonne as he dismounted wearily in the forecourt. He handed his horse's reins to a groom and ordered him to bring a fresh mount. As he turned, Charlotte and Abby cast off decorum and flung themselves into his arms.

"Papa, you're home!" Cécile exclaimed happily. "We didn't expect you for weeks."

"The news Chartres brought of your triumph against the British off Ushant has swept through the area and beyond," Lucien said with a broad grin.

Releasing the jubilant girls, Caledonne took in their smiles with a scowl. "*Sans doute,* he's being feted everywhere as a champion."

Uneasily Elizabeth noted that his normally impeccable uniform was rumpled and dusty, his mount lathered. "Yes he is," she said, suddenly apprehensive. "All of Paris greeted him with open arms, calling him the hero of this war."

"We were at the Opera yesterday afternoon when he was welcomed with a standing ovation that seemed to go on forever," Eugène added noncommittally. "An effigy of the British admiral was burned in the gardens of the Palais Royal last night."

"So I've heard." Caledonne's tone was taut with barely contained anger. "It appears he left early this morning to rejoin our fleet at Brest—quite prudently, I'd say, though I doubt d'Orvilliers will give him such a fine reception."

"Was the fleet recalled then?"

His eyes softened as he met Tess's concerned gaze. "The damage to our ships required repairs," he explained before continuing, "I've just come from meeting with the king. Unfortunately Chartres's report was inaccurate, to say the least.

All of them stared at him, nonplussed. To Elizabeth, Lucien appeared to be the most taken aback.

Frowning, Eugène said slowly, "Perhaps you'd better come inside and explain what really happened."

"I can't stay long. Sartine intercepted me at Versailles before I could get away. He's detaching my squadron, sending us back to the rest of my fleet with a new assignment." Taking out his watch, he glanced at it and shoved it back into his pocket. "I must leave within the hour."

"I'll have hot water brought for you to wash up, Papa," Lucien said hastily. "And wine," he added over his shoulder as he hurried up the steps into the château ahead of them.

Caledonne strode up and down the salon. "We inflicted considerable destruction on the British and crippled several of their ships. If Chartres had obeyed d'Orvilliers' orders to close on their rear squadron, we could easily have pressed our advantage, no matter the damage and casualties we'd taken."

He halted long enough to allow Lucien to refill his empty wine glass, gulped it down, then resumed his pacing. "Instead, the best that can be said is that the engagement was indecisive. The worst—" He shrugged. "Because d'Orvilliers withdrew instead of renewing the battle, the British are justified in claiming the victory."

"Then d'Orvilliers bears some responsibility in the matter," Eugène said.

"I can't second guess him. He acted as he thought best according to his orders."

"Which, according to our naval policy is to protect our merchant shipping, while avoiding battle," Eugène pointed out. "Warships are costly."

"It seems an eminently sensible policy, " Tess approved, nodding.

Caledonne stopped in front of her, arms folded, mouth twitching. "I, on the other hand, have always wondered why a nation should have warships if she did not mean to use them for the intended purpose."

She narrowed her eyes, but before she could respond, Lucien demanded, "But why was Philippe sent to report to the king?"

Sighing, Caledonne resumed his pacing. "He requested permission and was granted it. I've no idea why, but he left before we squadron commanders met with d'Orvilliers after we returned to port. When we compared our individual logs of the battle, it became apparent that Chartres's action, or lack of it, allowed the British to reform, and by then night was coming on. D'Orvilliers immediately sent me to report our conclusions to the king, but it was far too late for me to overtake Chartres."

"Isn't it possible Philippe misunderstood d'Orvilliers' orders in the confusion of battle, Papa, or possibly that the signal wasn't visible from his ship because of the gunsmoke?"

Caledonne's tension eased as he met Lucien's concerned gaze. "I'll grant you that. It's also much less likely, however, that it would have happened with an experienced admiral in command of the squadron. And I suspect d'Orvilliers will bring charges against him for refusing to engage the enemy."

"But you'll not testify against him if it comes to that?"

"I didn't have a clear view of *Le Saint Esprit* when d'Orvilliers signaled," Caledonne conceded, "and I won't try to judge his actions."

"When the report spreads—which I'm sure it will quickly—Chartres will be disgraced," Eugène pointed out. "He's placed himself in an impossible position by not only giving a false report, but also making himself out to be the hero in it."

Elizabeth glanced toward Lucien, who appeared quite crestfallen. What happened then was completely unexpected.

"I know you're close friends, and I'm sorry to bring such news," Caledonne said, gripping Lucien's shoulder.

Lucien met his father's sympathetic gaze with a rueful smile. "You're entirely justified, Papa. I'm not an expert in naval strategy. You are. Whatever Philippe's motives, I won't try to account for his actions or defend him. I've enough to account for on my own behalf, as I'm sure we all do."

She watched the two men embrace with stunned relief and gratitude. Tess and Cécile were also beaming at them, and even Eugène had relaxed his normally impassive demeanor into a broad smile.

Silently she thanked God that father and son had reached out to each other, and pleaded that their reconciliation would be complete.

TESS WAITED SILENTLY while Caledonne took leave of his family and Elizabeth. His glance toward her held unmistakable invitation, and she followed him outside into the courtyard.

A groom waited with a fresh mount. Caledonne took the reins and after dismissing the groom cast a cautious glance back at the château. Seeing no one, he said, "I don't suppose any word has come from Louis. Or Jonathan."

"Nothing at all," Tess replied. "Beth rarely speaks of Jon anymore, but I feel how deeply this continued silence distresses her."

"I also spoke with Vergennes briefly at Versailles. He just received a preliminary report of a battle at a place called Monmouth Court House. Apparently the Continentals gave a good account of themselves."

"That is good news. But no mention of Jon's being involved?"

He shook his head frowning. "This new assignment may give me time to investigate." He drew her into his arms, and she clung to him. "I wish I could stay longer. But when I return we'll speak of the matter you know to be very close to my heart."

"God forbid that anything happen to you—" Her voice caught, tears burning her eyes.

He bent to kiss her lightly, then with increasing passion. At last he drew back, whispered, voice rough, "I'll return to you, Thérèsa. Come heaven or hell, I will return to you. I swear it."

She wanted so dearly to tell him that he did not need to wait for her answer, that she would marry him gladly. But the words caught in her throat, and she could only say shakily, "I'll trust in that. Until then, my prayers and my love go with you."

DURING THE PAST WEEKS, to Elizabeth's relief, Lucien's manner toward her had for the most part returned to that of the kind, witty, insightful friend she had found him to be during their voyage to France. When Carleton's name arose, which it did infrequently now, he made no comment. The apparent easing of his tense relationship with his father also provided cause for rejoicing.

And yet Elizabeth remained wary, feeling that she could not trust him fully. Though she was careful to give no outward evidence of it, she guarded her heart more vigilantly than before, sensing in him still a possessiveness, a subtle assumption that an agreement existed between them that she neither felt nor wanted.

Increasingly she wondered whom she could trust with her heart other than Aunt Tess and Abby. Cécile, surely.

She had assured Caledonne that she trusted him. But the truth was that, having been a spy herself, she knew all too well that there were things he could not tell her, just as there had been things she'd been unable to confide even to Carleton. Or he to her.

Indeed, he had once told her that he did not trust anyone completely, not even himself. She was learning that lesson quite well.

Except that . . . she trusted *him* without reservation, she realized suddenly, pain stabbing through her so sharply that she could hardly draw breath. Even in his leaving her, she trusted him with her whole heart. For he had gone because he loved her with a true and deep passion and was convinced that for him to stay would be to hurt her even more.

For months she had fought with all her being to thrust away this inexpressible longing. The time she spent with Father Raulett, his gentle counsel and his prayers over her each time they met were having a good effect. The clouds that had hung over her spirit were steadily lifting.

In all but this one thing: the seemingly unquenchable hope that Carleton would one day return to her.

The frenzy of activity she engaged in—improving her mastery of pianoforte and violin; providing medical care for the château's servants; outings to the Opera, Theater, Comedie Français, and Bois de Boulogne; balls, salons, social calls—all of it was a futile attempt to drive him out of her consciousness. But time and again she was overcome by the ache for his arms strong around her like a bulwark against danger and disappointment and loneliness. She missed the light in his eyes when he looked at her. His keen gaze that pierced to her soul. His voice, husky with desire. His smile that melted her heart. The unutterable sweetness of his endearments, his touch, his kisses.

It mattered not that he had left her willingly. It mattered not that he belonged to a people so foreign and so fearsome. No matter his past, no matter what he had done or would yet do, the truth remained that who he was, *what* he was gripped her as no one and nothing else could.

The conviction that they belonged to each other would not relent. He was hers and she was his until death. Deny it though they might, it was a fact unchangeable.

And she prayed with a consuming passion that, despite all time and distance, despite the daily ebb and flow of life, he had not forgotten it, had not forgotten her. And that the Redeemer they both worshiped would bring him back to her nor ever tear them from each other's arms again.

Chapter Thirty-four

H IS EYE TO THE SPYGLASS, Carleton squinted against the glare of the sun breaking through storm clouds trailing low above an unsettled sea.

His gut clenched as the flash of white canvas came into focus against the misty horizon.

North northeast. Only the topgallants of the first visible at the moment three points off the larboard bow.

Leaning against the rail at his side on the quarterdeck, Captain William Eaden, commander of his 100-gun privateer *Destiny*, lowered his own spyglass and called up to the tops, "Can you make out their flags?"

"Not yet, sir," answered one of the sailors in the foretop. "But they've altered course. Heading fast in our direction."

Carleton kept his gaze fixed on the horizon. Gradually the second ship's topgallants came into view, then the third's. Over the next minutes the first ship came hull up, followed after too short an interval by the second.

"Four sail now," came the call from the foretop. Then a curse. "Nay, five!"

"British!" Stowe shouted down from the maintop shortly thereafter, confirming their worst fears. "Leadin' is a 90, and looks like a 74 with her. Can't yet make out the other three."

Carleton turned around and collapsed his spyglass. "We're in for a fight."

"Depending on what the other three ships are, we might still outgun them," Eaden returned cheerily. "But we'll try to outrun them first—provided we can get enough sails aloft."

Overrun by a massive storm two days earlier, they and their escorts had hauled in every shred of canvas, swayed down topmasts, and battened down everything that could be secured. Finally the torrents of rain had finally dissipated overnight, and the keening winds had eased. A cloud-darkened dawn revealed significant damage to rigging, spars, and sails; his squadron scattered from horizon to horizon; and a position well off course southwestward.

During the hours that followed the ships had reunited, then struggled back onto its former course, while their crews worked with all haste to clear wreckage and make repairs. Everyone aboard including the women and the youngest boys had pitched in. At last the four vessels were moving east, though sluggishly, buffeted by the still turbulent waters and a fluky wind.

Carleton assessed the progress of the gun crews feverishly cutting away the ropes they had used to bind the cannon lengthwise across the ports to ride out the storm. Then his gaze followed the lines of the towering masts upward to the sailors swarming high overhead in redoubled efforts to complete the repair or replacement of splintered yards, shredded sails, and torn rigging.

His tension eased briefly as he watched Red Fox lean out over the edge of the maintop as nonchalantly as though he'd been born there. He appeared not at all daunted by the long, dizzying arc the masts circumscribed from starboard to port and back more than 200 feet above the deck and the ship's graceful rise and fall through the rough waves.

Carleton grinned, remembering that the warrior had been sicker than a dog during their first week aboard. He and his two companions had slept on deck as did most of the crew in the intolerably hot weather, and Red Fox had risen only to hang over the weather rail, vomiting, or to stagger to the head and back, complaining pitifully and eating little.

Then one morning he'd suddenly discovered his sea legs and began strolling around the deck, taking in his surroundings with interest. From that moment he had been fascinated with everything about warships and sailing, had quickly made himself a favorite of the crew for eagerly joining in their tasks. One of the sailors had stitched him a pair of slops, while another knitted him a red cap. So accoutered, he was soon cautiously climbing the rigging, then scrambling to the tops, and even learning how to handle the sails.

His particular interest, however, was the guns. So much so that Midshipman Pete Moghrab, Isaiah's tall, handsome, eighteen-year-old son, had begun teaching him how to service, aim, and fire them during the gun crews' daily practice, and he had proven to be an apt pupil. Carleton was convinced the change in his cousin had to be a miracle of God.

Shouts echoed between the four privateers as the last of the storm's debris was cast away. He transferred his gaze to the patched mizzen sail as it unfurled and bellied outward, filling with wind. He could feel *Destiny* immediately gain speed, and one by one her escorts matched her pace.

All five enemy ships were well in sight now, sails full spread, a swift 40-gun frigate taking the lead, with the 90 and 74 crowding sail behind her. Another 74 and a two-deck 50-gun fourth rater ranged along the outer sides, bringing the odds distinctly in the enemy's favor.

Pete ran up the steps onto the quarterdeck and saluted. "Gun decks cleared for action and all guns back in place, sir."

"Thank you, Mister Moghrab." Eaden dismissed him and turned to Carleton. "What I wouldn't give to be able to bring our lower gun deck to bear!"

Carleton gave a short laugh. "Thankfully their 90 can't risk opening the lower ports in these seas either. Sinking the ship would be a tad counterproductive."

"I hate to see guns go to waste when we could use the extra firepower." Eaden sighed. "But I don't suppose fortune would favor us with glass-smooth water while denying the enemy."

"In my experience fortune's a fickle lover," Carleton returned wryly.

Dr. Lemaire and Marie Glasière had come up on deck, and they joined in Eaden's laughter. "The surgery's back in order. And it appears just in time too," Lemaire noted as he took in the squadron bearing toward them.

Carleton thanked the Almighty that Teissèdre had met him and his two companions at Baltimore, where he had been overseeing arrangements for their departure. The Frenchman had overridden Carleton's impatience at the delay and insisted they bide yet another day and a half, while 90-gun *Black Swan,* just arrived when they were on the point of sailing, hastily resupplied. She had provided a definite advantage against the three British sloops of war that intercepted them off the capes outside Chesapeake Bay only to think better of taking them on. And added to 74-gun *Eagle* and 50-gun *Pursuit,* back in fighting trim after tangling with Barbary pirates, they had a reasonable chance of fending off the approaching squadron despite the disparity in gun power.

His thoughts were interrupted by Second Lieutenant Francis Abbott, who ran up onto the quarterdeck to report that most of the sails and rigging were finally in good order. The fore topmast had been restored, he added, but there was no time to sway up and secure the main and mizzen topmasts. Which left them lacking the corresponding topgallants. In addition to the spanker. And the fore staysail. Replacements for these were being prepared, however.

Carleton drew in a slow breath, pressed his eyes briefly shut, then turned a calculating gaze on the three escorts spread out beside and behind *Destiny.* Only *Pursuit* boasted a full compliment of sails, while *Black Swan* and *Eagle* were missing topgallants altogether. At least their courses and staysails were all spread, and their crews were feverishly completing preparations for battle.

Eaden called across to the other captains through a speaking horn, ordering them to a southeast heading at all possible speed. At his command, the drummers began to beat. Sailors scrambled to sand the decks, while the gun crews hastily gathered their scattered sponges and rammers.

The young boys called powder monkeys scrambled up and down through the hatches, fetching shot, powder, and tubs of smoking slow matches from below.

Red Fox descended rapidly to the waist to join Pete's crew along the larboard side. The ships completed tacking to the new heading, and the sails took the wind, the expanse of canvas overhead snapping taut. The hiss of water increased along the ship's sides, and sea spray foamed up around the privateers' bows as *Destiny's* escorts spread out around her.

With England and France at war and the Atlantic bristling with British warships, Carleton had ordered his privateers disguised as Spaniards, still neutral in the contest though leaning toward entering on the Americans' side. Thus his ships flew the Spanish ensign and jack. For whatever the effort was worth. By now his privateers had become so infamous that there was little that could be done to conceal their identity.

Over the next hour their pursuers shrank the distance between them. The replacement of *Destiny's* spanker and fore staysail held their advance temporarily at bay, while the crew adjusted the set of jibs, staysails, and braces, taking every advantage of shifting sea and wind. But inexorably the distance between them and the enemy wore gradually away.

Suddenly additional sails emerged on the southeast horizon, directly ahead, these also British, traveling toward them at speed: another 74 accompanied by two 60-gun warships. Carleton swore violently under his breath. Eaden sent all the women below, and Lemaire hurried back down to his surgery.

Before Teissèdre had left them at Baltimore, pleading an urgent matter that required his attention, he had strongly advised taking a southerly route. "Admiral Howe is prowling after d'Estaing in the north," he'd warned, referring to Vice Admiral le comte d'Estaing, commander of a French fleet sent to the Americans' aid. "But he also has ships scattered all along your coast, and they're always on the lookout for your privateers. You don't want to run afoul of them."

They had heeded his advice and had run afoul of the storm instead. And now of two enemy squadrons that decisively outnumbered and outgunned them. The hope that they could outrun their pursuers was fading, the prospect of ever reaching France, and Elizabeth, melting away before Carleton's eyes.

He could not bear the thought of wasting the lives of so many men in a battle they could not win. Yet neither was surrender possible. That the British would hang him was the least of his concerns, though not an inconsiderable one; the vivid memory of his close encounter with a British gallows at Boston had not ceased to haunt him. But they would also hang every one of his officers as pirates and impress the crews under the worst conditions. And he didn't want to think of the fate of the women they had aboard.

Also troubling was that he hadn't received a reply from Elizabeth to his letter. Allowing for how long it would have taken to reach her, even if she answered immediately there would barely have been time for him to receive her response before he left the army's camp at White Plains, especially since they had been constantly on the move.. But it was possible his letter had gone astray. If so, then she would never know that his love had not failed, that he'd relented and was coming to her. He felt heartsick at the thought.

We've no other help but you, Father, he prayed silently. *If it be your will, please preserve the lives of all those aboard my ships. And mine.*

He heard Eaden order the helmsman to a new heading, then *Destiny* changed course sharply and fled southwest. Flanking her, the escorts kept pace. So did the enemy.

It was by now mid October. On their arrival at Baltimore, Teissèdre had related rumors that Black Fish and Black Hoof were leading a force against Boonesborough in reprisal for Daniel Boone's escape back to the fort early in the summer. He also told them that Congress was negotiating a treaty with Lenape at Fort Pitt. But with the majority of the tribes allied with the

British, Carleton feared it was destined to be as meaningless as so many previous treaties had been.

Each time his people came to his mind, he felt a painful tug to go to them, to find a way somehow to avert the disaster that loomed. Repeatedly he assured himself that he had done all he could, that their fate lay in their own hands—and the Creator's. It was Elizabeth who exerted the stronger sway over his blood now, drew him to her as surely as the moon draws the tides, all the more powerful for the months-long delay in gaining his freedom.

Monmouth had resulted in essentially a draw between the two armies, though the Americans jubilantly counted it as a win. The army's improved training had paid off, as they had proven they could hold their own against the Regulars in pitched battle. Even better from Carleton's viewpoint, in the battle's aftermath Lee had been court-martialed, found guilty, and banned from the army for a year. He hoped fervently that the general's sore pride would prevent his ever returning.

Another cause for celebration was that Congress had returned to Philadelphia at the beginning of July. And the following day d'Estaing's fleet appeared off Sandy Hook, though too late to prevent Clinton from transporting his troops to safety in New York.

From there, things had veered downhill, as it seemed to all too often. Clinton effectively blocked Washington's plans for attacking the city. Then the entire month of August had been mired in an ill-fated campaign to Newport, Rhode Island, under General Sullivan, while Carleton and his brigade languished at White Plains with the rest of the army.

With Sullivan's force bogged down, hampered by storms, desertions, and conflicts with d'Estaing, who was to act in support, Washington had again put off releasing Carleton. He had been left to temper Red Fox's increasing frustration—and his own raging impatience—as best he could.

By the time Sullivan managed to extricate his force and return to safety, his patience had evaporated, however. Resolved to tell Washington that he was leaving immediately for France and there was nothing anyone could do to stop him, he was on the way to headquarters when Laurens intercepted him with a summons from the General.

All things considered, their confrontation could have gone much worse. They'd had a sharp exchange over his neither alerting Washington to Lord North's warrant nor mentioning Elizabeth's presence in France.

But when Carleton had told him frankly that he meant to marry her, to his surprise, Washington had responded sympathetically, "This war has already lasted longer than any of us anticipated at the beginning, and there is no sign it will be over soon. The two of you have endured enough, I think. I wish you the joy of your lady that I've found in mine."

Carleton had thanked him, voice choking, then added, "I'll not forget your kindness."

"I'll hold you to that," Washington returned with a rare smile before handing him a thick packet of papers. Referring to President of Congress, Henry Laurens, he said, "Laurens asked me to entrust you with these letters to our commissioners. They've heard nothing from either Franklin or Adams and little from Lee for months and wish you to deliver these personally. You're also to send regular reports to Laurens and arrange for safe transport for the commissioners' future communications. And, of course, I expect you to keep me abreast of all that goes on in Paris."

At Carleton's nod, he added, "Godspeed, Jon. Come back to us with all due haste."

The voice from the foretop shattered Carleton's reverie.

"Sails one point off the starboard bow!" A pause, then, with dismayed awe, "Blimey, looks like a bleedin' fleet!"

He and Eaden jerked their spyglasses free at the same instant, swung in the direction the lookout indicated. With the sun declining in a cloudless azure sky, a clutch of sails emerged from the haze along the southwestern horizon. As they watched, the leading ships wore in their direction.

Carleton groaned. "Who are they?" he shouted to the lookout.

"Ye'll know soon's I do!" came the cheeky answer in a thick Irish brogue.

"More than likely the fleet these squadrons belong to." Eaden's voice was flat.

The words were hardly out of his mouth when the harsh, reverberating boom of cannon fire shook air and sea. Carleton raced after Eaden onto the poop deck, saw the billowing cloud of gunsmoke rising between *Black Swan's* stern and the bow of the leading British 74. Before it could clear, *Black Swan's* stern chasers blazed again, answered by the sharp report of the enemy's bow chasers.

"Point taken," Carleton muttered. "They're begging permission to board."

Eaden gave a short laugh. "It appears we're between the devil and . . . the devil."

"How far are we from the nearest French port?"

"That would be Brest. About 200 miles. And then there'll be Britain's Channel Fleet to dodge."

Even had they their topgallants, Carleton calculated, they wouldn't have enough speed to pass between the fleet approaching from the southwest and the squadron advancing from the southeast, while outrunning the first squadron directly aft. The grimfaced sailors and Marines clearly knew it too, and a palpable tension settled over the deck as they prepared to do battle.

For an agonizing interval the attention of everyone aboard see-sawed from the hot duel developing between their escorts and their pursuers, the closing second squadron rapidly coming abreast of *Destiny's* larboard bow in line to unleash a broadside, and the approaching fleet increasingly filling the horizon off their starboard bow, a duet of frigates in advance, racing toward them.

Suddenly the lookout in the foretop screamed, "French!"

A momentary silence, then jubilant cheers, shouts, and laughter accompanied by obscene taunts, jeers, and gestures aimed at the enemy erupted across the deck, immediately taken up by their escorts' crews.

Linking arms, *Destiny's* forward gun crews began to dance an exuberant jig, only with difficulty brought back under control by the midshipmen in command.

"You're certain of it?" Carleton demanded in disbelief.

" 'Less I miss my guess, sir," Stowe shouted back from the maintop, "that be Caledonne's pennant flyin' from what looks to be a hundred-twenty-gunner!"

Carleton began to laugh. He had not realized the intensity of his fear until his tension expelled in a harsh breath.

"Turns out I was right," Eaden said, echoing his mirth. "Except this one's our devil."

Carleton laughed all the harder, gasped, "And thankfully our devil far outmatches theirs."

Apparently that fact was impressing itself on the British squadrons as well. The crash of gunfire off their stern abruptly ceased. After a glance aft to assure himself that the first squadron was dropping back, Carleton turned to the 74 at the second squadron's van.

She did not slow. He could see the dark mouths of the guns lining her bearing side, menacingly close, but just out of range, he calculated. At least if she fired low, as British crews tended to. He prayed they would.

Only distantly aware that Eaden had left his side, that men were scrambling furiously across the decks of both vessels, that behind him the order to fire rang out, he stood mesmerized, watching as plumes of gunsmoke began to erupt from the 74's gun decks followed by tongues of fire, felt the timbers lurch powerfully beneath his feet as their own broadside unleashed.

The blast roiled toward him as a visceral force, and he clenched his hands on the weather rail, head bent, eyes closed, refusing to flinch as the deafening thunder engulfed him. Beneath its roar he heard the shot crashing into the sea not a yard off *Destiny's* hull, flinging heavy spray into his face as he staggered with her violent rocking. Then his ship heeled to starboard and salvation.

He shook off sea spray, drew in a long, slow breath before fumbling for his spyglass. Staring back through the wind-shredded gunsmoke at the 74, he saw with relief that she now bore away toward the retreating first squadron with the two 60s closely trailing.

His gaze found her captain, looking after *Destiny* though his own spyglass. Their eyes met, and fury darkened the man's face as he scanned Carleton, clearly recognizing him.

Without thinking, he came to rigid attention, holding his spyglass in his left hand as he deliberately touched the fingers of his right to his brow in salute. Then, breaking into a broad grin, he drew his hand away, palm forward, in defiant, mocking farewell as *Destiny*'s stern drew out of range.

The British captain's face went scarlet, his expression apoplectic. For the briefest instant, in Carleton's mind formed the image of General William Howe urging his horse to a gallop toward him too late when, having just narrowly escaped capture, he had dared the British commander to catch him.

But he shrugged off the memory and turned away laughing.

NÉRÉIDE HOVE TO off Destiny's starboard bow to cheers and whistles from the privateers' crews. By the time Caledonne and the captain and first lieutenant of his flagship were piped aboard *Destiny,* the leading ships of both British squadrons were hull down on the northeastern horizon with the rear vessels following apace.

Eaden ushered the officers onto the quarterdeck. That Teissèdre accompanied them came as no surprise to Carleton.

After making his addresses to Eaden and his lieutenants, Caledonne drew Carleton into an embrace and kissed him on each cheek before gripping him by both shoulders and stepping back to regard him with a smile.

"What's taken you so long, my boy?" he demanded. "And what are you doing in these waters? I'd have expected you to take a more northerly course."

Carleton turned a meaningful smile on Teissèdre. "We followed some excellent advice. And then we had the misfortune of running into a storm . . . and the enemy," he apologized dryly.

Teissèdre looked pained but held his tongue.

Caledonne took in the crews standing at attention, spilling across the ship's waist and forecastle. "I did have the impression that you were on the point of battle."

"You have our eternal gratitude for sparing us the trouble," Eaden put in.

Caledonne's regretful glance after the retreating British wasn't lost on Carleton, but he waved Eaden's comment off. "Bah. It was the least I could do since we were passing by, Monsieur Eaden."

"Passing by?" Carleton turned an enquiring gaze on Teissèdre. "I'm guessing this is the urgent matter that called you away from Baltimore."

Teissèdre's mouth twitched. "In an amazing coincidence, one of le comte's squadrons just happened to put in at Norfolk the day I arrived. My business didn't take long, and a trip home is well overdue."

In the midst of his cynicism, it occurred to Carleton that, had it not been for his delayed release, *Black Swan*'s late arrival at Baltimore, and the storm driving them off course, Caledonne's fleet would have passed by well south of his squadron, not knowing they had run into trouble. Once again he had chafed mightily that his plans had gone awry, only now to find himself immensely grateful.

His vision momentarily blurred. *Your mercy is great, Father.*

To Caledonne he said, "I seem to remember chastising you not so long ago for keeping watch over my ships. I was a fool. Please accept my apology. I do very much appreciate your care."

Caledonne regarded him with a twinkle in his eyes, but he only said, "I'll keep that in mind in case I need a favor someday. "

Carleton began to laugh, and the others joined in. "You'll never concede the advantage, will you, sir? Well, I'm pleased to give it."

Caledonne pursed his lips and cocked one eyebrow at him. "Now that our British friends have decided to hunt more obliging prey, we'll escort you on your way." Smiling, he added, "There's a very special lady in France, who, I think, would find your company not at all disagreeable."

Carleton's mouth quirked. "In Paris."

Caledonne spread his hands in apology. "In Paris. As you know, my elder daughter is not one to be denied."

I suspect you're the one not to be denied, sir, Carleton thought.

Eaden said something, but he did not hear it. For he was transfixed by the sudden realization that now no further obstacles stood between him and Elizabeth except one more small space of sea and land.

Chapter Thirty-five

ELIZABETH CLUTCHED the cart's rough plank seat with one hand, her heavy hooded cloak with the other, shivering as the conveyance jolted up the narrow, winding track from the estate's farm and fields on the plain to the château on the heights above. She took in her surroundings bleakly, the dull November landscape perfectly reflecting her emotions.

Will the consciousness of him that lies behind every thought, every word, every action ever fade? Yet if it does, then I'll truly have lost him.

It was a year to the day since Carleton had wrested her from the *Erebus*. A year since Pieter Vander Groot had fallen away from them into darkness.

Even after all these months it felt as though a jagged wound cut straight through her. For the only one who could truly comfort her on this earth was not there with her.

Yet her Lord was. Always. The God of all comfort. And to him she would cling until her heart's peace returned, though she wondered whether it ever truly would.

As though sensing her tangled emotions, grizzled old Gervais gave her a reassuring look, the creases deepening in his weathered face. She returned his smile, gratitude overflowing suddenly for the blessings that abounded to her and determined once again to find in them enough for that day.

Gervais slapped the reins across the sturdy pony's rump, and cresting the rise, they turned onto the road to the château. A brief ray of sunlight slanted through the brooding clouds, lighting a copse of trees at the roadside.

Amid the drifts of russet leaves beneath it, her eye caught a flash of scarlet. There a delicate spray of wild roses flamed on a withered branch.

Gervais followed her gaze and slowed the cart. "Shall I pick it for you, mademoiselle?"

She hesitated, then shook her head and patted his gnarled hand. "Let them brighten the day for another traveler."

He gave her a sympathetic nod and urged the pony on without speaking. The cart drew to a halt in the château's courtyard, He helped her down and handed over her medical case.

A footman took it along with her cloak and gloves when she entered the *salle*. A welcoming blaze crackled on the hearth, warming the huge space. The heavy draperies that swathed the doorways and openings to the passages to forestall drafts gave a gloomy cast to her surroundings, however, quite at odds with the château's sunny aspect in spring and summer.

Cécile, Tess, and the girls had gone to spend the day at nearby Moulin Joli with Madame Brillon and her daughters, while Eugène had business at the ministry offices at Versailles. As she walked toward the stairs the butler came to meet her and, bowing, held out a note from Lucien. Artois was getting together a gambling party, he explained, promising to return before suppertime.

She stared at the page as she climbed the shadowed stairs. *My dearest Beth.* With a frustrated sigh she thrust it into her pocket, her stomach churning.

What she was to do about Lucien remained a puzzle after all these months. When others were around he still adopted a playful, brotherly tone toward her. But his manner when they were alone had become unabashedly that of a lover.

The last thing she wanted was to hurt him, but nothing she said or did seemed to deter his attentions. When she tried to reason with him, he treated her like a small child to be petted and indulged. That he was her hostess's brother and Caledonne's son, that he treated Abby and Aunt Tess as affectionately as he did his niece and sister made things all the more awkward.

She realized now, too late, that she was partly to blame. In her grief she had at first been drawn to him because his affectionate, kind manner and quick mind reminded her of Vander Groot. Unconsciously she had sought in Lucien the brotherly companionship she had so treasured with the doctor who had been not only her colleague, but a dear friend. On closer acquaintance, however, the differences between the two men had become glaringly apparent.

In her chamber she shivered in front of the fireplace while Jemma helped her change from her plain linen gown into one of finely woven, supple moss green wool with creamy lace. Her hair had finally reached the middle of her back, and the maid swept the thick, unruly mass up and away from her face, leaving a few loose curls trailing onto her shoulders.

The effect was charming, Elizabeth thought, staring at her reflection in the mirror. But what mattered it anymore?

As throughout the château the suite's windows were heavily swathed against the cold. The candles' muted light served only to emphasize her loneliness, yet she did not want company. At her direction the housekeeper, Madame du Champ, sent up a dinner tray for both her and Jemma, and after they had eaten the maid settled down to sew.

Elizabeth wrapped a warm shawl around her shoulders and wandered downstairs to the salon, feeling entirely at loose ends. She was standing, disconsolate, at the terrace doors, staring across the frost-blighted gardens when she heard the château's outer door open, the butler speaking to someone whose voice she didn't recognize, then the door closing again. She dropped the draperies back into place and turned as the butler padded quietly into the salon and bowed.

"A message arrived from le comte addressed to la marquise, made-moiselle. Since both she and the marquis are gone and not due to return for some hours, I thought it advisable that you determine whether it is a matter of urgency."

She hurried to take it from him. "Yes, thank you." She broke open the seal and unfolded the wrapper, then the letter inside. Hastily she scanned the page and looked up.

"Le comte is on the way here with a party of four!" she exclaimed, her spirits lifting. "He estimates they'll arrive late this afternoon. Of course, there'll be escorts with them too."

A broad smile covered his face. "Excellent! I'll have Madame du Champ prepare food and accommodations for a large party."

Suddenly energized, she told him that she would be in the music room and instructed that she not be disturbed until Caledonne arrived. Bowing, he went to order candles to be lit and the fire built up there.

She entered the expansive music room at the chateau's rear to find maids and footmen already hurrying about. Near the pianoforte a brazier filled with hot coals added its heat to the fire snapping on the hearth. According to the clock on the wall above the instrument, it was a little past two-thirty.

Reassured that she had plenty of time to practice, she laid aside her shawl and warmed her stiff fingers over the brazier before looking through the scores she had recently practiced. As she paged through them, she pulled out one inscribed with her own notations.

Strains of the composition Carleton had performed for her and her family at Tess's home in Roxbury often haunted her mind. At their insistence he had played it several times before that terrible night of his leaving. And ever since, without confiding to anyone, she had been trying to capture as much of it as she could retrieve from memory.

Will Uncle Alexandre bring news of him? Hastily she buried the thought.

As she looked up, her gaze fell on his violin case, lying on a nearby shelf. So far she had only practiced on Cécile's violin, hesitant to try playing his. Cécile, however, played it daily, loving its rich tones, and she kept it tuned and in good condition.

On impulse she took down the case, removed the violin and bow, and pressed the instrument to her cheek, tenderly stroking the mellow, gleaming wood. Blinking back tears, she set it on a table behind and to one side of the pianoforte, then tested the resin on the bow. She applied a little more and carefully tightened the hairs. Taking up the violin, she ran the bow lightly across the strings and adjusted the tuning until she was satisfied.

She played the first measures of her efforts to transcribe the composition, frowned and repeated them. Then sighed, her shoulders slumping.

It was similar, but not quite as she remembered. And she certainly had not yet the skill to play with the ease he had nor to draw from the instrument such deeply evocative nuances.

With regret she laid violin and bow carefully back on the table and settled on the bench at the pianoforte. For some while she tried subtle variations in the effort to capture not only the notes, but also the emotions they evoked.

She had entirely lost track of time when she heard Caledonne's voice and laugh echoing in the great *salle,* the answering voices of several others. But she paid no heed, for all at once she could hear clearly in her mind the intense, sweet longing of the introduction as Carleton had played it. And now the notes flowed through her fingers onto the keys.

For a moment she froze, unable go further, for with them came a great tidal wave of anguish. Afraid to lose what she had gained, however, she drew a jagged breath and, eyes closed, forced her fingers to play through the measures again.

Behind her she heard someone quietly enter the room and approach with a familiar stride. She glanced up at the clock hanging above the pianoforte and saw that the hands stood almost at four o'clock.

Without turning she said huskily, "Welcome home, Uncle Alexandre. I'm trying to remember a song Jonathan once played for us at Aunt Tess's. Did he ever play anything like this in your hearing?"

Frowning as she concentrated on the keys, she heard him move something on the table behind her. The sound of the bow drawn lightly across the violin's strings followed. Then, with no hesitation, the composition's first measures filled the chamber, evoking more vividly than she could have the smoky sigh of wind and rain through forest reaches and continuing effortlessly, unfaltering and true, into a lilting Scottish jig.

Her heart contracted so sharply that she could neither breathe nor speak. The keys blurred before her eyes and, faltering, she struck a discordant note.

He bent to her then, so close his cheek brushed hers, and she breathed in the clean, masculine scent of him, of fresh wind and leather and linen, from the corner of her eye caught the glimpse of his strongly corded, deeply tanned hand and above it the edge of a charcoal grey cuff.

"Don't stop. Keep playing," he murmured, the unforgettable timbre of his voice rough with emotion. Straightening, he began again to play.

She could not look up. She dared not. Blindly she endeavored to continue, but she could no longer make out the keys and her fingers fumbled the notes. At last she dropped her hands to her lap, entirely broken, eyes squeezed shut, certain that it was the song that had summoned his spirit out of the very ether and that if she opened them, it would be only a dream, that he would evaporate even as he had vanished into the mist that winter morning when it had not been him after all.

He also stopped playing. "Beth."

That single word, spoken as tenderly as an endearment undid what little remained of her self-possession. She covered her face with her hands, tears streaming between her fingers. Behind her she heard him set the violin on the table, then he scooped her up into his arms as easily as though she weighed nothing. She buried her face against his neck, feeling the strength of him as steady as a bulwark against the months of sorrow and heartbreak and loneliness.

He carried her to the divan and sat down, settling her on his lap. For long moments they clung to each other. But at length he drew back and tried gently to turn her face up to his. Eyes still fearfully pressed shut, she kept head and shoulders bowed, and he had to bend to look into her face.

"Beth . . . look at me."

Afraid still to believe, she shook her head, pressed back into his arms, reveling in the feel of them sure and steady around her.

At last he pulled her shielding hands from her face, tilted her chin up. For a moment longer she kept her eyes downcast, finally, tentatively, raised her fearful gaze to meet his.

And found his eyes so full of love and pain that she could no longer hold back the sobs. Vainly she sought to brush her tears away, drinking him in as her gaze traced hungrily the well remembered, long ached-for contours of his face.

"Ah, dear heart, how my eyes have longed to see you!" he whispered, voice shaking.

And, oh, the deep blue-grey depths of them, impossible ever to forget, glimmering now with tears as were her own! She reached out to caress his cheek, feeling the wetness there with wonder, and a leap of joy as he enclosed her hand in his, bent his head until his forehead touched hers and their tears mingled.

"Shhh. Beth, don't cry. Dear heart, don't! You know I can't bear your tears—"

"You're not a dream?" she demanded, halfway between a laugh and a sob.

"Flesh and blood, I swear it."

Burying his fingers in her hair, he pulled her to him, kissed away her tears with a tender, aching sweetness that by swift degrees gave way to fire, kindling an answering passion in her bosom and erasing all consciousness of time.

"Don't ever let me go," she whispered at last.

She felt him shudder. "I won't—I can't . . . " He drew a quick, light breath. "And here I feared you'd have forgotten me by now."

She traced his cheek with her fingertips, returned his searching look with a reproachful one. "Don't tease me, Jonathan! I could as soon forget my very heart."

He smiled deeply into her eyes. "Forgive me. I only meant to make you smile."

She slipped her arms around his neck, clung to him. "I thought this time you'd truly gone forever."

"I was resolved," he answered, his words as broken as her own, "but Louis—"

"He found you then—praise God!"

"There's yet more to God's working, but I'll tell you all later." He held her away from him. "For now, only let me look at you—hold you." He pulled her roughly back into his embrace. "Ah, heart of my heart! The image I carry of you in my mind is more beautiful than any woman could possibly be. And every time I see you again, you're more lovely yet!"

"I told myself I could live apart from you, but I might as well try to give up sunshine and air," she returned with a rueful laugh.

"I'll do all in my power to keep it so! If you only knew the sway you hold over my soul, dearest, you'd never fear that your love could not draw me back again." He stopped, concern coming into his eyes. "Uncle Alexandre told me that you'd not received my letter by the time he left."

"Your letter? Then you did write!"

"As soon as I returned to Valley Forge. But it never reached you?" When she shook her head, he said urgently, "Beth, will you—"

A movement caught her eye, and she looked up, over his shoulder. Apparently he felt her stiffen, for he broke abruptly off and released her.

Lucien stood in the doorway, staring at them, his face contorted with such anger and hatred that her breath caught. How long had he been standing there watching them? she wondered. How much had he overheard? But as his gaze met hers, all trace of emotion erased from his features so completely that for an instant she wondered whether she had been mistaken.

She hastily got to her feet. Carleton rose with her and turned to face his cousin, the tenderness vanishing from his face as though a mask descended over it, leaving it hard and cold as marble. The look that passed between the two men made it clear that there was long history, and bitter rancor, between them.

"Lucien," Carleton said evenly. "It's good to see you again."

"You've been away from us far too long, cousin."

Lucien's smile did not reach his eyes. And the subtle irony of his words made Elizabeth think that what he really meant was that it hadn't been long enough.

Carleton responded with the slightest bow.

"It's good of you to leave your savages long enough for a visit. Though, *sans doute,* you'll want to return to them as soon as possible since you've made yourself one of them. And quite appropriately so."

The lazily drawled words came like a slap to the face and were accompanied by a quick, probing glance at Elizabeth. She went cold, felt the color drain out of her cheeks.

Carleton's laugh was soft, holding an edge of menace. Encircling Elizabeth's shoulders with his arm, he drew her protectively against his side.

"It's reassuring to see you haven't changed. But then, I didn't expect that you would."

For an instant Elizabeth had the horrifying sense that they teetered on the precipice of a duel. She opened her mouth to intervene but was struck dumb when Lucien turned on her the same dark, level look he fixed on Carleton.

She started when Caledonne appeared suddenly behind his son. Clapping Lucien briefly on the shoulder, he strode into the room.

"What's this?" he demanded, laughing. "Don't tell me the two of you have been left all alone without a chaperone! I'm scandalized, but not as much as my daughter will be when she learns that I'm the one behind the mischief."

The charged atmosphere perceptibly eased. Elizabeth joined in his laughter with relief and drew Carleton forward, leaning on his arm, grateful to feel him relax against her. His smile wry, he allowed her to lead him to his uncle, who immediately ushered all three of them out of the music room as though to forestall the very thing she feared.

✹ ✹ ✹

After a brief introduction to the rest of Carleton's party, Lucien excused himself and withdrew upstairs. Although his cousin's presence hovered at the edge of Carleton's thoughts like a black cloud, the joy of being with Elizabeth after long months of despair blocked it from his immediate consciousness. He watched, smiling as she greeted Teissèdre with delight.

"Thank you for bringing him back to me, Louis!" she exclaimed. "My heart overflows."

Teissèdre bowed, his face wreathed in a smile. "You doubted me, mademoiselle?"

"Never again! Clearly you're a miracle worker."

When she turned to Stowe, Carleton almost laughed outright. He looked extraordinarily uncomfortable in the fashionable clothing Carleton had purchased for him at Brest and insisted he wear, over his voluble objections. And her affectionate welcome and profuse admiration of his fine appearance brought a blush to his face.

Then her attention fixed on the last man of their party. She regarded the tall, swarthy, black-haired and elegantly attired man uncertainly before glancing around at the rest of them, evidently puzzled as to why no one introduced him. After scrutinizing him more closely, she burst out in astonishment, "Red Fox?"

Eyes glinting with amusement, the warrior swept her a graceful bow. "It is good to see you again, Healer Woman," he said in perfectly accented French.

Carleton stifled his mirth with difficulty as she threw her arms around the warrior. As usual at displays of emotion, he reacted stiffly, retreating into dignified reserve. But beneath it Carleton could tell that he was genuinely glad to see her, saw by her radiant smile that she recognized it too.

Just then the footman threw open the outside door, and Charlotte and Abby burst inside, trailed by Tess and Cécile. They all came to an abrupt halt, looking from one to the other.

"Jonathan!" Charlotte and Abby squealed in unison before flying to his arms, the two women trailing after them with exclamations of astonished surprise and welcome.

He stooped to gather the girls into his arms. "Here are my girls—but what fine ladies you've become. How I've missed you both!"

He kissed Charlotte soundly, then turned to Abby, who leaned in to press her cheek against his, her arms tightening around his neck. "I knew you'd come," she whispered. "I knew you love Beth too much to stay away."

He glanced up at Elizabeth, who was watching them with an emotion in her eyes that caused his heart to overflow. He still could hardly believe that all the months of painful separation were really ended.

He turned back to Abby. "Didn't I tell you that time would make all things right?"

Beaming at him, she nodded. "I never stopped praying."

"And surely your prayers brought me here."

They were interrupted by Eugène, who stepped in from outside and taking everyone in, broke into a grin. "Ah, you made it safely then."

Cécile rounded on her husband. "You knew and never breathed a word to me?"

He exchanged a smug glance with Teissèdre. "Is it necessary for a wife to know all of her husband's business?"

"*Certainement!*" she returned indignantly, drawing herself up. "How else is she to manage him—for his good, of course?"

"*Mais, bien sûr,*" he agreed dryly, and they all laughed.

Chapter Thirty-six

"A S I RECALL YOU WERE a mere captain when you visited us on your way back to Virginia four years ago," Cécile teased. "And now you've reached the exalted state of general—major general at that."

Carleton grimaced. "I don't know how exalted a state that is."

"You've had a meteoric rise, I'd say."

"Oh, please, Papa! Jonathan's head is swelled enough as it is."

Carleton grinned at his uncle.

Lucien had excused himself to his sister soon after their arrival, claiming yet another gambling party at Le Petit Trianon, and gone. Although they carefully avoided the subject, his abrupt departure cast a pall on the evening. But for Carleton it came as a relief, the delay of a confrontation he knew from experience would inevitably come.

He resolutely pushed the matter out of his thoughts. He could not keep his gaze off Elizabeth. Seated next to him, she wore a deep scarlet gown that in the glow of the chandelier sparked fiery tones in her dark hair.

He had changed from traveling clothes into a suit of fine, smoky blue wool. But although he had managed to browbeat Stowe into genteel clothing for the journey from Brest, the older man had dug in his heels when it came to joining them at table. Instead he had decamped to the servant's hall along with their Marine escorts, while Teissèdre had gone to, as he put it, visit his home.

Looking entirely like a Spaniard in black coat and breeches and with his hair grown out since leaving White Plains, Red Fox raised his wine glass. "Do not forget that my cousin White Eagle is first of all a war chief among the Shawnee."

Everyone lifted their glasses in response, and Cécile acknowledged the correction with a gracious inclination of her head. "I stand corrected, Monsieur Fox. But as fearsome as that rank is, I'm afraid you'll both find that the subtle deceptions our governmental ministers are skilled in are sharper than any blade."

"I can't believe that even you have so little confidence in my powers of discernment!" Carleton exclaimed in feigned outrage to Abby's and Charlotte's giggles.

Cécile lifted her shoulders in an expressive shrug. "When it comes to subterfuge, you're a mere amateur in comparison. But, after all, you are only half French."

In a loud whisper Carleton confided to Elizabeth behind his hand, "You see that my cousin is no more given to vain flattery than she was in our youth."

Elizabeth answered with a smile, eyes dancing with merriment.

Cécile tossed her head. "And what improvement could I expect in you if I were?"

"Hear, hear," Tess seconded, her mouth suspiciously pursed.

Caledonne rested his arm across the back of her chair. "It's been my experience that when criticized one does well to consider whether it might not be justified."

"Indeed. Did not my subtlety easily overcome you at your nation's great council, *mon ami?*" Teissèdre observed with a smug smile.

"I knew what you were up to, Louis. It was the extent of your temerity that stunned me." Carleton turned back to Cécile. "But I know when I've been put in my place. I bow at your dainty feet, oh Saint Cécilia!"

She rolled her eyes. "Spare me, cousin! I've no intention of playing the martyr to you or anyone else."

Eugène smirked. "I'll testify to that." Another gust of laughter greeted his comment as Cécile gave him a narrowed look.

"I, for one, firmly believe that a wife should rule the roost," Caledonne said, directing a warm smile at Tess.

She raised her eyebrows. "Oh, really?"

Carleton bent toward her. "Perhaps that's a proposition you'd care to test," he murmured meaningfully. Without waiting for her response, he lifted his goblet. "Shall we drink to the happy couple?"

Elizabeth had much to do to stifle a giggle as a wave of scarlet suffused her aunt's cheeks.

"Excellent suggestion!" Caledonne raised his glass, appearing inordinately pleased. "As I recall, I did give you an ultimatum before I left, Thérèsa. A loving one."

The two girls sprang impulsively from their seats and came to stand on either side of Tess. "Are you going to marry Uncle Alexandre?" Abby cried, hands clasped. "Oh, please say yes, Aunt Tess!"

"You'd never have to leave us," Charlotte echoed hopefully. "You'd become my own *chère grand-mère!*"

Tess looked around the table, her alarm clearly growing as she met the hopeful gazes fixed on her.

"Do say you will, Thérèsa!" Cécile pleaded as Eugène nodded encouragingly. "You do love Papa, don't you?"

Tess covered her face with her hands. Gently Caledonne took her by the shoulders and turned her to face him.

"You told me you do. You've not changed your mind, dear one?"

She dropped her hands, looked up to meet his gaze, then shook her head, tears glimmering in her eyes.

"And you do love my family?"

She scanned the others at table, and her shoulders drooped. "You know I do."

"And they love you. So what's to stop us?"

She looked up at him with an expression of doom that came near to breaking down Elizabeth's last defenses. She clapped her hands to her mouth to hold back her laughter.

"Oh, very well," Tess huffed, drawing herself stiffly erect and glaring at him. "I might as well try to hold back an earthquake as deny you!"

Elizabeth made the mistake of meeting Carleton's eyes, and they both dissolved into helpless laughter along with everyone else.

Regarding Tess with appeal, Caledonne gently took her hands as the girls crowded in to embrace them both. "But you are happy, aren't you, my love?"

She melted. "How could I not be?" Bending forward, she kissed him full on the lips.

As he drew her into his arms to return it with interest, they all burst into cheers and together raised their glasses high.

ALL THAT HAD CONSUMED HIM from the moment of his arrival was the desire for Elizabeth. And privacy. She clearly shared his feelings.

When he closed the door of her private salon behind them, it was as though a magnetic force pulled them immediately into each other's arms. He pressed light kisses upon her lips, her cheeks, her brow, the tender hollow beneath her ear.

Drawing her to the divan, with increasing passion he trailed kisses down her throat and to the silken cleft below until her breast was heaving and her cheeks were delectably rosy. His fingers found the pins in her hair, and he released the fiery flood, slid his hand down the curve of her back to her waist, feeling the quick intake of her breath as she arched against him. Then their lips met again while time stood still.

"Dearest, stop!" she gasped huskily at last. "We must . . . else . . . we'll not."

He managed a muffled, shaky laugh. "Beth, I've ached for you so fiercely that I feared it would be the death of me."

"You've haunted every dream, every thought until I was on the verge of going mad," she confessed. "Don't ever do this to me again!"

"Never, I swear it. Dear heart, marry me—say you will!"

She looked up at him in wonder. "But I thought it impossible until—"

"I talked to Washington, and he gave us his blessing. Red Fox is certain our clan won't stand in our way, and I'm persuaded your parents will accept it in time. Beth, we're finally free!"

"But when—"

"Now. Tomorrow. As soon as we can make arrangements."

She laughed shakily, on the verge of weeping. "I wish it were so easy! Unfortunately arranging a wedding will take weeks at least, if not months. If you'll remember, dearest, France is a Catholic country."

He released her, and with a frustrated exclamation, slumped back against the divan. "Of course it is. And we're both Anglican. At least one of us would have to convert before a priest could marry us."

"Well, Papa gave us strict instructions against that," she said with a rueful laugh. "And at any rate, I couldn't act so falsely. I'm content in my faith as are Abby and Aunt Tess. All three of us realized immediately, however, that it was impossible not to attend Mass with your family, and we've found great comfort in doing so. I deeply admire their devotion, especially as they express it in the good works they continually do. No one could be more concerned for those in need or kinder to everyone."

"I'm told my mother was a staunch Catholic, and I've always attended Mass whenever I visited Uncle Alexandre and my cousins. Is any more needed than to believe in our Lord Jesus Christ and to follow him as faithfully as we can?"

She nestled against his shoulder. "No. Nothing."

"However, if we're to marry, we're going to need an Anglican priest," he allowed with a grimace.

"If there's one in all of France, I don't know of it."

He grinned. "Come to think of it, this is France! We could just live in sin, and no one would give it a second thought."

She pulled away to glare at him. "Jonathan!"

He chuckled, then sobered. "My love, I swear that, come what may, I'll never dishonor you. I want you for my wife, not my mistress."

She blushed so adorably that his self-control almost melted again. To keep from snatching her back into his arms, he sprang to his feet and paced across the salon, rubbing the back of his neck in frustration.

"Red Fox and I must carry out the charge our sachems gave us, though it'll do no good. I'll be surprised if Vergennes even brings our suit before the king, but we have to go through the motions at least. It's more important, however, that I find a way to stop the destruction of my privateers and replace those I've lost."

"From what Uncle Alexandre told us, the situation has become somewhat dire."

He turned and came back to capture her hands and draw her to her feet. "I'm losing men and money by the day. If this continues, I'll eventually be unable to maintain my Rangers, nor will I have any means to provide for you."

She smiled up at him and reached to caress his cheek. "Whatever comes, from now until the end of our lives, we'll find our way together, dearest of my heart. We can always live among your clan, you know."

He pressed his hand over hers. "You're willing?"

"If you are there," she murmured.

He regarded her earnestly for a long moment, his heart swelling with love. Then, smiling, he bent to kiss her.

Chapter Thirty-seven

ELIZABETH HARDLY SLEPT that night, the heady memory of their shared passion and the anticipation of finally planning their wedding keeping her awake. As dawn broke cold and clear she could lie abed no longer. Eagerly she slid her feet into her slippers and wrapped herself in a morning robe.

She eased quietly out into the passageway, closing the door softly to avoid waking Tess, who had not returned to her chamber until quite late. Someone stirred in the early morning shadows, and she glanced up to see Stowe padding silently toward her from the direction of the spacious suite he, Red Fox, and Carleton occupied at the end of the wing.

He came soundlessly to her, looking more like a ruffian then ever clothed in his usual rough garments, a cheerful grin puckering the livid scar that creased the side of his face. " 'E'll be down direct," he confided in a low voice.

Thanking him, she impulsively kissed him on the cheek, causing his grin to broaden even though a fierce blush stained his cheeks. She hurried down the stairs and, catching the alluring scents of freshly baked pastries, coffee, and chocolate, stepped into the *petit* dining room.

Lucien sat alone at the table, a steaming cup in front of him. He started as she stopped abruptly on the threshold. Then he rose deliberately to his feet, his gaze level and cold.

"Good morning," she said, forcing her voice to remain steady.

Before she could say more, he cast his serviette onto the table without removing his gaze from her. "How fickle women are. Even you. I'd not have believed it—how quickly you abandon the understanding we had—"

"Understanding?" she protested in astonishment. "I've no idea what you're talking about. We had no such thing."

He gave a harsh laugh. "So you only toyed with me. And now you spurn my love like a plaything cast aside when it's no longer wanted."

"Lucien," she said carefully, "you knew I love Jonathan. I made no secret of it, nor that I've never felt anything toward you other than friendship. I repeatedly made that clear."

A spasm of what she could only define as lostness passed over his face, and her chest tightened. "You made me better as no one else ever could. Without you—" His face hardened, and he shook his head. "Well, what matters any of it now?"

He swung on his heel and strode to the door, brushing roughly past Carleton as he came through it. Carleton turned to watch him go, his expression unreadable.

Elizabeth ran to him. "He accuses me of making promises to him, but I did no such thing! I've tried and tried to make him understand—"

"Of course you have." He drew her into his arms, under his breath muttered, "It's just as I feared."

She pulled back to look up at him. "What do you mean?"

His smile was clearly forced. "Dear heart, don't trouble yourself. I'm here now and all will be well. I promise."

Eugène entered then, followed by Red Fox, and the rest of the family soon joined them. Carleton appeared to have dismissed the confrontation with Lucien, and Elizabeth also put it out of her mind, assuring herself that his ill temper would pass.

While everyone ate and chatted, she and Carleton exchanged glances and smiles so often that Cécile finally said, "You might as well tell the rest of us, though I'm sure we all know what's afoot. Have you set a date?"

Carleton chuckled, and his gaze settled on Elizabeth with an emotion that brought a blush to her cheeks. "I don't suppose there are any Anglican priests in Paris."

Glee erupted around the table. Tess and Cécile came to kiss both of them, as did Abby and Charlotte, while the men offered hearty congratulations. When the tumult at last died down, Caledonne promised to make inquiries for a clergyman, and Cécile pronounced a second wedding manageable, following Tess and her father's.

To this, Carleton took Elizabeth in his arms and kissed her before them all, to everyone's delighted approval.

❋ ❋ ❋

IN THE DAYS THAT FOLLOWED, Elizabeth and Carleton laid their hearts bare to each other, confiding without reservation everything that had happened during their separation. They shared their sufferings and temptations, their deepest fears and hopes and dreams.

He described what had transpired among the Shawnee, at Monmouth, and on the voyage to France. To her great delight he added that both Blue Sky and Spotted Pony's wife, Rain Woman, were pregnant again, and McLeod and Mary Douglas had married at White Plains.

In turn she told him of her struggles and that she was coming to rest in the confidence that through these difficulties God was leading her surely and steadily to the fulfillment of his plan for her. Carleton was a part of that plan, to be sure, but she found surprising encouragement in recognizing that his identity and purpose were not hers. Her life was the Lord's to dispose and order, and discovering daily all that entailed brought with it peace and joy.

"I feel this separation has done us both good," she told him earnestly, "for we come to each other now with a more mature devotion and steadfast love."

"The hardest things we do are often the best for us," he agreed, adding that for him being reunited with her had brought an unaccustomed sense of having truly found home.

He had wandered all his life never feeling that he fully belonged anywhere, he confided. Even among the Shawnee something essential remained missing: a family all his own. And deeper even than that, a father.

Sir Harry, then Black Hawk had stood in a father's place to him, and he loved and respected both. But neither *was* his father, not his real one. Sir Harry had adopted him, but the relationship between them had remained that of uncle and nephew, just as with Caledonne, while Black Hawk had seemed more grandfather than father.

"If I could only reclaim the man who sired me!" he told her. "If I could only learn what in me disappointed him so greatly that he had to send me away, I'd finally find peace."

As for Lucien, Carleton made no attempt either to avoid or approach him. It was becoming clear that whatever troubled him went deeper than the rivalry between them. As their paths intersected day by day, he remained scrupulously courteous, which Lucien countered with haughtiness, and increasingly with contempt.

Elizabeth he treated with a cold indifference that before would have been wounding. But seeing the two men together now, she found the differences between them striking. And unsettling.

Increasingly the undercurrents of dissipation in Lucien, entirely lacking in Carleton, troubled her. In Carleton there was an intensity of passion, something wild and free that made Lucien seem emotionally bound, unstable, and ruthless in comparison. Indeed there was nothing at all of those attributes about Carleton, and in his presence her blood thrilled with the instinctive recognition that he was her true match.

Sadly she acknowledged that her friendship with Lucien could not be restored if he did not choose it. Consequently she erected clear boundaries between them, which she enforced with quiet dignity, determined that she would allow no shadow to diminish her joy. At the same time she hated that she felt so much more at ease when he was absent.

Tess became so concerned about the tension that constantly disturbed the household's peace that she privately brought up the matter.

"What can Jonathan do?" Elizabeth responded in despair. "If he says nothing or answers peacefully, Lucien insults him. If he answers in kind, Lucien goads him. If he ignores Lucien altogether, he only becomes angrier."

Carleton made no further reference to the matter, and yet she felt a tense wariness in him. She knew that all of them were painfully aware of Lucien's brooding, his bitter antagonism toward Carleton, and now her as well, could see in their faces that he and his father again quarreled, often bitterly.

"No," Carleton said stonily.

Puzzled, Eugène said, "But it's not to be debated, Jonathan. When the king wishes a thing, it must be done if you're to be received."

Idly Carleton glanced around Eugène's spacious office where he kept all the estate's records and met with his steward and other official callers. Everything was, as usual, tidily stowed, with nothing out of place and no papers visible to any unauthorized eye, he noted with approval.

Caledonne turned from the long window that offered a sweeping view of the château's front lawn. Inclining his head toward Red Fox, he said, "If the two of you are to have any hope of presenting your appeal, then you must capture the king's interest. And what better way than this? Louis *Seize* has heard of your and Red Fox's presence in Paris—"

"As the entire city has by now," Eugene muttered, shaking his head ruefully. "Invitations to dinners and other fetes are pouring in, and already we've callers pounding at the door."

Waving off the interruption, Caledonne continued, "—and is very eager to meet you in spite of Vergennes' discouraging the affair. When we were on the hunt yesterday, he made a couple of kills, which put him in an excellent mood. In Vergennes' absence, I took the chance of circumventing his designs by arranging for your presentation at the *grand lever*. But he expects that you appear before him in Indian dress."

"Unless you wish for Vergennes to block your appeal altogether, you must immediately exploit this opening," agreed Teissèdre forcefully.

"With the queen nearing the end of her pregnancy, the king may be disposed to be generous."

Bemused, Red Fox demanded, "Why are you opposed to this, my brother?"

Carleton scowled. "To begin with, I don't look forward to being dragged into that den of gossips, rumormongers, and backbiters. Most of all, I detest being made a show of for the gratification of sycophants. If a certain nameless person hadn't persuaded our sachems to send us on this wild goose chase, I'd happily give it a pass."

His expression supremely virtuous, Teissèdre drew himself up. "Had said person not done so, you'd not even be here. And I've not observed you suffering any great distress on that score."

Carleton turned a narrowed look on him. "So we're to do penance by making ourselves a spectacle to courtiers in their fantastic court clothing and bizarre *maquillage*."

A broad grin spread over Red Fox's face. "I wish to see this!"

"You're eager to start a new fashion among our people?" Carleton enquired. As Red Fox considered the matter with happy anticipation, he added, "Can't we simply walk in, make our obeisance to the king, and bow ourselves out? We'll not be allowed to bring up our petition anyway."

"No! This is the first step toward receiving a hearing." Caledonne returned to his chair. "You're entirely too much of a republican, Jonathan."

"Guilty as charged."

"You're the son of a British marquess, who was incidentally a Scottish laird, and the grandson of a French comte," Caledonne pointed out.

"For whatever that distinction is worth to a second son."

Caledonne waved his objection away. "You may not like it, but you're inescapably a member of the privileged orders."

"To my shame," Carleton growled.

"After all these years, don't you think you ought to make peace with your position?"

Carleton looked away, frowning. "There are times when I don't know who or what I am."

Leaning back in his chair with fingers steepled, Caledonne considered him thoughtfully. "The nobleman, the republican, the warrior—all of these equally make up who you are. They complicate your life, to be sure, but they also complete you, not divide you. It's simply given to you to live within wider boundaries than is common to most men."

"Huzzah for me." Despite his cynicism, Carleton felt oddly as though somewhere inside a light glimmered, though a dim one. "However, the matter of what to wear to the king's *lever* is a moot point," he said hopefully. "I only brought uniform and civilian dress with me."

Red Fox had been listening with interest. "I have clothing enough—"

"Beggin' yer pardon, sir, but I packed yer best gear," Stowe broke in. He returned an obliging grin to Carleton's glare. "Brought paint, too, so's ye can compete with the courtiers."

Caledonne pushed back his chair and rose. "I'm afraid you've no choice but to endure, Jonathan. You will wear Indian dress to the king's *lever*."

ACCORDINGLY, AT MIDMORNING two days later, Carleton throttled rebellion with every step while stalking at Red Fox's side through Versailles' halls.

In obedience to his uncle's dictate, they were accoutered almost identically. Carleton wore a thigh-length shirt of cerulean; Red Fox, crimson. Both wore breechcloths and elaborately quilled and beaded leggings and moccasins. At their necks dangled a sheathed knife, and a tomahawk swung from a beaded sash at their waists. A silver brooch and white eagle feathers ornamented Carleton's roached hair; several turkey feathers and the tuft of a red fox's tail, Red Fox's. Silver armlets encircled their upper arms, and both their faces were painted in broad black and vermillion swaths.

Carleton resolutely ignored the raised eyebrows and astonished stares and murmurs that followed their path, his mood resembling that of a baited bear. Had it been up to him, they'd have presented the appearance of a two-man war party: naked and painted black.

For his part, Red Fox gave no evidence of being daunted in the slightest degree. He took in the courtiers' painted faces, towering hairstyles, brilliantly ornate clothing along with the gilded ornamentation and furnishings of the chambers they passed through with a wide-eyed appreciation that made it clear he intensely admired everything he saw. Carleton could almost hear his mind whirring with ideas. His cousin was going to become a celebrity among their people, he decided.

"Is the English court like this as well?" Red Fox enquired in a hushed voice.

"It's a matter of degree. The British are a more austere people, thus somewhat less outrageous in their clothing and adornments."

Disappointment furrowed Red Fox's brow.

Ahead of them blue-and-red-uniformed Swiss guards stood at attention on either side of the door to the king's bedchamber. By now several nobles followed in their train—those whose rank was not high enough to allow admittance to the earlier *petit* lever, Carleton guessed. As they approached, one of the guards scratched on the door. When bidden to enter, he swung it open and stood out of the way, bowing, as they passed into the sumptuous, gilded bedchamber beyond.

At its center, twenty-four-year-old Louis XVI, clad in shirt, breeches, and hose, patiently endured the elaborate morning ritual of being clothed by his nobles. Oblivious to the courtier who slipped his waistcoat over his arms and buttoned it for him, he stared at Carleton and Red Fox in unconcealed delight.

Their movements perfectly synchronized, they performed the required bows as Caledonne had instructed them. Clearly pleased, he came to usher them forward, Vergennes advancing at the same time, but looking as though his breakfast had disagreed with him. Before Caledonne could get a word out of his mouth, the foreign minister officiously presented the two of them to the king, keeping introductions short.

The French sovereign was of medium stature and, though corpulent, robust in appearance. Evidently somewhat myopic and none too graceful, he fumbled awkwardly closer to scrutinize them from head to foot.

"Astounding!" he exclaimed. "These men can teach us something about painting the face and dressing the hair, *n'est-ce pas vrai?*" A gust of titters greeted his words.

"We're most glad to assist you and your nobles, *Majesté.*"

The resonant tones of Red Fox's voice rolled through the chamber, causing a hush to fall and all motion to suspend. The courtiers stared at him, eyebrows raised.

Carleton slid a sidelong glance at his cousin, fighting to squelch a laugh. Red Fox gave no evidence of any discomfiture, however. He met the king's gaze with serene goodwill.

Far from being displeased, the king crowed, "The Indian speaks French—and like a Frenchman!"

Red Fox bowed as the nobles joined in the king's laughter. "*Mais, bien sûr.* As you may recall, we were your allies in the former war and hold your people in the highest regard."

Brilliant, Carleton exulted, sliding a glance at Vergennes. Except for a subtle tension around the foreign minister's mouth, his expression remained impassive.

Keeping a straight face, Carleton murmured, "We and our people stand at your service, *Majesté.*"

The king gave him a regally condescending nod and turned back to Caledonne, who had gone to hold his coat for him to put on. "We've heard much of your nephew's exploits, Alexandre, and would speak further with him and Monsieur Fox."

"With pleasure, Monsieur," Caledonne said with utmost deference. "I believe the queen met his fiancée, Mademoiselle Howard, this past summer."

The king settled the garment on his shoulders and turned back to

Carleton. "Indeed so. My dear wife commended her courage and resource-fulness to me, which Paris also lauds."

"I'm honored to hold the favor of an extraordinary woman, even as you do, *Majesté*," Carleton said, receiving a nod and smile in return.

Vergennes had clearly had more than enough of them. Diplomatically he brought up pressing matters of foreign policy that required the king's attention. Scuffing his feet into the shoes set out for him, the king nodded graciously to each of them, then led the way into an adjoining chamber.

Caledonne ushered Carleton and Red Fox out into the passageway.

As they strode back toward the salon where Elizabeth, Tess, and Cécile waited, Carleton said brightly, "That went well."

Caledonne grimaced. "As a matter of fact it went as well as it possibly could have, considering that Vergennes was stewing."

"When the king meets with us again, we will present our appeal?" Red Fox said hopefully.

Caledonne exchanged a glance with Carleton before saying with a shrug, "He might grant you an audience . . . if Vergennes allows it."

"Then we'll meet with this man soon?" Red Fox persisted.

"Negotiations with kings and ministers take an extraordinary amount of time," Carleton warned. "All we can do is to make every effort and be patient." Under his breath he muttered, "And hopefully someday we'll get to go home."

Chapter Thirty-eight

A S WORD SPREAD throughout Paris of Carleton's presence in the city and his and Red Fox's presentation to the king, a deluge of invitations to dinners, balls, concerts, the opera and theatre, and a host of other fetes descended on him and Elizabeth from everyone with a claim to importance. In a calculated move he insisted that they attend as many functions as they could endure and deliberately exercised all the amiability and charm that came so naturally to him.

Red Fox was soon equally sought out as he proved to be a delightful dinner companion, discoursing on subjects ranging from philosophy to politics to warfare with a grasp of the issues that invariably amazed his hosts. Though harboring no illusions that any of it garnered allies for the Shawnee's cause, Carleton hoped their notoriety, unwelcome though it was, and the goodwill it generated might break down Vergennes' foot dragging when it came to scheduling a meeting.

Always the thought of his people's welfare nagged at the back of his mind, as he knew it did Red Fox's, along with concerns related to his ships. But day by day he schooled himself to focus on the mission on which the Shawnee had sent them. Fending off blissful images of the future that lay before him and Elizabeth, however, was another matter altogether.

He was delighted by what a great asset she proved to be. Not only did she charm everyone with her beauty and grace, but she also showed genuine interest in others, which drew them to her even more. Yet her loving concern for the Martieu-Broussards' servants and farm workers and her medical skill in caring for their needs impressed him the most.

Constantly alert for any sign of danger, he went nowhere unarmed, always carrying a small dagger and loaded pistol concealed on his person. Red Fox and Stowe always accompanied them, both also armed, along with a couple of Eugène's guards.

Even so, whenever he and Elizabeth left the environs of the château, Carleton kept her close to his side, not only because of his concern for her safety, but because to have her company again after their long separation was doubly precious to him. He cherished every moment they spent together, each day falling more in love with her.

Toward the end of November Carleton and Caledonne were in Eugène's office conferring on several ships Teissèdre had located as possible replacements for those Carleton had lost, when Lucien stalked in. Both of them glanced up only briefly, then Caledonne continued outlining the meetings he had scheduled with the American commissioners, Sartine, and Chaumont to discuss financing their purchase and refitting.

Caledonne scowled. "Thus far your privateers have prevented any further losses to your merchantmen. But as a result there are a couple in port for repairs, which spreads the rest thin."

"If I'm to replace my lost merchantmen and bolster the size of the squadrons escorting them, I'll need new ships as soon as possible," Carleton told him. "I've a messenger waiting at Brest for *Destiny* to come in. I'm summoning Eaden here to give an assessment of all my ships' current condition and armaments. Louis' agents are visiting foundries looking for the new guns we'll need, so there's another expense."

"When he returns from the ministry Eugène wishes to talk with you about personally providing some financing. It'll be a good investment for him, and he'll offer favorable terms. And, of course, I'll continue to do all I can, so you're not to worry even should our meetings not go as we wish."

Lucien had listened silently, but now broke in. "Let France pay for this if it's so important. Why should you, a mere admiral?"

Caledonne faced him, arms crossed. "Both France and England are running this war on credit, a fact you well know. Both nations are consequently on the point of bankruptcy. This is a matter essential to the war—"

"I doubt his few small privateers are essential to winning the war," Lucien scoffed, directing a scornful glance at Carleton.

"Privateers fight on the front lines at sea," Caledonne snapped.

"The fact remains that you're spending my inheritance. Which means I'm paying for his ships."

Eyes narrowing, Caledonne said, "In case you've forgotten, while I live my estate is mine to do with what I will."

"How could I forget since the living you allow me is barely enough to cover my expenses."

The last thing Carleton wanted was to be witness to their argument. But Lucien blocked the door, giving him no line of retreat that lacked potential for precipitating an even uglier scene.

"Your living is a generous one. If you wish to gamble it away, that's your affair," Caledonne was saying, face and body taut. "But perhaps you'd prefer me dead so you can gain access to your inheritance all the sooner."

Pale with anger, Lucien drawled, "What would I lose? I hardly have a father as it is."

"Jealousy has been the root of your behavior all these years. It seems I need to remind you that you're my son, and—"

"Well, thank you, *mon père,* for finally acknowledging that," Lucien mocked.

Stung, Caledonne snapped, "I've always treated you so."

Lucien leaned toward him, his face hard as stone. "Then perhaps I'd be better off if you treated me as . . . your nephew."

Turning on his heel, he stalked out the door. Caledonne stared after him, and the devastation on his face stabbed painfully through Carleton's heart.

⊛ ⊛ ⊛

LUCIEN SPENT LITTLE TIME at the château now, most often returning late and going straight to his suite. His absence was a relief for a growing tension spanned the air whenever he joined them.

Abby and Charlotte avoided him as much as possible, clearly confused and upset by a conflict they could not understand, while Cécile, Eugene, and Caledonne repeatedly appealed to him in private. But he continued baiting Carleton when he was at home, making a point of doing so obliquely, but leaving no doubt as to his target.

Outwardly Carleton continued to shrug off the building conflict between him and Lucien, resolutely fighting the anger that was nearing the breaking point. It didn't help that Red Fox had reached a barely controlled seethe. After one confrontation Carleton heard him muttering something about scalping.

He was not as worried about Red Fox, however, as he was about Stowe. There was a cold, deadly glint in the older man's eyes whenever Lucien was present that from their long history together left Carleton so uneasy he had a frank talk with him—which did nothing to allay his concerns.

On the cold, blustery last day of the month, Lucien's remarks at dinner were especially sneering, clearly an attempt to push him into an explosion. Elizabeth and the girls were on the point of tears, Cécile flushed and angry. Both Eugène and Caledonne intervened repeatedly, attempting to reason with Lucien, while Carleton, as he had made his habit, only responded coldly to subtle insults directed at Elizabeth.

At last Lucien drawled, "I've had the misfortune of trusting women who appeared entirely virtuous, only to discover that they frequented masked balls in scandalous costumes to lure unwary men into their arms."

Stiffening, Carleton followed his scornful look to Elizabeth., and his chest tightened A crimson flush had risen to her cheeks, and she looked as though Lucien had struck her.

It was immediately apparent that Lucien referred to something she had not told him. His impulse was to defend her, but Eugène cut him off.

He sprang to his feet and sent the distraught girls out of the room with their governess. Rounding on Lucien, livid, jaw clenched, he said, "I'll thank you to remember that Jonathan and Elizabeth are guests in my home, as are you. I won't have them insulted at my table by you or anyone else. If you can't at least extend common courtesy to everyone under my roof, then I suggest you take your ill temper to your father's apartment at Versailles. He isn't using it."

Heat rose into Lucien's face, but before he could respond, Caledonne pulled a ring of keys from his pocket, detached one, and tossed it to him across the table. It bounced onto his half-empty plate with a loud clatter.

Lucien pushed to his feet, glaring at everyone around the table as he grabbed the key. "A plague on all of you."

He started to turn away, then paused and directed a look of cold rage from Elizabeth to Carleton. "You're going to regret this."

"YOU WERE QUITE FULL of yourself back then, you know—tall and mature for your age, quite self-assured. You and Frédéric were naturally drawn together in spite of the five years between you." Cécile directed a smiling glance at Elizabeth. "Both of them were magnets for the young ladies—and some not so young—handsome, blond, and blue-eyed."

"I don't doubt it a bit," Elizabeth said, rolling her eyes.

Carleton frowned down at her. "I don't remember attracting any extraordinary attention. It was Frédéric they were after—and justly so. It was that naval uniform." He grinned.

"If you think so, cousin, you're more naïve than I can imagine." Cécile waved the remark away. "But look at it through Lucien's eyes. You paid almost no attention to him. He's always been high strung, partly due to what Papa called Maman's coddling. The twins' death affected him deeply."

Elizabeth gave her a questioning look. "Twins?"

"A boy and girl. It was Maman's last pregnancy and didn't go well. They only lived a few months and died within days of each other." Softly

Cécile added, "Papa was at sea at the time, and when he returned he was sick at heart that he'd not been there when Maman needed him so. But Lucien seemed to blame himself for their deaths in some way."

Bowing her head, Elizabeth murmured heartfelt condolences.

"I remember how they still grieved during my visit some months later," Carleton said soberly. "I can't imagine a deeper grief than losing a child."

"Frédéric used to include Lucien in his activities as much as possible—except for the times when you came to stay with us, Jonathan. Then, in effect, you took Frédéric away from him."

"And now with him back again, Lucien feels he's taken your father away."

"I'm afraid so." Cutting off Carleton's protest, Cécile continued, "He idolized you at first as much as he did Frédéric. But then Papa began taking you along on his ship. You soon had a love of sailing in common, and Papa wanted badly for you to become a naval cadet, while Lucien was left out. He's only a year younger than you, but back then he was small and slight, quite immature and unsure of himself. And I think he settled on putting you down in order to puff himself up. That you simply laughed it off humiliated him."

"I'm sorry for it, but that doesn't excuse his treatment of me now."

"I'm not saying that his behavior's justified. It isn't. And ever since Frédéric's death you've made every effort to keep peace between you. The trouble is that when he feels himself wronged, he conceives a grudge and won't turn loose of it."

Carleton sighed and rubbed his forehead. "It's an endless circle. I can't win no matter what I do, and the rest of you are caught in the middle."

"I don't understand why he'd include me in it," Elizabeth ventured.

"You're not the first," Carleton said grimly. "Like a moth to a flame, he's drawn to beautiful young ladies who are suffering some distress. First he plays the part of her rescuer. But when she doesn't conform to his expectations, he begins to abuse her."

Elizabeth drew in a sharp breath. "Why didn't anyone warn me?"

A spasm of pain crossed Cécile's face. "Papa, Eugène, and I truly believed that it was only a matter of time before Jonathan returned to you and you'd marry. We assumed that Lucien would respect your relationship and wouldn't interfere with you. Papa even warned him not to get involved. It's been five years since the last episode, and I'm afraid we hoped too much that he'd put all that behind him. He kept saying he was a better man."

"He told me it was because of me, as though it was my responsibility to be his savior!"

Cécile bent her head, tears trickling down her face. "The last thing we wanted was for you to be hurt, Elizabeth. But the result was that we unwittingly allowed it. Please forgive us for being afraid to see what was before our eyes. Regardless of what he is, we still love him."

Carleton let out a sigh and took Elizabeth's hand. "If he were your son or brother, how would you feel?"

Elizabeth met his sympathetic gaze with a despairing one. "I can't judge. No one can truly understand the darkness that possesses another, even one so close to one's heart."

"We've all been praying for him." Cécile brushed her tears away before continuing, "Papa has spent as much time with him as possible and entrusted him with as many of his affairs as he can, hoping his influence will steady him. That's why he took Lucien along to Boston. And now he feels entirely responsible for this disaster."

"Well, whatever Lucien's motives, he did do everything in his power to keep me safe," Elizabeth said.

"That's to his credit," Carleton conceded, his face sternly set. "He has my gratitude for that much at least."

AT CARLETON'S INSISTENCE, later that evening in the privacy of her salon, she explained everything, certain that he must think the worst of her. Finally she stammered, "I-I don't know what possessed me to go through with it. It seemed all in fun until I got to the ball and saw how scandalously everyone was dressed." Hanging her head, she whispered, "As was I. I swore I'd never do such at thing again. Can you forgive my foolishness?"

She chanced a timid peek at him. Far from appearing outraged, he regarded her with what appeared to be amused speculation. The corner of his mouth twitched and the very devilment danced in his eyes.

"On one condition."

"What . . . what is it?" she asked nervously.

"That you model the costume for me. I want to know just how much controversy you stirred up."

She swallowed. "For . . . you . . . alone?" she ventured, her voice faint.

He grinned. "Would you rather we have an audience?"

"*No!* But . . . um . . . you mean now?"

"Of course now. Immediately. I must see it."

"It might be better if we . . . if we waited . . . until we're wed."

His gaze sharpened. "Why? I want a foretaste of the pleasures in store for me."

She could see he was trying hard not to laugh, felt a blush rising to the very roots of her hair. "Fine, then!" She tossed her head defiantly. "But I have a condition too. You must promise only to look. No touching."

His grin broadened. "I'll do my best."

Calling Jemma, she disappeared into her chamber, closed and locked the door. The maid's nimble fingers quickly transformed her once more into Diana.

Masked, she wrapped herself in the voluminous domino cloak and dismissed Jemma. Then, breathless, every nerve thrilling, she stepped back into the salon. He sat slouched in a chair, head resting on its back, arms crossed, waiting.

Her eyes fixed on the floor, she slowly unclasped the cloak and let it drop. She heard him suck in his breath and spring to his feet, looked tentatively up as his stunned gaze traveled from the top of her head to her sandaled feet. For a long, suspended moment he stood motionless as though frozen in place.

"Take off the mask," he said in a hoarse whisper.

She obeyed, more delighted than she cared to admit at the effect she clearly was having. Keeping a careful distance between them, he circled her with deliberate slowness, his tread light as a panther's. She could feel his eyes on her all the way, and a delicious tingle followed their course.

Stopping in front of her, he murmured, "My dearest, if you don't go take that off right away, I fear I'm going to break my promise."

He said it quite soberly, with a slight tremor in his voice, and the look in his eyes warned her that he meant what he said. For a moment she hesitated, both tempted and terrified at the thought of what he would do if she stepped into his arms instead.

His wicked grin made it clear he read her thoughts. "I'll want you to wear it again—but only for me," he said huskily, very softly added, "After we're married."

Her breath caught. Whirling around, she fled back into her chamber, shaken, not by his desire but by the strength of her own.

Chapter Thirty-nine

T HE MEETING WITH the American commissioners in early December turned out to be even less auspicious than the brief presentation to the king. Lee was apparently too busy to attend. And it didn't help that Carleton struggled to keep his mind on business instead of on the delectable vision of Elizabeth as he had kissed her before leaving.

It immediately became clear that Franklin and Adams were suspicious of his close ties with the French. The news of his and Red Fox's presentation to the king, which had been sown to the winds, had raised Franklin's hackles. He should have been present to take charge of "interpreting" America's Indians to the court, he lectured Carleton in front of Red Fox, as though neither of them was qualified to do so. Then he went on to speculate that Caledonne's intention in arranging it and a subsequent meeting with Chaumont before they met with their own country's commissioners—not to mention Vergennes with whom they had a close relationship—had doubtless been to create a division between them.

Coming on the heels of the blowup with Lucien, it was almost more than Carleton could endure. By heroic effort he wrestled his fury under control and directed a look of stern warning at Red Fox, who clamped his mouth shut.

He forced a smile entirely foreign to his emotions. It had all been a misunderstanding due to his own impatience, he apologized, then presented, with a bow, the packet of letters Washington had entrusted to him.

Adams snatched it and immediately sifted through its contents, which evidently pleased him. After they discussed Monmouth in detail, he asked about Carleton's privateers, the prizes and losses he had taken in service of their cause, the acquisition of new ships, and coordination with Congress's Marine Committee. Keeping in mind his discussions with his uncle and Elizabeth about Bancroft and the intrigues involving the commission, he told the two men nothing that was not already generally known, and he and Red Fox left with the promise of another meeting in the near future.

A courtesy call on the prize agent, Jonathan Williams, and another meeting with Chaumont went much better. And then there was the dull business of dispatching regular reports back to Washington and Congress. He felt keenly that time was winging by. And although Cécile had preparations for Caledonne and Tess's January wedding well in hand, his frustration mounted that no one had yet been found who could perform his own.

"I ASSUME MY COUSIN is plotting to get more money, supposedly for his privateers," Lucien drawled. "If I were you, sir, I'd guard my purse."

Chaumont was clearly taken aback. Glancing from Lucien to Caledonne, who had gone pale, he blustered, "I beg your pardon, Monsieur Bettár. General Carleton is well-known as a man of integrity and honor. Your own father vouches for him."

"Enough, Lucien," Caledonne growled. "You've no business here."

"Au contraire," Lucien said, giving him a triumphant look.

A week had passed since the disappointing meeting with the commissioners. The Chaumonts had invited Carleton and Elizabeth, Tess and Caledonne, the Martieu-Broussards, and Red Fox to dinner. After the meal they had just taken seats in the salon with the stout, balding comte and his plain, plump, good-natured comtesse, when the major domo unexpectedly ushered Lucien in. With him had come one of his friends, who, Carleton noted with a chill, lingered in the background.

Lucien swaggered over to him. "You've always had to put me down in order to prove yourself the hero, the conqueror above all others."

Carleton stiffened. "Can you seriously believe that I've lived my life for the purpose of spiting you? Believe me, sir, that is the least of my concerns. I've never spared the matter a single thought."

As color sprang into Lucien's face, Carleton silently cursed himself for giving rein to his temper after fighting so determinedly to contain it.

"I resent your constant attempts to alienate my father's affections from me."

"He's done no such thing!" Caledonne snapped as the others protested.

Carleton regarded Lucien for a long moment through narrowed eyes. "I've never made any effort at all to come between the two of you. What interest could I possibly have in doing so?"

"Your own father deemed you unworthy. He denied you your position and inheritance, thus you've always envied mine."

Feeling the last straw snap, Carleton answered curtly, "My position has never been in question. My inheritance from Sir Harry was substantial, to say nothing of the income from my business and privateers. I've made every effort to befriend you, Lucien—"

"Why would I ever wish to be friends with a liar and a cheat?"

A suspended hush hung over the salon as palpable as a living presence.

Fixing Lucien in a hard, level glance, Carleton said softly, "Don't do this."

"You, sir, are a base coward," Lucien sneered.

Carleton broke into a scathing laugh.

"Lucien, stop!" Caledonne implored, echoed by Tess and Cécile.

Trembling uncontrollably, Elizabeth pleaded, "Please, Jonathan, please let it go."

If he heard her, he gave no indication of it. With deliberate insolence he drawled, "Every man in this room, in this country and my own—by

God, in England!—knows that I'm no coward." Leaning over Lucien, he added in a clipped voice, "I've no need—to prove anything—to *you.*"

Lucien slapped him hard across the face. Elizabeth saw Carleton's head jerk with the blow, then he stood very still.

A gasp rose from everyone in the room, echoed by Caledonne's strangled outcry and Chaumont's outraged demand that they stop this insanity. The breath gone out of her, Elizabeth pressed her hand hard over her mouth, barely registering that Tess clutched her tightly as she watched Red Fox stride to Carleton's side, the tautness of his body and deadliness of his expression terrifying.

Straightening, Carleton gave him an unreadable glance, then with slow deliberation turned back to Lucien. "I'd say you're the one who has something to prove," he said, his tone laced with contempt.

"You've only gotten where you are by becoming a servile, self-serving—" Lucien's voice choked with rage, leaving him unable to continue.

"I believe the word you're searching for is *sycophant.* And if I were one, *you'd* have nothing to criticize."

Lucien struck him again, so hard that Elizabeth could see him draw in a sharp breath as he stepped back. Crying out, she pulled away from Tess and ran to him while the comtesse screeched and dismayed exclamations filled the salon.

Giving no sign that he was aware of her beside him, for a taut moment he stood as though paralyzed, the imprint of the successive blows rapidly staining his cheek. Then he deliberately swept his cousin in an assessing look from head to foot and, raising his eyes, met Lucien's hostile stare with a freezing one.

"As you wish," he said, his voice gone deadly soft. "You've been wanting this for a long time, so let's have it.""No!" Elizabeth turned to Caledonne, who observed the scene with horror. "Uncle Alexandre, please stop them!"

"It's too late," he rasped.

"But dueling's illegal!" Tess cried. "The penalty is imprisonment—or execution!"

"What weapon suits your pleasure?" Lucien mocked. "Bow and arrow?"

Red Fox brought his face menacingly close, forcing Lucien to take an involuntary step back. "We Shawnee fight in personal combat with *knives,*" he hissed.

Lucien's eyes widened, the color draining out of his face. "You . . . but that's . . . barbaric."

"Who's the coward now?" Seeing Lucien tense, Carleton dismissed the question with an elaborate shrug. "But no matter. Alas, I'm out of practice with the rapier. But not with pistols."

Lucien brushed past Red Fox, stepping toe to toe with Carleton. "Your choice. I'm equally skilled with both." He indicated his friend, who now came forward. "Here's my second. Name yours."

A wave of sickness rolled over Elizabeth at the memory of his nerveless calculation in shooting Veillars, and of Carleton coiling powerfully upward, his knife spilling Wolfslayer's blood. Fearing she would vomit, she turned back to Caledonne in desperation.

He appeared to her the perfect portrait of a father's grief, standing with arms crossed, one hand supporting his bowed head, eyes pressed shut. Anguish was written in every line of his body. Tess embraced him, and as though they were alone in the room, he blindly bent his head to hers.

Carleton slowly crossed the room to them. "If there were any other way, sir, you know I'd take it."

Looking up, Caledonne said hoarsely, "You made that abundantly clear. What else can you do now?"

Carleton returned to Elizabeth, his expression closed. Taking her hand, he bent and pressed it to his lips. When he straightened, he met her beseeching gaze with a probing one.

"You think he'll kill me."

"You're evenly matched, and he might," she answered tremulously. "Or you might kill him. Is that what you want—the guilt of his blood on your hands or yours on his? Uncle Alexander heartbroken. And Cécile. And me! We were parted for so long, Jonathan!" she cried out, despairing. "Will you now run the risk of separating us forever?"

She could see his defenses crumble. Flinching, he looked quickly away.

"I'd do anything else in the world to spare you this," he choked out. "But how am I to be a worthy husband if I abandon my honor? I cannot live with that—nor could you."

"As you said, your courage is unassailable," she returned, fighting to keep her voice steady. "Everyone knows it. Your honor will not be stained by refusing a challenge that is both foolish and illegal."

A taut silence stretched out between them while he regarded her intently. At last, conceding a faint smile, he murmured, "I said once that you're my better angel. And so you are."

He could feel her relax. Reaching up, she laid her hand tenderly on his throbbing cheek, and it seemed to him that her touch drew the sting from it. He kissed her lightly, then strode over to Lucien, battling a powerful sense of violation that demanded justice. And the greater urgency of forgiveness.

"I'll not fight you, Lucien" he said gruffly. Behind him he heard the sharp intake of Caledonne's breath, Tess's soft gasp as he continued, "You've always borne me ill will, but I bear none toward you. I forgive you for this, and for the past. If I've been at fault in any way, I ask your forgiveness. In God's name, let there be peace between us!"

Lucien stared at him as though he'd gone mad. In his eyes Carleton could see the realization that his carefully constructed plan—for so it had been—was collapsing.

"Must you always make yourself out to be the better man?" Shaking, he swung to face his father. "Well, you have your wish, *mon père.* Your precious nephew is too frightened to duel me, so he'll live, coward that he is, while I, your son, am dead to you."

❋ ❋ ❋

LUCIEN'S PARTING WORDS cast a pall over the entire family. Yet over the following weeks, Carleton saw how that one act of sacrifice rippled outward in blessings none of them could have conceived of.

Even as he had spoken forgiveness to his cousin, he had felt all the rancor built up between them over the years dissipate and pity take its place. Then because of his restraint, he and Caledonne grew closer, his relationship with Cécile more tender. Red Fox and Stowe treated him with noticeably greater respect, as did Eugène. And between him and Elizabeth grew an ever deeper and more confident love and trust.

Charlotte and Abby also mourned the break with Lucien and his subsequent disappearance. All of them did everything possible to console the two girls, while sharing as few details of the confrontation as possible, the subject too painful to be much spoken of. They in turn clung to Carleton, who gladly returned their affection without restraint.

The birth of a dauphine, Marie-Thérèse Charlotte, Madame Royale, to the king and queen at Versailles on 19 December provided some distraction, although celebrations were muted by near universal disappointment that France's sovereigns had not produced a son and heir to the throne. The *libelles* immediately churned out speculations about the infant's paternity in such vile terms that Elizabeth refused to hear anything more published in them.

Just before Christmas Caledonne's younger daughter, Julianne, arrived with her husband and two sons after sailing from the Bettárs' ancestral estate at Marseille to Le Havre and traveling by coach to Passy. They planned to spend the holidays and attend the wedding in mid January. With them came Eugène-Philippe, the Martieu-Broussards' son, a student at the Université d'Aix. The following day brought their elder daughter, Aline, with her husband and baby from Normandy.

A lively tumult took over the chateau, lightening the heavy mood that had hung over it for too long. To Tess and Elizabeth the new arrivals proved to be as warm and charming as the rest of the family, immediately adopting the two of them as their own and befriending Red Fox as well.

Every week they attended the Comédie Française and the Opera, which Red Fox embraced with unconcealed enthusiasm. He regarded the Comédie's tall Doric columns, the sky-blue theater's magnificent chandeliers ablaze with hundreds of candles, and the huge, exquisitely dressed throngs that crowded the hall with almost reverence. The elaborate plays with their grand backdrops and the superb, passionate performances kept him on the edge of his seat and drew his ecstatic applause. He found the Opéra equally thrilling, admiring the theatre's lavish decorations; the beauty of the dancers; their extravagant, if scanty, costumes; and the power of the music. Carleton and Elizabeth found as much enjoyment in his amazed wonder as they did in the performances.

Although Carleton basked in the happy clamor, the old, indefinable restlessness insisted on welling up in quieter hours. Elizabeth felt keenly the part of him that railed against being caged and would not be changed even by her. But she accepted this about him willingly, she told him, for it was a large part of what had drawn her to him from the beginning. For her own heart also yearned to fly free.

He had never spent much time in Paris, he explained. Here he felt the most keenly the decadence of French society that repelled him. All his happy memories were of Marseille, and he wanted more than anything to take her there, to share with her the places and fond memories of his youth.

But in the meantime he resolved to find contentment in the here and now. And when in her arms he did.

Chapter Forty

THE LONG-AWAITED meeting with Vergennes finally took place in the elegant ministry offices at Versailles early in January. Carleton deliberately donned his Rangers' uniform of a dun-colored hip-length French-dragoon-style jacket faced in forest green with gold epaulettes, and supple buckskin breeches that hugged the lean contours of his lean, muscular form. His sheathed sabre hung from a dark grey shoulder belt. Knee-length boots and a long forest green cloak along with the dark green leather helmet adorned with gold chains and flowing, blond horsehair crest that he carried in the crook of his arm gave him an even more commanding appearance.

Red Fox was equally striking, garbed in his finest ceremonial buckskins, with his hair roached and a brilliant vermillion stripe across each cheekbone. With great dignity he began by reminding the foreign minister of the good service the Shawnee had performed for France during the Seven Years War in fighting the British. He then presented their sachems' petition that the French government use their influence to press the American Congress to provide justice against the white settlers and stop their steadily expanding encroachment into the Shawnee's ancestral lands.

Vergennes listened politely, but noncommittally. When Red Fox finished, he said shrewdly, "It is true that your nation gave good service to France . . . at the beginning of the war." Carleton had been afraid of this, and his hopes plummeted as the foreign minister continued, "However, your nation, along with others, then turned their backs on us and allied with the British. This was a great blow to France and contributed greatly to our losing the war."

"France was already losing," Red Fox countered with a frown, eyes narrowed. "Your country stopped supplying us guns and ammunition, and food and clothing for our wives and children. Our people had no choice but to go over to the British, who brought in the goods we could not survive without. We spilled much blood on your behalf and would have spilled more had you maintained faith with us."

Vergennes allowed a faint smile. "Each nation has its own necessities in times of war. I'm told that your nation allies with the British in this one."

"Indeed some of our divisions do so, hoping they will keep out the settlers. But many of us remain neutral or fight, as White Eagle and I do, on the side of the Americans along with the Lenape, Oneida, Tuscarora, and Cherokee. If France will but reach out her hand to our people, then we will turn away from the British and help you to win the war. Then will not France be able to take Canada back?"

Vergennes dismissed this curtly. "Canada is of no account to us. France has more important interests."

Red Fox's face fell.

Turning to Carleton, Vergennes took his measure before saying, "It puzzles me that you come as a diplomat for this nation when you are not only a general in the American army, but also own a fleet of privateers that has been highly effective against British shipping."

His tone was not confrontational, but it was clear to Carleton that this was a confrontation. "I am the adopted son of the renowned sachem and warrior Black Hawk of the Kispokotha division of the Shawnee," he replied, meeting Vergennes' veiled gaze with a hard one. "I fight for the Americans in this war. But I will forever stand against those who seek to rob and kill my people regardless of who they are."

Vergennes considered him thoughtfully for some moments, at last dismissed both of them with a slight bow, saying, "I will bring this matter before the king at the earliest opportunity."

As they left the ministry offices, Carleton said to Red Fox, "Well done, my brother. You spoke strongly for our people."

Red Fox brightened. "He promises to bring our case before the king."

Carleton gave him a sidelong look. "At the earliest opportunity. Which means never."

Red Fox stopped in his tracks. "Then he does not speak truth."

Carleton also came to a halt. "It isn't in the nature of a French minister to tell you what he actually thinks or intends to do. If he says he will act a certain way, it is the thing least likely to happen."

"Then the French are as treacherous as the Long Knives!" exclaimed Red Fox, scowling.

"Are our sachems any more virtuous? All men harbor treachery in their hearts."

Matching his steps to Carleton's, Red Fox muttered, "It is so, my brother, to our shame."

TEISSÈDRE RETURNED a few days later, bringing Eaden with him. The agent's report on progress in acquiring the ships, crews, and armaments to bolster Carleton's merchant and privateer fleets, brought his simmering frustration to a low boil. It was counterbalanced, however, by Eaden's account of the British merchantmen his privateers had recently taken as prize. Best of all was the news that a squadron led by *Black Swan* had wrested his 74-gun privateer *Patriot* back from the British with her crew and restored her name.

The captain was staying at the Hôtel Valentinois, and Carleton accompanied him to the commissioners' apartment to to deliver the letters he had brought with him from Washington and Congress and to confer on the latest developments in the land and naval wars. After several more meetings in December, he had forged a reasonably amicable relationship with Franklin and Adams, and this day's offered some encouragement—much needed with Vergennes blocking any hope of the Shawnee's petition going forward.

When they left they almost bumped into a small, trim, dark-haired man with a weathered angular face and beak of a nose who was coming from the direction of Chaumont's offices. Carleton guessed him to be a naval officer although his uniform of a blue coat with gold epaulettes and a buff waistcoat did not identify him as either American or French.

The officer took in Eaden's plain, unadorned blue uniform, then Carleton's, with keen interest before sweeping off his cocked hat. "Sirs, I am Captain John Paul Jones," he said in a mild voice. "May I enquire as to your names and country?"

His easy, courteous manner was quite at odds with the reports Carleton had heard of his exploits—not only at sea but in the boudoir. He would have expected the man to be considerably more flamboyant, and he exchanged a glance with Eaden before making introductions.

Jones's gaze grew intent. "I've heard much about both of you and the success of your privateers against the British."

Carleton's mouth quirked. "We're well acquainted with your exploits as well, captain. Rumor and innuendo are the grist of Paris, after all."

"And its wheels grind out fame," Jones acknowledged in almost a whisper, eyes flashing. "It appears we have much in common. Would the two of you be so kind as to join me for some refreshments? My apartment is just down the hall, and I'd very much like to talk with you."

Intrigued, Carleton and Eaden agreed. In short order they were seated at ease in Jones's small but charming dining room in front of platters of cold roast beef, slices of cheese, and bread, and overflowing pints of ale.

He had come from L'Orient to meet Chaumont, Sartine, and the commissioners, Jones told them, in hopes of persuading them to purchase a ship for him called *Duc de Duras,* which he intended to rename the *Bonhomme Richard* in honor of Franklin. "Although she's of the old style, she's sturdily built," he said, speaking softly as appeared to be his habit. "I believe she'll be fast enough for my purposes. I'll have nothing to do with a slow ship as I intend to go into harm's way."

The determined glint in his eyes impressed Carleton and also, he could see, Eaden, who was as eager for action as a spaniel on the scent of game. For the next hour he listened noncommittally while Jones and Eaden compared experiences at sea, prizes taken, preferred naval tactics, and the frustrating delays in securing battle-ready ships and crews.

"What you need, gentlemen, is an adventure," Jones said finally, lifting his diminished pint in salute with a sly smile. "And to that end, I have a proposal to make that I believe you may be interested in. Once I've secured the *Bonhomme Richard* and she's ready for action, why don't you join forces with me in raiding the British coast? I mean to take every ship that comes into my sights. Although I cannot ensure success, I will endeavor to deserve it, and it's clear that you're men who'll do the same."

Eaden directed a questioning look at Carleton, obviously tempted by Jones's proposal. Carleton sensed a wariness in him that matched his own, however, and he hesitated, studying the captain for a long moment, keeping his expression neutral.

Admiral Howe's ships were freely patrolling the American coast, raiding ports at will, and had captured or sunk nine American frigates that year. Nor had the French done much better, achieving at best a draw at Ushant and proving useless in the campaign against Newport.

Jones had brought the Continental Navy the only glory it had achieved thus far. Yet Carleton had an uneasy feeling about him. Images of Benedict Arnold leading mad charges at Saratoga filtered into his thoughts. He had the distinct feeling that the two men were of a very similar character, with glory their first object.

Which was not necessarily a bad thing in combat. The trouble was that when not coupled with discipline and discretion, it was prone to disaster.

"What do you say, gentlemen?" Jones prompted, glancing eagerly between Carleton and Eaden. "We'll gain the prizes we seek, and fame will follow. What could be more gratifying?"

Carleton allowed a faint smile, then pushed to his feet. "I'll keep your proposal in mind, sir. First we need to find ships and crews. Then we'll see."

Chapter Forty-one

O N FRIDAY, JANUARY 15, Tess and Caledonne spoke their vows before the high altar of the cathedral at Passy. With the exception of Lucien, all his children and their families attended, along with Carleton, Elizabeth, Abby, Red Fox, and their servants. Caledonne had arranged for Tess to receive the title of comtesse over her objections, a battle she quickly recognized as futile and abandoned with resignation.

She was truly lovely in a *robe à la française* of a rich china blue silken damask, a soft blush coloring her cheeks. And he had never appeared more handsome in his ornate admiral's uniform adorned with a sash and his honors. A reception and festive wedding dinner followed at Château Broussard. All their close friends and neighbors, among them the American commissioners and Chaumont, joined them in addition to Sartine, Vergennes, Necker, a number of other nobles, and their wives.

Felicitations abounded, and Elizabeth's joy overflowed at the unconcealed devotion that brimmed between the newlyweds. She could see that Carleton's did as well.

At the beginning of the following week Julianne and her family left for home. With them went Eugène-Philippe, returning to the Université. Within days Aline and her family departed, and the château settled into the comparative quiet of everyday routines.

Elizabeth had never seen Tess so serenely happy. The very image of domestic bliss, she and Caledonne made no attempt to conceal their delight in each other.

"Alexandre is the most dear, tender man," she confided to Elizabeth. "Everything Cécile told us about him is true. I never conceived that I'd find such love in my older years, but it was worth every minute I had to wait. I am blessed!"

She had moved into Caledonne's suite the day of the wedding, and with Abby ensconced in Charlotte's suite, Elizabeth's felt depressingly empty. Her aunt's attention now understandably focused on her husband and his concerns, leaving Elizabeth mourning the loss of the close companionship they had shared for so long even as she rejoiced at her happiness.

That she and Carleton spent every possible moment together provided great comfort. But he was constantly pulled away by matters pertaining to his ships or writing endless reports to Washington and Congress. An Anglican priest had not been found, and with her movements restricted and no prospect of marrying until they could return home—a period that might stretch on indefinitely—she felt as though her life again hung in suspension.

All she seemed to do was wait. Joining in the family's activities raised her spirits, especially playing the pianoforte or violin on the many evenings devoted to music. Most of all she loved playing duets with Carleton as they did often, sharing meaningful glances and smiles across their instruments.

She also found solace in continuing to bustle about the estate, heavily bundled against the cold, snowy weather, to visit with the servants and farm workers and care for any needs that arose. Over the past months she had increasingly felt a clear leading that this was the ministry she had been made for. But now, too, she was coming to understand more and more that the waiting itself held purpose and blessing.

THE FOLLOWING WEEK they were just rising from dinner when the butler came quietly into the room. Drawing Carleton aside, he said, "A man named George Winton just arrived asking after you or Mademoiselle Howard. I told him you were here, and he asked to speak with you. He claims to have been valet to your father, Lord Carleton, during your infancy."

It was so unexpected that for a moment Carleton could only stare blankly at him.

Elizabeth came to his side. "Perhaps this man knows something of his reasons for sending you away. You've wondered for so long—"

"I doubt he has anything to say that I care to hear." With an impatient gesture, he said gruffly, "Very well. We'll meet with him in the salon."

The others quickly dispersed, Caledonne gently squeezing Carleton's shoulder as he passed. Moments later, seated before a crackling fire, Carleton took the caller's measure.

Winton was not at all what he expected. In his early fifties, of medium height and slender build with reddish brown hair and mild blue eyes, the man held himself with a quiet dignity. His manner and steady, warm gaze gave the impression that what was confided to him would be neither judged nor disclosed to others.

"Thank ye for seein' me," he began in a rich Scots accent, nodding at both of them. Fixing his gaze on Carleton, he continued, "I've been under conviction for some years now that I was to find ye. Unfortunately the way never opened. But the burden's weighed all the heavier on me since the news o' yer privateers' attacks began spreadin' throughout England. And once the warrant for you and Miss Howard became known and finally your presence in Paris, I couldna put off seekin' ye out any longer."

"Why? What have I to do with you?"

The only effect Carleton's curt demand appeared to have on Winton was that his expression softened. "Mayhap much," he said, his gaze keen.

Feeling Elizabeth clasp his hand, Carleton tightened his fingers around hers, while keeping a wary gaze on Winton. "Then let's hear it."

"First off, ye need to know yer brother, Edward, died two months ago."

Carleton stiffened. "Of what cause?"

Winton cleared his throat and looked around him as though searching for a tactful explanation. Finally he said simply, "He died in a duel with the brother of a young woman he'd debauched."

Giving a short laugh, Carleton said, "I can't say that surprises me."

Winton shook his head sadly. "Och, but he was a *thrawn* man. It grieves me to say it, but none mourned him." Delicately he added, "But wi' his death . . . ye stand to inherit the title and lands."

Carleton dismissed the matter with a shrug. "Let the next in line have it. Even had I ambition for an English title, were I to set foot on Britain's soil, I'd immediately be arrested and beheaded."

"Surely not after the war, sir," Winton protested. "That is, as long as ye Americans win it—which appears to me to be in the offing now wi' France enterin' the fray. Britain canna afford to fight this war forever. And believe me, followin' Edward, the tenants would welcome ye with open arms."

"A peace treaty will change nothing. I'm counted a traitor to the crown, a charge the king will never set aside. Besides, for me to succeed Edward would doubtless be against my father's wishes since he had no love for me."

Winton's mouth dropped open. "No love fer ye? Ye've nay believed such all these years? Why, sir, the decision to send ye to Sir Harrison, though the hardest he ever made, was in yer best interests."

"It's in a child's best interests to remain with his parents," Carleton said, his voice steely. "My father gave me away as though I was a piece of property to be bought and sold."

"Nay, sir, he did no such thing!" Winton exclaimed, looking horrified. "Ye belonged exactly where yer father put ye. He knew things ye couldna ken. Ye were but a bairn. He was a grown man, wi' experience and wisdom ye did not ha'."

Carleton rose and paced restlessly across the salon. Veering to the fireplace, he propped one arm on the mantel.

"Wisdom and experience told him to give away his son?"

"Were ye not born August 30 in 1743?" Winton questioned. When Carleton inclined his head, frowning, he continued, "I remember the day well. I remember what a bonny, braw lad ye were, and how Lord Carleton near burst wi' pride. But he feared greatly to see ye ruined by a corrupt society the way Edward ha' been: the child of a loveless marriage for convenience only, who from birth was mean, malicious, self-seekin', spoiled —wantin' his own way and carin' naught for anyone else.

"Lord Carleton couldn'a bear to see how Edward teased and tormented ye," he went on, "ye, whom his heart loved, the son o' the wife he cherished. And he could do nothin' to provide for ye since Edward, as his firstborn, would inherit near everythin' he ha'. Och, yer father did what he could for ye, but English law is strict and canna be broken. And one winter night Edward lured ye out into a storm and left ye to die—I doubt ye remember it—"

"I do," Carleton cut in grimly. He stalked away, putting more distance between him and Winton.

"Then ye remember how long it took for yer father to find ye, and how ill ye were as a result. He feared he'd lose ye, and he saw the wisdom o' Sir Harry's pleas to take ye far from such a life and raise ye up free to be the man God made ye to be."

Carleton slouched into a chair on the far side of the fireplace. Regarding Winton darkly, he said, "That's essentially the story Sir Harry told me. I've always doubted it was the full truth."

"Did he tell ye any more?"

Carleton glanced at Elizabeth, who perched on the edge of her seat, brow furrowed, hands clasped in her lap. Returning his gaze to Winton, he said gruffly, "He broached the subject several times when I was older. By then I wasn't interested, and I let him know it. He finally dropped the subject."

"Did he tell ye anythin' about *Bliadhna Theàrlaich*—the Year o' Charles?"

Carleton studied him, eyes narrowed. "The Jacobite Rising of '45? He told me more of Sheriffmuir."

Winton nodded. "Ah, the Risin' o' 1715. Yer uncle fought 'longside o' yer grandfather and was knighted for his gallantry though he was hardly more than a youth. The Risin' o' '45 began scant days afore yer second birthday and ended at Culloden in April the followin' year—"

"What of it? Lord Carleton had no sympathies with the Jacobites, as he went to great lengths to prove. In fact, it always puzzled me that he and Sir Harry kept a close relationship."

A faint smile tugged at Winton's mouth. "Aye, that's what yer father desperately needed everyone to think. He stood to lose everythin', ye see—least of all his life—if anyone found out how involved he was in the plannin' o' that campaign and how much o' it he financed verra carefully through a few trusted men."

As Carleton stared at him, stunned, he continued, "He had extensive properties and tenants who depended on him, a beloved wife dyin' as the result o' a bad birth, a son he cherished who'd be left destitute and mayhap exposed to those who'd harm him—"

Carleton sprang out of his chair and retreated to the terrace doors, pushed back the draperies with one hand and, trembling, stared through the panes into the bleak, clouded afternoon. But all he saw was the hazy image of his father's face, branded in his memory by the terror of that night in the dark winter forest when Lord Carleton had snatched him up off the cold ground and away from the slavering hounds.

Elizabeth was beside him then. He turned blindly to her, felt her arms go around him, and laid his cheek against the crown of her head. Silence stretched long before Winton spoke again.

"Lord Carleton had with long and careful effort earned a powerful position at court, but George the Second was a difficult, changeable man. And after Culloden, rumors were swirlin'. All the lairds were suspect . . . and yer father was married to a young Frenchwoman, who on her mother's side was blood relation to the Auld Pretender."

"I was never told that." A shock went through Carleton as sudden realization struck him through. "That's why I was named Stuart."

"So it is." Winton sighed. "It fair tore his heart right out o' his chest to send ye away and grieve yer mother so on her deathbed. But he had no way o' knowin' whether he'd be betrayed—and thank God he wasn't! And he had no other choice if he was to keep ye safe. So he sent ye to the only one he knew would rear ye to hold yer freedom dear and let no man wrest it from ye ever."

Carleton drew in a shaky breath. "Sir Harry told me of Sheriffmuir, and then Culloden so often when I was a child that I dreamt of them," he said slowly. "At times I still dream I stand on a dark battlefield amid men whose faces I can't see. They grapple sword to sword and cry out, *'Saorsa! Saorsa!'*" Glancing down at Elizabeth, he translated softly, "Freedom."

"Aye," Winton said. "Ye do remember some Gaelic, I see."

Carleton shrugged. "Little. It's been years since I've had anyone to speak the language with."

"Interestin' that Sir Harrison told the story to ye that way since what the Scots shouted as they charged was the name o' the Stuart king. But he taught ye exactly what Lord Carleton knew he would."

Carleton remained speechless for some moments. At last he said raggedly, with wonder, "My father loved me."

"Och, sir, ye were the very apple o' his eye! I stood by him that last night while ye lay fast asleep in yer cot w' tears on yer cheeks from cryin' yerself to sleep. Lord Carleton knelt there beside ye, laid his hand on yer wee blond haid, and whispered a prayer over ye that's in my mind still. 'Ne'er forget that your mother and I love ye wi' all our hearts, my wee lad,' he said. 'Be brave and strong, and may our Father keep ye in the shadow o' his wings all yer life.'" Winton paused, then continued hoarsely, "Not a day passed that he didna long to ha' ye by his side."

The piercing memory of kneeling beside Elizabeth's bed while she lay asleep and praying over her before leaving for what he thought would be forever suddenly overwhelmed Carleton. Biting his lip hard to keep from crying out in anguish, he drew her tightly to his side.

Oh, Lord, you've answered every cry of my heart! And I thank you!

When he looked down, he read understanding in her tearful gaze. Brokenly he murmured, "I spent all these years striving to somehow earn my father's love—even after his death—not knowing that it was always mine! What might my life have been had I only known it?"

"But you know it now," she returned, smiling tremulously up at him. "Our Lord gives us a new beginning every morning. You've had the life you were meant to, as I have. And in the coming years we'll make an even more blessed one together."

Leaning on her, Carleton glanced out through the glass panes as a shaft of hazy golden sunlight slanted through the clouds. Though the winter gardens were blurred to his sight, for a moment it seemed to him that he could see the first tentative signs of spring's flowering.

The light faded. Drawing a deep breath, he pulled out his handkerchief, wiped away her tears and his, then led her to the divan and sat beside her.

"Did you serve Lord Edward Carleton too?" she asked.

"Bless me, no!" Winton exclaimed with a laugh. "I'd never ha' survived it. In fact, I left service not long after Lady Carleton's death. Lord Carleton knew that I felt called to the ministry, and he most generously financed my education at Christ Church, Oxford. After I was ordained, he set me up as curate. But while at Christ Church, I came under the influence o' the Wesleys and have become what ye'd call a Methodist. I'm currently rector o' one o' their affiliated churches."

While he was speaking, Carleton and Elizabeth exchanged astonished glances. "But you are an ordained Anglican minister," Carleton prompted. When Winton nodded, he said, "Which means you're authorized to perform weddings."

Winton's smile broadened. "Aye, sir. Baptize, marry, and bury."

"We're both baptized Anglicans, and hopefully we've no need of burying just yet," Carleton responded wryly.

Eyes narrowed, Winton glanced from one to the other. "Then considerin' this is a Catholic country, do ye mayhap have need o' marryin'?"

"As a matter of fact, we do," Elizabeth assured him with a smile. "You're not in a great hurry to leave, I hope."

Happily, he was not, and Cecile and Eugène were quickly summoned. In short order maids were readying Winton's accommodations for the next several days, while wedding preparations were finalized and invitations to the wedding dinner and reception hastily sent out. Eugène immediately sent a messenger to the priest of the local parish, and within the hour arrangements had been made for him to be present as witness to the ceremony so the marriage could be legally registered.

"We've frustrated ourselves for nothing," Elizabeth told Carleton with a rueful laugh. "All the time our Lord was preparing the perfect solution."

"As he always does," Carleton answered gruffly as he drew her into his arms, "if we'll only learn it."

Chapter Forty-two

LATE IN THE AFTERNOON the following day, Elizabeth stood between Cécile and Rev. Winton in the *salle's* center, surveying the expansive space speculatively. An abundance of flowers had been brought from the orangerie and distributed throughout the entire château in arrangements that delighted the eye. The *salle's* stone walls made the perfect backdrop for their jewel tones and greenery, while their heady fragrances wafted on the warm air rising from the blazing fireplace.

"There's plenty o' space. It'll do quite nicely," Rev. Winton approved, nodding. "I'll lead everyone in, and we'll gather in front o' the fireplace."

Elizabeth turned to Cécile, who answered her smile with one equally pleased. "It's perfect. Thank you!"

"It's going to be so beautiful!" Abby exclaimed, throwing her arms around Elizabeth's waist and laying her head on her shoulder. "Two lovely weddings in a fortnight! If only Mama and Papa were here."

Elizabeth hugged her and said longingly, "That would make the day even sweeter."

"But your gown isn't finished," Charlotte broke in plaintively. "What will you wear?"

"She has others that are suitable, *ma chère*," Tess assured her, brushing a stray curl back from the young woman's face.

Elizabeth turned a glowing look on Carleton, who stood nearby with

Caledonne, Eugène, and Red Fox, while their servants clustered behind them. "It matters not at all to me."

With a wicked smile Carleton murmured, "Mmm . . . perhaps a reprise of the goddess Diana."

She felt heat rush to her cheeks. Eugène and Caledonne smirked, while Rev. Winton and Red Fox looked puzzled.

"Jonathan! Must you always be such a scoundrel?"

"You could wear rags, dearest, and you'd still be the loveliest woman in all of France." He added earnestly, "I love you with all my heart."

She melted, tears springing to her eyes. Before she could run to kiss him, however, the butler passed through the salle into the spacious vestibule. She heard him throw open the outer door, followed by the murmur of voices borne on a cold draft. The door closed and he stepped back into the salle.

"Doctor and Madame Howard," he announced.

It seemed to Elizabeth that time stood still, for her mother and father appeared in the inner doorway then. Shivering, their faces reddened from the cold, he removed his hat and she pushed back the hood of her cloak, both glancing from one face to another as though taken aback to see all of them gathered there. Hastily he bowed, while she sank into a deep curtsey.

"Mama! Papa!" Abby cried, breaking the spell.

With her sister and aunt, Elizabeth flew across the room to embrace and kiss her parents, tears overflowing. Stepping back to hold her mother at arm's length and look from her beloved face to her father's, Elizabeth said, "You've come—you're really here!"

"We are!" her mother answered, laughing as she brushed away her own tears. "And quite a journey we've had."

Everyone clustered around them talking all at once.

"If you wrote to tell us you were coming, we never received the letter," Tess broke in.

Nodding to Carleton, Dr. Howard explained, "Before he sailed, Jon wrote to explain his intentions. He asked us to let go of what was past and to come as soon as we could . . . that we'd be welcome." He stopped, overcome by emotion.

"We immediately wrote to him here, in care of la marquise, with our arrangements and when our ship would sail," Anne supplied. "We wanted to surprise you."

"You certainly have!" Abby exclaimed, clinging to her mother. Beckoning Charlotte forward, she added, "We've so much to tell you!"

Frowning, Dr. Howard turned to Carleton. "You're not already married?"

"Not until the day after tomorrow." Keeping his voice neutral, Carleton assured them that he had received their letter, then briefly explained the difficulties he and Elizabeth had encountered in finding a priest and his concern that they might not arrive in time. "So you're most fortuitously come, sir, madame," he concluded.

To Elizabeth's surprise, her father said gruffly, "We'll have no formalities between us, Jon. Let us be as before. Indeed, we're sorry for . . . for what happened. Although there's still much that's hard for us to accept in your actions, we understand more now than we did then."

Stopping, he cleared his throat. He fixed on Elizabeth an earnest gaze in which moisture shone before turning back to Carleton. "Beth loves you, and her mother and I have no doubt of your love for her," he said, his voice husky with emotion. "We believe you'll be a faithful and true husband to our girl. That's our greatest wish after all."

They clasped hands, though with some reserve, then introductions were quickly made and pleasantries exchanged. Last of all Carleton said evenly, "This is Red Fox, the commander of my warriors."

Her father's brow furrowed and the color drained from her mother's face as they stared, nonplussed, at the tall, dignified warrior dressed and coifed as fashionably as any Frenchman. His expression remained unreadable and her father's guarded as they reached warily to clasp hands.

Cécile broke the tension by saying to the Howards, "We were delighted to learn that you were coming. A suite has been prepared, and you've time to get settled and rest before supper."

"Our governess, Madame Verignay, will go over Abigail's studies with you at your convenience," Eugène broke in. "And I believe you'll be greatly pleased at both your daughters' progress on the pianoforte, and Elizabeth's on the violin."

"They'll play for you this evening," Cécile insisted warmly. "And Elizabeth must tell you of all the good she does in providing medical care for our servants."

Beaming, Elizabeth's parents looked from her to Abby. "Both our girls look so well and happy," Dr. Howard said. "This change has indeed been good for them."

Caledonne drew Tess forward. "Before you go upstairs to refresh yourselves, Thérèsa and I wish to make an announcement."

"Don't tell me you've married!" Anne cried gleefully.

Tess rolled her eyes. "As you may have noticed, Alexandre is not a man to be denied," she said, lips pursed. But as she looked up to meet his fond gaze, her face softened into a smile. "And he's made me a very happy woman indeed."

Bending to kiss her, he murmured, "I doubt I've the power to make you as happy as you make me, dear one."

While Anne exclaimed in delight, Dr. Howard regarded the two of them with complete astonishment. "Married! Didn't I once have a sister who swore that if she were to wed at all, which was doubtful, it would never be to a nobleman? What happened to her, and who is this stranger?"

Tess bridled, color rising to her cheeks. "I meant a *British* nobleman, not French," she returned haughtily.

All of them gave way to a gale of mirth. "Allow me to introduce you to la comtesse de Caledonne," Elizabeth said finally, fighting to contain a giggle as she indicated Tess with a sweep of her arm.

"And titled too!" Dr. Howard burst out, thunderstruck.

"Let's see," Carleton said, stroking his chin as he studied Tess thoughtfully. "It just occurred to me that once Beth and I are married, you'll be my aunt on both sides. Surely that includes some privileges."

Eyes narrowed, she retorted, "For me, indeed, not for you. You'd better be on your best behavior, Jon."

When their merriment subsided, Cécile shooed the women upstairs, where the Howards' baggage had already been delivered to their suite. After admiring their accommodations with amazement, Anne turned to Elizabeth.

"Sarah insisted I bring along my wedding gown. She told me that when you and Jonathan first planned to wed you'd wanted to wear it."

"Oh, Mama, thank you!" Elizabeth gasped. "Rev. Winton is only here for a few days, and the gown I'd ordered won't be ready in time."

"It may require some alterations," her mother warned.

"As soon as your things are unpacked, bring the gown to me," Cécile urged. "My seamstress will make any changes needed."

TWO DAYS LATER Elizabeth stood before Rev. Winton at the *salle's* great fireplace facing Carleton, her hand on her father's arm. Their families and closest friends clustered around them, with the local priest, Father Moreau, observing from a seat nearby, and all the higher ranking servants gathered along the *salle's* perimeter.

Jemma had woven fresh flowers from the orangerie into her elaborately coifed hair, and the seamstress had done wonders with her mother's gown in hardly more than a day. The bodice and stomacher of the silvery satin gown could not have fit more perfectly. The open front edges of the full outer petticoat were now trimmed with snowy French lace, the sides and back drawn up in elaborate flounces over the matching embroidered under-petticoat. Lace generously finished off the gown's elbow-length sleeves and décolletage as well, both edged with a delicate tracery of beading.

The ancient words rolled richly off Rev. Winton's tongue. "Jonathan Stuart Alexandre Carleton, wilt thou have this woman to thy wedded wife, to live together after God's ordinance in the holy estate o' matrimony? Wilt thou love her, comfort her, honor, and keep her in sickness and in health; and, forsakin' all other, keep thee only unto her, so long as ye both shall live?"

His grave gaze fixed on her, he said quietly, "I will."

Rev. Winton turned to Elizabeth. "Elizabeth Anne Howard, wilt thou have this man to thy wedded husband, to live together after God's ordinance in the holy estate of matrimony? Wilt thou obey him, and serve him, love, honor, and keep him in sickness and in health; and, forsakin' all other, keep thee only unto him, so long as ye both shall live?"

Tremulously she repeated, "I will."

She did not turn her gaze from his as Rev. Winton took her right hand from her father, who stepped back, then laid it into Carleton's. Time and their surroundings blurred as he repeated the vows to her after the priest.

"I take thee, Elizabeth, to my wedded wife, to have and to hold from this day forward, for better, for worse, for richer, for poorer, in sickness and in health, to love and to cherish, till death us do part, according to God's holy ordinance; and thereto I plight thee my troth."

"I take thee, Jonathan, to my wedded husband," she followed, forcing her voice to steady, "to have and to hold from this day forward, for better, for worse, for richer, for poorer, in sickness and in health, to love, cherish, and to obey, till death us do part, according to God's holy ordinance; and thereto I give thee my troth."

From the moment she had descended the stairs on her father's arm, Carleton's gaze had hardly turned from her, the light in the depths of his smoky blue-grey eyes leaving her breathless. Nor could she withdraw her gaze from him. He had never appeared more handsome to her, his tall, lean, broad-shouldered form clad impeccably in a suit of deepest blue with sky blue facings and a matching, intricately embroidered waistcoat, his blond hair brushed neatly back and tied at the nape with a narrow dark blue ribbon.

He released her hand and took from Red Fox the gold wedding band. The warrior had been following the service with great interest and now glanced from Carleton to Elizabeth with a smile, echoed by Stowe beyond him. She returned an unsteady one to both, then to Abby and Charlotte, who stood on either side, each holding a small fragrant bouquet, before seeking her mother's tearful gaze.

Carleton laid the ring on the open Book of Common Prayer Rev. Winton held. He blessed it, then handed it back to Carleton.

Slipping it onto the tip of the fourth finger of her left hand, he repeated after the priest: "With this ring I thee wed, with my body I thee worship, and with all my worldly goods I thee endow: In the name of the Father, and of the Son, and of the Holy Ghost. Amen." Gently he slid the ring all the way onto her finger.

Looking up, he mouthed silently, *I love you.* Tears blurring her eyes, she mouthed back, *I love you.*

He steadied her as they both knelt. And into the hush, Rev. Winton prayed, "O eternal God, Creator and Preserver o' all mankind, Giver o' all spiritual grace, the Author o' everlastin' life; send thy blessin' upon these thy servants, Jonathan and Elizabeth, whom we bless in thy name; that, as Isaac and Rebecca lived faithfully together, so Jonathan and Eliza-beth may surely perform and keep the vow and covenant betwixt them made, whereof this ring given and received is a token and pledge, and may ever remain in perfect love and peace together, and live accordin' to thy laws; through Jesus Christ our Lord. Amen."

From the assembly echoed a muted amen.

Rev. Winton raised them to their feet, and the three of them faced the assembly as he said, "Those whom God hath joined together let no man put asunder. Forasmuch as Jonathan and Elizabeth have consented together in holy wedlock, and have witnessed the same before God and this company, and thereto have given and pledged their troth either to the other, and have declared the same by givin' and receivin' o' a ring, and by joining of hands; I pronounce that they be man and wife together, in the name o' the Father, and o' the Son, and o' the Holy Ghost."

After everyone again repeated the amen, he continued, "God the Father, God the Son, God the Holy Ghost, bless, preserve, and keep you; the Lord mercifully with his favor look upon you; and so fill you with all spiritual benediction and grace, that ye may so live together in this life, that in the world to come ye may have life everlastin'. Amen."

IMMEDIATELY FOLLOWING the ceremony, Franklin and Adams, Chaumont, Teissèdre, the Brillons, Sartine, Vergennes, and other nobles and their wives close to Caledonne and the Martieu-Broussards began arriving for a celebration that clearly impressed and gratified Elizabeth's parents.

The reception, elaborate wedding dinner, and dancing in the upstairs ballroom stretched long into the evening. It was late before their guests began to take their leave. After embracing and kissing her parents and sister, Tess, Cécile, and Charlotte, Elizabeth retired to her chamber, softly illumined by candlelight and a warm fire. Jemma helped her to change into a silk négligée, took down her hair and brushed it, then turned down the bed and quietly withdrew.

Early that morning Stowe had supervised the transfer of Carleton's possessions into the chamber that had been Tess's before her marriage. When Elizabeth heard him enter it with Stowe, her heart began to pound and anticipation bubbled through her like the champagne she had drunk at dinner.

All through the afternoon and evening each lingering gaze, each brief touch of their hands, every smile and precise step as they came together and parted in while dancing had heightened a passionate desire in her that set every fiber aflame. Sitting by fire now, hearing Carleton's and Stowe's muted voices in the adjoining room, she thought of all the years of waiting they had endured, the separations and repeated disappointments. Yet God's plan for them had been perfect after all.

To every thing there is a season, and a time to every purpose under heaven, she thought, smiling. *A time to be born and a time to die . . . a time to weep and a time to laugh; a time to mourn and a time to dance . . . a time to love . . .*

Let our love always remain, oh Lord.

Quietly the door opened, and he stepped inside, wearing a silk banyan the deep blue-grey of his eyes. As she rose he came to take her in his arms, tenderly turned her face up to his. Slipping her arms around his neck, she tip-toed to claim his mouth, every nerve thrilling.

Let him kiss me with the kisses of his mouth: for thy love is better than wine. Behold, thou art fair, my love; behold thou art fair . . .

Pulling away, she caressed his face, studying each angle and plane, with her fingers traced his jaw to his neck, then slid her hand beneath the collar of his banyan and slipped it back, reveling in the tautness of his skin, the hard muscles beneath rippling at her touch. She bent her head to kiss the scar of the wound he had suffered in battle just days after their first meeting, heard and felt his breath catch.

"Ah, Beth," he murmured, "we've waited so long for this night."

"Let's not waste a moment of the rest of our lives, beloved," she returned huskily . . .

He brought me to the banqueting house, and his banner over me was love . . .

His senses filled to overflowing with her sweet fragrance, her eyes deep pools of love and desire, the seductive curves of her slender body pressed to his, trembling. He slid one hand down her back, embracing her with the other and trailing light kisses down her throat to her breasts, straightened then, tangling his fingers in the silky flood of her dark tresses. Passion ignited into flame, and he found her mouth again.

"Dearest of my heart, I love you so," she said shakily at last.

Ah, flesh of my flesh and bone of my bones! Beloved helpmeet . . .

His cheek to hers, he whispered into the soft curls at her ear, "With my body . . . I thee worship."

He drew her to him with rising hunger, feeling her respond without restraint, every doubt, every fear, every barrier falling away with each article of clothing until they stood together with nothing between them but skin, she as pure and lovely to him as she had been in that brief glimpse on the riverbank at her adoption by Blue Sky—surely as wondrous as Eve must have been to Adam at his first sight of her.

Rise up, my love, my fair one, and come away. For, lo, the winter is past, the rain is over and gone; the flowers appear on the earth; the time of the singing of birds is come . . .

Sweeping her up into his arms, he brought her to the bed and lay with her, full certain that heaven itself could not hold in store greater blessings than all the joyous years that lay before them. And as she gave herself into his keeping eagerly, joyfully, all else melted away until they were truly one, their love to him a sacred fire—life to his soul and health to his bones, and sustenance to last him all his days upon the earth.

Thou hast ravished my heart, my sister, my spouse; Thou hast ravished my heart with one of thine eyes, with one chain of thy neck. How fair is thy love, my sister, my spouse! How much better is thy love than wine!

Chapter Forty-three

T HE NIGHTMARES that had still occasionally plagued Elizabeth quickly became a thing of the past as she spent each night in Carleton's arms.

She had not imagined the contentment she would feel to have their relationship finally settled and a future together before them. She could tell that he also felt a new assurance and greater peace, especially with the shadows of his childhood finally dispelled. The dark cloud of Lucien's bitter leaving retreated further into the background as well. Everything seemed new and fresh and full of hope to their eyes despite winter's continued grip on the land.

To Carleton's gratification, after all the frustration and delays, by early in February Teissèdre had secured three ships that with few alterations would be both fast and sturdy enough to bear the heavier guns he wanted. A search was being made for these at the foundries, while the ships were readied at Brest and L'Orient, and crews enlisted.

A welcome letter also came from Andrews with assurances that the brigade was at full strength and that, for the moment at least, quiet appeared to reign on the western frontier. He also shared news that delighted them both: Blue Sky expected the birth of their second child in December—thus born by now—with Rain Woman's baby to follow this very month.

Carleton took less joy in the news that the army had encamped for the winter in the Watchung Mountains at Middlebrook, New Jersey, to keep watch on Clinton's force occupying New York City and its immediate environs. He remembered the place all too well from their brief encampment there in the spring two years earlier.

"This is becoming depressingly predictable," he said to Elizabeth. "We're right back where we started."

"We'll prevail through persistence if nothing else," she assured him, eliciting first a grimace, then a reluctant smile.

With no more reason to stay and impatient to return home, early in February Red Fox accompanied Teissèdre and Caledonne to Brest, where one of Caledonne's squadrons was preparing to escort a merchant convoy loaded with war materiel to Boston. From there he would return to Carleton's brigade. And soon after he had gone Elizabeth's parents took their leave with many embraces, tears, and blessings before traveling to Amsterdam to board a Dutch merchantman bound for home.

After he returned from Brest, Caledonne suggested to Carleton that while the guns were being sought for his new privateers, they travel to Marseille. "I've no immediate need to sail with my fleet, and we're both newly married. Surely our brides deserve a wedding trip! We might even find that other ship you've been seeking for your merchant fleet at the shipyards there," he added.

The temptation was too strong to resist, and Carleton agreed eagerly. Nor did Elizabeth and Tess needed any persuasion.

They left for Marseille in mid March, with the weather warming, escorted by a small detail of Caledonne's Marines. The women rode with their maids in one spacious coach, the men's servants in another, with a third carrying their baggage, while Carleton rode alongside with Caledonne.

Stowe had gone to deliver Carleton's and the commissioners' official dispatches to Eaden at Brest, where *Destiny* was being resupplied after bringing in a fat British merchantman as prize. He would then sail aboard her to Marseille before she returned to prowling the African coast.

One revelation clouded their eager anticipation as they set out on the journey. Sartine's agents had located Lucien in Rotterdam, Caledonne confided privately to Carleton.

"He has no contacts in the area that I know of," he said. "I can think of only one reason he'd go there."

He did not need to say what that was, for Carleton read it in the devastation his face reflected. Lucien meant to go to England.

SITTING ACROSS FROM ELIZABETH in the coach, Carleton could not keep his eyes off her, and his gaze brought a soft blush into her cheeks. There was a glow about her recently that enchanted him even more than usual.

"I've never seen anyone as besotted with each other as your aunt and my uncle. Except for us."

She returned his teasing grin. "We are fiercely in love, aren't we?"

He fought back the impulse to span the space between them and snatch her into his arms. "I thought I loved you before," he murmured, overcome. "But now my heart is bursting. I never conceived it possible to adore anyone as I do you."

Her blush deepened and her answering smile was so sweet that it was all he could do to keep from scooping her across to his lap.

The period since their wedding had been the happiest of his life. It had taken a month to reach Marseille, traveling the almost six hundred miles at a leisurely pace, frequently changing horses as they followed the glorious spring just beginning to wash over forested mountains and picturesque valleys, across verdant fields, orchards, and vineyards, stopping at charming small towns along the way.

By the time they reached Provence and descended to the coast, a riot of wildflowers swathed the craggy, stream-cleft valleys in vivid colors and rich, sun-baked fragrances. Red poppies, violet wisteria and wild thyme, yellow broom, and the grey-blue leaves of lavender just beginning to bud mingled with a profusion of gnarled shrubs and evergreen oaks amid vineyards and groves of olive trees in full leaf.

A few miles east of the busy port of Marseille, the magnificent four-teenth-century château dominated a rugged cliff from which it over-looked the sparkling blue waters of the Mediterranean. Their first glimpse of its high, weathered stone walls awash in the golden sunlight of late afternoon, made it appear as though it had sprung from the cliff's rocks.

Visiting again with Julianne and her family and seeing the affection growing stronger between them, Elizabeth, and Tess had been an equal joy. Together they had shopped and dined on the local cuisine in between tak-ing in all the sights the port city offered: ancient St. Victor's Abbey with its fortified tower perched on the southern hills; the forts of St. Jean and St. Nicolas that guarded opposite banks of Rhône River; Chateau d'If, a square prison fortress with a round tower at three of its corners that brooded over the bay from a small rocky island; the arsenal, quays, and shipyards where scores of merchant and naval ships, fishing boats, and private vessels plied the busy harbor. And, as Caledonne had proposed, the two of them had indeed found the perfect ship for Carleton's merchant fleet at the shipyards.

The last week had been the sweetest of all. Caledonne and Tess sailed for Brest with a squadron from the Toulon fleet. From there they would travel to Paris. After arranging financing for the ship, he would return to Brest to sail with his fleet, while she remained at Passy.

Left to wander as they would by their hosts, with only Stowe and Jemma attending them, Carleton and Elizabeth traveled widely through the area, visiting more of his favorite youthful haunts, basking in the sunny days and often following paths beaten by farmers and donkeys through the rocky hills to find a secluded niche for a picnic.

Yet with each passing day the vast reaches of the American wilder-ness drew him more powerfully, coupled with the nagging concern for the fate of his people, his warriors, his brigade. Elizabeth also made no secret that she increasingly longed for home, and in the end the decision to return had been an easy one to make.

The coach jolted, jerking his thoughts back to the present. Seeing Eliza-beth's grimace, he asked anxiously, "You're all right?"

"I'm a little queasy, that's all. Nothing unusual. It's much better now that we're on paved road—or was until we hit that bump," she added with a laugh.

It was the last week of May, the day sunny and warm. At his insistence they had again taken the journey slowly, making frequent stops for her sake. Several hours earlier, to both their relief, the ride finally smoothed out as they passed onto the pavement beginning thirty miles from Paris.

He lifted a corner of the curtain that covered the window on his right and glanced out, assuring himself that Stowe held his position, appearing more a ruffian than ever as he kept a keen eye on their surroundings. More guards rode ahead of their coach and behind the two following that carried Elizabeth's maid, other servants, and their baggage—which had expanded considerably due to all the shopping he had happily encouraged her to do. He had taken every precaution to ensure their anonymity, and so far the journey had been peaceful.

He returned his attention to Elizabeth. "I hadn't thought this would happen quite so soon," he admitted ruefully.

"It's the natural course of things, after all. Are you as happy as I am?"

He leaned forward and captured her hand. "Can you doubt me? It feels as though I've waited all my life to become a husband—your husband—and a father."

"You have, actually," she teased.

He grinned, but after a moment sobered. "Shall we tell everyone right away?"

"Let's wait a little while longer."

"You're certain, though?"

"I know all the signs well enough, though this is the first time I've personally experienced them. And yes, I am certain." Hesitantly she added, "It's not quite three months, and . . . things can go wrong." As he studied her with concern, she added, "Please don't worry, dearest of my heart."

"You know what happened to my mother—"

"From what Rev. Winton told us, she wasn't strong. I am."

"It hasn't been all that long since I brought you off that cursed ship," he pointed out. "You were so ill that even your father was terrified. I can't express what I felt. We came far too close to losing you."

She gave him a stern look. "But you didn't. If I can survive battle and the worst the British can do, a pregnancy is nothing."

He transferred to the seat beside her and enclosed her in his arms, marveling, as always, at how naturally she nestled against him. Bending over her, he pressed his lips to hers and surrendered himself to the answering passion of her kisses.

At last he drew back to look down at her, heart clenching, tears stinging his eyes and blurring his vision. *Dearest love. Wife. Mother of our child.*

Thank you, Father, he added silently. *Your goodness is without measure.*

He laid his cheek against the crown of her head, caring nothing for her fashionable coiffure, nor did she protest. By now her hair had grown until the curls tumbled almost to her waist when released. One of his greatest pleasures was the nightly task he had appropriated of pulling out the pins that held them demurely in place during the day. Then he brushed out the glorious, dark flood that glittered in the candlelight with shafts of flame, reveling in the feel of the silken strands between his fingers.

On impulse he lifted one hand to do so now, but she pulled away, warded him off with her hand and a steely, "Don't you dare. We'll be at Passy shortly, and I don't want to have to stop for Jemma to make me decent again!"

He threw back his head, laughing. And as quickly stopped and took a painful breath.

"There are things that can go wrong, as you said. Too many. If I were to lose you now, and our baby too—"

Looking up, she pressed her fingertips gently to his lips. "We're never in control of our future. All we can do is to trust the one who is. Against all odds he's brought us this far, and I feel in my heart that he'll complete the work he's begun in us no matter what may lie ahead."

He forced a nod and cheerful agreement though his chest still felt as though it was painfully compressed by a steel band. Which she must have sensed, for she quickly nestled back into his arms and changed the subject.

"Boy or girl?"

He looked down at her, smiling. "As long as you and the child are well, I don't care. Well . . . I might favor a wee lass as beautiful as her mother, with dark auburn hair, large brown eyes, the prettiest blush, and a smile that always takes my breath away."

"And as sweet tempered," she suggested mischievously.

He cocked one eyebrow. "There may be some dispute on that score."

She pushed him away. "Wretch!"

They fell back into each other's arms, laughing. Holding her tightly, he pressed his lips against the fine tendrils that in spite of all effort to subdue them insisted on escaping to curl against her temples. "I can't wait until I can take you home," he whispered.

"And I can't wait to go. Where will home be?"

"With my brigade until this war's over, I'm afraid. Then Thornlea. But someday I want to build you a home in Ohio Territory nearer my people, where they can come safely to us."

She looked up at him, hope brimming in her gaze. "Do you think we'll be home in time for Blue Sky to 'catch' our baby—as my sister says? I do miss her so, and the others too. How wish I knew how she and Rain Woman and their newest little ones are!"

He cupped her cheek in his hand and gazed deep into her eyes. "If God wills it, we shall. And I promise you'll have all the help you need. The changes will be greater for you than for me, and I don't want you to ever feel confined."

She gave him an arch look. "I suppose sometimes I will. As I've warned you, I'm entirely useless when it comes to domestic duties." When he began to protest, she leaned to brush a kiss across his cheek. "I shall revel in caring for our babes, however. As you, I've wanted this for so long that the reality of it fills me with nothing but joy. And I've seen how the Shawnee women help each other with the children. Surely they'll help me too."

Fighting to contain his emotions, he nodded, then captured her hand and pressed it to his lips. Voice choking, he murmured, "I know they will. Gladly."

✳ ✳ ✳

THEY STEPPED INTO Château Broussard's salon, then came to an abrupt halt. A sudden chill fell over Carleton as he took in Caledonne's ashen face and Teissèdre's grim one. Eugène's frown and Cécile's distraught expression were no more reassuring, and Tess' eyes were red-rimmed as though she had been weeping.

"Thank God you're finally here!" she exclaimed, rushing forward to embrace Elizabeth, then him, the others following to cluster around them. "We expected you days ago."

Carleton glanced at Elizabeth, but she gave a slight shake of her head. "What's gone wrong?" he demanded, turning to Caledonne, his voice tight. "I assume it's a greater disaster than usual since you've returned so soon. With Louis," he added, indicating Teissèdre.

Teissèdre met his wary gaze with one that caused his breath to catch. "There's no easy way to tell you this," he said gruffly.

"Then just say it."

Teissèdre's mouth worked for a moment, then he rasped, "*Destiny's* lost."

Staggered, Carleton stared blankly at him. Of all the possible disasters he could imagine, he had not foreseen this one.

But he should have, he realized, feeling sick as the memory flooded back of his mocking salute to the captain of the attacking British 74 when her broadside fell short. He should have learned by now that one never fared well by taunting the devil.

Dimly he felt Elizabeth press close to his side, clasp his hand tightly. But all the rest of the world had ceased to exist.

"*Destiny* . . . sunk?" His voice sounded brittle to him, that of a stranger.

Teissèdre shook his head. "Perhaps worse. *Sans doute* they deemed her too valuable a prize to destroy. She suffered heavy damage, a fire, was forced to strike her colors, and they took her with her surviving crew."

"We just learned this morning that she was towed to Portsmouth," Caledonne supplied. "My guess is that they mean to repair her and turn her against us."

"I'm so sorry, Jon," Tess murmured, horror in her voice.

"How many men—" Carleton stopped, the words impossible to speak. He saw Eugène and Caledonne exchange glances.

"Most of the crew," Caledonne told him. "The British did save some. Able seamen are hard to come by, and those who survived the battle would have been impressed."

"Surely they wouldn't fight against us!" Elizabeth protested.

"They won't be given a choice," Eugène returned, his voice hard. "Privateers are considered pirates, and they'll either obey their new masters or suffer execution."

She drew a sharp breath. "Pete—Colonel Moghrab's son!" She pressed her fist to her mouth, her voice muffled as she added in dismay, "Dr. Lemaire and Marie!"

Shaking his head, Caledonne spread his hands helplessly.

Carleton covered his face with one hand. For a long moment he said nothing, finally looked up and in a voice that shook, said, "Eaden?"

"Impossible to know who survived and who was lost. For now, at least. If he survived, as a former British naval captain he may well be hanged. My agents should be able to discover his fate and possibly that of the others, though it'll take time."

When Cécile tried to press Carleton down into the nearest chair, he shook her off, released Elizabeth's hand, and retreated to the long windows overlooking the terrace. Behind him, as from a far distance, he heard the muted murmurs of the others' voices, then his uncle's footfalls approaching.

"Admiral Howe evidently learned that my fleet's charge was to protect American privateers," Caledonne explained hoarsely, his hand on Carleton's shoulder. "And especially yours. He sent a strong force against us, and while we fought them off, another large British squadron struck *Destiny* with her escorts and convoy of merchantmen several miles ahead of us. From what we've been able to learn, Eaden put up a determined resistance. Judging by the destruction we're told he wrought on the British, no one could have fought harder or more effectively. But in the end your ships were outnumbered and outgunned, and the only choice left was to strike or lose every man."

"The rest of the convoy?" Carleton said through gritted teeth.

"*Eagle* was also forced to strike and was taken prize with her crew. *Invictus* was sunk. *Wolf* suffered considerable damage, but a fog came up as night fell which, added to the gunsmoke, allowed her to slip away." He hesitated. "They were escorting your merchantmen *Faire Winds, Horn of Africa,* and *Mandarin.* They also were taken . . . with their surviving crews and full cargoes."

Carleton let out a low groan. The disaster could not have been more complete.

"After we drove our attackers off, we came across the debris of the battle. We picked up a few survivors drifting in *Destiny's* wrecked cutter and found *Wolf* and her crew at Brest. Louis got the full report of what happened from them."

Teissèdre had come to join them, and Carleton told him, "I want all my ships still at sea ordered into the nearest French or neutral port, with the rest to remain where they are. I can't afford to lose any more."

"I'll send a squadron to intercept those at sea first," Caledonne said. "Louis, give me the list of all their routes and ports of call."

Teissèdre nodded. "It'll take some time to reach them all, I'm afraid. There could be more attacks in the meantime "

"As quickly as possible then," Carleton said gruffly.

When Teissèdre had gone Elizabeth and Tess came over to them, their expressions reflecting their dismay.

For a long moment, Caledonne stared into the air, looking entirely broken. At last he said, "The worst is that Sartine's found evidence of Lucien's involvement. He went to London as we feared he might. And he knew which sea roads we typically sail—all the British would need to intercept us. Clearly I trusted him with more than I ought to have."

"He's your son. Why wouldn't you trust him?"

Caledonne met Carleton's bleak gaze with a despairing one. Bitterness edging his tone, he said, "I've known all along what he was—what darkness his soul harbored. But I persuaded myself that I held some influence over him, that he was capable of changing. He warned that he'd make you and Beth regret the injury he conceived you'd done him. I'm just afraid he isn't finished yet."

Turning abruptly away, he cried out, "How could Luciana and I from our love have produced a monster like this?"

Tess drew him gently around and forced him to face her. "You didn't. He's the man he's freely chosen to be. But he's not irredeemable, Alexandre. Nothing is impossible for God. He may yet repent. Like the prodigal son, he may come home again."

He straightened and nodded, tears trickling down his cheeks. Pulling her to him, he whispered hoarsely, "I will trust in that. And pray."

A sharp pang cut through Elizabeth to see that Carleton's face had gone hard, his eyes the wintry grey she recognized with a sinking heart. *My husband is become the warrior again, and I must release him. But it's so much harder now. And how often will it be so until this war is finally ended?*

"I must find them, Beth. I can't—"

"I know all too well what they're suffering." She forced a smile, with difficulty kept it steady. "We can't abandon them as long as there's hope they're alive."

The tension of his body eased, but worry still creased his brow. "I swore I'd never leave you to bear our child alone," he said in a low voice. "But I may have no choice."

Taking a deep breath, she raised her chin. *Other soldiers' wives have borne this, and so will I.*

"I'll not be alone in any case, my love. I'll be safe and well, praying every moment that you find and rescue the captives. And come home to me. You know I'll be waiting when you do."

He drew her into his arms. "One thing I promise you, dear heart. Our children will always know that I love them—and you." He kissed her tenderly, and she pressed into him, heart aching, never wanting to let him go.

Too soon, however, he released her. Caledonne drew him aside, and Tess's arm went around her then. As she leaned on her aunt, watching the two men, it occurred to her how alike they were not only in appearance, but in the fierce eagerness for battle clearly visible in their eyes and the taut line of their bodies as they stood together, speaking in low tones. Turning to Tess she saw her face crumble as she recognized it too.

"I was just on my way to meet with Sartine when you arrived," Caledonne said urgently. "Come with me, Jonathan We can't give in to despair. If they're still alive, we'll get them back. *Destiny* too. And if that proves to be impossible, we'll cause as so much wreckage they'll wish they'd never challenged us."

Through gritted teeth Carleton said, "I want someone who has a fast ship and is determined to go in harm's way. And I think I know just the man."

Caledonne studied him for a moment, frowning. "Your Captain Jones?"

"When all appears lost," Carleton returned with a grim smile, "what's needed is a madman."

FORTHCOMING

Forge of Freedom

In the seventh and final volume of The American Patriot Series, the Americans' war for independence finally concludes in triumph—and the renewed fight of the native nations for survival in their ancient lands.

If you enjoyed this story and would like to offer feedback, we invite you to email the editor, Joan Shoup, at jmshoup@gmail.com. We'd love to receive your comments. We always appreciate thoughtful reviews posted on the book's detail page on Amazon, Christianbook.com, Goodreads, Barnes and Noble, and other online sites. Thank you for telling other readers about this series!

Glossary

FRENCH

affaire de coeur: affair of the heart.

allée: path.

a la mode: in style.

Anglais: English.

ami, aimie (masc., fem.): friend.

Au contraire: on the contrary.

bien: good.

bon, bonne (masc., fem.): good, fair, beautiful.

bonne chance: good fortune.

bosquets: ornamental groves.

Canadien: Canadian.

certainement: certainly.

charmante: charming.

château; pl. châteaux: a castle or fortress.

chèr, chère (masc., fem.): dear.

Dieu: God.

Dieu Merci, en effet: thank God indeed.

écarté: a popular card game.

enceinte: pregnant.

exquise: exquisite.

fleur: flower.

française: French.

friseur: hairdresser.

Général: general.

Grands-Lacs: Great Lakes.

grand-mère: grandmother.

jardin: garden.

le eau d'égouts: the fragrance of sewage

libelles: pamphlets filled with sensational and scandalous attacks against notable persons.

libellistes: publishers of libelles.

lustrine: lustring, a silk fabric with a shiny finish.

maman: mama.

mon, ma (masc., fem.): my

Majesté: majesty

mais, bien sûr: but, of course.

maquillage: makeup.

marchand: merchant.

merci: thank you.

mère: mother

Mère de Dieu: Mother of God.

naturellement: naturally.

n'est-ce pas; n'est-ce pas vrai: Is it not so?

non: no.

ottomane: upholstered and usually backless seat or couch.

oui: yes.

pardonne-moi: pardon me.

père: father.

peste: plague (an exclamation).

petit: little, small.

plaisir: pleasure, enjoyment.

quinze: fifteen.

renarde: vixen.

roi: king

Sacré Dieu: dear God.

salle: hall, reception room, auditorium.

sans doute: without doubt.

savoir faire: capacity for appropriate or polished social behavior.

seize: sixteen.

serviteur: Your servant.

tant mieux: so much the better.

trés: very.

votre: your.

GAELIC

auld: old.

bairn: child, baby.

braw: fine, splendid, brave.

soarsa: freedom.

thrawn: perverse, ill-tempered.

MIAMI

Myaamia; pl. Myaamiaki: Miami, or Twightwee, tribe.

Waapaahšiiki: Wabash River (Fr., Ouabache); it shines white, or water over white stones.

SHAWNEE

Cakimiyamithiipi: the Little Miami River in Ohio.

Goshochking: Coshocton, Ohio, on the Muskingum River.

Hathennithiipi: the Mad River in Ohio.

killegenico: tobacco mixed with dried sumac leaves.

Long Knives: originally Virginians, later all Americans, so called because their soldiers carried swords.

mattah: no.

Miyamithiipi: Miami River.

Moneto: the Shawnee's Supreme Being of the universe.

msikahmiqui: a large building that served as council house and temple for religious rites.

neahw: thank you.

opawaka: a token the Shawnee believed was given by Moneto to transmit power to an individual.

pepoonwi: winter.

psaiwi nenothtu: great warrior.

seela: yes.

Sciotothiipi: Scioto River.

shemanese: white men.

Spelewathiipi: Ohio River.

Twightwee: Miami Indians.

wampum: strings, belts, or sashes made of shell beads used either as ornaments, tribal records, a medium of exchange for goods, or to transmit messages of peace or war.

wigewa: a large rectangular or square dwelling for one family framed with poles and overlaid with bark, woven mats, or animal hides.

Appendix

THE FIVE SUBNATIONS (SEPTS) OF THE SHAWNEE

THE CHILLICOTHE AND Thawekila septs controlled political matters that affected the tribe, as well as relationships between the Shawnee and other native tribes. Although there was substantial intermarriage between them, the Thawekila were considered to be the southern Shawnee, and the Chillicothe the Northern Shawnee. The Shawnee's principal leaders and tribal historians were always chosen from among these two septs until the Thawekila separated from the tribe during the American Revolution and withdrew across the Mississippi River.

The Maquachake sept controlled matters pertaining to health and medicine. The Piqua sept was in charge of the worship of Moneto, the Great Spirit, and lesser deities and spirits. As the Shawnee's warrior clan, the Kispokotha provided the tribe's warriors and war chiefs. Although their chief leader was ineligible to become the Shawnee's principal chief, in power and prestige he stood second to the tribe's chief.

Each sept's chief leader was autonomous in matters that pertained to his own sept. In matters concerning the whole tribe, however, the leaders of each sept were subordinate to the nation's principal chief.

HAUDENOSAUNEE

THE IROQUOIS LEAGUE. Originally the Five Nations, the League consisted of the Mohawk, Onondaga, Oneida, Cayuga, and Seneca tribes. In 1722 they accepted the Tuscarora tribe into the League and became the Six Nations.

SHAWNEE CHARACTERS

Black Fish: the Chillicothe sept's principal sachem and war chief who favored war with the Americans.

Black Hoof: principal war chief of the Maquachake sept.

Black Snake: principal war chief of the Kispokotha sept.

Blue Jacket: a sachem of the Piqua sept who attempted to form an alliance with other Native American tribes to stop the Americans from forcing them out of Ohio Territory.

Cornstalk: the principal sachem of the Maquachake, one of the five subnations of the Shawnee, and of the Shawnee nation. After defeat in Lord Dunmore's War in 1774, he refused to fight the Whites and counseled the tribe to honor the peace treaty. Murdered at Fort Randolph on November 10, 1777.

Kishkalwa: Thawekila sachem who separated from the Shawnee over warring against the Americans and led the division across the Mississippi to settle among the Spanish.

Nimwha: Nonhelema's brother, who became the principal sachem of the Maquachake and of the Shawnee nation after Cornstalk's death.

Nonhelema: Cornstalk's older sister, a women's peace chief who sided with the Americans.

Silverheels: Nonhelema's youngest brother.

OTHER NATIVE AMERICAN LEADERS

Dunquat: Wyandot half king.

White Eyes: Lenape sachem influenced by the Moravians. Although he did not convert to Christianity, he protected Native American Christians who moved to the vicinity of his town, Goshochking, in Ohio Territory.

CHRISTIAN MISSIONARIES TO THE NATIVE AMERICANS

Samuel Kirkland, Presbyterian.
David Zeisberger, Moravian.

SHAWNEE MOONS: THE CYCLE OF LIFE
Moons correspond roughly with the designated months.

January	*Ha'kwi kiishthwa*	Severe Moon
February	*Haatawi kiishthwa*	Crow Moon
March	*Shkipiye kwiitha*	Sap Moon
April	*Pooshkwiitha*	Half Moon
May	*Hotehimini kiishthwa*	Strawberry Moon
June	*Mshkatiwi kiishthwa*	Raspberry Moon
July	*Miini kiishthwa*	Blackberry Moon
August	*Po'kamawi kiishthwa*	Plum Moon
September	*Ha'shimini kiishthwa*	Papaw Moon
October	*Sha'teepakanootha*	Wilted Moon
November	*Kini kiishthwa*	Long Moon
December	*Washilatha kiishthwa*	Eccentric Moon